IN
ALEXA'S
SHOES

CAPTURED BY THE NAZIS.
CAN SHE TRIUMPH OVER TRAGEDY?

IN ALEXA'S SHOES

CAPTURED BY THE NAZIS.
CAN SHE TRIUMPH OVER TRAGEDY?

ROCHELLE ALEXANDRA

AUTHOR
ACADEMY elite

Published by Author Academy Elite
P.O. Box 43, Powell, OH 43035
www.AuthorAcademyElite.com

Paperback ISBN- 978-1-64085-614-1
Hardcover ISBN- 978-1-64085-615-8
Ebook ISBN- 978-1-64085-616-5

Library of Congress Control Number: 2019935712

DEDICATION

This book is dedicated to the memory of my
beautiful grandmother, Alexandra,
'My sunshine, my diamond, my heart . . .'
who passed away on April 15, 2019
at the age of 92,
two months before this novel was published.

. . . and to the memory of all the many
innocent victims, whose lives were taken
and forever changed during the Holocaust
at the hands of the Nazis.

We must never forget!

PREFACE

As a young girl growing up, I knew my Polish grandmother had endured a harrowing personal experience during the Second World War. I was told she had been forcefully rounded up along with her mother by the Nazis and then taken to Germany, where she spent the next several years of her life. That was all I knew.

I was born and raised in Scotland and only got to visit my grandmother every other summer, during the school holidays with my mother. Our visits together were always happy times. We adored each other, sharing only pleasant and enjoyable times and an unconditional love.

It wasn't until 2002, when I visited my grandmother in Kraków for seven weeks, that she finally opened up to me and shared her heartbreaking story. We talked about it many more times over the years when I would visit, and each time she would share some new chapters and experiences from her life with me. She always said I should write her story down for her one day, as she was now too old to do it herself. I said I would, and now I have.

What you are about to read is her story.

NOTE TO THE READER

Thank you for taking the time to read my grandmother's amazing life story and for your interest in it. I always knew it would make for a powerful and inspiring read, and from the wonderful feedback I've received since *In Alexa's Shoes* was published in June 2019, my belief has been confirmed. Thank you kindly for the many letters, emails, and messages from readers around the world who have taken Alexa into their hearts and kept her memory alive.

How wonderful a journey it has been so far in becoming a debut author. I only wish Alexa could've been around to witness it all and the outpouring of love towards her and the incredible woman she was. As you know from the Preface, I always promised my grandmother I would write her story one day. I believed I would but didn't really know how. I started writing on January 1, 2018, and by the end of September that same year, I had completed my first draft.

I next discovered a collaborative publishing company in the USA and, after interviewing with them, signed an 18-month contract to learn how to write, market, and publish my novel the best way. Alexa's health was deteriorating rapidly and I was in a mad rush to get the book out so I could hand Alexa her very own copy, keeping my promise to her.

Sadly, Alexa passed away on April 15, 2019, only two months before the book's release day. I immediately searched for flights to Poland in time for my grandmother's funeral.

It was a very sad day but Alexa would've been touched to see the sun gloriously shining, flowers in abundance, and her family who loved her, surrounding her as she was laid to rest next to the man she'd always loved.

After flying home, I went horseback riding to try and lift my deep sorrow. Unfortunately, I was thrown from my large Clydesdale for the first time in six years due to someone spooking the horse. The fall was a violent one and I ended up in hospital with a broken bone in my back. It was total agony, and yet I still had to get the book out.

I had hired an independent editor to do a final copy edit and almost had a heart attack when I received the edited manuscript. There were more errors than when I had first sent her my manuscript! But I was determined to stick to my deadline and release date; out of respect for my gran, I had to keep my promise. The charges for correcting the multiple errors were adding up, so I fixed as many as I could myself so as to not have to pay a fortune in correction charges, which turned out to be a very good idea.

I pushed the button to publish in June and immediately went to *Number One Best New Release* on Amazon, even before my book had gone into pre-sales. Then I reached the *Number One Bestseller* spot in a category in the USA, and then in the UK. This has happened multiple times since then, and today, as I write this, *In Alexa's Shoes* has achieved its 1000th Amazon number one best seller spot.

Alexa would've been as amazed as I am, if not more so. The majority of reviews for my novel have been five-star ones, which pleases me greatly. There have, however, been some lesser ranking ones referencing the poor editing, and I cannot disagree with them on that point. A great editor is so important. I have learned much in my writing journey so far and look forward to perfecting the art in my future books.

Finally, *In Alexa's Shoes* has now been re-edited. Better late than never. And so, to everyone who was kind enough to see past the bad punctuation, grammar, and point of view (POV) errors and *still* fall in love with Alexa's story, my heartfelt thanks. This revised edition is how this story should read.

CHAPTER 1

In September of 1940, Alexa was one week into the start of her new school year. A blisteringly hot summer had finally come to an end throughout Europe, and as autumn began, the leaves on the trees were beginning to slowly turn color.

Alexa sat close to one of three large picture-framed windows in her classroom, which looked out onto a large field at the back of the school. The field was surrounded by a forest at its far edge and Alexa had a front row seat as the seasons put on a natural performance for her. The scenery was ever-changing, and although ever so slowly, the trees always entertained her. Autumn was her favorite season; she loved the vibrant colors and the dance of the leaves. Often accompanying her view, she would hear Vivaldi's *Four Seasons* playing in her head. He was the composer of whom she was fondest and whose music she knew very well from listening to it with her mother over the radio at home.

Alexa watched the seasons change with great anticipation and pleasure. As autumn shed its colorful beat, she was in awe of the rich vibrant reds, the golden yellows, burnt oranges, and copper rusts on display. Then ever so slowly, day by day, one by one, the leaves would gently fall to the ground. She could hear violins play in her head as the autumn leaves fell swirling, spinning, twisting, and turning on their descent before being added to the cushioned pile on the forest floor below.

Some days they fell faster than others, especially when the elements took over, blowing strong winds that frantically tossed them through the air, tearing the dry leaves from the safety of the branches that once held them securely. Eventually the winds would die down and calmness would be restored. It was nature's way. Everything had its time and its season. Life, death, and rebirth. Nothing could stay the same forever. This, however, was the constant, safe, peaceful place in which she often found herself daydreaming.

Alexa was a model student, a smart, creative girl who learned fast and worked hard in class; always obedient, always doing as she was told. It was usually only after her schoolwork was completed that Alexa allowed herself the luxury of letting her thoughts drift off.

It was late afternoon on Friday, and as Alexa looked out the window, she noticed some sudden movements at the field's edge where the forest began. There were what seemed to be three dark-colored military trucks parked on the grass verge, with groups of men filing out the back of them. They were German military trucks. These had become a very common sight around Poland since the German invasion the previous year.

Alexa looked harder and focused more than she had done previously, squinting her eyes until they were almost closed, as she tried to see more clearly into the distance. She had never seen any gatherings of people or group activity there before. The men seemed to be carrying something over their shoulders and every now and then as they moved, the sun would reflect a bright silver glint, as if from metal. The men then disappeared off into the woods, through the trees, and were gone from sight.

Alexa lived at her home in Lublin, in the East of Poland, with her mother, Sophia, aged thirty-seven, and her eight-year-old sister, Asha. Their father, Alexander, had been older than their mother and had died after a long and painful illness when Alexa was only seven years old. He had been a wonderful man, a devoted father and husband who loved his wife and family dearly.

He had adored Alexa, who was named after him even though she was a girl. Being that she was his first-born child, he spent most of his free time playing games with her and encouraging her creativity. He made a habit of sketching and drawing regularly with Alexa, as he tried to teach her and pass on his artistic talents. He was an accomplished artist who had many of his original oil paintings displayed in art galleries for sale throughout Poland, as well as in some other main European cities. Although he had given up painting commissions for clients and creating new works of art, he took great pleasure in showing Alexa how to mix colors and how to make a blank canvas come to life. He taught her about the great masters of the past as well as their various painting styles and encouraged her to develop a style of her own.

He tried to share all things he viewed as beautiful and important in life with her, sensing he only had a short time to live. This contributed to them being a very close and loving family, extremely attentive to each other's needs.

Sophia's mother, Sarah, also lived with them since the death of her husband and helped to care for and raise the girls. Sarah was a religious woman, a good Roman Catholic lady who had a real love for God and the Bible. She shared this love with both her granddaughters, teaching them Bible truths as they grew up. Sadly, Sarah had died suddenly, two years earlier, when Alexa was only eleven. It was a deeply painful loss for them all. Sarah had been such a big influence in all of their lives, and her good habits, morals, and teachings remained very much alive in their home life and in their hearts.

That Friday afternoon, as she waited for the school day to be done, Alexa was full of anticipation. Her mother had promised to buy her a new pair of shoes for school in town the coming weekend. Alexa knew her mother worked hard and was careful to save money for important necessities, which made this promised purchase an extra-special treat. Alexa was so excited she could think of little else. She had passed by the town square's only shoe shop many times, stopping to peer through its windows, her nose pressed up against the glass as she imagined wearing several pairs of the pretty shoes inside. There was a royal blue leather pair with a reasonably-sized small, square heel, a side strap, and a shiny silver buckle. Alexa thought these were especially beautiful, blue being her favorite color. A black pair was more practical but she wasn't too keen on them.

Deep down, she really wanted the one pair of shiny red patent shoes in the shop. They were a brand-new style and so eye-catching but she knew her mother would never allow her to get those. After all, they were also the most expensive pair in the shop. No, her shoes needed to be a practical pair, comfortable and durable—ones that would last.

As Alexa sat in the classroom, daydreaming about the blue shoes, her thoughts were brought back to reality when the bell rang, bringing Friday's school day to an end. However, the bell had rung an hour earlier than it normally did and the confused teacher told the children in her classroom to remain in their seats while she went to investigate. A little while later, she returned with a serious expression on her face.

"Children, I need you all to quickly put away your books, bring your coats and bags with you, and follow me out of the building, now," she said.

The children murmured their confusion but did as they were told. They packed up their bags and followed their teacher along the corridors towards the main doors, excited to get outside and into the freedom of the open field. But their smiles soon faded as they saw SS soldiers with large and mean-looking German shepherd dogs outside the school building and guarding the gates. Freedom was most definitely not to be found there.

The large group of children came to an abrupt stop. Eight armed soldiers motioned them to line up in twos along with their teachers. A tall German officer, sharply dressed in his grey Nazi uniform and shiny black jackboots, instructed the children in a firm, loud voice that under no circumstances must they go near to or walk through the field at the back of the school. Nor were they permitted to freely go play in or explore the woods anymore. This area was now out of bounds to everyone except the German soldiers. Instead, they were to use the main road in the front of the building to the right, to walk away from the school area and back towards their homes.

It was abundantly clear to everyone this was an order, not an invitation. There was no personal choice in the matter. The teachers knew better than to ask questions and immediately motioned the children under their care to quickly walk out onto the roadway. The soldiers told them to keep walking briskly together along the side of the road, to keep to the left, and to continue going until they arrived home.

"Don't look back or come back here for anything!" they barked at the children.

The teachers began the long walk together. There was an air of fear surrounding them all. As the last of the children joined the long procession, two SS soldiers stood guard outside the school gate and six armed soldiers followed along behind them.

"*Schnell!*" the soldiers shouted.

Alexa was afraid and longed to be with her mother, safe and secure in her arms. The other children's pale, drawn faces and trembling lips showed her she wasn't alone in her fear.

Alexa had paired up with her best friend, Helena, who lived near her. They held each other's hands tightly as they quickly marched along the road. Alexa silently began reciting her favorite prayer to herself. Her grandmother had taught her a version of the 91st Psalm from the Bible when she was only five years old, and every night before lights out and sleep, she'd say the prayer out loud in rhyme form. Once Asha had finally learned it off by heart, they would recite it together, and this became their bedtime ritual. Even after her grandmother's death, Alexa faithfully continued saying the prayer out loud, in the morning and at night. Now however, Alexa silently repeated the prayer as hard and as sincerely as she could, with the firm belief that God would hear her and help. *'You are my refuge and my stronghold, Oh God . . . Rescue me from the bird catcher . . . Protect me under your wings . . . You are my Salvation.'*

A few seconds later, two of the six soldiers marching them along pulled back, stopping off on the roadway to stand guard with their barking dogs beside them. A few miles farther along the road, another two of the soldiers halted, also taking up guard positions along the route.

For the first twenty minutes into the long walk, none of the group spoke at all due to the uncertainty of what was happening and the heightened sense of fear which they all felt. Finally, as they reached the edge of town, the last two soldiers peeled off and took up their posts on the side of the road, as the other soldiers had done previously. With the teachers now leading the group alone and the soldiers no longer with them, light chatter began amongst the group of children once again.

"What do you think was going on in the woods, Alexa?" asked Helena. "What's this all about?"

"I don't know, but in school as I looked out of the classroom window across the field, I saw some German army trucks parked at the edge of the forest. There were groups of men getting out of the trucks and disappearing through the trees."

"I don't like the sound of that," Helena said.

"I know, me neither. Oh, and they were carrying something that seemed silvery over their shoulders because I saw the sun reflect off whatever shiny metal-looking things they were carrying," Alexa added.

They walked on for a few more minutes in silence, lost in their own thoughts, until a new one floated in. Helena changed the subject.

"So, what pair of shoes have you decided on, Alexa?"

"Well, you know I'd really love the red patent ones, but realistically I think it's going to have to be the royal blue ones. I really love them too and they are so much more practical."

"Blue is your favorite color and I'm sure they will look so good on you. Plus, they'll go with anything. Can I try them on when you get them?" Helena asked.

"Yes, for sure. I'm getting them tomorrow morning in town with my Mama, so I'll be wearing them to school on Monday. You can try them on during our lunch break."

"Oh, thanks Alexa, I can't wait."

"Have a good weekend and I'll see you on Monday at school."

The two best friends briefly hugged goodbye. Alexa watched as Helena quickly crossed the road and headed off towards a side street, close to where she lived. Before she disappeared out of sight, she turned back, raised her hand high in the air and waved. Alexa smiled and waved back, blowing a kiss in the wind, and then Helena was gone.

Alexa's little sister, Asha, had not been at school that day. Their mother had said she could stay and rest at home as she had taken ill with a sore throat and bad cough and hadn't slept much through the previous night. Alexa was now quite relieved that Asha hadn't been at school that day.

Asha was quite different from Alexa. She had always been the frailer of the two sisters and she was a worrier. Perhaps the early death of her father and grandmother, at such a tender age had affected her character formation. Alexa always took extra special attention and care when it came to her little sister, always trying her best to protect her from life's cruelties, knowing how fragile she was.

Alexa finally arrived home safely and breathed a deep sigh of relief as she closed the door behind her. "Mama I'm home; I'm safe and I'm home."

Sophia came out of the kitchen as Alexa ran into her arms.

"Whatever's the matter, my dear child? What's happened to you?"

"The SS, the soldiers, they came to the fields at the back of the school in trucks this afternoon. They sent groups of men with what I think looked like shovels into the woods. I saw them from the window in my classroom. When the bell rang early at 2 o'clock, they were waiting outside the school. They ordered everyone to stay away from the fields and the forest and made us all march together along the roadway. We had to take the long way to get home. I was so scared, Mama!" Alexa spoke very fast, trying to give her mother all the pertinent facts of what she had gone through.

"Oh, my darling girl, are you alright? Are you hurt?"

"No, I'm okay; they never hurt us. The German guards followed behind us with their rifles and their big scary dogs barking at our heels, but they didn't hurt us. The teachers were with us and I walked next to Helena the whole way. Oh, Mama I'm so glad I'm home."

"Me too, sweetheart. There, there, it's all okay. You're safe now. Sit down and I'll make you some hot tea. There's some cake left, and the sweetness will help you feel better. Sit, darling."

Alexa sat at the kitchen table while her mother quickly boiled some water on the stove. She kicked off her tight, well-worn shoes under the table. She had outgrown them.

"My feet are sore, Mama."

"Don't you worry, Alexa. Tomorrow is Saturday and I'm still taking you into town to buy your new pair of shoes, as I promised you. Your feet will feel great in them and then you'll forget all about today's drama," Sophia said.

"Thank you, Mama, I can't wait. Would it be alright if I got the pretty royal blue pair of shoes with the silver buckles?"

"Yes, my beautiful girl, I knew you would pick the blue ones in the end." Sophia smiled at her daughter as she placed a slice of cake on the table in front of her. Just then, they heard Asha coming out of her bedroom where she had been asleep. "Let's not tell your sister about what happened today, Alexa," Sophia said quietly. "We'll tell her before school on Monday."

Alexa nodded in silent agreement, knowing how worried it would make Asha. She watched as Sophia poured out three cups of hot tea and Asha joined them at the kitchen table, comforted by the normalcy of the scene.

"How are you feeling now, Asha? Any better?" Sophia asked. "Here, drink some tea; I put some lemon and a little honey in it for you. It'll help soothe your throat."

"Thank you, Mama. My throat's still sore and I feel so hot," Asha said, coughing.

Sophia leaned over and felt her forehead.

"You do have a bit of a temperature. Let's get you back into bed, sweetheart. Tomorrow morning when Alexa and I go into town to buy her new shoes, I will ask Magda from next door to look after you until we get back. Come on, I'll carry your drink through to the bedroom for you. Now back into bed."

Alexa promised she would go through and read to Asha a little later, after she had finished helping their mother prepare dinner. Asha was happy with the plan. The sisters loved each other very much and enjoyed every moment they spent together.

Alexa was now thirteen and a half years old and was blossoming into a beautiful young woman, the very image of her mother. Her soft, smooth, unblemished skin had a golden glow from the summer sun that gave her a healthy bronzed complexion. Her eyes were like deep pools of blue sapphires, which drew you into her gaze and held you there for a while. Her hair, falling soft and straight to just beneath her shoulders, was a beautiful shade of light golden blonde and shimmered as the sun kissed it. Her figure was shapely and perfectly proportioned, giving the impression that she could have been older than she actually was. She appeared strong and healthy and was indeed a stunningly beautiful young Polish teenager.

Sophia told Alexa she wouldn't be gone long and went next door to her neighbor's house. Magda was a German woman who lived in the adjoining house with her husband, Michael, and their nine-year-old twins, Eva and Peter. Five years earlier, they had moved from Berlin to Lublin. Over the years they had become good friends as well as neighbors, with Asha and the twins often playing together at each other's houses or in the garden. Sophia knocked on Magda's front door.

"Hi Magda, I need a favor. Asha is feeling poorly with a sore throat and running a slight temperature, and I wondered if you could look after her in the morning for about an hour or two while I take Alexa into town to buy her new shoes?"

"Yes, it's no problem, I would be happy to watch over her. Just let me know what time."

"We'll leave at around nine, if that's okay?"

"Yes, Michael will be home, and he can look after the twins."

Sophia thanked her friend and returned home to make dinner. After they'd eaten, Alexa read a little to Asha as promised while the hours ticked away and darkness fell. Alexa got ready for bed, brushed her teeth and combed her long blonde hair. Sophia came into the bedroom to say goodnight, and tell her girls she loved them, as she always did. Alexa then began their ritual prayer of Psalm 91.

"Anyone dwelling in the secret place of the Most High will lodge under the shadow of the Almighty.

I will say to the Lord: 'You are my refuge and my fortress, my God in whom I trust.'

For He will rescue you from the trap of the bird catcher, from the destructive pestilence.

He will cover you with his feathers, and under His wings you will take refuge.

His truth will be thy shield and a protective wall.

Thou shalt not be afraid of the terror by night, nor the arrow that flies by day.

Nor the pestilence that walks in darkness, nor for the destruction that ravages at midday.

A thousand will fall at your side and ten thousand at your right hand, but to you, it shall not come near.

Only with thine eyes shall you behold and see the reward of the wicked.

Because you said, 'God, is my refuge,' you have made the Most High your dwelling.

No evil will befall you, neither shall any plague come nigh upon thy dwelling.

For He will give his angels a command concerning you, to guard you in all your ways.

They shall bear thee up in their hands, less thou dash thy foot against a stone.

On the young lion and the cobra, you will tread;

You will trample underfoot the maned lion and the big snake.

God said: Because he has set his love on me, I will deliver him.

I will set him on high because he knows my name.

He shall call upon me, and I will answer him.

I will be with him in distress.

I will rescue him and honor him.

I will satisfy him with long life, and I will cause him to see my acts of salvation."[1]

"Amen," they said in unison.

Sophia leaned over and kissed each of her daughters on their foreheads. "I love you my beautiful girls; sleep tight," she said as she turned out the light and left the room, leaving the door slightly ajar behind her.

CHAPTER 2

Saturday morning arrived with a deep red sun rising up from the horizon. The early morning birds sang a wake-up call as they flew about their daily business. Sophia was first to awaken in the household and went about the kitchen preparing breakfast for her and her two daughters. Alexa was first to appear from the girls' bedroom. She hugged her mother good morning then sat down at the kitchen table.

"Did you sleep well, my darling?" Sophia asked.

"Yes, Mama. At first, I was too excited to sleep, thinking about getting my new pair of shoes today. So, I started counting sheep but that didn't work so I started counting shoes in my mind instead and must have lost count and eventually dozed off at about 300."

"You're so funny, Alexa." Sophia smiled as she walked behind her chair and began affectionately stroking her daughter's long blonde hair. "Was that 300 shoes, or 300 pairs?" They looked at one another and burst out laughing.

From the bedroom, Asha could be heard coughing, so Sophia fixed a warm cup of black tea with lemon and a spoonful of honey and took it through to her.

"Good morning, sweetheart, are you feeling any better today?"

"Morning, Mama. No, I feel even worse today I think." Asha coughed again.

"Don't worry, my love, I'm sure it will clear up soon. Drink your tea while it's hot. Magda is going to come and sit with you this morning while Alexa and I go into town to buy her new shoes. I'll go into Carl's shop on our way back and get something to help your cough. We won't be away too long," Sophia reassured her.

"Okay, Mama, thanks."

Alexa had finished her breakfast, washed, dressed, and was ready to go. "What time is Magda coming, Mama?"

"She said she'd be here at 9 o'clock, so we have about fifteen minutes yet."

While Alexa cleared the table and washed up the few dishes they had used for breakfast, Sophia reached up into the back of one of the kitchen cupboards and pulled out an old glass jar. Inside, wrapped up in a handkerchief, was the money she had saved to buy Alexa's new shoes. She screwed off the lid and emptied the contents onto the wooden table. It seemed there were more coins than notes but after Sophia had counted out the amount, she gave an approving nod, content she had enough money for what she needed to buy that day.

Sophia and Alexa went through to the bedroom where Asha was still curled up under the covers. Sophia placed a second cup of warm lemon and honey tea on the table next to her bed and asked if there was anything else she needed before they left.

"No thanks but come back quickly. I miss you both already."

"Aww, darling don't worry; we'll be back as soon as possible. Two hours maximum."

"Mama, can I wear your rings while you are in town?" asked Asha.

"Okay, darling, I suppose it's alright since you're going to be in bed the whole time," Sophia said. She took off her gold wedding band along with her engagement ring, which was also made of gold. It had a raised rectangular-cut amethyst stone in the center, held securely in place by four gold claws. Sophia still wore them every day, as if her husband were still alive and with her, and Asha often liked to try them on her little fingers and pretend. Her mother handed the rings to Asha. "Be good for Magda."

The doorbell rang. Sophia leaned over and kissed her daughter's cheek. "I love you."

Alexa opened the front door to let Magda in, put on her coat, then ran back to Asha's bedside. She leaned down and kissed her forehead.

"See you soon, little sister. Feel better."

It was 9 o'clock when Sophia and Alexa closed the door behind them and began the twenty-minute walk into town. The red morning sun had long since disappeared from the sky and it began to get cloudy and slightly overcast. Alexa took her mother's hand as they crossed the road.

The town was fairly busy for an early Saturday morning. Many of the locals were out grocery shopping for the weekend at the farmers' market, set up in the town square. Friends chatted on the streets, while children looked for mischief to amuse themselves. Most of the local shops were already open with customers browsing and buying their desired goods. Alexa noticed her friend Karolina walking out of the butcher's shop across the street, with her mother and little brother. She waved to them. They all smiled and waved back.

A few more steps and finally they reached the shoe shop. "Mama, we're here," Alexa said, bursting with excitement.

"Okay, let's get your new shoes first. Everything else can wait until after that."

The shop wasn't very big. Two wide concrete steps led up to a wooden-framed glass door, flanked by two large framed display windows. Sophia reached up for the handle and opened the door. A small brass bell rang overhead announcing their arrival. They both stepped inside and as the door closed behind them, the brass bell rang once again. Alexa immediately ran over to where the royal blue pair of shoes were on display.

"Good morning, ladies. Can I help you with something?" asked a well-dressed woman in her late fifties, her hair tied up neatly in a bun and very politely spoken.

"Yes, thank you," said Sophia. "Could my daughter please try on those pretty royal blue shoes over there with the silver buckle, in her size?"

"Yes of course, let me get them for her. What size is she? Perhaps a 28?" estimated the shopkeeper.

"Maybe a size 30 would be better? So she has some room to grow in them. You know how fast these young teenage girls grow, and I want these shoes to last her," Sophia said.

The shopkeeper nodded. "One moment please." She disappeared behind a long burgundy velvet curtain at the back of the shop to locate the shoes.

Sophia told Alexa to come and sit on a chair next to her, where she could comfortably try on the shoes. Alexa took off her coat and placed it neatly on the chair beside her.

"Oh Mama, I'm so excited. You're so good to me, thank you for today." Alexa threw her arms round her mother's neck and kissed her cheek.

"Oh sweetheart, you're so welcome. You deserve them. You've always been such a good and pleasant girl. I'm so happy you are my daughter and no one else's," Sophia said.

The shopkeeper reappeared from behind the velvet curtain, opening the shoe box she held in her hands. "Here we go, size 30 for the young lady to try on."

Alexa took the shoes and stared at them for a few seconds before carefully placing them on the floor. She could smell the new leather. Kicking off her old shoes, she gently slid her right foot into the right shoe first. She pulled over the leather strap and fastened the silver buckle. She smiled blissfully as she slipped her foot into the left shoe and fastened the buckle.

"Stand up, darling, try walking in them. They look beautiful on you," Sophia said.

"Walk over to the mirror and you can see how you they look on you," the shopkeeper suggested.

Alexa walked over to the long ornate mirror leaning against the back wall of the shop. She could see the reflection of the street outside behind her, as the sun briefly peeked through the clouds in between the buildings, casting random shadows and shapes onto the ground. She was much more interested in the new blue shoes and looked admiringly at her feet, pointing her toe to the left and then to the right. She turned sideways to see the small heel and then swiveled to see how they looked from the back. As the daylight caught the silver buckle, it glistened brightly in the mirror.

"How do they feel? Are they comfortable?"

"They feel great on. I love them, Mama."

"Then you can have them, my love."

Alexa walked the entire length of the shop, looking down at the shoes on her feet the whole time. Her mother spoke with the shopkeeper, telling her she would buy the new shoes for her daughter. They continued to admire them on Alexa while she modeled them with a tremendous smile across her face.

All of a sudden and from out of nowhere, there was what sounded like a loud roll of thunder. Alexa's smile faded. Sophia and the shopkeeper appeared to be puzzled by the noise too. It was strange as there had been no thick dark clouds in the sky that morning and no obvious signs of bad weather on the horizon. Alexa shrugged it off, turned around and with a spring in her step walked back to the mirror. But this time, the reflection she saw behind her had changed— and had changed for the worse. All traces of her beaming happy smile disappeared in an instant.

"Mama, look. The German soldiers are outside in the street!" Alexa gasped, her voice full of panic.

Both Sophia and the shopkeeper immediately turned to look out the window, their eyes growing wide with horror as they stared at the terror unfolding outside on the street. The thunderous noise they had all heard was the sound of large army trucks rolling along the cobbled streets of the town square. The heavy vibrations made the shop windows rattle in their wooden frames. Alexa's heart filled with fear, even more so as she looked at her mother and the shopkeeper's pale faces and open mouths.

Sophia shook her head as if to snap herself out of her terrified paralysis. She pulled Alexa close to her, took a firm grip of her hand and asked the shopkeeper if there was a back door leading out of the property. But the woman shook her head.

"No, there isn't," she said, chewing her bottom lip.

Through the windows they could see a line of about five or six large grey-colored German military trucks parked to one side of the street, along with a dozen or so military armored cars. On the other side of the street, people were being brutally pushed and shoved into lines by the Nazi soldiers. The locals were being dragged out of the shops at gunpoint and forced to stand together in the middle of the town square.

"Mama, there's Karolina . . . they've got Karolina!" Alexa shrieked.

Sophia held her daughter's hand even tighter. "Don't worry darling, just try to stay calm," she said, not really knowing what to say for the best in the situation into which they had now been thrown.

The door of the shoe shop burst open, the brass bell above the doorjamb clanging loudly as if in warning.

"Get out. Everybody out. Get out onto the street now. *Raus! Schnell!*" barked an angry-looking German soldier as he pointed his rifle at them menacingly. A second soldier strained to hold a snarling German shepherd dog on the end of a long chain, its saliva splashing the shiny shoes set out on display.

Sophia moved hurriedly towards the door, grasping hold of Alexa's hand. There was no time to think, only to do. To do as they were ordered. To go outside with all the others. They spilled out onto the street and lined up with all the other people being forced against their will.

The woman from the shoe shop began to protest her innocence aloud, insisting there had been some kind of mistake. "Why are we being treated like this? We are not Jews! We are good, honest, hard-working Polish people. There must be some mistake. I have identification papers and I *own* this shop."

The SS commander standing closest to the woman and who seemed to be in charge of the operation laughed loudly. "Good and honest . . . ha! Now I've heard it all," he laughed sarcastically with his fellow SS officers and soldiers. "Good for nothing is more like it and honest liars, she should actually say." The soldiers all laughed again. "Hard workers, eh? Well let's hope so for your sakes. I hope you Poles work harder than the lazy Jews do."

The woman became hysterical and began begging the commander to let her go. She moved closer towards him in the middle of the street, her pleas becoming louder, more desperate and out of control. Sophia quickly whispered to Alexa to close her eyes as the commander laughed again and reached for his pistol. Pointing it at the woman he shouted, "Now you can go. Go directly to meet your maker."

Taking aim, he pulled the trigger. The single bullet hit its intended target and the woman became limp, collapsing to the ground in a heap. And just as fast, the life left her body. Her head connected with the cobbles making a loud cracking noise, then a slow stream of deep red began to fill the channels between the stones, her blood staining the mortar.

A few horrified screams could be heard from the group, mainly from some of the women and children. Several of the men gasped deep breaths, their eyes wide in shock at what was taking place before them. The commander blew the smoking tip of his pistol, then returned it to his holster. "Now let that be a warning to you all, to shut up and follow orders. Don't speak," he ordered.

Alexa could feel her mother's heart pounding, while her own body shook with fear. Sophia again squeezed her hand, the hand she hadn't let go of since they were inside the shop, only tighter this time. Some of the children in the lineup were crying hysterically.

When the commander turned his back on them, Sophia whispered to Alexa, "Don't let them see you're scared. Concentrate, darling. Look down at your shoes and say your prayer over to yourself."

Alexa looked down at her new blue shoes and fixed her stare upon the silver buckle. She closed her eyes and began silently reciting the 91st Psalm she knew so well, and gradually her trembling reduced. *'You are my refuge, my God in whom I trust. Cover me with your wings, shield me.'* All of a sudden, she became still, a strange calmness spreading through her whole body. When she opened her eyes, she spotted her friend Karolina standing in the lineup with her little brother, holding their mother's hands. Alexa was relieved Karolina was with her family. As their eyes met briefly, through their fear, they gave a slight smile of hope to one another.

The town clock chimed the hour out of its tower in the market square, its bell ringing loudly. It was 10 o'clock in the morning. Alexa suddenly became overwhelmed with thoughts of Asha who was back at home with Magda, and her heart began to beat even faster. How were they going to get home to her now? She was filled with a heightened sense of fear, and each chime that echoed through the town square seemed to jar her entire body to the core. She wished desperately that she could stop time, or rewind it, back to before she and her mother had left their home that morning. But such thoughts were futile. Like chasing after the wind.

The commander gave orders in German to half a dozen of his officers and more than two dozen other soldiers who gave him their full attention before he sent them off to their allotted positions. They quickly began selecting all of the men from the lineup who were over fifty years of age—about fifteen in total—and ordering them to run over to the first parked truck.

"Leave your bags and packages on the ground; you will get them back later," commanded one of the officers in Polish.

Next, they ordered all the women over fifty years in age to run over to the first truck, where the older men were already standing, bringing the total of that group to about forty-five. Next, they ordered all the younger men, aged from sixteen to fifty, to go and stand behind the second truck.

Half the soldiers held loaded rifles in their hands, aiming them directly at the men. The remaining soldiers carried solid wooden batons in their hands and used them to restrain the group with brutal force. Some of the soldiers fired a few warning shots up into the air while others swung their batons haphazardly. The group of younger men, about twenty-five in all, reluctantly began making their way over to the second truck.

Alexa felt her mother's grip on her hand tighten and her body begin to shake as the officer ordered all the women aged sixteen to fifty to go and stand next to the third parked truck. Alexa, only thirteen and a half years old, wouldn't be included in that group. They held each other tightly, desperately, like many of the other mothers and children in the street with them.

Some soldiers rushed over to them, their barking dogs snapping and snarling at the women, as they forcibly pulled the children away from their mothers, while swinging their batons to divide them and break the tight clasping of their hands. Sophia's hand slowly let go of Alexa's as she was rushed over to the third truck with the other women and mothers who had also been forced to abandon their children. There were about thirty of them in total.

Sophia and Alexa never took their eyes off each other. Alexa stood alone, staring at her mother, tears slowly trickling down her cheeks. Sophia didn't make a sound, but inside she was silently screaming. Tears brimmed in her eyes, but she didn't allow them to fall.

Alexa glanced to her left and saw her friend Karolina standing with her little brother, grasping his hand tightly, her other arm wrapped protectively around his shoulder. She too had tears rolling down her face, as they stood, alone, without their mother.

The officer ordered the children who were under the age of eight to go and stand next to the fourth truck; the smaller children were left abandoned on the ground. The soldiers pushed and dragged them over, about twenty children in all. Karolina and her four-year-old brother were now forcibly pulled apart. He, along with the other infant children, were violently pulled by their arms across the square. The soldiers threw them up into the back of the fourth truck. Spine-chilling screams from the helpless parents filled the air, as they looked on in horror. The children could be heard screaming and crying hysterically from inside of the truck. An SS soldier fired his rifle up into the air multiple times as a reminder for everybody to keep themselves in check.

The ferocious-looking German shepherd dogs continued to bark and growl at each group, straining to break free from their chains as they were made to stand guard, merely inches away from the terrified people. These were blood-hungry hounds that were deliberately fed minimal amounts of food in order to make them more threatening. Their presence was terrifying.

Now all who were left in the lineup were the terrified boys and girls aged eight to sixteen years, about eighteen altogether, including Alexa. They were told to run over and stand next to the fifth parked truck. The commander in charge made his way down the street to the first truck and ordered all the older people, male and female, to climb into the back of the vehicle. He walked to the second truck and ordered all the men to get into that truck. At the third truck he told all the women to get inside. Then he passed by the fourth truck, already loaded with the smaller younger children, still frantically crying out in vain for their mothers and fathers.

As he got to the fifth truck, he looked each child up and down from head to toe, examining their appearance as well as their physical build. When he got to Alexa, he seemed quite surprised. He stopped, looked down at her shoes for a few seconds then continued upwards to her sapphire blue eyes. Alexa suddenly became filled with feelings of guilt and thought frantically, *'Oh no, we didn't pay for the shoes!'* He stared into her eyes intensely, which made her even more nervous. So, she shifted her eyes and looked away, down towards the ground. The commander took his baton and placed it under her chin.

"Look up girl, lift your head. Look at me," he demanded.

Alexa did as she was told. With his baton, the commander lifted up her chin, turning her head to the right and then to the left. Next, he ran the baton slowly down the length of her long blonde hair, then stepped backwards. He walked over to one of the officers who was standing in front of the fifth truck and pointed to Alexa, as he said something to him in German.

Alexa lifted her eyes from the ground at which she'd been staring. Turning to her right, she could see the third truck down the line, onto which the women were now being loaded. She managed to catch a glimpse of her mother's blonde head as she was being forced into the back of the truck.

"Alexa! Alexa!" her distraught mother cried out, as if unable to keep silent any longer. She locked eyes with her daughter and began waving her hands frantically in the air. She now sensed they were saying goodbye, and a grey shadow fell over her face as if all the blood had drained from it.

"Mama!" Alexa yelled back. "Mama!" she screamed.

"My Alexa!" were Sophia's final hysterical words as she was pushed into the back of the truck, disappearing from Alexa's sight. Alexa stood rigid, staring at the truck into which Sophia had been shoved, hoping to catch another glimpse of her mother.

The children and teenagers, including Alexa, were all finally loaded into the back of the fifth truck. Almost simultaneously, all of the military trucks started their engines and revved up, filling the air with diesel fumes. Over the sound of the loud, angry, growling engines could be heard desperate and anguished voices calling out random names: parents for their children, children for their mothers. Blood-curdling screams, wretched cries, and frantic despair blended into a hopeless cacophony of grief-stricken panic.

Two heavily-armed soldiers climbed up into the back of each truck, along with two bloodthirsty barking German shepherds under their command. As the crazed dogs barked and snarled their handlers ordered the terrified people to be silent; if not, they would be shot and the dogs would be set upon them, they threatened.

The commander ordered two of his soldiers to remove the dead shopkeeper whom he had shot earlier from where she lay in the middle of the square and for her to be loaded into the first truck. The soldiers immediately obeyed, dragging her lifeless body off the cobbled street and throwing it up into the back of the truck in amongst the older men and women already there.

Alexa heard the dead woman's body land in the truck with a heavy thud, like a sack full of wet sand. The men and women already in the truck stepped backwards, their eyes wide with shock and terror. One of the soldiers shouted that this was a warning to remain quiet and follow orders or they would suffer the same consequences. An overwhelming sense of hopelessness seemed to fall upon the reluctant prisoners, their cries and screams reduced to whimpers.

The soldiers appeared to be unaffected by the anguish of their prisoners as they dropped the rear canvas covers of their trucks down so that no one could see in. But it also meant no one could see out. Before their cover was dropped, Alexa noticed the clouds had darkened in the sky and rain had begun to fall. On the street, two gaunt-looking Jewish prisoners in dirty old raggedy clothing, with yellow Stars of David sewn onto armbands on their jacket sleeves, appeared. They were ordered to collect all of the bags and packages left on the ground by the locals and to pile them onto a nearby wooden cart. An armed soldier then instructed them to load all of the items into the rear of an empty military vehicle, before they too were told to climb inside and placed under his guard. The prisoners inside of the trucks wouldn't be getting their belongings back later, after all, thought Alexa sadly.

Alexa's truck, the one with all the youths loaded onto it, was the last to join the convoy. She caught sight of the first truck, carrying the older men and women, as it headed towards the edge of town and then turned in an easterly direction, with an armored car in front of it and another at its rear. The second and third trucks, carrying the younger men and women, also headed out of town, each with an army vehicle escort, heading for the railway station. The fourth truck, with the youngest children in it, followed the route of the first truck, traveling east. It was also escorted by armored vehicles. The fifth truck, the one in which Alexa sat with the other youths, hadn't pulled off yet. Alexa strained to hear the diminishing engine noises of the other trucks as they rumbled away.

Alexa huddled at the back of the truck with her friend, Karolina. They didn't say anything to one another. They hugged each other tightly, trembling with fear, as they waited to learn their fate. Alexa said her prayer silently over and over again to herself. Suddenly, the truck began to roll forward. Picking up speed, it reached the edge of town and turned towards the railway station.

CHAPTER 3

The rain had started to fall lightly at first, but soon became torrential. The first truck, carrying both the males and females over fifty, had been driving for approximately fifteen minutes when it pulled off from the tarred roadway onto softer, more uneven ground. The heavy black rubber tires were now rolling through wet mud, trying to hold their grip as they drove along the edge of the field where it met the forest. Finally, the truck came to a stop and its engines were shut off. The prisoners inside remained silent, apart from the sound of their nervous heavy breathing.

The rain pelted down on the canvas roof and poured small streams of water into the truck through little holes above them. Having no view outside of the vehicle, the prisoners remained in the dark as to where they had been driven. Outside the truck, boots could be heard squelching in the mud. Orders were shouted in German while dogs barked loudly, all to the background noise of the heavy falling rain.

Suddenly, the two soldiers in the back of the truck pulled up the rear canvas cover and fastened it open, allowing daylight to somewhat illuminate the interior of the vehicle. They jumped down onto the muddy wet ground with their dogs and turned to point their rifles at the prisoners. Another soldier ran and placed a large, empty wooden crate to serve as a step down for the people inside, in order to speed things up.

The fourth truck carrying the twenty youngest children under eight years of age, had also traveled in the same easterly direction. It pulled off the road at the point where the forest met the edge of the field and forced a track through the thick grassy mud, overtaking the first truck. It came to an abrupt stop next to an opening in the trees, and its engines were turned off.

The officers ordered the older men and women to get out of the truck. The men exited first.

"Everybody out, quickly," yelled a German officer. "*Schnell!*"

The men moved as fast as they could, conscious of the rifles aimed at them all the entire time. They clambered out and then assisted the older women to climb down, some with great difficulty. The group of forty-five people stood silent and shivering in the pelting rain.

"Move up ahead of the first truck. All of you. Do it now," shouted the officer. "*Schnell!*"

The canvas cover was pulled up on the rear of the truck carrying the children. As they were callously yanked down off the truck by the soldiers, some of them recognized where they were. Up to the left, beyond the field, was their familiar school building. The children were lined up in front of the older men and women until they were all standing in the rain at the opening to the trees.

"Attention!" shouted one of the German officers. "All of the adults will hold the hand of the child in front of you. Do it now."

They all did as they were instructed, with the elder ones taking the lead, picking up the infants in their arms. Not all of the adults had a child to themselves.

"Good. Now everyone will follow the soldiers into the woods, where we can get out of the rain and have some refreshments. Go now, quickly," ordered the officer.

A soldier led the way and the group of about sixty-five fearful and bewildered adults and children followed him into the woods as instructed, taking some comfort from the hand of a stranger. They walked for at least ten minutes until reaching a wide opening deep in the forest. Through the heavy rain and trees, they could see up ahead what looked like a row of about ten Jewish prisoners, all wearing yellow Star of David armbands. They were standing completely still, staring down at the wet, muddy ground under their feet.

As the group came closer to where the wretched-looking men were standing, they could see a large, deep ditch between them, like a huge crater in the earth. The young children seemed oblivious to the imminent danger as they held on to the hands of their elderly chaperones. But the adults were filled with even more terror than they had felt before, as they began to figure out in their minds the nightmare which was about to occur. Like lambs to the slaughter, there was no way out for them. They squeezed the hands of the children tighter and pulled them closer, in a nurturing and protective manner as if they could somehow protect them.

"Walk up, right to the edge. It's time for you to leave us now," said the commander, his voice harsh and cold.

Some of the adults quickly scooped up the smaller children into their arms and held them close to their chests in an attempt to shield their small innocent faces. Behind the last prisoners standing at the very back of the group, a line of German soldiers with automatic rifles had formed a firing squad. They took aim at the helpless crowd in front of them and, once the order was given, began firing their weapons at full blast.

A murder of crows flew out of the treetops, as though even they couldn't bear to watch.

One by one, the human bodies became limp corpses, their legs buckling underneath them before they collapsed into the cold, wet mud. Most of the adults who were shot first were at the back of the group. But quickly, the bullets reached the children near the front, the shots drowning out their blood-curdling screams.

Finally, a mass pile of death lay at the edge of and inside the ditch, and the continual rapid gunfire eventually stopped. The Jewish prisoners were then called to action and ordered to quickly throw the remainder of the sixty-five dead bodies down into the ditch. While they carried out this gruesome task, several of the German soldiers stood smoking cigarettes and drinking shots of schnapps together, satisfied with the success of their murderous act. Two soldiers fired random shots from their pistols at any of the victims in the ditch of death who still showed the slightest remaining signs of desperate life.

After the last body was thrown down into the death pit, two of the Jewish prisoners, escorted by an armed soldier, were ordered to go back and remove the body of the dead shopkeeper from the rear of the first truck. They struggled to drag her dead body over the muddy forest floor in the torrential rain, but finally managed to throw her limp body down onto the mass pile of dead corpses. The Jewish prisoners were then each given a silver metal shovel and ordered at gunpoint to fill in the ditch with the surrounding earth and sodden mud.

The massacre and ensuing mass burial were over within two hours, with all evidence well obscured and hidden out of sight. The soldiers walked back out of the forest, unfazed by the events they had enacted. They marched their forced labor digging-crew into the back of an empty truck, then loaded their dogs in to guard them. With their weapons and tools loaded onto a separate truck, they climbed into their vehicles and drove away from the scene of the crime as if nothing had ever happened there.

Magda looked up at the clock again; it was almost noon. She tried not to let Asha see how anxious she felt, but couldn't help looking at the clock every ten minutes or so. She had peered out of the window multiple times and regularly stood at the front door, staring down the street for signs of Sophia and Alexa's return.

Magda couldn't think of any more excuses to tell Asha to ease her worried little mind. Something was obviously very wrong. She told the little girl to get dressed so they could go next door to her own house to wait. Asha was very reluctant at first and began crying, becoming very upset.

"I don't understand. Where's my Mama and Alexa?" Asha sobbed, "They . . . they said they'd only be gone an hour. I need my Mama. Why can't we stay here in my house and wait for them to come home?" Asha began coughing uncontrollably through her tears.

"Look Asha, I don't know what's happened to them, or why they are so late. I think it's best we go next door to my house for now. There you can play with Eva and Peter. I will take the key and lock the door so, you see, your Mama will have to come next door to my house to collect you. Please don't worry. When they get home, we will know," explained Magda.

Magda forced a smile and took Asha next door to her house, hoping the distraction of playing with her young twins would take the child's mind off worrying for a little while. Eva and Peter greeted Asha kindly and took her into their bedroom to play while Magda started preparing lunch. She closed the kitchen door and spoke quietly to her husband, making sure the children wouldn't overhear her.

"Michael, something is very, very, wrong. I just know it. Something bad has happened to Sophia and Alexa. There's no way they would take this long to go into town and back, with Asha lying in bed ill. It's been over three hours."

"I know, it doesn't seem right to me either. Look, you stay here with the children and I will go into town and see if I can find them near the square. I will ask at the shoe shop and see if anyone knows anything."

"Okay darling, please be careful. Take your German identification papers with you just in case."

"Alright, I will. I'll try not to be long."

"Please come straight back home. I can't be worrying about you as well."

Michael gave Magda a reassuring hug, kissed her on the cheek, and headed out the front door into town.

The second and third military trucks traveling in the convoy together drove along the road for about ten minutes before they approached the town's train station and continued along, parallel to the railroad tracks. The truck carrying the twenty-five men aged between sixteen to fifty had not had a smooth ride. Two of the men had protested loudly during the journey, voicing their anger over the whole ordeal, and of not knowing what was happening to them or their families, or where they were being taken to. The soldiers couldn't let that go unpunished, and when the men started to make threatening moves by advancing towards them, the soldiers took aim with their pistols and shot them.

One of the men lay injured on the floor of the truck, after receiving bullet wounds to his right thigh and side. The other lay dead, his lifeblood seeping out of multiple bullet wounds.

One of the soldiers lengthened out the chain attached to the leash of the dog under his control and the ravenous animal tore into the flesh of the corpse.

No doubt motivated by the will to survive, to be reunited with their families again, and to get out of that death truck in one piece, the remaining men in the truck were silent in their horror. Therefore, they remained as controlled as possible, restraining themselves and obeying the orders given to them and stood well back, huddled together with strangers.

The third truck, carrying the younger women, had continued to follow the men's truck as part of a smaller convoy, accompanied at the front and back by armored cars. Inside, Sophia had managed to position herself next to Karolina's mother and they sat together on the floor, holding hands. The majority of the women were still terribly upset, especially the mothers in the group, who were distraught about not knowing where their children were or when they would be reunited with them—or if indeed they would ever be reunited with them again. A few had fainted, falling in and out of consciousness on the floor of the truck, while others sobbed and whimpered.

Sophia's mind kept running back to Asha, who was still at home with Magda, waiting for her return. 'How will my fragile daughter cope? Who will look after her?' Then her thoughts turned to Alexa, who'd been loaded onto the fifth truck. 'Is she in the next truck in the convoy? Is she still with Karolina? Are we all going to the same place? Will I ever see either of my girls again?' She thought she would go mad. Then she began to pray the 91st Psalm silently to herself.

Finally, the truck slowed down, took a sharp turn, and came to an abrupt stop. The soldiers jumped out of the rear of the truck first but left the dogs chained on guard inside. Sophia heard German voices talking outside to the background sound of heavily falling rain. Everyone inside the trucks spoke only Polish, so they were no wiser as to where they were or what would happen next.

The fifth truck, carrying the youngsters and Alexa, had been on the road traveling on the same route towards the train station for a relatively short time, until it made a sharp turn to drive alongside the tracks as the other two trucks had done. In the train station stood a large steam engine train with at least ten cattle wagons—the kind designed to carry livestock. Some of the wagons seemed to have already been fully loaded, but not with animals. Instead, people had been crammed inside them, and the doors firmly bolted shut.

Heavy rain continued to pour relentlessly from the dark clouds above, making a tremendous noise as it pelted down onto the hard metal roofs and struck the stones on the ground. There were more armed German soldiers at the station than there had been in the town center. They formed a line leading from the trucks to the remaining empty transport wagons. Every fourth soldier held a vicious, barking, bloodthirsty German shepherd dog on a long chain, while all the others held either pistols, loaded rifles, or manned machine guns.

Two soldiers headed over to the truck with the men inside and pulled up the rear canvas cover, allowing some daylight to enter the vehicle. They yelled at the men to jump out of the trucks at high speed, while the entire time they aimed their guns at them. The prisoners began jumping down out of the truck. Some fell as they landed but wasted no time in getting back up as the barrels of the soldiers' guns closest to them struck their heads and backs. They were rushed along the gauntlet to a vacant cattle wagon and for the first time could see the train in front of them. From some of the other already locked wagons, people's hands could be seen, grasping the few small railings near the roof, where a tiny window was, covered with barbed wire. The fear-stricken men, harried and chivvied by the shouting SS troops and their hungry hounds, were rushed into the empty wagon.

Meanwhile, the bodies of the two prisoners who had been shot were dragged out of the truck, along the platform, and thrown into the men's wagon. The dead man's partly chewed, bloodied and lifeless body landed on the floor with a heavy thud, like a sack full of heavy mud. The injured man yelped like a wounded animal in excruciating pain, as though wishing he too was dead. He was thrown violently into the wagon and landed at the feet of the other prisoners all crammed in together. Once all the males were loaded inside, the doors were quickly and firmly bolted shut.

Sophia and the other women in the second truck could hear the frightened cries from outside; it was terrifying. Sophia and Karolina's mother held each other's hands even tighter than before, trembling with fear. As the train's engine let off a blast of steam, the canvas cover of their truck was thrown open by two soldiers.

The gauntlet of German soldiers now awaited them. They were ordered to get out of the truck and run into the empty wagon selected for them less than a hundred yards away. With rifles aimed at them and the hounds wildly barking and growling, the women ran through the pouring rain towards the wagon. Sophia tried to look around as she ran, desperately hoping to catch sight of Alexa. But with too little time to scan the area properly, there was no visible sign of her daughter.

Once the women were all pushed inside, the wagon door was quickly slid shut and firmly bolted. Although it was still daylight outside, inside the locked wagon it was dark. Karolina's mother stood next to Sophia and grabbed hold of her arm.

"The children will probably be in one of the other wagons, and we'll be able to see them when the train finally comes to a stop and we can all get off," she said tearfully.

"I pray to God you're right," said Sophia. "Please God, let them be alright."

The soldiers threw open the canvas at the rear of the final truck carrying the eighteen youths aged eight to sixteen, and let the barking dogs out first. Alexa had already deduced they were at the train station and thought they may be loaded onto a waiting train, but she was convinced they would not be going to a good destination. She had a bad feeling, like when you sense deep down in your bones that bad weather is coming. But the weather already was bad and the feeling she had now terrified her.

There were soldiers everywhere, most standing guard while others pulled the children quickly from the truck and still others brutishly pushed or threw them up into the wagon, almost throwing them inside. Once the petrified children were loaded inside, the door was slammed shut and firmly bolted. At least now they were a little safer, away from the ferocious dogs and the soldiers' guns. However, being confined in the foul stench of the dirty wagon, not knowing where they would be taken, brought them no comfort at all.

The train pulled slowly out of the station, hissing as it blasted steam into the atmosphere, causing large billowy clouds to form. The train's whistle sharply pierced the air. As it picked up speed, the loud noise of the steel rails beneath the barreling train vibrated loudly, and continued a four-beats-to-the-bar rhythmic tune that became almost hypnotic. For the remainder of the journey, Alexa and Karolina huddled together in the corner of the wagon on the cold, filthy floor. They didn't say much to each other but drew a little comfort from being together.

It was dark inside and cold winds blew through small gaps in the wagon walls as the train sped on its journey. Feeling the cold pierce her skin, Alexa wished she was still wearing her navy-blue coat, which she had left behind in the shoe shop. She began to pray silently. *'I shall not be afraid by the terror of night, nor the pestilence that walks in darkness. Give Your angels a command to guard me.'* She wondered where they were traveling to—perhaps to the far north of Poland? In reality, that couldn't have been further from the truth.

After a more than seventeen-hour journey, the train transporting all the locals rounded up from Lublin's town square finally arrived at its destination near Munich and slowly screeched to a halt. The rain had stopped falling but the sky was dark. It was 3:30 am, and suddenly a flood of light shone onto the train, knifing through the cracks of the wagon walls. The door to their wagon was unbolted and slammed open with a loud crash. Nazi troops ordered the fatigued children to come out and jump down onto the ground below.

As Alexa quickly did as she was told, she heard the other heavy cattle wagon doors being thrown open and everyone being ordered to quickly get out. Once again, the Nazis with their tumultuous shouting, threatening voices, and their wild bloodthirsty barking German shepherd dogs, struck terror into the hearts of those helplessly forced to stand in front of them. It was as if the soldiers could taste the fear of the prisoners under their control and they binged on it, with all trace of humanity absent from their faces. A line of soldiers kept their rifles aimed at the crowd of new arrivals, while army officers wielding heavy batons moved through the crowd as if making assessments and sizing up each individual's worth at a glance.

Now that the prisoners were finally out of the train wagons, they began frantically scanning the crowd for any trace of their children and other family members. Some mothers had already spotted their children and had immediately reclaimed them, pulling them in close to their bodies, and holding them tighter than they'd ever done before. However, the majority would never find their infants or their youngest children, nor would they ever learn what had happened to them. This was the case for those adults in the group looking around for their mothers, fathers, or grandparents—there was no trace of them and no explanations were offered as to their whereabouts. All who now remained from the Lublin square roundup were the youths and the adults up to fifty years of age. Karolina's mother had found her daughter, but frantically searched around them looking desperately for her four-year-old son. She would never find him.

Alexa was half pushed down into the milling crowd on the platform. Recognizing some of the adults she'd seen in the square, she started jumping up and down, trying to spot her mother in the chaos. Suddenly, there she was, pushing her way through the crowd, her eyes wild and her hands reaching.

"Mama," Alexa cried with a sob as Sophia caught her up in a fierce hug. They even laughed a little in relief; knowing they were alive and together again. It was going to be alright; they would get through this madness. They gripped each other's hands as if they'd never let go again.

"Attention!" yelled a commandant taking the lead. "Everyone face forward and pay attention to me."

The prisoners did as they were told, falling into an uneasy silence. He had their attention.

"You have now arrived at Dachau. This is a labor camp and here you will all be put to work, working hard for Germany and for the fatherland. The officers will tell you where you are to go, either to the left or to the right. Do as you are told and follow the orders quickly if you want to stay alive."

As he finished speaking, a few of the officers worked their way through the group of prisoners with their batons, selecting and directing them which way to go. Hurriedly, the wretched people began to run, spurred on by violent random strikes from the swinging batons. Sophia and Alexa were directed to go to the right and quickly ran in that direction, their hands still tightly locked together.

Most people were instructed to run to the left and to stand outside of a windowless brick building. A soldier, seated at a small desk, began recording everyone's pertinent information on sheets of paper in front of him. As they stood waiting to receive their next order, Alexa looked over to the group who'd been instructed to go left. To her surprise, she saw them start to undress, forced to remove their clothing and jewelry at gunpoint out in the cold air. She gasped and Sophia quickly placed Alexa in front of her, as if to shield her daughter's innocent eyes from seeing the things behind her. But it was too late. Alexa stared up at her mother with an expression of horror and shock.

They stood silently in line in front of another desk where two soldiers asked each prisoner for their full names and dates of birth, their town of birth and their religion, as well as any special skills or talents they possessed. Next, the adults were told to remove their jewelry and watches and to empty their pockets, handing over any money or items of value they still had on them. Alexa squeezed her mother's hand, remembering Sophia had left her rings with Asha the previous morning. Sophia darted a sharp glance at her daughter, as if telling her not to make mention of it. The soldier motioned them forward to a large barracks without checking Alexa.

"Move now, everyone inside," ordered a female *kapo* for that building.

Alexa looked around the group in which she and her mother found themselves. They were all women and young girls and they all had something very obvious in common: they all looked the same. They were all blonde-haired and blue-eyed.

Alexa and Sophia ran with the rest of the group of twenty-eight females into the building in front of them as instructed, not knowing what they'd find there. Once they were all inside, the door was bolted shut behind them and no further instructions were given. Alexa peered around the gloomy interior. They were now inside of what appeared to be a long, narrow, barracks-style wooden hut. On either side of both walls were crammed rickety-looking wooden sleeping bunks, stacked three levels high. They were already packed full, with other women and teenage girls on them. Another row of three-tier bunks ran down the middle of the hut. There were no pillows or blankets; only a flimsy sack stuffed with some loose straw, supposedly a substitute for a mattress. There was no other furniture in the hut, no tables or chairs, nowhere to sit. It was a most inhospitable place.

Some of the new arrivals began looking for empty bunks, but they were already occupied. A number of the bunks had fewer people crammed on them than others so some of the women took the initiative to squeeze in and lay claim to their spots early on, next to random strangers. A few of the women already there seemed to treat the newcomers with a resentment, that came across as unwarranted. They were, after all, in the same desperate situation. No one was there by choice or of their own free will.

Sophia spotted a bunk with only one woman on it; she quickly tried to position herself next to the woman and told Alexa to climb on the end. That way she'd be the buffer between her daughter and the stranger. But the woman became difficult and stretched herself out to take up all the surface space on the bunk.

"Please can you move over so my daughter and I can lay down here?" Sophia asked.

"No. There's no room here for two more people. Go try somewhere else."

"But if you moved over a little bit . . ."

"Who are you to tell me what to do? You've only just arrived. Get lost." The woman became more aggressive and hostile, so Sophia took a few steps back still grasping Alexa's hand tightly.

"Sophia," a voice called out from one of the bunks two rows down. "Come over here. You can share this bunk with me."

The invitation had come from a younger woman who knew Sophia. She had worked as a nurse in the local hospital in Lublin; she had nursed Sophia's sick husband, Alexander, before his death. "Come," she said again. "There's enough room here for you both. Climb in."

Sophia and Alexa headed over to where the young woman was and climbed onto the bunk with her.

"Thank you so much, Angelica. I don't know what we would have done next."

"I'd much rather be next to someone I know than a complete stranger, anyway, so it's a better solution for all three of us. I think we are going to need all the friends we can get in this God-forsaken place."

"Yes, I think you're right."

"Mama, I'm so hungry. Can we get anything to eat or drink before we go to sleep?"

"Ha," the woman in the bunk above them sneered. "Get real child. Where do you think you are, in a hotel?"

"Sorry my darling, not tonight," whispered Sophia. "But in the morning, I'm sure when we wake up, we'll get something. Try and sleep for now."

There was nothing available to kill their hunger or to quench their thirst. Not a stray crumb, nor a droplet of water to be found anywhere. Sophia wrapped her arms tightly around Alexa, who felt comforted and a little safer. Her empty stomach rumbled while her mother stroked her long blonde hair.

"No talking!" ordered the stern *kapo* in a loud voice. All of a sudden, the lights went out and the large dormitory was shrouded in darkness. Even the shadows hid in the sanctuary of blackness, sensing evil in the air. It must have been well after 4 o'clock and, as the morning crept in, time passed by very slowly. Alexa was aware that Sophia was awake, her arms around her tense and her head turning this way and that at the slightest noise. After a long time, an exhausted Alexa finally fell asleep.

Sunday morning gave way to daylight. The sun shone outside as roll call was announced at 8 o'clock. The newest women and girls to arrive at the barracks followed the lead of those who had been there longest and who already knew the drill. The prisoners crawled stiffly out of their sorry excuse for a bed and quickly stood in front of their bunks. Their names were called out by the *kapo* to whom they all had to answer loudly, making their presence known. There were no further orders given at that point and the *kapo* abruptly exited the barracks, closing the wooden doors firmly behind her.

Most of the women climbed back onto their bunks and lay down. At the very end of the barracks, two buckets were the only unsanitary latrine provisions. Unable to hold their bladders anymore, a few women reluctantly swallowed their pride and relieved themselves into the buckets as best as they could, gagging from the stench of the foul odor surrounding them.

Alexa and Sophia lay back in their bunk with Angelica, with very few words shared between them. There wasn't much to say, but they took comfort from being together.

A little before midday, the *kapo* returned to the barracks with two male armed Nazi soldiers. She began taking a second roll call so everyone jumped out of their bunks and stood to attention, answering when their name was shouted out. Once the roll call was completed, the *kapo* began calling out another list. Those whose names were called out were told to immediately go and stand outside. One by one, the young girls were selected, rounded up together and forced to run outside the barracks. Sophia clenched Alexa's hand tightly.

"Alexa Szewczyk," the *kapo* barked. That was the next name called from the list and Sophia gasped, clutching Alexa close to her.

"No! Please don't take my daughter," she pleaded.

The *kapo* ran over to Sophia and without hesitation swung her baton with full force towards the side of her head. It was a perfect aim and made a loud crack as the hard, wooden object struck Sophia's temple area and she immediately collapsed to the floor. Alexa still had hold of her mother's hand and knelt down on the ground, leaning over Sophia's unconscious body in shock and dismay. Her mother's head was cut and blood began streaming from the deep gash.

The *kapo* used her baton again, this time hitting Alexa's hand with excess force, causing her to reluctantly let go of her mother's hand. One of the armed soldiers ran over, grabbed hold of Alexa's hair and dragged her outside the building to join the other selected youths already gathered there.

"Mama," she screamed. "Mama!"

But her mother remained unconscious on the cold, hard, dirty floor, unaware of her daughter's desperate cries for help. Tears of pain streamed down Alexa's face. The fierce soldier threw her onto the ground outside the barracks and ordered her to shut up.

A group of young boys had also been rounded up and forcefully taken from inside of the adjacent barracks. Together with the girls from Alexa's barracks, the group of selected youths numbered about twenty-six. They were all ordered to climb into the back of a waiting military vehicle. Two SS soldiers climbed up after them and sat on guard in the back of the truck, their snarling German shepherd dogs and pistols aimed at their young captives.

The prisoners sat on the floor in silence as the truck began to move, their eyes wide with fear. They stared with terrified faces at the soldiers who lit cigarettes and callously stared back at them through the smoke, their cold eyes and vicious dogs trained on them. The men reeked of violence and seemed eager to show it. Sensing this, their young prisoners were riveted to the floor where they sat, too afraid to move. Their survival instinct was still alive so despite the pangs of hunger rumbling and raging inside them, they obeyed the soldiers' commands, in the hope they'd soon be given some food and water.

After a four-hour journey, the truck finally reached its destination and came to a stop inside the gated courtyard of a large ornate, grey stone governmental-looking building. It was decorated and draped with large Nazi flags. The unmistakable bright blood red backgrounds with centered white circles and bold black swastikas were proudly on display.

Alexa looked at the other children fearfully, but unlike on her last truck journey, she had no friend's hand to hold on to this time. Karolina hadn't been loaded into the truck with her, and for the first time in her life she really felt what it was like to be alone.

The two soldiers who had journeyed with them lifted up the rear canvas cover of the truck and let the two dogs jump down first. They then ordered the youths to get out and line up in a row in order of their age, starting with those who were eight years old up to sixteen. Alexa stood sandwiched in between three other thirteen-year-old Polish girls in the center of the lineup. Two of them were also blonde like her, and the other was dark haired, carrying a little more weight on her than the others. While they all stood to attention, a German officer came out of the building, marched over to where they were standing and began looking them over from head to toe.

"If I tap you with my stick on your shoulder, run over to the left immediately and stand next to the soldiers waiting at the bottom of the stairs," he said.

He continued down the line of youths and tapped the shoulders of only fourteen of them. He tapped Alexa on her shoulder and she immediately ran over to stand at the foot of the stairs. She assumed the other three girls standing next to her would follow her over, but that never happened. Only two of them were chosen, the two blonde teenage girls; the dark-haired girl wasn't.

The selected children were ordered to run up the stairs and were guided through a large iron door. Alexa glanced back over her shoulder as she reached the top of the stairs and saw the dark-haired girl along with the other similar-looking children, numbering twelve, being marched off in a different direction before the heavy iron door slammed shut behind her, blocking her view.

The fourteen children were taken to a large room where four female German soldiers were waiting for them. It was their job to make the children presentable and look their best. First, they gave each of them a cup of milk and a piece of buttered bread, which they all scoffed down. Alexa hadn't had anything to eat or drink since breakfast the morning of her capture and was famished. The sparse food and drink hardly made a dent in the starving children's hunger levels.

The female soldiers separated the eight girls from the six boys, and each took a few children to place their attention on. They began to wash their faces rather forcefully and towel-dried them just as roughly. Next, they began brushing their hair. The boys were fairly easy as their blond hair was short and fell into place with little fuss. Some of the girls' long blonde hair was tangled so the women worked quickly, forcefully detangling them with metal combs. Alexa's hair was smooth and untangled as she always took pride in her appearance, so didn't need as much attention as the others were getting. She was relieved as some of the other girls showed visible signs of pain.

Next, their clothing was inspected. Again, Alexa was dressed very smartly and needed no changes made to her outfit. She had deliberately worn a blue skirt, white blouse and matching blue cardigan to match the new royal blue shoes she was going to buy with her mother the day before. She still had the new royal blue shoes on her feet but in her heart, she now wished they had never gone into town that day to buy them. *'If only we had stayed home . . . If only I'd have kept wearing my old shoes . . . If only . . .'*

A few of the other children were given some smarter, cleaner clothes to put on rather than the ones they had been wearing. Then finally, they were all taken to use some toilets and told to wash their hands well afterwards.

Alexa unbuttoned the top button of her blouse and began to wash her hands. She looked into the mirror over the sink and noticed her necklace hanging around her neck. A silver chain with a small silver cross on it, it was a gift from her mother and had once belonged to her grandmother, who had always worn it. She was grateful the soldier at Dachau had missed it when checking all the others. She hadn't made any reference to it in the camp or in the truck, as she was afraid it might be taken from her. She quickly buttoned her blouse, hoping nobody would spot it.

The female soldiers hurried them all into another larger room where they were placed in another line-up and told to look forwards. They stood stationary for at least five minutes, staring ahead, before getting distracted and looking curiously around the room, as children often want to do. They were immediately prompted by the soldiers to be still and look straight ahead again.

Suddenly, the tall double doors opened and multiple heavy footsteps in both heels and boots echoed across the shiny wooden floor. A mix of fourteen SS and Gestapo officers and their wives came into the room and one by one they began to inspect the children in the line-up.

One of the wives seemed very interested in Alexa. She walked over to her, motioning for her husband to join her. He stood looking at Alexa. His SS uniform made Alexa nervous so she dropped her eyes to the floor away from his direct stare. The wife said something in German to her husband and then raised her hand towards Alexa's neck. She moved the collar of Alexa's white blouse and pointed to the necklace.

"Are you Catholic?" the woman asked in German, reaching for the little silver cross.

Alexa couldn't speak much German but she understood the word Catholic and nodded.

"Good, then you'll come home with us," said the wife.

"We'll take this one," The SS officer announced. He spoke to the head officer in the room for a moment, signed some papers at his desk, and then rejoined his wife in front of Alexa. "Come now girl, you will leave with us."

The other children also began to be selected by the remaining couples and as Alexa left the room with her new keepers, she finally figured out what the fourteen children all had in common. They were all blonde-haired and blue-eyed, very attractive, healthy, and fit-looking. *'That must be it,'* she thought. She had heard stories about the Aryan race in school. *'The other girl in the courtyard had black hair and was a little overweight; that must be why she wasn't selected to be in this group,'* she reasoned to herself. Some of the others who hadn't been selected also had brown hair and didn't look as fit as the children in her group. *'That definitely must be why. We are all blonde, blue-eyed, and Aryan looking. We could almost pass for real Germans.'*

The SS officer led his wife and Alexa down the stairs, out the building and across the courtyard to his black Mercedes 260D sedan. He told Alexa to climb into the back seat as he took off his long, black leather coat and threw it over onto the seat next to her. Then he and his wife got into the front of the car and he started the diesel engine, revving up his powerful chariot. Alexa looked out of the side window as the loud car pulled out of the gates and rumbled along the cobbled stones and onto the streets of Frankfurt. Alexa had never been out of Poland before; nothing looked familiar and she knew she was now far, far away from home.

"What is your name?" asked the wife, turning her head to look at the girl in the rear seat.

"My name is Alexa," she replied with a nervous quake in her voice. In school, Alexa's class had been learning some basic German so she understood the question and tried to answer in her best German. The wife told her that her name was Emilie and her husband was named Fredrick but she should call them Herr and Frau Klauss whenever she addressed them.

"Ja, Frau Klauss," Alexa said.

CHAPTER 4

Alexa stared out the window at the strange landscape, desperately trying not to break down and burst into tears. She was terrified and totally heartbroken over being separated from her mother and sister. As hard as it was, she managed to control her feelings, remembering what her mother had whispered to her back in the square in Lublin. "Don't let them see you are scared. Keep strong." She did her utmost to quell and purge the overwhelming and telling signs of fear from her face, thinking instead of how proud her mother would be of her for not showing her real emotions.

The long car journey took roughly three hours until they reached their destination on the outskirts of the city of Bitburg in the far west of Germany. They drove along the dark country roads and eventually pulled off onto a long, private and tree-lined driveway leading up to a large, remote farmhouse. Alexa had dozed off in the back seat at some point and was awakened by the sound of Herr Klauss saying her name.

"Alexa, wake up. It's time to get out of the car. We are home."

Alexa awoke suddenly with a jolt, opened her eyes and quickly got out of the car, with the word "home" echoing in her head. As she looked around, she saw nothing familiar and quickly became aware she most definitely was not at her own home.

"Come, come here with me," ordered the SS officer's wife.

Alexa followed her into the farmhouse and they headed down a long hallway that led straight into a large kitchen. Once there, Herr Klaus appeared behind them a few seconds later with another German soldier.

"Explain to the girl," ordered the SS officer, handing the soldier a sheet of paper to read out to her.

The soldier took the paper and began to read. "First of all, you must not think or talk about Poland anymore. Nor will you speak in Polish. From now on you will learn all things German. You will learn to speak only in German. This will be your German home. You will live and work for the Klauss family here in Bitburg," the soldier said, ironically in Polish. "You will begin work at 4 am, milking the cows, collecting the hens' eggs, mucking out the barns, etc. Then you'll bake fresh bread daily and will prepare breakfast for Herr and Frau Klauss by 6:20 am each morning. You will attend to all of the family's clothing needs, laundry, ironing, and mending. Then you will waken their three children at 7 am—Richard aged nine, Anna aged seven, and Rudy aged four—getting them washed and dressed and then preparing their breakfast by 7:45 am. The older children will go to school at 8:30 am, while you will look after Rudy here at home. You'll be expected to clean the entire house except for the study. You must not enter Herr Klauss's study at any time, for any reason. This will be the only room in the house you will not be allowed to clean. You will prepare dinner for the family and attend to all chores required of you. The cows need to be milked twice a day, so you will milk them in the morning and once again in the afternoon. You will be expected to work in the field ploughing and planting and taking care of the vegetables in the greenhouse. When the children arrive home at 3 pm you will give them a sandwich to eat, make sure they complete their homework and reading assignments, and let them have some playtime before dinner. You will cook every meal and serve dinner at 5 pm on weekdays, earlier on holidays and weekends, and after dinner you will bathe the children and make sure they are ready for bed. You will make sure the kitchen is clean and tidy as well as the rest of the house. Their parents will read a story to the children and kiss them goodnight at 9 pm, Rudy at 8 pm. At this time, you will clean out the animal barns, feed the animals, and put down fresh hay. You will also check that Herr Klauss's Mercedes is clean and polished, ready for him to drive off in each morning. Do you understand all of what I have told you?"

"Yes, I do." Alexa answered.

"You will not leave this farm alone, unless you have Herr or Frau Klauss's permission. Do you understand?"

"Yes" Alexa replied.

"You will wear a letter 'P' sewn onto your outer jacket for the times you are permitted and instructed to leave the farmhouse and be outside. You will have no days off, nor holidays, and your workday will finish at 11 pm, unless you have completed everything before then and have been dismissed by Frau Klauss. In which case you can retire to your bed earlier. Is this all clear?"

Alexa's heart had sunk a little more with each job description the soldier had read out from the list of chores, and when she thought it couldn't sink any lower, she heard she was expected to work every day without a break.

"Yes, I understand," she said in a small, broken voice.

"Good! You will not eat with the family. Only after they are finished eating may you fix a small plate of leftovers for yourself and eat it in the kitchen pantry after your chores are completed. Here is a sandwich, an apple and a cup of milk; pick them up and follow me. I will take you to your room now. You will start work tomorrow at 4 am sharp."

The soldier turned to the husband and spoke in German to him, confirming he had told Alexa all that was expected of her from the long list he had been given. Herr Klauss answered him back very matter-of-factly and then dismissed him. The soldier saluted him with a "Heil Hitler" then turned sharply on his heels and walked out of the kitchen door, motioning for Alexa to follow him.

He led her up to the top of the stairs and pointed out the children's bedrooms and the parents' bedroom, then led her through a little door and up some more stairs into the attic. At the rear corner of the attic was another door into a tiny windowless room, and inside was a small bed with a plain wooden side table, an old lamp, a wooden chair, a dresser, and some coat hangers hung on a hook on the back of the door.

"This is your room where you will sleep. There are some clothes that might fit you in the drawers and whatever else you find in this room you can use. Be ready to go downstairs to the kitchen at 4 am to start work. The woman whom you are to replace will come for you in the morning. If I were you, I'd follow her routine closely and learn your duties very quickly, as she leaves here on Friday. Any questions?"

"Only, where can I use the toilet, please, sir?" Alexa shyly asked.

"There is a bucket in the corner," the soldier said, pointing. "Use that and empty it in the morning. There's a well outside near the barn if you want water to wash yourself in the morning. Now I must go." He turned un-empathetically and left the room, closing the door behind him. Alexa heard a key turning in the lock, confirming to her she had no way out.

Alexa was totally disheartened and completely demoralized. She felt as though she were falling deeper and deeper into a never-ending nightmare. *'How can this be happening to me?'* She sat down on the bed, placing the cup of milk, sandwich, and piece of fruit onto the side table with shaking hands. The fruit began to roll, fell off the little table, and rolled across the dirty floor, coming to a stop against the leg of the dresser. Alexa stared at it, making no effort to pick it up. As hungry as she was, her appetite was completely gone.

The tears began to stream down her face now she was finally alone. Alexa buried her face in the pillow and cried uncontrollably. She hadn't cried like that since her grandmother had died. *'Now I'm in the bird catcher's trap. Now the bird catcher has me. How can I ever escape from here?'* her thoughts screamed. She eventually cried herself to sleep, curled up in a ball on top of the bed in the lonely, dismal attic room.

Some hours passed but Alexa had no concept of the time as she opened her eyes. It must have been around one o'clock in the morning so she had been asleep for about four hours. At first, she had no recollection of where she was. Immediately panic engulfed her as she feared she had spent another night on one of the shared bunks of the horrific work camp at Dachau. She quickly realized, however, that her mother wasn't next to her, and her new reality dawned on her.

As her eyes adjusted to the darkness, she was acutely aware she wasn't in the comfort of her own bed either. She wasn't in her pretty bedroom she had shared with her little sister in their family home, not resting her head on her own comfortable feather pillows, nor tucked up warmly under her pink feather quilt her mother had made for her.

Her eyes stung with tears as she recalled the soldier locking her into her dismal new bedroom earlier that night. It was a stark contrast to what she was used to. The bed was metal and hard, with no soft mattress. There was a thin grey woolen blanket on top and below it were two thin, scratchy old sheets. They didn't match the pillow, which was more of a cushion— an old stained cushion, rather fusty and stale-smelling. This was certainly not the kind of place where a cared-for young girl would sleep.

Alexa's eyes caught sight of the cup and sandwich on the table next to her and was suddenly aware of the hunger pains clawing at her stomach. She recalled she hadn't eaten anything since she had been groomed for selection with the other blonde children, when they had been given some bread.

Alexa sat up, reached for the cup and drank half the milk. She picked up the plain-looking sandwich; it was made of two thick and unevenly cut slices of bread, with a thin spread of butter and four slices of German sausage placed in between. Alexa opened the sandwich and split it in half, laying two pieces of sausage on each slice of bread. She ate the first half, then drank some more of the milk. It didn't taste so bad, so she quickly devoured the second half, and her hunger subsided slightly.

Alexa remembered the soldier telling her there was some clothing in the dresser that she could wear. She lifted her feet off the wooden floor and looked down at the pretty new royal blue shoes she was wearing. *I never thought in my worst nightmares that I'd walk in my dream shoes to a place as horrid as this.*

She moved off the bed and walked over to the wooden dresser, which had two large drawers in it. Opening the top drawer, she found two plain white blouses, two white cotton vests, three pairs of white socks, and three pairs of underwear. In the bottom drawer was one grey plain dress, a grey skirt, one grey woolen cardigan, and a pale blue nightgown. Underneath the dresser on the floor was a plain pair of large wooden clogs.

Alexa didn't like the look of any of the clothing she had found, and she certainly didn't like the look of the clogs. *I hope I don't have to wear any of these clothes, and definitely not those clogs. Now I'm glad I have my new shoes.* As she looked down at the floor, she spotted the apple that had fallen off the table and picked it up. Sitting back down on the bed, she cleaned it off by rubbing it against the grey blanket and took a bite. The apple was sour and not to her liking, so she put it back on the table next to the bed. Soon after, hunger got the better of her and won over her tastebuds.

Alexa felt a chill so she pulled up the grey blanket and crawled underneath it. She positioned her arm across the cushion so she could rest her head on her sleeve without her hair touching it.

"I really don't want to be here; please God don't let it be for long. Please God, rescue me from the trap of the bird catcher. Remove the terror of this night. Please guard and protect me. Please protect my sister and Mama too, wherever they are right now. Rescue me, dear God," Alexa prayed aloud, ending as always with a firm "Amen."

Alexa's thoughts became filled with her mother's condition after she had received such a violent blow to her head that morning. How would she ever know if her mother had recovered and was still alive? How would her mother ever know where she now was? The nightmare held and consumed her, giving no solutions or hope to cling to. Emotionally and physically exhausted, Alexa drifted off to sleep.

Magda's husband returned home about an hour or so after he had headed off into town to look for Sophia and Alexa. Magda remained at home with Asha and her twins, waiting anxiously to hear some news. The front door opened and Magda went to meet her husband. He gestured to her to go through to the privacy of the kitchen where they closed the door behind them.

"Darling, it's not good news," he said in a low voice, with a look of despair.

"What do you mean? What's happened?" Magda whispered, her voice hoarse with worry.

"Well, when I got near to the town square, it was unusually quiet—eerily quiet, almost deserted. The market stalls were still set up but the two blocks of shops on Slawka street were completely empty of people."

"What do you mean?" Magda repeated. "Where was everyone?"

Michael checked the kitchen door to make sure the children were not within listening distance, then closed it firmly. He turned back to his wife, uncertainty and worry furrowing his brow.

"There were some abandoned food packages lying on the streets around the square—broken eggs, cake, shattered glass, even a child's doll—and some of the shop doors were left wide open but there was no one in sight. It was hauntingly quiet, like a ghost town, and there were a few German army barriers placed at either end of the street surrounding the town square."

"Didn't you see anyone?" Magda's hands flew to her face, which was ashen.

"As I was heading away from the market square and back towards home, I spotted Jack and asked him what had happened. He said half a dozen Nazi trucks had driven into town and soldiers had started pulling people out of the shops at gunpoint and rounding everyone up." Michael pulled his wife close and she leaned her head against his chest.

"Jack said everyone was separated into groups," Michael continued, "men, women, old, young, and even children, and then loaded into trucks and driven off."

"Oh no, say it's not true," Magda begged.

"Jack said he thinks they were perhaps taken to a labor camp but he didn't know for sure."

"No!" Magda cried out.

"Quiet Magda," Michael hissed. "The children will hear you."

"Not Sophia and Alexa, no it can't be true," Magda moaned. "And not everyone who was shopping in town. I can't take it all in."

Magda began to shake, tears running down her face, while she tried to absorb the information she'd been given. Michael sat her down at the kitchen table. His steps heavy, he walked over to a kitchen cabinet and took out two small glasses, reached for an old bottle of brandy and poured two shots. He carried them over to the table and handed one to Magda.

"Here, drink this down quickly, it'll help calm you."

They both drank the brandy in one swift gulp and Magda composed herself as best as she could. She picked up the glasses, placed them in the sink, and turned to face her husband.

"What should we do now?"

Michael pulled her close again. "We won't say anything to the children just yet and we'll keep Asha here with us until we know for sure. Try and act as normal as possible. I know it won't be easy, but we must try." He hugged his wife tighter for a long minute and then kissed her on the cheek. "I'll go check on them now," he said, heading for the kitchen door.

Magda had a really bad feeling in the pit of her stomach; she'd felt something wasn't right, that something must have happened to keep Sophia and Alexa from coming back home on time, but she'd never thought of such a terrible outcome as this.

She began to imagine the horrific scene of Sophia and Alexa being dragged out of the shops with all the others. '*How terrifying it must have been for everyone. Who else was taken that I know from town? Were they taken because they were Polish?*' For a moment she felt relieved she was German and in the next second she was disgusted she was German. '*How can my own people be so cruel, so wicked and so evil?*' She searched her powers of reason, but no answers came. There was no reasoning. She could not fathom how any human being could ever be that evil to their fellow humans.

Magda began to pray.

The time was approaching 3:50 am when a key began to turn in the locked door of Alexa's room. She was still asleep but awoke to a female's voice ordering her in German to get up. Alexa opened her eyes to see an older woman in her fifties standing next to her bed. A large, white, stained apron covered most of the black dress she was wearing underneath. Alexa thought she looked almost like a nurse.

The woman opened the drawers and selected clothes for Alexa and then motioned to the girl to get dressed quickly. Alexa did as she was told with no argument until the woman pointed down to the clogs and told her to put them on. Alexa didn't want to take off her new blue shoes and sat back on the bed, shaking her head. The woman picked up the clogs and dropped them on the floor in front of the girl, and again Alexa shook her head, no. The woman scowled angrily and then, lifting her right arm, she slapped Alexa across her face.

Alexa had never been hit like that before. She had always been a well-behaved, obedient, and pleasant child who did what she was told when asked, but she really didn't want to take off her new shoes. She hadn't even removed them when she had gone to sleep the previous night. In fact, they hadn't been off her feet since she had first tried them on in the shoe shop.

The woman reached for Alexa's left leg and forcefully pulled the left shoe off her foot. She then grabbed the large clog and pushed the girl's foot inside it. She was about to do the same with the other leg but Alexa quickly reached down, slid the shoe off her right foot and placed it into the other clog. She could see this woman had no patience and wasn't playing with her. Her own clothes were left on the bed and the pair of new blue shoes lay abandoned on the floor.

The woman motioned for Alexa to stand up and she stood behind her. Taking hold of Alexa's long blonde hair, she pulled it all together tightly in one hand and with her other hand she tied it up with a thick rubber band. Twisting it up into a bun, she fixed it in place so it was out of Alexa's face.

"Come," the woman said, as she led Alexa out of the attic, down the stairs, and into the kitchen.

Alexa's first day as an unpaid slave had begun.

CHAPTER 5

The large clock in the kitchen showed 4 am. It was Monday morning but it was still dark outside, as the sun hadn't risen yet. The woman handed Alexa an apron and told her to put it on, which she did. It was the woman's responsibility to quickly teach Alexa all the many daily jobs and duties that would be expected of her. The woman would be leaving the Klausses' home that Friday for good and Alexa would be her full-time replacement, so she had to learn fast.

First, the woman handed her a pencil and notepad and then led Alexa over to the gas stove. She turned the oven on, setting the dial to two hundred and fifty degrees, and lit the two back burners. She filled a large pot with cold water, placed it on the stove, and then filled a large iron kettle with cold water and placed it over the second burner. Alexa watched, wide-eyed. Would she be able to carry even one kettle full of water by herself? She quickly started thinking of a way she could fill them up on the stove by using a smaller pot and making several journeys to and from the sink.

Next, the woman led Alexa outside to the barn where the animals were kept. She handed her a basket and showed her where to collect the freshly laid eggs from the hens. They collected twenty eggs before she instructed Alexa to put them on the table in the kitchen and then come straight back out to the barn.

The woman then grabbed a metal bucket along with a small wooden stool, which she set up next to one of the five large cows, motioning to Alexa to come closer. She reached both hands under the cow, placed her fingers and thumbs on the udders, and began to gently squeeze the teats as she milked the first cow. The woman was very well built with large muscly arms and a very full figure. It took her about eight minutes to milk the first cow.

When she had finished, she stood up, moved the bucket over to the next cow, and pointed to Alexa to bring the stool over. This time she motioned to Alexa to sit down on it. Now it was her turn to milk the cow. Alexa had never been on a farm. She had never been up close to such a big animal before and so was understandably apprehensive. She wasn't looking forward to the task but feared the woman might slap her again—or worse—if she didn't do what she was told.

Alexa positioned herself on the stool as she'd been shown and placed her fingers around the two front teats. She pulled gently but nothing came out. She was anxious and very aware of the woman standing behind her and watching her every move. The woman leaned in and squeezed Alexa's fingers harder, pulling in a firmer manner, and the milk began to squirt out slowly. Alexa gradually got the hang of it after much practice but it took her much longer to finish milking the cow than it had taken the woman.

The woman told Alexa to milk one more of the cows. Her small, soft hands and arms were hurting already. It was hard work. She didn't have big muscles like her teacher but she did the best she could.

The woman stopped her and lifted the stool away while instructing Alexa to bring the bucket and carry it into the kitchen. There, she showed her where the milk had to be cooled down.

It was now 4:45 am. The woman lifted a tin of flour onto the large wooden table and reached for a big mixing bowl. Alexa watched everything closely while trying to write it all down in her notebook at the same time. Into the bowl went several measures of flour, some salt, yeast, warm water, and oil; the woman mixed it all together vigorously with her hands. After a few minutes she told Alexa to wash her hands and knead the dough for a further five minutes before covering the bowl and leaving it to sit near the stove for an hour and a half.

Alexa was told to strain the milk through some cloth into two large milk jugs and put them in the fridge. After that, they went back outside again to fill a bucket of coal and gather logs of wood. They shoveled the coal into a door opening at the bottom of the stove. They carried the logs into the lounge and then the dining room, placing them in the fireplaces in each room. Kneeling down in front of the dining room fireplace, the woman scrunched up some old newspapers and placed them in between the logs with some dry twigs. Taking a box of matches from a pocket in her apron, she carefully lit the paper. The twigs slowly began to catch on fire, and the flames gradually spread to the logs. She placed an iron guard in front of the fireplace and told Alexa to light the fire in the lounge, as she had seen demonstrated. Alexa had never lit a fire herself before but she did exactly as she had seen the woman do and had the fire going well in a relatively short time.

Her next chore was to set the dining room table for breakfast: tablecloth, china plates, bowls, egg cups, glasses, cups and saucers, cutlery and napkins for five people. This she managed with little trouble as she had often set the kitchen table at home for their family meals, although they were only three people.

Back in the kitchen again, the clock showed ten minutes past five. The woman told Alexa to first empty the fresh eggs from the basket into separate cartons and then to wash the empty milk bucket and take it back to the barn, as she now had the other two cows to milk.

One of the cows seemed to catch her attention more than all the others. All of the cows had names. This particular cow was named *Blümchen* meaning *Little Flower*. For some strange reason, Alexa felt the cow was sympathetic to her situation, as if Blümchen somehow knew how she was feeling. It stared at her continually and seemed to shed a tear from its sad-looking eyes. Alexa shook her head and turned her attention back to the milk squirting into the bucket. She must be imagining it because she was feeling sorry for herself. She finished up as quickly as she could and moved on to milk the last cow.

The woman next showed Alexa how to open the rear gates and lead the cows out to the field to graze. This chore went a little easier for Alexa, and she was soon on her way back to the kitchen with the bucket of fresh milk. She washed her hands and glanced at the clock. 5:45 am.

The woman uncovered the dough mixture and shaped it into a metal baking tin. Opening the oven door, she placed it inside on the middle shelf, and firmly closed the door. Alexa wrote all this down in her notebook; the woman took the pencil from her and wrote the number *30*. The bread was to be baked for thirty minutes.

She turned to the fridge from where she removed a selection of cold meats and sausages, which she began slicing thinly, placing them neatly onto a small platter. Next, she sliced some tomatoes and cucumbers and added them to the platter. Cheese was next to be sliced, and it completed the platter, ready to be served.

It was now 6:10 am, and the woman brought a carton containing eight eggs to the table. She cracked six of the eggs into a bowl, added salt, pepper, and some milk, and began to beat them together quickly. She fetched a metal saucepan, put a tablespoon of butter into it, and placed it on top of the stove, lighting one of the front burners. She poured the egg mixture into the pan and cooked it over a medium heat, stirring it continually.

Alexa continued watching and writing everything down. The woman dropped the two remaining eggs into the pot of boiling water and held up three fingers to Alexa, meaning three minutes cooking time, and told her to write that down. Both kinds of cooked eggs were ready at the same time. The woman used a large slotted spoon to retrieve the boiled eggs and set them down on the table. Then she removed the scrambled eggs from the heat and covered them with a lid.

Next, she filled a teapot with boiling water from the kettle, spooned four teaspoons of loose tea leaves into the pot, and replaced the lid for it to brew. She did the same with a pot of coffee, making it strong and black.

As the clock neared 6:15 am, the woman opened the oven and carefully removed the freshly baked bread, setting it to cool on top of the kitchen table. On a tray she placed a butter dish, a jug of fresh milk, a sugar bowl, salt and pepper, sliced lemon, and told Alexa to carry it through to the dining room table. She prepared another tray with the meat platter, the two kinds of eggs, and the freshly sliced loaf of warm bread, and carried it through to the dining table. She told Alexa to go and get the tea and coffee pots while she set the items in place on the table. As Alexa came back into the room, Herr Klauss appeared through the door behind her with his wife at 6:20 am sharp.

"Good morning," he said in German.

"Good morning," said the woman, motioning to Alexa to answer him as well.

"Good morning, Herr and Frau Klauss," said Alexa timidly.

The woman asked if she could get them anything else and then left the room with Alexa, returning to the kitchen. Alexa was pretty tired already. She had only been working for a little over two hours but she had already filled up six pages of work notes in her notebook. The woman handed Alexa a piece of thick bread with a slice of meat and cheese on it, along with a small glass of milk. Alexa was quite hungry and was grateful for the food. She thanked the woman and began eating and drinking quickly.

Their breakfast eaten, it was now time to go upstairs to the first floor. They started in the largest bedroom, which belonged to Herr and Frau Klauss, and began making up their bed. They collected their already worn clothes from the previous day, which lay scattered around the room, and placed them in a pile for the laundry. Then they headed into their bathroom, collected the used towels from the floor, cleaned off the excess water around the bathtub and mirrors, and wiped down the surfaces. Their arms full of dirty laundry, they headed back downstairs, walked through a rear door in the kitchen into a utility room. The woman separated the white articles into a pile and left them to soak in a sink full of hot water.

They returned to the kitchen while Alexa continued writing down all the chores in order. The woman walked back into the dining room and placed a newspaper on the table at Herr Klauss' right hand. She asked the couple if they would like anything else but they seemed quite satisfied with all they had before them.

The woman collected Alexa from the kitchen then led her back upstairs to wake the children. First, they went into Richard's bedroom. The woman opened the curtains, letting the sunlight pour into his room.

"Good morning, Master Richard. It's time to get up," she said.

Richard rolled over in his bed and then sat straight up, starting at Alexa. "Who are you?" he asked but Alexa didn't understand him.

"Her name is Alexa. She will be living and working here from now on," the woman told him.

"Oh yes, my mother told me about her. But isn't she too young? I mean she doesn't look much older than I am."

"Don't you worry about that, Master Richard. She will be able to do all the things I do for the family and more. She will be my replacement when I leave on Friday."

"Yes, but will she be as good as you, Olga?" Richard asked.

"Well, it's too early to say. Let's just get on with today, shall we? Now let's get you out of bed and dressed, young man. Your casual clothes are laid out on the chair ready for you to wear. No school today; it's a holiday," she smiled.

That was the first time Alexa had seen her smile all morning. Now she also knew her name: Olga. She seemed a little bit more human by actually having a name and the ability to smile. They walked out of the door and into the next bedroom; it belonged to Anna, the Klausses' seven-year-old daughter. Olga opened the curtains and walked over to the young girl's bed. Placing her hand on her shoulder, she gave her a little shake.

"Good morning, Anna. Time to wake up," Olga said.

Anna was harder to wake than her older brother and pulled the covers up over her head.

"Come on, it's a brand-new day outside. No school today, it's a holiday, so let's get you up and dressed in some fun clothes," encouraged Olga. "And there's someone new here to meet you."

That sparked Anna's attention and she peeked out from beneath her blanket to take a look.

"Who is she?"

"This is Alexa. She will be living and working here in the house from now on."

"Why? Doesn't she have a house and family of her own?"

"Anna, don't be difficult. Get up out of bed and stop wasting time."

Olga and Alexa left the girl's room and went into the last bedroom where young Rudy, aged four, slept. Olga again began by opening the curtains but the boy was already awake.

"Good morning Olga. I'm awake already."

"Yes, I see that, Rudy. Let's get you dressed and ready for breakfast. This is Alexa, she will be living and working here every day from now on."

"Oh good, someone new to play with," Rudy said.

Rudy hopped out of bed and walked over to Olga who was taking out some clean clothes from his dresser for him to wear. She motioned to Alexa to make Rudy's bed and gather his dirty clothes for the laundry pile, while Olga removed the boy's pajamas and began dressing him. She took him through to the bathroom in the hall to wash his face, brush his teeth, and comb his hair. The two older children were dressed already and Olga brushed and styled Anna's hair while Alexa made up both their beds and gathered their clothes worn on the previous day. Once presentable and ready, they all headed downstairs together into the dining room for their breakfast.

Herr Klauss had finished his breakfast already and disappeared into his office, locking the door behind him. Frau Klauss was still in the dining room and welcomed her children like a mother hen.

"Good morning, my little angels," she said as she kissed them all on their foreheads, one at a time. "Did you sleep well?"

Alexa's mind drifted to memories of her own mother who was always so happy to see her and her sister Asha first thing in the morning, and of how happy they both were to see their mother too. By the way Sophia would hug her girls and kiss them affectionately, they always felt their mother's unconditional love.

Olga grabbed Alexa's arm, interrupting her reminiscing, and led her out of the dining room and back through to the kitchen. They now had to prepare breakfast for the children: three boiled eggs and some scrambled eggs for them to choose from. Olga beat the eggs together in a bowl while she motioned to Alexa to quickly fetch the laundry pile from upstairs and bring it down to be washed. Alexa did as she was told, then caught up on the note-taking of her chores so far, adding everything to do with the children to her list.

Olga placed some more sliced bread, sausage and cheese on a plate and carried it, along with the bowl of eggs, through to the dining room table for the three children. She poured two large glasses of milk and a smaller one for Rudy, and placed them next to their plates. At that time, their mother left the room. Olga peeled the shells from the boiled eggs and dished out the scrambled eggs onto their plates, followed by some meat, cheese and bread.

"Now eat up, children. I will be back in a few minutes," she said, and then told Alexa to follow her.

Alexa was tired after her four hours of continual manual labor. Her feet were sore as she hadn't quite mastered how to walk comfortably in the large clogs she was forced to wear. She couldn't imagine they'd ever become comfortable to wear. *If only I had on my new blue shoes, I could walk faster and work better.'* She wanted to crawl back into bed, but not the strange horrible one she had slept in the night before. She wanted to climb into her own warm, cozy, inviting bed in her own bedroom. She wanted to be in her own home, with her own family, eating breakfast prepared by her own mother, at their own family table. She was all too aware, however, that such thoughts were wishful thinking. This was her new reality and she'd have to accept and get used to it.

Olga went back into the utility room with a large stick where she stirred the water with the white laundry in it. She showed Alexa a bar of laundry soap and a scrubbing board, and motioned with her hands for the child to roll up her sleeves and start scrubbing. Alexa did as she was told. She had no choice. She had never done laundry before. Her mother and grandmother had always taken care of that but she had seen it done and did her best to get the clothes cleaned.

Olga left Alexa alone in the small utility room, leaving the door open so she could still keep an eye on her from the kitchen. She checked on the children who had finished eating their breakfasts, then dismissed them from the table to their playroom, while she began clearing their plates and carrying them through to the kitchen.

Olga called Alexa to come clear the dining room table of all the remnants of breakfast, and then had her wash the dirty dishes in the kitchen sink while she herself covered the leftover food and placed it into the fridge. That done, Alexa returned to continue washing the laundry by hand. *'Will this day ever end?'* she wondered.

CHAPTER 6

Herr Klauss hadn't ventured out of his study since he'd gone in right after breakfast that morning. He had shut the door firmly and locked it behind him; presumably, he had important work to attend to. He was not to be disturbed, which was clearly understood by the entire household and was a rule that was strictly adhered to. Alexa wondered to herself if this was a daily occurrence, or his Monday ritual.

As the clock neared noon, Herr Klauss finally emerged from his study, closing and locking the door once again behind him. He called for Olga to bring him fresh coffee, which she began making immediately. Alexa was also in the kitchen and set about arranging a tray with two cups, saucers, teaspoons, cream, and sugar. Olga handed her a plate with a selection of premium fancy-looking chocolates, which were also to be placed on the tray. Alexa stared at the plate enviously, her mouth beginning to water as she salivated over the delicious-looking chocolate temptations in front of her. She would have loved to have had even the tiniest taste of those fine delicacies. But she didn't dare to take so much as a crumb from one of them.

Olga added the fresh pot of coffee to the tray, which she snatched up with both hands and carried it away to the lounge where Herr Klauss was patiently awaiting its arrival with his wife. Apparently, this was a regular occurrence for the couple on holidays and weekends, and Olga motioned to Alexa to make a note of it in her book: *At 12 noon, coffee and chocolates for Herr and Frau Klauss in the lounge*, she wrote.

The next chore was to prepare dinner for the family. The older children had been playing out in the courtyard on their bicycles since after breakfast, while young Rudy had spent most of the morning with his mother in the children's play-room upstairs. She was keeping him occupied so Olga could concentrate on teaching Alexa her long list of new duties.

Olga took Alexa out to the rear of the farmhouse and across the courtyard to where there was a large glass greenhouse. She showed the girl what was growing there—fresh lettuces, several tomato plants, cucumbers, spring onions, radishes, and green beans. They picked some of each, placing them in a wicker basket. From there, they headed further outside to a small plot of land with various vegetables growing in it. Olga began selecting some fresh carrots and with a digging trowel, she chose some large potatoes from the patch. She pointed out to Alexa where the cabbages, onions, beetroots, peppers, and broccoli were grown.

Alexa continued to make notes of everything Olga was showing her, both mentally and in her notebook. It was a lot to take in and although she had spent nine hours working there so far, she could sense she'd have a lot more work to do before the day was over. There were no signs of her load lightening up anytime soon.

As they headed back into the farmhouse with the basket of gathered vegetables, they passed Anna and Richard playing in the courtyard on their bicycles. Suddenly, a black car drove up the driveway. It came to a stop at the farmhouse and out stepped two SS officers, sharply dressed in their uniforms and shiny black boots. Olga told the children to put their bikes away in the shed and to come inside the house after they had saluted the officers. She told Alexa to go with them up to the playroom and to stay there out of the way while the officers were in the house.

Herr Klauss walked out to meet the visitors. They all gave a *Heil Hitler* salute, raising their open right hands upward, extending their arms out straight while clicking their heels loudly together. One of the officers carefully lifted a large, narrow rectangular sealed wooden box out of the car. The other carried a similar but square-shaped wooden box in his hands. Herr Klauss led the way to his study and closed the door firmly behind them.

Alexa did as Olga had told her but she had been shocked to see the officers arrive in their uniforms at the farmhouse. It was, after all, only two mornings before that she and her mother had been forced out of the shoe shop by men dressed in those same kinds of uniforms. It was men like them who had separated her from her mother in the street, who had forcefully loaded them onto trucks and trains, and then driven them far away from their home. She couldn't help but think they had come for her again. She immediately thought of hiding.

"Let's play hide and seek," Alexa suggested. She took little Rudy's hand and hid behind a curtain with him. Then she began to count to ten out loud in German, the best she could. Rudy corrected her pronunciation and filled in the numbers she got wrong. Richard and Anna had been preoccupied while they hid, so they hadn't seen exactly where they were concealed in the large playroom. They both began seeking and in a relatively short time, Richard pulled back the long, green velvet-lined curtains to the side of one of the windows, revealing Alexa and Rudy.

"Now it's our turn to hide," said Richard. "Close your eyes and count to twenty."

Alexa continued the game and began to count in German, even though she'd only learned the numbers up to ten in school. The three children hurried about looking for the best place to hide in the spacious room.

"Eighteen, nineteen, twenty, here I come," Alexa said, counting the teen numbers in Polish.

She deliberately took her time to search out the three children, wanting them to be as quiet as possible for as long as possible. Four-year-old Rudy did not have a great deal of patience; as Alexa passed nearby his hiding place, he couldn't contain himself.

"You missed me," he shouted, jumping out from behind the chair where he was hiding. Alexa tried to act surprised so as not to let on that she knew where he was all along. Rudy announced he would help her to find his sister and brother and then proceeded to look in all the best hiding spots he could think of, dragging Alexa with him. The game continued for twenty minutes or so with Alexa always doing the counting and seeking, before the door opened and Olga entered the playroom.

"What are you children doing?" Olga asked. "Or rather, what have you done with the children, Alexa?" The three of them were nowhere in sight.

"They are hiding," Alexa answered.

All of a sudden Rudy jumped out from his hiding place. "Boo!" he yelled. "She's not very good at this game. It's taking ages for her to find us."

Olga had left the door ajar and Alexa could hear the men talking in the hallway downstairs. The voices became faint as they left the house and headed outside to their car. The engine started up and the car drove off with the two officers inside. Herr Klauss returned to his study and locked the door behind him.

Olga left the children to play upstairs and took Alexa with her to the kitchen to begin the task of making dinner for the family. Potatoes and carrots had to be peeled and chopped, then placed in pots to be boiled or steamed. Olga took chicken pieces out of the refrigerator; first, she tenderized the meat, then dipped each piece into flour, eggs, and breadcrumbs, to be fried. She put a chopping board, bowl, and knife in front of Alexa and had her prepare a salad with the fresh lettuce, tomatoes, cucumber, onion, and a carrot. Olga took the boiled potatoes and proceeded to mash them together, adding some butter, milk, salt, and pepper. She then fried the chicken pieces in some hot oil in a pan on the stove and steamed the carrots.

Alexa took note of it all and as the aroma of tasty food filled the kitchen, she became hungrier by the minute. It was approaching 2 pm when the meal was finally cooked. Olga gathered five dinner plates, bowls, and sets of cutlery, and sent Alexa to place them on the dining room table. The family came into the room and sat down at the table. Olga placed a glass of milk in front of each child and then served the meal. After she was content she hadn't forgotten anything, she left the room while Herr Klauss opened a bottle of wine and poured two glasses, one for himself and one for his wife.

Olga told Alexa to return to washing the family's clothes in the utility room. Alexa was tired and longed to take the weight off her feet, and to get out of those most uncomfortable clogs. But she had to carry on with her demanding chores. Olga handed her a book and pointed to the title on the cover a few times: *Learn German*. Alexa knew that German would be replacing her own Polish language and the sooner she learned it, the better it would be for her. However, she did wonder at what time of day she would be able to look at the book and learn any German, as she hadn't had even five minutes to herself so far.

It was now three o'clock in the afternoon. Alexa had completed washing the laundry, had rung out the excess water using the old hand-turned clothes wringer, and had hung it all out to dry. Olga made her clear the dining room table after dinner. It was also her job to wash all the dishes, cooking pots and pans, and to clean the kitchen. Her delicate young hands were red raw and sore by that point, but she carried on until everything was clean and put away where it belonged.

To Alexa's surprise, Olga placed a small bowl of leftover food from dinner in her hand, together with a spoon, and pointed to the utility room where the girl was to go and eat her cold food. Alexa, being hungry, said thank you and took the bowl into the small room where she had done all the laundry and, for the first time since milking the cows that morning, she finally got to sit down.

She slipped her throbbing feet out of the large, heavy clogs and placed them on the cold stone floor. She quickly devoured the food she had been given and could almost feel it land in her empty stomach. She wasted no time, as if the bowl could be snatched away from her at any moment.

After a few minutes, Olga approached her with the metal milking bucket and told her it was time for the cows' second milking of the day. She led Alexa back out to the barn and opened the rear gate out to the field where the cows were grazing. She began leading the cows back into the barn.

"*Fünf*," she said in German, pointing to the cows, meaning all five cows were to be milked again.

Alexa placed the stool under the first cow in readiness to begin the process again. Olga watched over her as she milked the first cow and then she walked out of the barn, closing the large doors behind her and sliding the locking post securely into place.

Alexa continued to milk the cows one after another. As she got closer to Blümchen, she noticed the cow staring at her continually, with its sad eyes and lowered head. As she began milking Blümchen, she began to speak to the cow in Polish. "I hope you can understand Polish," she said. "Why do you look as sad as I feel? Are you sad for yourself, or are you feeling sorry for me?"

She continued to milk the cow and when she next looked up, she could see a visible tear rolling out of Blümchen's left eye. She looked round to her right eye and it too had a tear trickling down from it. *'Well I never. I think this cow's crying for me.'* Alexa stood up and gently placed her hand on the cow's head, softly stroking it. She wasn't afraid anymore.

"Don't cry, Blümchen," she murmured. "We will be good friends and then I won't feel so awfully alone in this place. I can talk to you secretly every day in Polish, and you will help me not to forget my own language."

She finished milking all the cows then heard the barn door opening. She shared a silent glance with Blümchen. Olga came back into the barn with Alexa's next chore, after the milk was removed to the chilling area. It was Olga's job to guide the cows back out to the nearby field for grazing, then to securely bolt and lock the gate. The cows set off while Blümchen kept her head raised up, staring at Alexa until she was out of sight.

Olga led her to one of the sheds on the property where there were several large baskets of apples being stored from which she collected about two dozen. On their way back to the kitchen, Olga pointed out to Alexa where the apple trees were in the garden. Alexa figured out she'd probably have the job of climbing up and picking the apples when they were ripe—more manual labor.

They took the apples back into the kitchen; Olga told her to wash her hands and then handed her an apple peeler and a large bowl, instructing her to start peeling. Once the apples were peeled, Olga cored and sliced them thinly, after which she began preparing the ingredients to make an apple pie. Alexa wrote down all the steps, including what temperature the oven was set to.

Before the pie was ready, Olga took Alexa out to the barn where the animals were and showed her how to rake up the soiled straw and renew the barn floor with fresh straw and hay. The cows were still out in the field grazing. Then they added fresh hay to the sty where the pigs were kept. The day's leftovers were poured into the pigs' trough for them to eat. In total there were four pigs with six piglets.

After that, it was the chicken coop that had to be cleaned out. There were eight chickens in total, seven hens and one cockerel. They weren't kept in the coop during the day but roamed freely around a fenced-in area at the back of the barn. Alexa couldn't help but think that, in comparison, the animals had a lot more freedom than she did.

Next up was the stable, which was home to two horses. Only one was in the stable. Herr Klauss had saddled up the other one and taken it out for a ride after dinner. Olga pointed to a shovel for Alexa to use to lift the horses' mess into a nearby wheelbarrow. She was then to rake up the straw and hay that was on the ground and replace it with fresh, along with a bale of hay for the horses to eat. After that, the water for the horses needed to be refreshed, along with all the other animals' drinking water; this Alexa had to draw from the well out in the courtyard and carry by the bucketful.

After that chore was completed, it was time to check on the apple pie. Its aroma filled the kitchen, and Alexa's mouth watered as Olga removed it from the oven, carefully placing it on a metal rack on top of the kitchen table. She motioned to Alexa to wash her hands after she had cleaned hers and then told her to get five bowls and dessert spoons and to place them on the dining room table.

Alexa did as she was told, as she had done all day. It was now 5:30 pm; voices could be heard from the children who had gone for a walk with their mother after dinner and had now returned to the house. Olga served the warm apple pie with cream to the family and stoked the fireplace with a steel poker, adding another few logs of wood to the pile. She collected a large jug of fresh fruit compote and five glasses from the kitchen and poured everyone a refreshing drink.

By 6:30 pm, the family had finished their dessert and left the dining room. Alexa cleared the table and carried the dishes through to the kitchen sink where she began washing them. Olga followed her through with the glasses, placing them at the side of the sink, while Alexa put all the clean dishes away.

Herr and Frau Klauss had retired to the lounge to relax, followed by their children. Alexa understood the family usually spent some time together in the evening before the children were taken upstairs to get ready for bed. Meanwhile, Olga took Alexa upstairs to prepare the children's bedrooms—switching on the lights, laying out pajamas, pulling back the bedding, and running warm bubble baths, starting with Rudy's.

Once Rudy was bathed, clean, and dry, Olga dressed him in his pajamas, ready for bed. She then ran baths for the other two children and laid out fresh pajamas and a nightgown for each of them. Anna, being seven, still needed assistance bathing, especially in washing her long blonde hair, but Richard was nine and insisted on privacy in the bathroom. He bathed and dressed himself, quite the independent young man. However, he had no interest in picking up after himself or cleaning up the mess he left behind him. That was Olga's job, and now it would be Alexa's.

Richard's parents had ensured he joined the German Youth movement, and it was obvious from his words and actions that the classes were having a major influence on the young boy, who was full to brimming with nationalistic pride.

Olga told Alexa to clean up the bathroom after the children were finished. Then she was to collect all the wet towels and soiled clothes, take them downstairs to the utility room, and wash them. It was after eight o'clock and the night sky had already turned dark when Alexa went outside to collect and fold the dry laundry.

While Olga showed Alexa where to put the clean laundry in the children's wardrobes, Herr and Frau Klauss came upstairs to say goodnight to their children. Rudy was the first to get some attention. As his mother sat on his bed, ready to read him a short story, his father kissed his forehead and left his room. Carrying a large book with a bold swastika symbol displayed on the front cover, he went into Richard's bedroom, closing the door behind him.

After Rudy's mother finished reading his story, she tucked him into bed, pulling the blankets up below his chin, and kissed his cheek. She switched off the bedside lamp and pulled the door behind her, leaving it slightly ajar. She then went to her daughter's bedroom, where Anna was waiting with her book of choice. First, Frau Klauss took a soft brush and began gently running it through her little girl's hair, before reading her bedtime story. And so, Herr and Frau Klauss spent about an hour with their children before kissing them goodnight and heading downstairs.

Once Alexa had completed hand-washing the bath-time laundry, she hung it up to dry. She was beyond exhausted with every bone in her body seeming to scream for relief. Olga took her outside to the field and showed her how to bring the chickens into their coop, and then the cows into the shed. Thankfully, this was Alexa's last chore of the day; she could hardly stand, her feet throbbing in the heavy wooden clogs—as she walked back into the kitchen, she could feel them blistering.

Olga cut two slices of the leftover apple pie into two bowls, one bigger than the other, and covered them with cream. She took one bowl for herself and gave the smaller one to Alexa to eat. She poured them each a glass of fruit compote to drink.

Once they had finished eating and cleaned up their dishes, Olga led Alexa back upstairs, stopping at the children's bathroom where she motioned to her to go in and use the toilet. She then led Alexa up another flight of stairs to the attic and over to the small room in the corner where she had slept the night before. It was now 10:30 pm. Olga told her she'd be back for her in the morning at 4 am. Olga switched on the lamp before leaving the room without another word, closing and locking the door behind her.

Alexa kicked off the clogs and collapsed onto the bed in sheer exhaustion. Then she thought of her new blue shoes. She hadn't seen them since she'd been forced to take them off that morning. She got off the bed and searched the small room but there was no sign of her new shoes. Her heart sank. They were gone. Alexa recalled the last conversation she'd had with her best friend, Helena, as they had walked home from school that last Friday, only three days before. Now she wouldn't be able to keep her promise to let Helena try on her new shoes. Worse, it didn't look like she'd ever get to wear them again either. She thought how disappointed her mother would be with her for losing them, and the tears began to fall.

She climbed back onto the uncomfortable bed, feeling totally alone. She said her prayers, reciting her Psalm, with a whispered "Amen" at the end. Burying her head in her exhausted, aching arms, Alexa drifted off to sleep, the tears still trickling down her cheeks.

CHAPTER 7

As time went on, Alexa's long list of chores for the Klauss family became like second nature to her. Olga had taught her well during her final week before leaving the Klausses' farm, and Alexa was a quick learner. She became very familiar with the family's routine, their likes and dislikes, and soon she had the household running smoothly, like a well-oiled machine.

Alexa kept telling herself her situation was only temporary and would eventually come to an end, that she would be reunited with her mother and sister again one day soon, and would be able to go back home to the life she knew and loved. No matter how many times she told herself all this, there was still a small part of her that didn't fully believe it. All the same, she kept her hopes alive, choosing to ignore her doubts and instead fuel her positive thinking. She knew she wasn't free to physically leave whenever she wished, being kept against her will as she was. *'I'm basically a slave,'* she thought. *'I'm as good as a prisoner here. But I still have my mental and spiritual freedom.'* And that, she would consciously try to preserve.

In her mind and in her thoughts, she could be free. There, she could escape from the pain, suffering, and separation she felt so deeply in her heart. There, she could be her own liberator and dismantle her prison walls, brick by brick. She would choose to be happy, rather than depressed. She'd choose to be hopeful over being miserable and bitter. She realized it was her choice, and she chose joy and freedom of mind. She would hold firm to her faith and trust in God. She would muster the needed courage to allow the worst situations to bring out the very best in her. She reminded herself daily that this nightmare was only temporary. *I will survive today, and tomorrow, I will be free. As long as I still have hope and faith, I will live. I will survive this.* These thoughts sustained her and helped her endure even her most difficult days.

Her father had always taught her when she was little that if a job was worth doing, it was worth doing well, and so no matter what task was laid before her, Alexa did the very best she could. In time, Herr and Frau Klauss could see she did a great job with each chore given her and that she was especially good with their children, her nurturing manner showing sincerity and genuine affection.

The three children quickly grew very fond of Alexa, and enjoyed spending time with her. Alexa shared her love and talent for art with the Klauss children, creating little masterpieces to amuse them and art projects to involve them in, much as her father had done with her when she was a small child. Herr and Frau Klauss saw she was trustworthy and honest, so as time went on, they began to give her certain privileges.

The first privilege she received was that she no longer had to sleep up in the tiny attic room, which was dreary, dark, dismal, and more like a dirty, windowless old cupboard than a bedroom. Instead, she moved into a real bedroom in the main house on the floor below. Of course, it wasn't as nicely decorated or as beautifully furnished as the three children's rooms were, but it was clean, bright, and more spacious than the farmhouse attic. It had a proper bed with clean bedding, pillows, and a warm feather quilt. Furthermore, she didn't get locked into this room at night.

On the opposite wall from the bed was a small window that gave a good amount of natural light, although as Alexa was always busy working during the daylight hours, she never really got the pleasure or benefit of it. Her room faced towards the greenhouse and over the fields at the rear of the farmhouse, which reminded her of the view from her old classroom window where she used to sit at school. She recalled how she and the other children used to dream of being free from that classroom most days, away from all the hard work that was given to them there. Now she wished more than anything that she could go back to the safety of the school classroom. She would have given anything to trade in the incredibly hard work she was now forced to do each day for those few hours of daily education, Monday to Friday, from her teacher. *'To be able to do math, science, reading, indeed any subject would be better than this,'* she thought.

The war battled on, year after year, with no sign of any immediate let-up, and Alexa's daily chores for the Klauss family continued without any slackening. Alexa quickly became an expert at her job, and the set of individual skills she had developed became very refined and professional for such a young teenager.

The Klausses' farmhouse in Bitburg was only a few kilometers away from the border with Luxembourg, and when Alexa was roughly sixteen and a half, the Klausses decided she could be trusted to make the journey on foot to run a new errand for them—an errand that would extend their trust in her. A little way over the border was a little village called Vianden, and in it was a small shoe shop where the Klausses would place orders and have their shoes custom made. Previously, Herr Klauss had always sent an officer to collect them by car, but this time, his wife had convinced him it would be good for Alexa to go alone and that she could indeed be trusted.

The Klausses gave Alexa straightforward directions, telling her how to get to Vianden. Once she crossed the nearby border, she was to go over the wooden bridge crossing the river; adjacent to the large white church, she would find the quaint little bespoke shoe shop. They gave her the necessary documents in order to collect the shoes, along with the money to pay for them. She put on her jacket with the letter 'P' sewn on it, identifying her as being Polish, and headed off on the hour's walk to Luxembourg, unaccompanied for the very first time.

Alexa felt a mixture of emotions on her journey. On the one hand, she was very pleased with the trust placed in her by both Herr and Frau Klauss, who believed in her enough to allow her the freedom to go so far unescorted and come back alone. On the other hand, she couldn't help but want to take advantage of her short window of freedom—the first real window of opportunity she'd had. She thought over and over how this could be her chance to escape, perhaps her one and only chance to ever escape. *'I could run away and just keep running. It would be hard to find me,'* she thought. But then more realistic thoughts came to mind. *'Where would I run to? How could I even run anywhere far in these big clumsy clogs? What would I survive on? Where would I live? I have no food and the money wouldn't last long. What if someone else captures me?'* Alexa came to the conclusion she'd be better off to simply collect the shoes as she was instructed, and take them straight back to the Klausses' farmhouse.

Her thoughts drifted back to the last time she had gone to buy new shoes with her mother in Lublin; what a horrific event that had turned out to be. It couldn't have been any worse and she began to worry that this journey to the shoe shop might also be a bad experience. As the flashbacks went off in her mind like fireworks, she began to pray her familiar Psalm 91.

'You are my God and my stronghold, in whom I trust. Let me not fall into the trap of the bird catcher. Let me take shelter under your wings. Have affection for me and rescue me, my dear God, that I will see your acts of salvation. Please keep me safe. Amen.'

Alexa crossed the river by way of the bridge and eventually neared the large church, as she had been told, and there in front of her was the small shoe shop. Alexa walked into the shop and approached the woman who stood behind the counter.

"Good afternoon, can I help you?"

"Good afternoon, I have this card to collect a pair of shoes."

"Ah! So, you are Polish I see. We never see any Polish people here. What are you doing in Luxembourg?"

Alexa found the woman to be endearing as she engaged her in conversation. She had a kind face and seemed to be genuinely interested. Alexa began to explain her situation to the woman who listened attentively until, all of a sudden, she shook her head vehemently.

"Oh no!" the woman said. "In that case, you are not going back to slave away for the mean Germans anymore, child. I have some lovely cousins in Belgium; I will arrange for you to go and stay with them tomorrow. My husband is a politician and he can drive you there in secret in his car. You don't ever have to work for the Germans anymore. How dare they!"

Alexa liked what she was hearing but was still very anxious over what the consequences of her not returning to the Klausses' home that night might be. The woman closed the shop early and took Alexa to her large family home in the nearby mountains where she was told she could spend the night and decide what she wanted to do. The woman told her that her name was Alice, then introduced her to her family. She made Alexa a tasty meal to eat and some fresh fruit compote to drink.

Alice encouraged Alexa to tell her story of how she had ended up in Germany and was visibly moved as she listened intently to Alexa's every word. It was late in the evening and dark outside, so Alice showed Alexa to one of her comfortable spare bedrooms where she was invited to sleep for the night. Alice gave her a clean, fresh nightgown to wear and some fresh towels to use, while she ran her a warm bubble bath and made her feel as much at home as possible.

Alexa settled into the comfortable bed with ease that night. It reminded her of her childhood home and of her own pretty bedroom in Lublin, which she'd never forgotten. She wished more than anything that her mother would walk through the door and come to tuck her in, kissing her forehead as they said their nightly prayer together before she turned out the light. But no matter how hard Alexa stared at the door, she knew her mother would never walk through it. She turned out the light, pulled the covers up around her neck, and said her prayer alone, thanking God for the kindness of strangers.

In the morning, Alexa was awakened by loud voices and a commotion coming from outside. There was heavy arguing, and Alexa could hear Herr Klauss's angry voice. Alexa made her way downstairs.

"Look," Herr Klauss shouted, "I know the girl is here because we sent her to your shop yesterday. She had nowhere else to go and didn't come home last night. I have come to collect her and if you don't produce her immediately, I will report you to the German army. Then they will have you, your family, and Alexa all arrested and sent off to a work camp. Is that what you want?"

"Look, please let's all calm down and go inside the house," said Alice. "I'll make some fresh coffee and we can talk about it. I'm sure there is a simple solution to all of this."

Alice's invitation calmed things down slightly. Perhaps it was all those years of her husband being a politician that helped her defuse the situation. She made the coffee and they all drank some together, discussing things more calmly until a mutual agreement was finally reached and agreed upon.

"Alexa will go back to Bitburg to work for your family from Monday to Saturday, but on Sundays she will be allowed to come freely to Luxembourg, where she can relax with us, eat good food, and enjoy fine company every Sunday, as her day of rest," proposed Alice's husband.

This arrangement was finally agreed to by Herr Klauss, who had known Alice's husband since they were young boys. As this longtime acquaintance was a politician, Herr Klauss had called on him for special favors over the years and therefore felt obliged to grant his request regarding Alexa. They all returned to the shop to collect the new shoes Alexa had originally been sent for, and then she returned to Bitburg with Herr Klauss in his car that morning.

The following Sunday, Alexa walked to her retreat in Luxembourg as agreed. She was welcomed warmly and enjoyed a taste of normality with her new-found friends. It gave her something to look forward to all week as she worked, and she cherished her visits with Alice and her family, along with the freedom she felt when with them.

At the end of her second Sunday visit, Alice gave Alexa a new pair of shoes, which they had made as a gift for the Klausses' older son. When the Klausses received them, they were very pleased, and the following Sunday they dispatched Alexa with a parcel full of fine cheeses and fresh meats for them in return.

At the end of that day, the shoemakers gave a pair of shoes for young Anna as a gift. The following week they gave her a pair for Rudy, and then a new pair of shoes were made for and given to Frau Klauss. The Klausses continued to show their appreciation to the shoemakers and never allowed Alexa to visit them empty-handed, always sending her off with a bag full of gifts in return.

Alexa spent almost every Sunday in Luxembourg, relaxing with Alice and her family for about four hours each visit. These special times allowed her to unwind, and gave her the endurance she needed to continue working for the Klauss family.

After the first month of getting to know her, Alice and her family presented Alexa with a beautiful pair of new black shoes, which they had custom made especially for her. Alexa was overcome with emotion and gratitude. The kind gesture made her feel special. These became her Sunday shoes, and the Klausses allowed her to take off her clogs and leave them behind at the farmhouse while she wore her beautiful new, comfortable shoes for her walk to Luxembourg and back. Alexa had a youthful spring in her step once more.

CHAPTER 8

Roughly five hundred and fifty kilometers away from Bitburg was the city of Munich. There were large numbers of SS officers in all the cities, with their offices in various locations. Munich was one of the largest Nazi strongholds, and it was where Hitler and Goebbels happened to be when they instigated "Crystal Night" on November 9, 1938.

Continuing on into the next day, Nazi storm troopers conducted an all-out attack throughout Germany. It was impossible for Jews to live a peaceful, normal existence anymore. Hundreds of their synagogues were torched and left to burn to the ground; German fire fighters standing nearby were instructed not to save the synagogues, but instead only to fight a fire if it threatened to spread to an Aryan-owned building. Jewish businesses were severely vandalized and glass-fronted stores were smashed during the Pogrom. Local German police officers joined in the horrific events, arresting thousands of innocent Jewish men, both young and old, and sending them off to labor camps or worse—never to return to their homes or families again. From then on, the Germans continued segregating the remaining Jewish population and setting harsh, almost impossible rules and regulations for them to live by.

Rapidly, the hate for all things Jewish spread like wildfire from the busy cities to the small countryside villages.

The German youth movement recruited many youngsters, teaching them to hate all Jews from childhood, even if they had had young Jewish friends a few years earlier at school or as neighbors. They were now to be despised, to be hated at first sight. The majority of adults who were once friends with Jewish work colleagues and neighbors now betrayed and turned their backs on them. The Nazi regime made Jewish life and survival virtually impossible in Germany, as hatred of them spread like wildfire.

Life rapidly became harder for the Jews throughout Europe, but especially in Germany and Poland. Their stores were boycotted, attacked, and vandalized, so that making a living became near impossible. Many highly qualified, professional and intellectual Jews were no longer permitted to work or to practice in their chosen fields. Their children were no longer permitted to attend regular schools, and further education was out of the question. They were treated as less than second-class citizens and were forced to wear a Star of David. Made out of yellow fabric and visibly sewn onto the outer sleeves of their jackets and coats, it clearly identified them as being Jewish, a visible label they couldn't avoid. Stars of David were also painted on their few remaining businesses, homes, and windows. It wasn't long before Jewish people were being forcibly removed from their homes during night raids and transported to work in concentration camps, while their valuables were confiscated by the SS and Nazi army.

The wealthiest Jews who had the finances, connections, and the foresight, obtained visas—frequently by bribing officials—and bought tickets for their families to leave Germany. Those lucky ones escaped to go stay with other family members or migrate to other countries by any means possible. Such arrangements were usually made very hurriedly, with families disappearing under the cover of night, carrying very few belongings or valuables with them, which meant there were many homes with valuables left behind. Priceless works of art, famous paintings, valuable antiques, and jewelry were all left with no guardians.

The Nazi party needed no invitation or permission to take possession of these valuables, taking their fill of the abandoned bounty. The German museums had already been pilfered and stripped of their greatest assets, antiquities, and masterpieces. Now, the SS plundered the homes of private collectors and Jews alike. Their hoards became massive as they looted their choice of priceless art from across Europe, which they stashed in a variety of safe and secluded locations all over Germany and occupied Poland.

Herr Klauss travelled to the SS Headquarters in Munich once a week, and on a daily basis to the Frankfurt offices, which were closer to where he lived. There, he oversaw operations locating desirable masterpieces and artworks the SS were still trying to acquire from a secret "list."

The *List* was exactly that—a meticulously kept record of several million famous and priceless paintings and sculptures, all inscribed in a collection of large and sequentially numbered ledgers, bound in black leather. Along with the title of each piece of art, the List noted the names of the artists who had created them, the date and country of their completion, and their last known location and owner. In addition, the details included a full description of the actual artwork, including the colors, mediums, frames, settings, scenery, and characters. It was, in short, Hitler's ultimate collector's wish-list.

Herr Klauss was intensely passionate about art; he took his position and responsibility very seriously, with an enormous amount of pride. His job was to guard the List as top secret, so privacy was paramount. He was head of his office in Frankfurt, with six senior officers under his command and direction, who in turn had a few dozen Nazi footmen under their control, whom they would order out on reconnaissance and retrieval missions.

Three years into the Second World War, this team already had three quarters of the List successfully gathered and safely stored in secret locations across Europe. Herr Klauss had several dozen personal favorites which he had always loved, but there were still some of his own favorites that he was yet to trace and lay his hands upon for the Führer. He was committed to the cause, and it was his duty to help obtain them by any means possible. The plan was that eventually, all the individual pieces of art would be housed in a new, enormous German mega-museum to be purposely built for the Führer in Berlin. It would be the greatest museum the world had ever seen, and Herr Klauss and his officers took tremendous pride in the part they played, working towards its creation.

Herr Klauss was a popular man and well respected by his peers. He was well known in German society and amongst the local townspeople where he lived. The SS uniform he wore gave another dimension to his personality, an added air of authority and inevitably, many people feared him on sight. However, although he was a highly decorated SS officer, he had a certain quality of kindness that shone through, and when in a good mood, he was quite approachable and pleasant. He viewed himself as a good Christian man. He and his family were Catholics and every two weeks, his first cousin, Edgar, a Catholic Priest, would come and visit with him at his farmhouse. This always seemed to make him feel as if God approved of him somehow.

From the German point of view, the war was going quite well. However, for the millions of Jews and innocent Europeans caught up in the crossfire, the same could not be said. Towards the end of 1943, Herr Klauss had the idea of entertaining groups of officers at his farmhouse and hosting private parties to boost the morale among his junior officers, soldiers, and staff. His wife thought this was a wonderful idea and took charge of inviting several young local women whom she knew, as well as some of her attractive single female friends. There would be music and dancing, tables of fine foods, delicacies, wines, vodka, and cognacs for all to enjoy. This was the very distraction the Klausses needed as the war roared on.

Alexa was now seventeen and blossoming into a beautiful young woman, quite the head-turner, although she was completely oblivious to her attractiveness. She still worked almost every hour of the day, except from a five-hour reprieve from eleven o'clock at night until four o'clock in the morning, when she finally got to take the weight off her tired feet, worn out from walking all day in the heavy, oversized clogs. It was no wonder she so looked forward to her Sunday afternoons and some much-needed respite with Alice and her family.

Despite the mundane, monotonous, and demanding nature of her chores, Alexa became the perfect housekeeper, an excellent cook, meticulous cleaner, and wonderful childcare provider. She was hard not to like and almost everyone who met her took an immediate shine and warmed to her.

Over the years, Alexa had met a few other young European girls who had also been taken from their homes and families in a similar and horrific manner. They too had been made to work as house slaves for other SS officers and their families in some of the other farmhouses nearby. Occasionally they would be dropped off at the Klausses' farmhouse with the children they looked after, so the young ones could have some supervised playtime together. This gave Alexa the opportunity to make friends with some of the girls.

These moments in time would be amongst the most enjoyable ones during her years of captivity and forced labor. Alexa was now fluent in German and could communicate very well indeed, as though it were her mother tongue, so there was no language barrier with the other girls who had also been forced to learn German. She was especially fond of Eva, who was originally from Luxembourg, and Elizabeth, who was Belgian.

Frau Klauss gave Alexa the details of what she wanted for the upcoming party. It was Alexa's job to decorate the main barn for the dance, as well as to prepare all of the food which was on the list she had been given. A day before the event, an SS truck delivered stacks of chairs, folding tables, several crates of soft drinks, fine wines, and beers.

The party was coming together nicely. Frau Klauss told Alexa she too was invited to attend, along with Eva, Elizabeth, and some of the other local girls. Much to Alexa's surprise, Frau Klauss gave her a beautiful new powder blue dress to wear for the night of the party. All of a sudden, overwhelmed with joy and genuine excitement, she threw her arms around the lady of the house, and thanked her. Frau Klauss was surprised by her reaction, but her motherly instinct seemed to kick in for a split second and for the first time she showed some genuine affection for Alexa, putting one arm around her and patting her shoulder. She then gave her a pretty blue velvet bow for her hair and told her to take both that and the dress upstairs to her room, out of the way until the party the following evening.

The day of the first party finally arrived, and Alexa's morning began as had all her other days at the Klauss residence—at 4 am. She set about attending to her many regular daily chores, as always, but also began preparing the food she'd be making for that evening's event. Frau Klauss had told Alexa to cater the party for sixty people, which was a new challenge for the seventeen-year-old girl. She had never cooked for more than twelve people at one sitting before, and so the task was very daunting; but as always, she did her very best.

As the day went on, Alexa worked tirelessly while her imagination drifted off into thoughts of how much fun the party would be that evening. The prospect of interacting with new people and spending some time with her few friends from the surrounding farmhouses, when they wouldn't be working either, excited her. She wondered what Eva and Elizabeth would wear to the party, and if they'd been given a new dress to wear, as pretty as hers. These girlish thoughts helped the hours fly by and her pile of chores reduced rapidly.

With all the food prepared, glasses set out on tables, and the barn decorated and ready for the guests to arrive, Alexa was excused from further duties and allowed to go upstairs to get dressed and make herself look pretty. She peered in the old mirror in her bedroom as she let down and began brushing her long blonde hair, and then she attempted positioning the blue velvet bow in place. It took her several tries as she had worn her hair in the same clinical style every day for the past four years, tightly pulled back and tied up in a bun, out of the way.

As she stared at the reflection looking back at her, she couldn't help but notice she bore a strong resemblance to her mother, Sophia, when she was that age. Alexa specifically remembered a black and white photograph of her mother that used to hang in a picture frame in their old house. In the photograph, Sophia's hair was long, straight, and blonde, which seemed almost identical to how her own now looked, as she peered back to the memory in her mind's eye.

There was a knock at Alexa's door, and Frau Klauss entered her room. "You look very pretty, Alexa."

"Thank you."

Frau Klauss held a folded-over brown paper bag, which she passed to Alexa. "Here, open this and put these on, then come downstairs," she said and then left the room.

Alexa opened the bag and reached inside. To her complete and utter surprise, she pulled out a pair of shoes. But these weren't simply any pair of shoes. These were the very same pair of brand new, royal blue shoes she'd been shopping for with her mother in Poland, that fateful day in the town square. The same shoes she had been taken away in. The same shoes she'd worn when she'd arrived at the Klausses' home four years earlier but which she'd never seen again since that first night—until now.

The only shoes Alexa had been given to wear at the Klausses' were the big, uncomfortable wooden clogs, and the reason for that became clear to her as time went on. All the captured young foreign girls forced to work in the farmhouses locally were made to wear them so as to deter any attempts to escape. Running away on foot wouldn't be a wise choice in the large clogs, being that they were so uncomfortable, and definitely not a shoe for gaining speed or distance in.

However, none of that mattered now to Alexa; she had her shoes back, and a wave of comfort and overwhelming emotion flooded her. She quickly slipped her feet out of the ugly clogs and, one by one, put on her own pretty royal blue shoes. To her amazement, they still fit her feet, but only just. There was no extra growing-room room left. Her mother had chosen the size wisely that day in the shoe shop, when she'd said it would be better to allow Alexa's feet a little room to grow. Alexa had to loosen the straps of the silver buckle by two holes, so they weren't so tight on her feet. This way, she could get away with wearing the shoes—just and no more.

She didn't care that they were snug on her. As she looked down at them on her feet, they were the perfect complement to her blue dress, and they were still in brand new condition. For the first time in four years, the young girl felt attractive and comfortable in her own shoes. She closed her bedroom door behind her and walked downstairs with a spring in her step and joy in her heart.

There were a few cars parked in the courtyard already, and more were making their way up the driveway. The lights in the barn were lit, and music was playing on the record player housed in its stand-alone wooden console, positioned against a wall in the middle of the barn. Herr Klauss was welcoming his friends and colleagues as they arrived at the party and told Alexa to take the coats from their guests and hang them up. Junior officers were placed in charge of the music and the task of serving the drinks. The food was laid out for all the guests to help themselves freely, buffet style, and the party was underway.

Herr Klauss was the first to move onto the dance floor. Taking his wife's hand, he led her out in a waltz. A round of applause erupted, and gradually a few other couples joined them on the dance floor, getting the party off to a fine start.

Eva and Elizabeth arrived, and Alexa made her way over to greet them. They were both also wearing pretty dresses, and it was the first time they all looked like normal, attractive young females, freely enjoying life without the burden and yoke of forced labor around their necks.

Frau Klauss had allowed her two older children, Anna and Richard, to say hello to their guests and spend half an hour at the party. The agreement was that they'd then go upstairs to their bedrooms to join Rudy, who was already tucked up in bed. The children were reluctant to leave, but Alexa led them out of the barn and into the main house where she got them ready and settled for bed.

After about twenty minutes, Alexa returned to the party. All the guests had now arrived and were enjoying their evening together. Both Eva and Elizabeth were dancing with two handsome young soldiers in their smart uniforms. Alexa looked on, and seemed quite happy about the attention her friends were receiving. There were a number of single German soldiers at the party, and several of them had also selected a dance partner from among the attractive young foreign and German girls who were present.

The soldiers seemed quite interested in their dance partners and were visibly enjoying having a pretty, young female close in their arms. When the music ended, the girls began to make their way from the dance floor back to their seats, but the soldiers pulled them back for another dance. Both Eva and Elizabeth appeared to be enjoying the male attention they were receiving; however, there was also an air of unease about the situation. They were, after all, dancing with German soldiers, the very people who had ripped them away from their homes and families, from the lives they had once lived. They were responsible for robbing them of their freedom and forcing them to work as unpaid slave girls.

Even with that knowledge, the young girls still seemed rather enamored and quite swept away by all the interest and male attention shown them. Being asked to dance by the handsome soldiers after being treated and regarded as nothing less than a second-class citizen for so long, gave them a feeling of being special and worthy of not only the attention of a man but of the attention of a German man, and a soldier no less.

The girls left the dance floor when the music ended and headed back to their seats to join Alexa. Both girls were giddy with excitement and, as young girls do, they quickly shared their thoughts and feelings about their dance partners. They commented as to who was the most handsome and who had held whom the closest.

The soldiers returned to their seats across the room to join their fellow soldier friends; they were also sharing comments about the girls with each other over a few steins of beer. However, their eyes shifted from their two dance partners onto someone else who had caught their attention. Another soldier jumped to his feet and made his way over to where the three girls were sitting together. Suddenly, his two friends who had danced with Elizabeth and Eva, hurried over to join him.

Eva turned to her girlfriends. "Here come the good-looking soldiers again and look," she said, "there's one for you too, Alexa."

Alexa looked up and, as the soldiers arrived at her seat, she became suddenly aware that all three of them were directing their attention completely towards her. The soldiers had large, flirtatious smiles on their faces and couldn't seem to take their eyes off Alexa.

The first soldier approached Alexa. "Would you like to dance with me?" he asked.

The soldier who had danced with Elizabeth took at step forward. "No, don't dance with him," he said, "dance with me!"

The excited smile quickly disappeared from Elizabeth's face, replaced by a puzzled expression and visible signs of disappointment.

"He can't dance," jibed the soldier who had been dancing with Eva. "Don't waste your time with him, come and dance with me."

Like Elizabeth, Eva's mood changed and she was obviously displeased by what she was hearing. Alexa could sense and clearly see her two friends were getting upset and angered by the attention she was receiving. So, she politely thanked the soldiers for their dance invitations and turned them down.

"I'll dance with you," Elizabeth said to the soldier with whom she'd already danced. But he rather abruptly declined her offer and once again asked Alexa onto the floor. Alexa now felt extremely uncomfortable; she really didn't want to dance with any of them, so she stood up, declined once again, and excused herself from the group.

The soldier who had first asked her to dance took hold of her hand forcefully as she attempted to walk away, pulling her close to him and trying to hold her in a waltz position, but Alexa tried to break free. He became a little more forceful and, using more strength, he wrapped his left arm around her waist while firmly taking hold of her right hand, pulling her in close to his chest, and began waltzing with her to the melody of the music. Alexa was overpowered and realized it would be better for everyone there if she went along with him, so she stopped fighting it and followed his lead across the dance floor. The other two soldiers took Eva and Elizabeth back onto the dance floor but as they danced with them, it was blatantly obvious that their eyes were fixed on Alexa.

As soon as the music ended and Alexa was free from the soldier's grip, she walked swiftly out of the barn, across the courtyard, and ran into the farmhouse, where she closed the door behind her and headed straight upstairs to check on the children. She used that as her convenient excuse and stayed there for the remainder of the evening.

Her absence was noticed by the three soldiers who eagerly waited and anticipated her return, only to be disappointed. However, Alexa's friends were well aware she had left the party. In a way, they were very pleased, as it meant they would have the full attention of their soldiers and dance partners again for the rest of the evening.

Alexa had been wise in her decision. Sensing her two girlfriends were getting upset by all the attention she was receiving, she had deliberately declined the advances of the German soldiers so as not to hurt Eva and Elizabeth's feelings. Her lasting friendships with the girls were far more important to her than any short-term physical interest the young men might have had in her. For her, the best option had been to remove herself from the situation so as to not upset her friends any further. This also meant she would avoid any further uncomfortable and awkward situations.

Alexa went to her room and took off the pretty dress and hung it up in her wardrobe. She put her work clothes back on and tied up her hair, gathering it back into a bun. However, she couldn't bring herself to take off her blue shoes, so she kept them on. As the clock approached midnight, Alexa knew she would still be required to clear up the mess and remove any leftover food from the tables, so she headed downstairs and back over to the party.

The music had finally ended and some of the invited guests had already started to leave. Next to an armored car, Eva and Elizabeth were talking and laughing with the soldiers they had danced with and were getting pretty close with them. Or rather, the soldiers were getting up close to them. Alexa began to clear up, and collected the food that could be saved to store away in the kitchen.

The party had been a great success and the Klausses were very happy with the event's turnout. From then on, they made the dances at their farm a regular monthly occurrence. And every month, Alexa kept her wits about her, slipping away early on or at certain points throughout the evening with various excuses, so as not to be compromised or to upset any of the other girls there.

CHAPTER 9

The war had roared on in Europe unmercifully for almost six years at the power-hungry hands of the German army, under Hitler's brutal and inhumane command. Millions of Jews from many countries had been murdered as part of the Führer's "final solution" and along with those victims were also many European non-Jewish prisoners who were captured for simply being in the wrong place at the wrong time or for having the wrong political, religious, or sexual preferences.

It had been a particularly cruel and evil war, full of much violence and devastating destruction. As the Allied troops from Russia, Britain, France, America, and other countries finally drew closer to bringing an end to the German tyrant's reign of terror, there was much movement as German troops made a run for it to avoid capture for their heinous crimes.

Now aged eighteen, Alexa had spent the previous five years working in the Klausses' farmhouse as their unpaid slave and attending to all their family's needs. Although this was not of her own free will or choice, and considering Herr Klauss was an SS officer, Alexa had actually been more fortunate than some of the other young Christian girls who had also been taken captive. She had never been sexually or physically abused, nor was she ever beaten by the Klausses, which was not something that could be said by many of the girls in similar circumstances.

Early on, when Alexa had first arrived at the Klausses' farmhouse, Herr Fredrick Klauss's cousin, Edgar the priest, had reminded them they were baptized Christians and they had a Christian duty as good Catholics to take care of Alexa. He told them that in fact, she was an orphan with no mother, father, or family of her own to care for her, and so it was their responsibility to make sure no harm came to her under their roof or on their watch. Edgar's reminder was effective and stayed with the Klausses for as long as they were Alexa's keepers.

After the first few years of Alexa's enforced labor, the Klauss family had grown rather fond of her and had given her more privileges, such as being allowed to eat with them and the children at their dinner table on the weekends and during the celebrations of various holidays. They had even given her small presents at Christmas time.

Of course, this was by no means where she wanted to be, and not a day went by when she didn't think of where her mother and little sister were and when she might be reunited with them once again. She kept her faith and hope alive that the day would eventually arrive. She continued to recite her prayer of Psalm 91, which she could now say in perfect German. Anyone meeting Alexa for the first time could easily have been convinced she was a natural-born German citizen. She spoke German fluently, and along with her beautiful appearance, her blue eyes, and lovely long, blonde hair, she looked the part too.

In the final months of the Second World War, there were many bombing campaigns across Germany, aimed at certain targets as the Allies tried to take out as many of the main German army positions as possible. Of course, there were many stray bombs as well, and inevitably, many innocent Germans were caught up and killed in the crossfire. Properties were destroyed and buildings leveled in the Allies' quest to defeat the German army and regain power.

One cold day in early December of 1944, Herr Klauss and his wife called Alexa into his study. Alexa had never before been permitted to enter his home office in all her time at the farmhouse; Herr Klauss had always kept the door locked when he wasn't in it. It was the one room in the house Alexa had never been allowed to clean, and she never knew why.

As she stepped into the room she looked around, but there didn't seem to be anything unusual about it that might warrant it being kept under lock and key all the time. All she could see was some matching wooden furniture, a desk, a bureau, bookshelves with a large collection of books, and a black leather chair. Hanging on the walls were an assortment of paintings. Alexa figured there must be a very important matter to be discussed for her to be invited into Herr Klauss's study. However, she could never have guessed the words which were about to be spoken to her.

With his wife standing behind him, Herr Klauss sat at his desk, dressed in his uniform. "Alexa," he said, his voice very serious, "the war is ending, and we are giving you back your freedom."

Alexa couldn't believe her ears. She heard the words but she couldn't quite take them in. She stared at the Klausses with a puzzled expression on her face and said nothing.

"Did you hear me, Alexa? Did you understand what I said to you?"

"Yes, I think so."

"The war is almost over, and you can go home now."

"But . . . I don't know the way," stammered Alexa. "I don't remember how to get back to my home."

The husband and wife looked at each other for a few moments in silence, and then Herr Klauss addressed Alexa again. "Don't worry, we will help you to get back to your home. I have arranged some fake German papers for you to use so you can travel within the country as a German citizen. If anyone asks, you are a German. Once you cross over the border to Poland, of course, you can dispose of them."

He opened his desk drawer and pulled out the documents he was referring to, and showed them to Alexa. She took them in her hand and examined them, her eyes wide in disbelief.

"Thank you."

Frau Klauss moved around the desk and took a look at the papers; then she handed them back to her husband who placed them back in his drawer.

"You will leave here on Friday afternoon," Herr Klauss announced. "I'll buy you a train ticket for Berlin tomorrow, and then I'll tell you all the pertinent information you'll need to know for your journey."

It was already Wednesday evening and Alexa was suddenly filled with great excitement at the realization that so very soon, she would actually be making her way home. She was facing the prospect of being reunited with her mother and sister again after so long. Freedom was finally within her reach. The day she'd hoped, prayed and dreamt about for five years was so very near to her now and it consumed her every waking moment, her every thought.

Alexa still had chores to attend to, but they now seemed so much lighter since the knowledge that her captivity was soon coming to an end and her release was in sight. This made everything seem less burdensome. She could almost taste her freedom, and it was sweet.

Throughout the evening and into the early hours of Thursday morning, many bombing campaigns rumbled loudly through many German cities and towns. Dresden and Leipzig were almost completely annihilated in the Allied attacks. Meanwhile, through SS intelligence, the word of impending defeat spread, and many officers started removing records of their crimes, attempting to destroy all incriminating evidence of their pillaging.

Frankfurt was another center of Nazi activity which was heavily targeted by the Allied bombing campaigns. Hitler's art collection was nearing completion, but there were still some masterpieces on the List that had so far escaped the reach of the SS.

Very late that evening, two army trucks arrived at Herr Klauss's farmhouse; under the dark cover of night, some soldiers emptied their contents into the smaller of the two barns. There were various crates and wooden boxes of different shapes and sizes. The larger ones were carried into the barn first and the smaller ones were stacked carefully next to them.

Finally, after all the crates were stored in the barn, two soldiers carried three smaller, numbered wooden crates into Herr Klauss's office. He held a leather-bound notebook in his hand and seemed to be checking off all the items that corresponded to numbers on his list as they were brought to him. Once this task was completed, the two trucks, emptied of their precious cargo, left the farmhouse, but not before Herr Klauss handed a black leather briefcase, full of German marks, to one of the soldiers taking the lead. The soldiers climbed into their empty trucks, started up their engines, drove off down the long driveway, and turned out onto the road, away from the Klausses' farmhouse.

Herr Klauss locked up the barn and then disappeared into his office, locking its door securely behind him. There before him, in his own office, lay his heart's desire. He now had in his possession some of his ultimate masterpieces. Three of his most favorite works of art were now finally his. He had saved a special bottle of the most expensive and rarest red wine especially for this occasion, an 1869 *Château Lafite*. He carefully opened the bottle, gently popped the cork, and set it aside to breathe.

Taking a chisel, he carefully began prying open the lid of the wooden crates he had directed to be placed in his office. These were the ones he had personally bought with his briefcase full of German marks. They were now his, separated from the many other listed paintings in the barn. The barn pieces were all logged and accounted for and even had documentation confirming where they had been moved to for safe storage that night. But the three stolen paintings Herr Klauss had paid for had been listed as missing in action, destroyed or burned, and all trace of them had gone cold before the soldiers left the Frankfurt office.

Herr Klauss slowly eased the lid off one of the wooden crates; there, to his sheer delight, sat one of his most favorite paintings. He carefully lifted it out and placed it onto an empty easel he had set up and, after centering it in place, he stepped back. He walked around his desk and sat down in his black leather chair. He reached for the priceless bottle of wine and poured out a generous measure into one of his finest crystal glasses. He breathed in the aroma as he swirled the rich, red liquid inside the glass, then finally took a sip of his as he drank in the vision that lay before him. '*It's magnificent,*' he thought, '*and it's mine!*'

About an hour later, Herr Klauss got up from his desk and began opening the other two crates to reveal the other wonderful masterpieces he had paid for by dishonest means. Even long after daylight had broken, he remained in his office with his treasure of the three priceless paintings and the bottle of *Château Lafite*.

It was now Thursday, and Alexa was eager to complete her day's chores. She got the three Klauss children ready and off to school, then prepared the day's food for the household. Herr Klauss left the farmhouse in his car at 2 o'clock and was gone for several hours. Frau Klauss found Alexa in the kitchen and told her to come through into the lounge with her.

"Here is a small suitcase you can use for your journey home. There is no need to take everything you have, just enough for an overnight stay. That way you won't attract too much attention to yourself," Frau Klauss told her.

"Thank you, Frau Klauss. I will do exactly as you say."

Alexa didn't have a lot of possessions to her name. She had never received a wage for any of her hard work, so she had never been able to buy things she liked. She didn't even know what she liked. She very rarely left the Klausses' farmhouse, so she'd never really had the opportunity either. All she had was what she had been given, but the few things she did have she had taken good care of and valued.

She had a few outfits mainly, for working in and one smart one, which she'd wear on special occasions only, along with the pretty dress for the dances. Since the night of the first dance in the Klausses' barn, she had been allowed to keep her blue shoes, which she treasured, even though they didn't fit her anymore. They were more of a comfort item which she associated with her mother. She had her Sunday shoes from Alice. She had also been given a German Bible by the Klausses one Christmas, which she cherished and read daily. Beyond that, she had a hairbrush, some bows, a few hair combs, and a scarf. Not much to show for the life of a young eighteen-year-old girl. The good thing was that it made her small suitcase easier to pack.

Frau Klauss instructed Alexa not to tell the children she would be leaving, saying it was something she would rather tell them. Alexa agreed, but inside felt rather sad about it. She had grown very close to the children over the five years she had cared for them, but it wasn't something she was going to argue about. Her main concern was to return home to her own family. That was her priority now.

Herr Klauss returned home after dark, and while Frau Klauss kept the children busy upstairs, he called Alexa into the dining room. "Alexa, I have your train ticket. You will leave on the 1pm train to Berlin. I bought you a first-class seat in the first carriage. It's important you get on carriage A, and your seat is number 18. A18. Do you understand?"

"Yes, Herr Klauss, I understand: A18," she answered while thinking it was easy to remember: A for Alexa and 18 was her age.

"Good. Speak only if someone speaks to you. Answer only in German and keep it short. Don't give away too much information. If anyone asks, stick to the story that you are traveling to visit your sick aunt for the weekend." He waited for her to reply.

"Yes, Herr Klauss, I understand."

"You will be on the train for a little over five hours. Then you will get off at the Potsdam crossing, which is just before Berlin, where you will take the road towards the left. You will then need to walk for another five hours, leaving the roadway and going through the woods on foot until you reach the town of Kreuzberg. There you will find a convent where you will stay for one or two nights. The nuns are expecting you."

Herr Klauss walked over to his drinks cabinet and poured himself a double brandy into a short crystal glass. He raised it to his lips and took a large sip.

"From there, you will need to walk or find transportation towards Ahrensfelde. After that, you can use the money I'll give you to buy a bus or train ticket to make the connection to travel to your hometown of Lublin, where you will hopefully find your home and your family waiting for you." He took another large sip of his brandy.

"I've written down all the instructions and directions for your journey on these pieces of paper. You must memorize them and then throw away the papers before you leave here tomorrow; throw them into the fire in the morning. Don't take the papers with you, understand?"

"Yes, Herr Klauss, I understand. I will memorize them tonight. Thank you."

He handed her the papers with all the directions written down on them along with her new German identity papers. "I will give you your train ticket to Berlin and the money tomorrow. Leave your packed suitcase in the wardrobe in your bedroom, hidden well out of sight. Don't let the children see it."

"Yes sir, I will do exactly as you have told me. Thank you for letting me go home."

Herr Klauss took one final, large gulp and finished his brandy, then looked at Alexa. "You have always been a hard worker and have taken good care of my home and my family," he said. "You have earned your freedom. Be ready to leave at 12:30 pm tomorrow. My cousin Edgar, the priest, will drive you to the station in my car." He turned and headed out of the dining room door, disappearing into the privacy of his office.

Alexa put the papers which Herr Klauss had given her safely into the pocket of her apron, out of sight, and headed upstairs to run baths for Rudy and Anna. Richard was almost fifteen years old now and ran his own bath when he wanted, before going to bed. Alexa knew it was her last evening with the family and it brought her mixed emotions. She tried to act as normal as possible with the children. It was something she had mastered well over the past five years—the art of masking her true feelings. However, she was still human and had a tender heart. She knew she'd miss the family, but she would not miss the laborious, never-ending chores and the hard work of looking after all their demanding needs.

Finally, Alexa's chores were done for her last evening with the Klausses. She cleaned up the kitchen, turned off the lights, and headed upstairs to bed. She closed her bedroom door quietly and tightly behind her. In the bottom of her wardrobe was the small black suitcase Frau Klauss had given her.

Alexa began selecting the few items she would take with her on her journey. First into the bag were her royal blue shoes, which she placed at the bottom. Even though they didn't fit her anymore, they were of great sentimental value to her and, apart from her grandmother's silver cross necklace, they were the only things she had from her past. She wanted to show her mother how well she had taken care of them all these years, once they were reunited.

It didn't take her long to pack the case with her few possessions: her Bible, a pair of pajamas, a change of clothes, her hairbrush, some clean socks and underwear. Then she closed the suitcase and placed it back in the bottom of her wardrobe. She hung the good outfit she would wear on one hanger inside the wardrobe, ready to be worn before she left for the train station in the afternoon.

At last, she climbed into bed, and began reading the white pieces of paper Herr Klauss had given her with the travel instructions intently, over and over again, until she knew them off by heart. Then, she recited her prayer of Psalm 91, emphasizing certain parts with deeper feeling, tailoring it to fit her needs.

'You are my fortress, my refuge, my God in whom I trust. Rescue me from the bird catcher. Shield me with your mighty wings. Let me not be afraid, and let evil not come near me, nor disaster befall me. I beg of you to protect me, dear God almighty, on my journey home. Amen.'

Full of anticipation and excitement for her great day of release, Alexa finally fell asleep.

CHAPTER 10

The cold winter's morning broke through the cover of darkness with the birds singing their morning welcome. Alexa was wide awake before 4 am on that, her very last day serving the Klausses. She made her way downstairs and began her chores, as she had done every morning for the past five years, but this morning was different.

Her approach and attitude were far more joyous than ever before. She recognized the finality of the tasks before her—it was the last time she would milk the large smelly cows, collect the hens' eggs, clean out the mucky barns and stables, and shovel the manure. No more would she have to do all the laundry for the household, clean the farmhouse, work the land, or cook the family's meals. She now thought only of the joy she would have being able to cook for her own mother and sister, and of how proud they would be of her when tasting her delicious dishes.

The morning eventually gave way to sunrise, but it was a red sky with highlighted clouds—the shepherd's forewarning of unpleasant weather conditions on the horizon. There had already been a significant amount of snowfall earlier that month of December, and the signs of it were still visible on the ground.

Alexa made her way to the barn where the animals were, to begin milking the cows. She approached Blümchen first and reached her hand up to gently stroke her head.

"I'm going to miss you, my friend. Today I leave this place and won't ever see you again," Alexa said in Polish. "Herr Klauss is letting me go home. I'm finally going back to Poland to find my Mama and sister."

A tear trickled down from Blümchen's eye as she continued to stare at Alexa, as if the cow really understood what she was being told.

"You've been my best friend and my confidant through these difficult years, and I'll never forget you," Alexa whispered.

She finished milking the other cows before returning to give a final farewell to Blümchen as she wiped a lone tear from her own eye.

The hours passed quickly for Alexa as she meditated on her journey home. After breakfast, Herr Klauss took the children off to school, and that was the last Alexa saw of them. She had wanted to hug them goodbye but she knew she mustn't let them know of her planned departure. So, she refrained and watched them leave from behind a curtain of one of the upstairs windows, tears brimming in her eyes.

Alexa cleared up the remains of breakfast, made all the beds in the household, did some loads of laundry, and prepared dinner for the family. She made a few sandwiches for herself and wrapped a slice of cake in some paper to take with her on her journey. Then at noon she went upstairs to her bedroom for the last time and dressed in her good clothes, which were neatly hanging inside her wardrobe. She put on a warm woolen sweater and brushed her long blonde hair, then took one last look in her mirror.

"It's time. I'm coming home, Mama!" Alexa said out loud, before turning and walking out of the bedroom for the last time.

When she got downstairs, Frau Klauss called her into the dining room. To Alexa's surprise, the woman told her to take off her clogs.

"We can't have you traveling in those; it would be too obvious and give your identity away. Here put these on; I think they will fit you."

Alexa removed the heavy wooden clogs and tried on the black shoes Frau Klauss had handed her. They were not brand-new shoes, but they were in fairly decent shape with only a little wear and tear. They seemed to fit her quite well and they completed her look—that of a normal young German woman. Alexa was so relieved to finally be freed from the burdensome clogs that had been like shackles to her.

It felt very liberating to wear normal shoes on her feet, which to her were as good as new shoes. She thought of the parallel of the time she had gotten her new pair of shoes with her mother in Lublin; that dreadful day had led to the long journey away from home and a whole new nightmarish chapter in her life. *This* pair of shoes would take her on another long journey, but this time back home again to begin a brand-new chapter, reunited with her family.

Alexa was filled with excitement but also with much anxiety and fear. She thought of the wonderful gift of the new pair of handmade shoes Alice had given her a few years earlier in Luxembourg. They didn't fit her anymore but that had been a wonderful, unexpected surprise, and theirs had become a beautiful friendship. Alexa was sad she wasn't able to tell Alice in person that she was finally going home or say goodbye. There wasn't time; she had to leave today, and Sunday was two whole days away. Optimistically, she reasoned these shoes from Frau Klauss could lead her on a positive journey, this time with a happy outcome.

Herr Klauss emerged from his office at 12:30 pm with Edgar and told Alexa it was time to go.

"I'm ready, sir," Alexa said as he stood in front of her.

"You'll not last very long out there without a warm coat, and especially not with one that has the letter 'P' on it. Here take this one," Frau Klauss said, handing Alexa a long, black woolen coat to put on. "There are a pair of gloves in the pocket; you'll need them as it'll be cold on your journey."

Alexa put the coat on and buttoned it up. Frau Klauss wrapped a woolen scarf around her neck and said, "Now you are all ready to go home, Alexa."

Alexa hugged the woman, thanking her for the kind gestures. She was filled with pure gratitude towards them as they willingly freed her. Alexa knew they didn't have to do that.

"Okay, now you must leave," Herr Klauss announced and headed out the door towards his car, Alexa and his cousin Edgar following behind him.

"Sit in the front seat," Herr Klauss said.

Alexa picked up her suitcase and got into the black Mercedes. With the door still open, Herr Klauss handed her some German marks and her train ticket.

"Did you memorize all the instructions I gave you on the pieces of paper?"

"Yes sir, I did, and then I tore them up and threw them in the fire this morning."

"Good. Edgar will let you out of the car a few minutes' walk from the station, and you will go to the train by yourself. Don't forget to sit in the first-class compartment, on seat A18."

"Yes sir, I will. I won't forget," Alexa said.

Herr Klauss closed the car door, and Alexa took one last look out of the window as the car drove off down the long driveway and away from the farm along the country roads. Alexa could taste her freedom and tried hard to control her emotions. The clock on the car's dashboard read 12:45 pm as Edgar pulled the car over on the roadside, drawing to a stop underneath the railway bridge. He instructed Alexa to get out with her suitcase and continue on foot towards the station, which she could see in the near distance.

"Your train is departing at 1 pm, so hurry along to the platform and remember to follow Herr Klauss's instructions exactly. I sincerely hope you have a safe journey back home to your family, Alexa. Now go, and may God bless you, child."

Alexa thanked the priest and closed the door. The car drove off, and Alexa took a deep breath. Her first real breath of freedom. Now she belonged to no one. She quickly began walking along the road towards the small station, and within a few minutes she made her way onto the platform. The sky had become grey and it looked like more snow was on the way.

A smartly-dressed elderly man wearing a hat and his wife sitting next to him on a bench awaited the arrival of the train, but no one else. Alexa sat down on another bench, placing her suitcase on her lap as she waited. She stared blankly down onto the train tracks before her and at the cold-looking hard steel rails, firmly bolted down to hold the wooden sleepers in place. It made her think back to when she was first transported from Poland to Germany. Alexa vividly recalled being loaded into the cattle wagon with the other youths, herded in like livestock for the long and terrifying overnight journey to Dachau.

At least this train journey was guaranteed to be a far more comfortable one, seeing she had a first-class ticket this time. She wondered where her mother was at that moment. Had she been moved out of Dachau, as she herself had been? Maybe she had already managed to make her own way back home to Poland and was waiting for her there.

As Alexa's eyes followed the train tracks, she became aware of how the parallel lines of the two steel rails, although separate, seemed to join and meet up again in the distance. She made her own parallel in her mind: she and her mother had been separated but would meet up again farther down the line.

On the station wall hung a large clock which showed the time as approaching 1 pm. Alexa heard a faint sound of rumbling vibrating on the steel tracks, which grew louder as the train came closer. The train's whistle shrieked a double blast, announcing its imminent arrival in the station, followed by the screeching sound of brakes as the long and powerful train gradually slowed and came to a complete stop.

The elderly couple got up from the bench and walked along the platform, looking for their carriage. Alexa picked up her suitcase and headed towards the first carriage, which was marked "A" for first class. She reached her hand up to the door handle, pulling it down to open the train door. She climbed up the three steps and pulled the door firmly closed behind her. She turned to her right, took a few steps forward, and approached the door marked "A" leading into the first-class carriage. She turned the door handle and stepped inside.

As Alexa looked up, she became frozen with fear and was sure the shockwaves shooting through her body would surely stop her heart. Her survival instinct kicked in, and her brain engaged the well-trained skill set she had developed, those of masking her true feelings and emotions to become the character she needed to be at any given time for the situation she found herself in. Now she was indeed in a situation.

Alexa closed the door behind her and walked into the carriage; which, was full of SS officers and male German army soldiers who occupied almost every seat. They had all seen her walk in through the door and were staring at her intently. Alexa looked at the seat numbers, praying hers was vacant. Finally, she reached number 18 and found that it was. Number 17 had no one sitting in it but there was an army jacket and cap resting on it. Alexa slowly eased herself into seat number A18 and sat down. Placing her suitcase on her lap, she gave a general smile, but to no one in particular.

"Good afternoon, Fräulein," said one of the SS officers sitting diagonally across from her.

"Good afternoon," Alexa replied in her best German accent with all the confidence she could muster. She then turned her head with self-assurance to look out of the nearby window. Inside, she was stricken with panic and fear, but on the outside no one could tell. On the platform outside, the station master blew his whistle, waved his flag, and the train slowly pulled off from the station.

Snowflakes began to fall.

There were about thirty German soldiers and SS officers all together in the first class carriage. Several of the soldiers had been playing card games and gambling on the tables in front of them, to which they returned almost immediately when the train started moving again. Others were reading and smoking, some chatting while drinking schnapps and beers, which they ordered from the small bar at the end of the carriage.

About ten or twelve of the men continued to fix their stare on Alexa, which made her feel even more uneasy and very uncomfortable, although she didn't show it. Instead, she prayed silently, repeating her familiar Psalm 91 over and over again. Sometimes she would close her eyes too, which prevented her from having to make direct eye contact with any of the soldiers.

The door on the opposite side of the carriage opened, and in walked the train conductor. He quickly noticed there was now a female civilian in the compartment with all the soldiers and officers and immediately walked over to where Alexa was sitting.

"Let me see your ticket please!"

Alexa reached into her pocket, took out the train ticket Herr Klauss had given her, and handed it to the conductor. He took the ticket from her and looked at it; suddenly enraged, he began shouting at Alexa.

"What are you doing sitting in this seat? This is not a first-class ticket. You shouldn't be here. This is a first-class seat!"

"I'm so sorry, sir. The ticket was bought for me and I was told it was for first class. I'm so sorry," Alexa tried to reason.

By now, all the soldiers were looking over towards the commotion between Alexa and the conductor, who was now furious. He seemed to have a valid point and was no doubt concerned for his own job.

"You cannot stay here. You'll have to leave this carriage. Get up!" he shouted.

Alexa's face turned red with embarrassment. She didn't know what to do next for the best. Suddenly, the SS officer who was sitting diagonally across from Alexa stood up and walked over to where they both were.

"What seems to be the problem here?" he asked the conductor, who was now showing signs of fear himself.

"My apologies, sir, but this woman should not be here in this compartment; she does not have a first-class ticket. I shall move her out of your way immediately."

"Tell me, how much will it cost for her ticket to become a first class one, so she can continue to sit here in this seat?" asked the SS officer.

The conductor seemed puzzled at the unexpected question, but he was becoming more and more fearful over the ticket discrepancy as the minutes ticked by, as if he were to blame in some way.

"It would cost another eleven marks," the conductor answered.

The officer reached into his rear pocket and pulled out his wallet. He took out eleven marks and handed them to the conductor.

"There's the additional money. Now give the pretty young lady a first-class ticket and apologize for shouting at her," ordered the officer.

The conductor nervously took out a new first-class ticket which he handed to Alexa and said he was sorry for shouting at her, his voice quivering a little.

"Okay, now you can leave our carriage, and don't come back here until we have left the train. Do you understand?"

"Yes sir, I understand. I'm sorry, sir, to have bothered you."

The conductor turned and hurriedly left the carriage by the same door he had come through.

"I'm sorry he was so rude to you, Fräulein, but now you can sit here for the rest of your journey," said the officer.

Alexa had thought her cover was surely going to be blown but kept her composure.

"Thank you, sir, that was very kind of you. I'm terribly sorry for the misunderstanding."

"Where are you traveling to?"

"I'm getting off at the stop just before Berlin, sir, at Potsdam. I'm going to visit my aunt for the weekend."

"Well, it should be about five more hours until then," he informed her as he looked at his pocket watch. He smiled, and returned to his seat.

Some of the other soldiers were still looking over in her direction, puzzled at why one of their senior officers had paid the rest of the young lady's ticket to keep her in the same carriage with them. Some derogatory comments were made by some of the soldiers. She was, after all, a very beautiful young woman, unaccompanied and alone in their midst.

Alexa tried to figure out in her mind what had happened. *'Why did Herr Klauss give me an incorrect ticket? Why did the officer insist I stay here in first class? Why did he pay for the rest of my ticket? What does it mean? Do I now owe him? Why are all these German soldiers staring at me? What are they going* to do with me? Can they tell I'm Polish?' All these thoughts spun around and around in her head until she thought she would go mad.

After an hour had passed, Alexa stood up and placed her suitcase on her seat along with her gloves. Excusing herself, she made her way to the small toilet she had passed on her way into the carriage when she had first boarded the train. Several of the soldiers followed her with their eyes, then returned to their business at hand. She closed the toilet door behind her and locked it. *'Oh, dear God above, please give me the strength beyond what is normal to endure the rest of this journey and to make it off this train alive and in one piece. I beg of you, help me get home safely! Amen.'*

Alexa turned on the tap over the small sink and splashed some cold water onto her face. She rinsed off her clammy hands and dried them with the towel. She took some deep breaths and felt safe, alone in the privacy of the small space with the door locked; she didn't want to leave.

She had been in the toilet for about fifteen minutes, but she knew if she stayed there much longer, she would attract unnecessary attention from the soldiers. She flushed the toilet, then straightened her hair in the mirror. Reluctantly, Alexa unlocked the door and stepped out into the hallway, then confidently made her way back into the carriage and back to her seat. A few of the soldiers smiled at her; others carried on their intense staring in her direction, while the rest drank schnapps and made her the brunt of their jokes.

When she sat down, she avoided making eye contact with the soldiers again and stared out the train window, looking at nothing in particular. The train moved at speed through the countryside, and the trees nearest to the tracks sped by as a blur, their individual leaves and branches indistinguishable. The noise of the train hurrying along the tracks had an almost hypnotic sound, and Alexa found herself lost in the rhythm.

After a while, she opened her bag, took out her Bible, and began to read the book of Psalms from its beginning.

The train continued on its journey, drawing closer to its destination. It seemed as though the soldiers were no longer paying much attention to Alexa, which made her feel a little more at ease. Of course, for as long as she was still alone in the carriage with all the German soldiers and SS officers, anything could happen to her—of that fact she was all too aware.

Some of the soldiers were readying and repacking their bags and loading their guns and pistols with ammunition, which brought home to Alexa what a dangerous situation she really was in. If they even had the slightest suspicion or inclination of her true identity, that she was actually a released Polish slave trying to return home after five years of capture, she knew they'd shoot her or even worse. Alexa knew she had to hold it together for a little bit longer.

The train blew its whistle as it approached the Potsdam crossing, the last stop before Berlin. This was where Herr Klauss had told Alexa to get off the train. She closed the Bible and placed it back in her suitcase. She buttoned up her coat, tucked in her scarf, and stood up from her seat. Most of the soldiers noticed her getting ready to leave the carriage and watched her carefully. Alexa walked along the carriage towards the door at the far end, then placed her hand on the handle to open it.

"Stop!" came the voice of the SS officer who had been sitting diagonally across from her during the journey.

Alexa froze on the spot and slowly turned around to search out the voice. She could feel her legs shaking beneath her and was sure she'd collapse from fear. The train's brakes began to screech, gradually slowing the train down and, as it jolted, Alexa had to steady herself by holding onto the back of one of the soldier's seats. With rising hopelessness, she looked up at the officer.

"You forgot one of your gloves. It's there on the seat," said the officer.

Alexa couldn't believe her ears at first but began walking back towards her seat while one of the other soldiers picked up the glove and handed it to her.

"Thank you, sir. Thank you very much indeed," she said. Then taking the glove, she turned and headed for the door once again, stepping down from the train onto the snow-covered ground below. There wasn't much of a station at Potsdam. It was more of a level crossing train stop without a platform.

The snow was coming down heavily, and several of the officers and soldiers had stood up from their seats and moved towards the windows. Alexa could see them out of the corner of her eye and began walking in the opposite direction, away from the train. From behind her, she could hear some of the windows being lowered in the first-class carriage she had been traveling in with all the soldiers.

She tried not to look back, but then she thought to herself, '*If I'm going to be shot, I won't be shot in the back of the head, I won't make it easy for them. They'll have to see my face and look me in the eyes.*' She looked back in defiance and sure enough, several of the officers were staring at her out of their open windows as she slowly walked away. Alexa couldn't see any of them taking aim at her, so she continued putting one foot in front of the other as she walked alongside the railway tracks towards the roadway. '*Dear God, please protect me,*' she repeated to herself, over and over again.

The train slowly began to pull off, and Alexa took one last look back at the carriage. She could still see the soldiers, staring at her out the carriage windows until the train picked up speed and finally disappeared out of view.

Alexa let out a deep sigh of relief mixed with sheer disbelief. She had made it. She had survived the train ride, from right under the nose of all those German Nazi and SS officers. Despite not even having the correct ticket, she had managed to convince them she was a real German woman, a German citizen. She was convinced that God had heard her prayers, and he had indeed answered them by keeping her safe. She offered a sincere prayer of thanks as she continued walking along the road until it joined the forest.

CHAPTER 11

The fresh new powdery snow continued to fall steadily, adding to the accumulation of the older snow lying frozen on the ground beneath it. The time was approaching 6:30 pm and the winter sky was already dark. Alexa had memorized the list of instructions Herr Klauss had given her, but she couldn't help but wonder if he had got the next part wrong as well, as he had with the mistake over her first-class train ticket. Having no other options available to her, Alexa decided to follow the directions she had been given and had memorized in her head.

At the end of the road leading away from the Potsdam train crossing was an adjoining road. It led off to a main intersection, then veered to the right as it followed the edge of a deep forest and a line of trees. Alexa had been instructed to go to the left, but she had also been told not to walk on the roadway. Instead, the pages of notes had said she was to walk into the woods for about three quarters of a mile so she could still see the roadway through the trees, but the forest would hide her from the traffic traveling along the road. The roadway didn't seem very busy to her, but she trusted there must be a good reason for the instructions and headed off into the woodlands, away from the road's edge.

The terrain was very hard going on her feet. Not only was there the forest floor to deal with, full of uneven tree roots, sharp branches, jagged bushes, and thick undergrowth, but it was covered and hidden under deep snow upon which it was hard to get a firm footing. It crunched and cracked under her feet. After she figured she was far enough into the forest, Alexa began her long, lonely walk, keeping an eye on the roadway through the trees.

The natural daylight was long gone, and the cloak of darkness made her journey all the more strenuous and arduous. The full moon above illuminated the sky. It poured down between the pine trees and lit up some of the terrain ahead of her, as well as casting long dark shadows across the frozen forest floor. The tall, bare birch trees appeared silver in the moonlight and, having been stripped of their foliage, looked like tall lightning rods to Alexa.

After about an hour of painful walking in the freezing cold, she chose a large tree to sit against to take a much-needed rest. She opened her suitcase and took out the extra pair of socks she had packed; she put them on, doubling them over the ones she was already wearing, pulling them as far up her legs as they would go. Next, she took out her pajama bottoms and climbed into them, tucking the legs down into her socks. She loosened the scarf from around her neck and pulled it up over her head, covering her hair, and then crossed the two ends under her chin and tied them at the back of her neck. She pulled up the collar of her coat and did up the very top button. She smiled to herself and thought how glad she was that no one could see how ridiculous she must look.

After she had layered on some warmth and a little protection from the harsh freezing elements, Alexa reached into her suitcase and took out the sandwiches she had made earlier that day and unwrapped them. Leaning against the tree, she began to eat half a sandwich. She couldn't see very well, with all traces of daylight long gone, but as she looked through the trees in the direction of the roadway, she could see the distant headlights of army trucks and cars, randomly coming and going in both directions.

She finished off the other half of the sandwich, and then ate the piece of sweet cake she had brought. She wished she had also brought something to drink with her, as she felt a real thirst in her parched throat, but she hadn't. Then Alexa had an idea. '*There's all this fresh snow around; I'll have some of that, life's water free*,' she thought. As cold as it was, she took handfuls of freshly fallen snow and let it melt on her tongue inside her mouth, quenching her thirst.

She also thought the aid of a tree branch as a walking stick would assist her in her journey, and looking around the forest floor, she soon found the perfect one, about the right length for her height. After a fifteen-minute rest, Alexa gave both her feet a good rub to warm up her circulation before putting her shoes back on. She closed her suitcase, put her gloves back on, and continued her treacherous walk through the night forest.

The night air was full of an array of familiar and unfamiliar sounds. In the far-off distance, Alexa could hear the dull noise of explosions, as the Allied forces' bombing raids pummeled various prime targets in and around Berlin and other surrounding areas. She could faintly hear the sound of engines and tanks as they drove along the roadway at the edge of the forest. Occasionally, the hum of a bomber's engine could also be heard flying overhead.

With every step Alexa took, twigs and branches snapped under her feet along with the crunch of the frozen snow lying below the newly-fallen fresh powder. From high up in the trees, the hoot of an owl echoed through the forest, then another in reply from farther away. The cries of crows and the various whistles of other birds made their presence known. Nature's wildlife, the creatures of the night, were awake.

Alexa suddenly wondered if there were wilder, more dangerous animals in the forest around her like foxes, wolves, and bears. Her familiar prayer came to mind, especially the parts of Psalm 91 that petitioned protection from the bird catcher and the snare of the fowler, from the terror by night, and the pestilence that walks in darkness, for the foot striking against a stone, and from the maned lion and the snake under foot. She was quite sure she didn't have to worry about any lions, but she couldn't have the same confidence that there were no bears in the area. As she meditated and pondered on the phrases in the verses she knew so well, she gained comfort and had faith that she would be protected.

However, walking in the dark through such harsh terrain for so long did cause Alexa some pain, her legs received cuts from brushing against the sharp branches and prickly thorns. After she had been trekking for over two more hours, she decided to take another break to tend to her wounds, rest a little, and eat the other remaining sandwich. She found a tree with a low thick branch and sat down upon it, slipping off her shoes one by one to examine the damage.

The shoes weren't holding up very well at all. There was a cut in the sole of the right shoe which was letting in cold water that soaked through to her sock. Her legs were very cold, almost frozen, and she could feel the sting of cuts as a few of her open wounds were exposed to the cold air. One cut in particular, on her left leg above her ankle, seemed to be the worst. Alexa lifted up her pajama leg and could see the blood still seeping from it, so she took some fresh snow and rubbed it against the wound to clean it, then took her cotton handkerchief and tied it tightly around it. She pulled down the trouser leg, tucked it back into her sock, and cleaned her hands in the fresh snow. She took some more handfuls of fresh snow to quench her thirst, all the time shivering down to her very bones.

Alexa estimated she must have been walking through the forest for about four hours by that point, and that she probably only had another hour or so left to go until she could finally exit the woods and get back onto a road again. Her destination that evening was a convent on the outskirts of the small town of Kreuzberg. She had been told the nuns were expecting her there.

Herr Klauss's instructions had said that after walking through the forest for five hours, following the line of the roadway, the trees would stop and there would appear a large opening like a field she would have to walk across. Once she crossed the field, there would be another road in front of her which she would have to cross; this time, she was to walk to the left, which would take her in a westerly direction for about ten minutes, until she reached an intersection.

The snow finally stopped falling. She stood back up and continued walking for at least another hour. Finally, the trees stopped, and she could see the field she had to cross. After reaching the roadway, she walked on it to the left, continuing along it for about ten minutes as she had been instructed.

Suddenly, she heard the dull sound of engines growing louder as they came nearer. She could see some headlights off in the distance, so she threw her suitcase into the ditch and jumped down off the road, laying as flat as she could, out of sight. A convoy of large SS military trucks drove by along the road, above where she was hiding. Soon they had passed by, and the sound of their loud engines became a dull hum again, then disappeared into the night. Alexa's heart was pounding, and her young nerves were shattered. She threw her suitcase back up onto the roadway and climbed carefully out of the ditch. Wiping herself down, she composed herself and then continued on along the roadway once again, shivering in her shoes.

There was a full moon in the clear night sky, and Alexa appreciated it illuminating the road stretching before her. She could see in the distance she was approaching the intersection, but she couldn't remember in which direction she was to go. With each step, she tried harder and harder to recall which road she was instructed to take, but the answer wasn't coming to her. The road was dark and deserted; there were no signs to read, no houses to enquire at, and no people to ask. She was all alone and now she was lost.

The intersection ahead of her had three options. She could either take the road to the left, go straight, or follow the road to the right, but only one of the options would lead her to the correct destination. Alexa stood looking at all three roads, but it was no use—she couldn't recall which one she was to take and besides, they all looked the same. The young girl was physically exhausted and felt totally alone and defeated. As always when feeling alone and fearful, she began to pray.

'Dear Almighty God above, please guide me with your wisdom as to which way I should go. To the left, or to the right? Please make me know the way. I'm so cold and so tired, and I need your help to carry on. Please keep me safe. Amen!'

She looked up at the brilliantly shining moon in the night sky and gazed at it as it floated there, suspended upon nothing in the pitch of black night. As it shone down on her, a tear fell from her eye and rolled down her cheek.

Suddenly, a voice from behind her asked, "Are you lost?"

Startled, Alexa whirled around, and to her surprise, she saw an elderly gentleman with a walking stick, carrying a small cloth bag.

"Oh yes, sir, I am. I'm lost, and I don't remember which road I am supposed to take," Alexa said.

"Well don't worry, young girl, I'm sure I can help you. Where is it you are trying to get to?"

"I'm trying to get to the St. Clemens Convent near Kreuzberg. They are expecting me."

"Aha, yes, I know where that is, and it's on the road I am taking. We can walk together if you'd like," suggested the old man.

"Oh yes, please, sir, that would be wonderful. Thank you ever so much," said Alexa, who was so relieved she wanted to hug the old man.

"Shall we go?" asked the old man, pointing his walking stick to the roadway on the right.

"Yes, and would you like me to carry your bag for you, sir?"

"That's very kind of you to offer, but no; you have your own load to carry and mine is not too heavy."

"Okay, if you're sure, sir."

They began walking along the road together and, strangely, the old man seemed to have such a calming effect on Alexa that after a short while, she could no longer feel the pain in her feet and legs, nor the cold temperatures of the freezing night.

"My name is Alexa," she said.

"I'm very pleased to meet you, Alexa. It's nice to have some company on my walk."

"And I'm so very pleased to meet you, sir. I don't know what I would have done if you hadn't come along when you did."

"Well, I'm glad I could be of some assistance. It's not very often an old man like me is of any use to young people these days, it seems."

"Oh, I'm sure you know many useful things, sir, and I'm ever so grateful that you know the way and are able to help me tonight," Alexa said.

After they had been walking for about fifteen minutes, the old man suggested they take a short rest on a nearby log. He sat down and reached into his bag, and from it he first pulled out a bar of chocolate.

"Do you like chocolate, Alexa?"

"Oh yes sir, I do."

"Good, let's have some then. I find it always gives me a little boost of energy, and it will help us on our journey."

"That's a great idea, sir. Thank you very much," said Alexa as the old man opened the chocolate bar and gave her some. She took a square and popped it in her mouth, letting it slowly melt as it sat on her tongue. It was delicious. Alexa hadn't had chocolate in a very long time and sat in complete silence as she ate it.

"Here, have some more."

Alexa took another square, and again said thank you. Next, the old man reached into his bag and pulled out a bottle of fresh milk. He took off the lid and handed it to Alexa.

"Would you like some, Alexa?"

"Oh yes, I would, if you are sure, sir."

"Yes, I'm sure; go ahead drink."

Alexa thankfully drank the milk; it was refreshing and wonderfully complemented the flavor of the chocolate. But she was careful not to take too much and handed it back to the old man.

"Thank you, sir, for sharing with me."

The old man took the bottle of milk and had a drink himself before replacing the lid and putting it back in his bag. Then he reached for the chocolate once again, and with a big smile on his face, he told Alexa to take a whole row of squares this time. Alexa snapped off a row of chocolate and gave him a great big smile in return.

They both sat and finished their chocolate, and then the old man put the remains of the bar back in his bag. Alexa put her arm around the old man and thanked him for his kindness towards her. Standing up, they picked up their bags and continued on their journey along the road. It had been the most refreshing rest for them both, and Alexa was still savoring the taste of the chocolate, long after she had swallowed the last of it.

They continued to walk a while, with the old man leading the way, until after half an hour or so they came to another intersection. The old man stopped and turned to face Alexa.

"This is as far as we go together. I'm taking the road to the left, but you are going to continue straight for about three kilometers until you reach a bridge. Cross over the bridge and then go left and walk alongside a row of houses. Once you pass by the last house, you will see a sign that says St. Clemens Church and Convent. Turn right and walk up the long driveway, and then you will be there," instructed the old man.

"Okay, thank you so much for all your help, your generosity, and your company too," said Alexa as she leaned forward and gave him a big hug.

"You're welcome, child. It was a pleasure walking with you. God bless you," he said, then walked off towards the roadway on the left.

Alexa had felt safe walking with the old man and had enjoyed his company immensely, but now she was alone again. She stopped walking and turned around to look at the old man once more, but there was no sign of him. He was gone from sight, with no trace of him to be seen anywhere. Alexa thought this was very strange, as it had only been about ten seconds since they'd had parted and the old man hadn't walked at great speed when he was with her. Nonetheless, he was gone.

'I didn't even ask his name,' she thought. *'Did I imagine him? Was he an angel?'*

Alexa continued walking straight along the road as the old man had instructed her. The freezing winter's night seemed darker and so much colder now she was traveling alone again.

Suddenly, snow began falling heavily once more and it quickly became blizzard-like.

After a few kilometers, the houses which the old man had mentioned came into view. By now, Alexa was exhausted; she was beyond tired as well as frozen through to her bones. She felt as though she couldn't go on any further and so decided her best option would be to knock on the doors of the houses to see if anyone would kindly let her rest there for the night.

Unable to muster up the courage to approach the first house, she continued to the second house, telling herself to be brave. The house was dark with no visible lights on inside, but she approached it anyway and knocked on the front door; after all, what was there to be afraid of? There was no answer at the door, so Alexa continued to the third house as the wind picked up, blowing and swirling the snow around her.

Finally, at the third house there were signs of life, and the downstairs windows had light shining through the curtains. Alexa made her way down the snow-covered garden path and knocked on the door. After a moment or two, the door opened to reveal a short German woman, roughly in her mid-fifties. Alexa wasted no time introducing herself and explaining her predicament.

"Good evening, I'm sorry to bother you so late, but I'm journeying to visit my old, sick aunt and I'm still a little far away from her house. It's so late at night now; I'm cold and tired and wondered if I might be able to rest somewhere for a little while?" said Alexa.

The woman seemed very sympathetic and motioned for the girl to step into her small hallway. "It's okay dear, come in out of the snow before you catch your death," she said.

Suddenly, the woman's husband appeared to see what was going on at such a late hour of the night. As Alexa looked up at the tall, dark-haired man, she caught sight of a wooden coat rack fitted against the wall behind him. Her heart seemed to stop on the spot while she subtly tried to catch her breath and disguise both her shock and horror. There hanging on the coat rack was the decorated uniformed jacket of a German special police officer, along with his leather gun belt. On the shelf above the rack sat his police hat, decorated with the eagle emblem. Alexa couldn't believe it. Of all the houses along the row she could have chosen to approach, she had picked the very one where a German special police officer lived. She had willingly walked straight to his door; he hadn't even had to find her. She thought she would die on the spot. She thought this was her end.

"You see? Look what this war has done. Look at this poor young German girl trying to get to visit her sick aunt. It's late at night, it's freezing outside, and bombs are dropping everywhere," said the woman to her husband. "What is the point of this war?"

"The war is the war!" he replied, waving his hand in the air in front of his wife. Then, disinterested, he disappeared back into the room from which he had come.

The woman invited Alexa to come into the house and sat her in front of the warm log fire in her living room. Then she hurried into the kitchen and made some hot cocoa and sandwiches for the girl to eat, along with a slice of home-made cake, and placed them on the table for her. As hungry as Alexa was, she couldn't eat anything. Her heart was still in her mouth and her nerves were shot over the identity of the woman's husband.

The woman could see Alexa wasn't eating anything and decided it was because she was tired, so she encouraged her to drink up her hot drink and showed her to a downstairs bedroom where she could comfortably sleep for the night in a clean warm bed. Alexa agreed, but as she sat in the bedroom worrying, her discomfort would not subside. She lay in the bed but could not sleep, as hard as she tried.

Alexa began to pray as was her routine. '*Dear God Almighty, here I am in the trap once again, with the bird catcher right outside my door, this time by my own hand. But this time no one will know my fate. How will I ever be found? Help me I pray. Amen.*'

An hour went by with Alexa still wide awake and unable to relax. She heard a set of footsteps come down the stairs and go into the kitchen, then the noise of dishes clattering in the sink. Alexa straightened herself up and cautiously tiptoed her way through to the kitchen. Thankfully, it was the woman of the house whom she found there.

Alexa began explaining to her that she couldn't sleep as she had to get to her sick aunt who was all alone, awaiting her arrival. The woman tried to talk Alexa into staying until the next day but eventually listened to her reasons. She insisted Alexa have one more hot drink before setting off again, then she wrapped up the sandwiches and cake for her to take away with her. Alexa thanked the woman for her kindness and hospitality then left the house.

The snow had stopped falling, and Alexa walked up the garden pathway, stepping back into her very own footsteps as she made her way out of the gate and back onto the roadway.

CHAPTER 12

Alexa continued walking in the direction the old man had told her to go and soon saw the signs for the convent. She felt such a relief that Herr Klauss had gotten the convent information correct and began walking up the long driveway towards the large main stone building.

As she approached the front of the structure, the moon lit up the entrance. Several arches cast long curved shadows across the ground before her. There were two huge wooden doors, framed and overlaid in cast iron. Alexa wasn't sure what time of night it was exactly, but she figured it had to be well after 1 am or even later. There were no visible lights on in the building, and she was reluctant to start banging loudly on the doors.

She looked around and began exploring the perimeter of the building in search of another entrance. She noticed the property appeared to be in three sections. The first seemed to house an old rectory with its own garden; the second section looked like a traditional church building—a purpose-built house of worship with large, arched stained-glass windows—and attached at its rear was a convent with a separate yard of its own. Behind that was a much larger and newer looking brick building consisting of several floors reaching up high off the ground; with tall windows it resembled a large school or residential complex of some kind.

Alexa decided the second building would be the best place to try and get someone's attention, so she walked around into the yard and searched for a side door. She found one at what she guessed was the convent and gently began knocking on it, but there was no reply. She knocked again several times, harder and then a little louder. A few minutes passed by, but there was still no answer. Then suddenly from the rear of the building came the sound of a bolt being unlatched, and a woman appeared from out of a side gate.

"Come around this way," she said. "Quickly!"

Alexa followed her through the side gate.

"Are you Alexa?" the nun asked.

Alexa nodded yes.

"You are late, girl. Follow me," instructed the nun sharply.

She led Alexa into the convent, closing the door firmly behind her, then picked up a lit lantern and led her down a stone spiral staircase into a cold, damp, eerie and unwelcoming basement. The woman didn't fit the preconceived idea Alexa had in her head of what the nun would be like. She did wear a black habit, which covered her from head to toe, but her character seemed to be as dark as her cloth. Alexa had assumed that when she arrived at the convent, she'd be greeted by warm and kind little old Catholic nuns, helpful women who'd welcome her and make her feel at home for the night. Now she thought she couldn't have gotten things more wrong.

The nun led Alexa to the end of a long corridor, past many closed doors until finally stopping at the very last one. She opened the heavy solid wooden door and walked inside, beckoning Alexa to come in after her. The nun rested her lantern on a small wooden table; she reached into her pocket and took out a candle, which she proceeded to light from the flame in her lantern.

The flame illuminated the small room, which looked more like a dungeon. She placed the lit candle on the table, securing it with some hot melted wax she had dripped as it burned. There were no windows in the small space, and the walls were constructed of cold bare stones, which were full of dust and cobwebs. There was a single metal bed with an old flat pillow, a table, a chair, and two buckets on the floor, one empty with a dirty towel draped over its side and one half filled with cold water. Alexa realized this was where she was to sleep for the night and cringed at the very thought of it.

The nun pointed to some sheets and old blankets lying on the ground in the corner and told Alexa to make up the bed for herself and that someone would come for her in the morning. Then she picked up her lantern, turned and walked out of the room, closing the door behind her. It happened so fast that Alexa didn't even have time to ask her any questions. And then she heard the nun put a key in the door from the outside and lock it. Alexa panicked.

"Oh no, please don't lock the door, Sister," she shouted out as she ran towards the door. But the door was already locked and there was no reply as she heard the nun's footsteps become more distant as she walked back down the long corridor.

Alexa was exhausted on all levels. Physically, she could feel the pain of her wounds and the throbbing of both her feet from the many kilometers of walking she had done that night. She had endured a sea of emotions, and her nerves were shattered. She had gone from excited to terrified, elated to deflated, scared to relieved, lost to found, from freedom to being captured again and so much in between, all within less than a twenty-four-hour time scale.

Alexa picked up the bedding, threw it onto the uninviting bed, and climbed under the blanket, curling up into a ball with all of her clothes still on her. She kicked off her shoes, left the candle burning and pulled the blanket up over her head. *'At least it's only for one night,'* she thought. Then she tried to recall the instructions given to her by Herr Klauss for the next part of her journey home. As exhausted as she was, she soon drifted off to sleep.

At some point in the night, the candle burned itself out, but Alexa was oblivious to that fact as she slept soundly, mainly due to exhaustion and fatigue rather than any feeling of being relaxed and comfortable. She didn't even hear the key in the lock the next morning when two nuns entered into the room.

"Wake up, girl. Get up!" ordered one of the nuns abruptly while she shook Alexa, who was still fast asleep. Alexa opened her eyes, sat up, swung her feet out from under the blanket to touch the cold stone floor. She began feeling for her shoes with her feet, but the nun nearest to her kicked the shoes away and out of her reach.

"Here, put these on," ordered the other nun and threw a pair of heavy wooden clogs over to her. They made a loud and familiar noise on the cold stone floor as they landed at her feet. Alexa thought she must be in the middle of a bad nightmare. She rubbed her eyes hard, but the picture in front of her didn't change in any way. She reluctantly placed her feet into the large clogs.

"Okay, up you get and come with us," said the nun near the door. Alexa got up and followed them down the long corridor and up the stairway at its end. Then they walked towards a large kitchen where there was a group of about thirty nuns sitting eating breakfast together.

"Sit down here," ordered one of the nuns, pointing to a spot on a wooden bench next to the long table.

Alexa did as she was told while she felt each pair of the nuns' eyes staring at her, looking her over from head to toe. She was still wearing the clothes she had arrived in the previous night, except for the black shoes. Her blood-stained pajama trouser leg was still tucked into her dirty sock, now pushed into the ugly clog. She quickly became aware that only she was wearing the wooden clogs. She knew she must have looked a sight but didn't really seem to care about that. A younger nun walked over to where she was and placed a cup of warm milk in front of Alexa. A few seconds later, she put a plate of warm lumpy porridge down in front of her.

"Thank you," said Alexa as the nun turned her back on her and walked away. Alexa reached for the milk and drank half of it down, then wasted no time beginning on the porridge. She was famished. Apart from the hot cocoa at the German police officer's house, she hadn't had anything to eat or drink since her short respite with the old man on the roadway the night before, when he had shared his milk and chocolate with her.

The porridge was lumpy and didn't taste as good as what she could make herself, but she ate it anyway. Once she had finished eating, the Mother Superior came over and stood next to her. She snapped her fingers, and two younger nuns came running over to where she was.

"Sisters Mariska and Julia will take you to get cleaned up and give you fresh clothes to wear. Go with them now and report straight back to me when you are done," she ordered, "and don't take all day about it."

Alexa stood up and the two nuns led her out of the kitchen. After a while of walking along corridors, turning corners, and walking upstairs, they arrived at a bathroom. The nun named Julia told Alexa to get undressed while they filled a metal tub with several buckets of water from the sink. Embarrassed, Alexa was reluctant to take her clothes off, not to mention the bathroom was cold and by the looks of things, so was the water. However, it didn't appear the matter was up for discussion as Sister Mariska moved closer to her and began to undo her coat buttons.

"Okay, okay," Alexa said. "I can do it myself."

She climbed out of her clothes and slowly stepped into the bath, letting out an uncontrollable shriek as her skin felt the pierce of the cold water. She tried to step back out, but the two nuns pushed her back down into the water and shoved a bar of soap into her hands. Alexa decided it would be better for her in the long run to do as she was told, so she washed her wounds clean and finished the cold bath as fast as she could.

Sister Julia had a towel waiting for her; it was rough and scratchy but at least it was clean and Alexa dried herself quickly, shivering all the while. Next, she was handed a small pile of clothes to put on. They were not her own clothes and didn't look like they were particularly her size, but they looked clean and she began to put them on.

Sister Julia pointed to her neck and said, "What is that? Take it off."

Alexa reached her right hand up to her necklace and took hold of the cross part.

"Oh no, please don't make me take it off, it was my grandmother's," she tried to explain.

"Take it off!" the nun said again.

"No, you don't understand, I've had it on every day since I was a little girl. I can't take it off. Please don't make me," Alexa begged.

"If you don't take it off, we will pull it off. Is that the way you want it? Do you want us to break it off?" Sister Mariska threatened.

Alexa shook her head as she slowly reached up and gently opened the clasp of the necklace. She held it in her hand and took one last look at it before reluctantly handing the necklace over to Sister Julia.

"If you behave and do as you're told, you might get it back," announced the nun who seemed to be enjoying bullying the young girl.

Alexa felt tears welling up in her eyes, but she was determined not to show her weakness and fought them back, flipping her inner switch to activate her instinct of masking of her true emotions, becoming the person she needed to be. She put her feet into the cumbersome clogs, tied back her hair, and said, "I'm ready."

The two nuns told her to pick up her dirty clothes and follow them, then they led her back down to the kitchen and stood her in front of the Mother Superior. Sister Julia handed the older nun Alexa's necklace, which she took a good look at and then said to Alexa, "It's very nice. I'll take good care of it for you and if you do a good job, maybe I'll give it back to you one day." She then placed it around her own neck and had Sister Julia fasten it securely for her.

Alexa tried to look unaffected by the nuns' actions, but deep down she was hurting badly. This was the one thing she had of her grandmother's, the one precious item from her childhood, from her home life, which she had managed to keep hold of all these years. This was the priceless item that in her mind had saved her life, the thing which had attracted the Klausses to her when they first selected her from the line-up. Even they hadn't been so wicked as to take it from her. She'd get it back, she resolved; she'd do whatever it took, but she'd get it back—somehow, someday.

"Time for you to get to work now, girl," announced the Mother Superior. "You will be doing laundry duties this week to start with. Sisters Julia and Mariska will show you where. Go with them."

"But I thought I was only to stay here overnight," said Alexa, "and then continue on my journey home to Poland."

"Well, you thought wrong, didn't you? Now go," ordered the nun.

Having no other choice and being greatly outnumbered, Alexa followed Sisters Julia and Mariska as they led her to a large laundry area and set about putting her to work. The piles of dirty laundry were huge; mountains of white sheets and towels filled one entire corner and black clothing another.

For the first time, Alexa wished she was back working at the Klausses' farmhouse, but she made a start on the mammoth task that lay before her and concentrated all of her energy on working hard towards getting her grandmother's necklace back. She couldn't give up hope, not now. Nor could she allow her thoughts to become dark and negative. Again, she reminded herself that this situation was only temporary and she'd be free from it soon. She made the choice to rise above the suffering and not become a victim of the circumstance she now found herself in. She had done it before, and she'd do it again.

After her first full day of work at the convent, Alexa was taken to a different room where she was to sleep at night. This room was a lot larger than the first room she had been placed in when she arrived. It looked a little more comfortable, although not by much. This room had four single beds, so it quickly became apparent to Alexa she would likely be sharing it with others, although she didn't know who the others would be.

It wasn't too long before her new roommates arrived, escorted by two of the nuns. They too had experienced a long day of hard, forced, manual labor. They were three girls who all spoke German, but it was apparent that German was not their mother tongue. The three girls were also blondes and seemed to be from another part of Europe. As their individual stories unfolded, it became clear they had also been taken from their homes against their will, some years prior, just like Alexa. The nuns locked the door behind them, as was their routine, and the girls were left alone in the room. One of the girls introduced herself to Alexa.

"Hi, my name is Marta and I'm seventeen years old, originally from Belgium. What's your name?"

"Hello," replied Alexa. "My name is Alexa and I'll be nineteen in March. I'm originally from Poland."

"Nice to meet you," said Marta. "This is Henrietta; she's eighteen and comes from Holland." Marta pointed to the tall blonde girl sitting to her right, and Henrietta said hello in response. Marta then pointed to the other girl in the room. "This is Greta and she is from Denmark originally but lived in Belgium also. She's nineteen and the oldest of the three of us."

Greta smiled at Alexa as she leaned forward to shake her hand. Alexa extended her hand to meet Greta's. Now the four girls had all introduced themselves to one another. Alexa realized they were all in the same boat, with the same goal: they had all been taken against their will from their families, and they were now all desperately trying hard to get back to their own individual homes. They were also all wearing the heavy oversized wooden clogs on their feet. Henrietta pointed to one of the beds closest to her and told Alexa it was where she slept.

"Marta sleeps on that one and Greta on this one, so that one there will be yours." Henrietta pointed to one of the beds.

"Ok, thank you, but I really don't intend to be here for very long," Alexa replied.

"Ha, that's what we all thought when we first arrived here too," Marta said.

"How long have you all been here?"

Henrietta answered first, "I've been here since the beginning of September this year."

"It was two weeks into October when I was brought here," said Marta.

"I got here the first week of November," said Greta.

Alexa thought if she shared her story of when and how she was taken, it might encourage the others to speak out about their experiences too. "I was thirteen years of age when my mother and I went into town to buy me a new pair of shoes. The Nazis drove into the square and started rounding everybody up. We were separated into groups, loaded onto different trucks, put into cattle wagons, and transported to a labor camp. I got to spend one night there with my mother before she was beaten and knocked unconscious. The next day I was separated from her. It's been more than four years since I last saw my mother. I have no idea what happened to her. I was taken to Frankfurt, where I was selected and sent to work as an unpaid house slave for a German SS officer and his family at their farmhouse. I was freed by them only yesterday and have journeyed to this place, where I was only supposed to spend one evening. That's my story up until now, what's yours?"

Greta was first to speak after Alexa had related her experience. "I was fourteen years old when I was taken. I was fast asleep in bed in my family home, when all of a sudden, our front door was forcefully and violently kicked in, and a bunch of Nazi soldiers with rifles charged into our home. We had no time to run or hide. Immediately we were pulled out of our beds and were rushed outside into the streets without any of our belongings. I was separated from my mother, father, brother, and sister. I was sent to Germany as an unpaid domestic slave for four years, and now I find myself here with you three girls."

The three girls looked at her empathetically; they knew how it felt to walk in her shoes for they had all trodden similar paths to the point they were now at.

Next up was Marta's history. She began by speaking of her happy childhood in Belgium and then led into the circumstances of her capture. "I was twelve years old and it's a day I will never forget as long as I live. My father had just said the prayer as we sat down to dinner, me and all six of my immediate family. As my father passed me the bread, we heard the engines of trucks outside in the street followed by the heavy footsteps of German soldiers and their barking dogs. My father told us to quickly go and hide in the places, as we had often rehearsed, for a day such as that. We all ran away from the dining table and I hid with my brother in the secret loosened panel behind the kitchen cabinet; we crawled inside the tiny space. Then I heard our front door burst open and soldiers running into our house, shouting and then shooting. I heard my father shout out in protest, but very quickly he was silenced mid-sentence with a bullet, and we heard a great thud as he fell to the floor. My mother was holding my baby brother, and my four-year-old little sister was standing together with her in the dining room. The soldiers screamed at her, demanding to know if there was anyone else in the house. They said if there was anyone hiding, she and my siblings would be shot. So, my brother and I crawled out of our hiding places so my mother and the others would not be killed. We were all marched outside onto the street and separately loaded onto different trucks. I haven't seen any of my family since that day. My father was left lying for dead, alone on the floor. I was selected by the Nazis with some other blonde, blue-eyed youngsters like me, and brought here to Germany as a slave. And the rest I'd rather not talk about. I just want to get back home to try and find any of my family who might still be alive."

Greta, being the oldest of the girls, took it upon herself to take the lead, summarizing that they had all individually been through horrific, nightmare ordeals, which bonded them all together, but that they also shared a common goal.

"We have all survived up till now, and there must be a good reason for that. I'm sure if we stick together and do our jobs here as the nuns expect of us, we will make it out of here alive and get back to our homes and find what's left of our families. Somehow, we will find a way together," encouraged Greta.

The girls all agreed and seemed to be empowered by Greta's words. They took some comfort in the fact they all had shared similar ordeals and that they were also not totally alone anymore. The exhausted girls settled into their beds, said goodnight to one another, and lay silently with their own thoughts as they drifted off to sleep. Alexa said her prayer silently to herself.

CHAPTER 13

Over the national radio broadcasts came news reports that the Second World War was finally coming to an end. The Allied troops were trying to capture as many Nazi soldiers, SS officers, and high-ranking SS officials as possible—those responsible for so many of the atrocities that had occurred since the start of the war.

Towards the end of January 1945, some of the Nazi concentration camps and forced labor camps were beginning to be liberated throughout Germany and Poland. And the world began to receive the first photographic evidence, film footage, and firsthand survivor accounts of the terror that had actually taken place in these horrific and most hellish places on earth—accounts of the undeniable, unimaginable, brutal, and inhumane treatment, torture, and murder of millions of innocent Jewish men, women, and children—and many others—at the hands of Hitler's Nazi army, Gestapo, and evil henchmen.

The nuns had an old radio they kept in a large wooden cabinet in the main dining room of the convent where they would sit and eat dinner together. After they ate their main meal, they would turn the radio on to listen to the latest news updates being broadcast. The four workhouse girls were always seated at the small table in the far corner of the dining room to eat their meals together, away from the group of nuns but always remaining within their sight. It was now the beginning of April, and Alexa was nineteen. She had been kept there against her will for four months, forced to slave away in the laundry room every day.

One evening, after her meal, Alexa lingered to hear the radio broadcast warning of bombing campaigns led by the Allied forces in one town after another, as they aimed to take out key German army targets in and around Berlin. Reports also told of Nazi soldiers running for cover across the country, trying to hide their long trail of evil. At the end of the update, it was reported there was a mass of freed innocent prisoners, mainly Jewish but also others who had been taken from across Europe, who were now on foot—refugees trying to make their way back to their various homes. The broadcaster said the German civilian population in general should assist these unfortunate people in any way they could and it was their duty as human beings. The Mother Superior looked over at Alexa and the other three girls at the table. Seeing they were all listening intently to the radio broadcast, she said loudly, "That doesn't apply to you girls, now get back to work!"

Two nuns got up from their seats and took them all back to the laundry room. They were never permitted to go there unaccompanied nor to leave by themselves, and were never left in the laundry room alone either. There were always eyes watching over them. Someone came and took them to morning prayers and then to breakfast afterwards. Next, they were escorted to work in the laundry rooms, and the same at dinner time. After they had finished their work for the day, two nuns would escort the girls back to their room down in the basement.

Alexa had tried to think of ways to escape—they all had— but there really weren't any opportunities she could think of. That night, as she lay exhausted in bed in their shared room, Alexa prayed hard as she did every night, but this time out loud, for all the girls to hear.

"Dear Almighty God in heaven, we desperately need your help to escape this prison which we now find ourselves in. Please hear my pleas and make a way out for me and my friends so we may continue on our journeys home and find our families. Guide and protect us, dear God, we beg of you. Amen." The other girls said "Amen" too. Alexa closed her eyes and soon fell asleep.

When morning came, she and one of the other girls were collected by two of the nuns and taken upstairs to breakfast, as per the normal routine. The other two girls were then collected and escorted upstairs separately by two other nuns. After prayers and breakfast were over, they were all taken to the laundry room area and guarded as they began slaving away, scrubbing and washing, rinsing and hanging up the never-ending piles of laundry.

Henrietta and Marta were ordered to collect the large pile of clean and dry black nuns' clothing and were then led out of the main room through a door in the corner into the next room, where their duties consisted of ironing the nuns' habits and white linen sheets.

While Alexa attended to her monotonous chores, she heard overhead what sounded like airplane engines, flying low in the vicinity; she immediately continued her work with caution. The airplanes seemed to pass over them and go off into the distance, but after a few minutes they came back, the hum of their airplane engines growing louder, followed by the whistling noise of a fast-approaching, falling bomb.

The nuns began to scream in terror. Alexa ran towards the large stained-glass window on the far-left side of the room; crawling under the large, solid wooden table which was directly underneath it, she buried herself in a massive pile of dirty sheets for protection. The bomb hit its target, and a tremendous explosion erupted as it hit the rectory at the front of the property. Then immediately after, a second bomb hit the rear of the convent building.

The entire stone structure shook violently as a mass of bricks and mortar began to crumble and fall in all around the interior. The stained-glass window shattered with the impact of the second explosion, and large sections of glass shards shattered and landed everywhere. The large table under which Alexa was taking shelter split in half at its middle from the weight of the falling debris above it; fortunately, Alexa had been cowering under the rear legs section, which still provided her with some protection.

Alexa slowly became aware of the relative silence that now existed in the laundry room, except for the loud ringing in her ears. There were no more screaming nuns, nor were any of them crying out for help that she could hear. More importantly, she couldn't hear Greta either.

Alexa crawled out from under the broken table and kicked off the laundry sheets in which she had wrapped herself for protection. She seemed to be uninjured, apart from the knock to her head she'd received when the table above her had snapped in the middle. She stood up, squinted her eyes, and looked around the room to assess the damage. Through the unsettled dust that filled the air like a white mist, she saw part of the roof had fallen in on the right side of the room. It had damaged the adjoining room also, knocking down part of the wall and blocking the doorway. Looking for any signs of life, she discovered the bodies of the two nuns who had been guarding her and Greta before the bomb had hit. Both were now buried under a large pile of rubble. Alexa looked around the room desperately trying to find Greta who had been working nearest to her, calling out her name until finally she saw her.

"Greta, you're okay!" yelled Alexa as she hugged Greta.

"Yes, and you are too, my friend. Who would have thought these dirty sheets would actually end up saving my life?" said Greta. Alexa pointed to her ears, shook her head, and gestured that she had a problem hearing. Greta saw the nuns' dead bodies lying on the ground under piles of rubble. The girls realized that, for the first time, there was no one guarding them anymore, or watching their every move.

"Let's go and try to find Marta and Henrietta," said Alexa. Greta nodded in agreement and the two girls carefully made their way over the debris, out of the devastated laundry room and into the next destroyed room.

There were no immediate signs of life in the next room. This was where Alexa believed Henrietta and Marta had been taken to work that day, in the area where the ironing was done. The extensive bomb damage was obvious and there were few to no areas that weren't covered with fallen bricks, mortar, wooden beams, and piles of large stone. Eventually, they discovered the shoes of one of the nuns, showing out from under one of the large stone piles. It was obvious there was no way she could have survived and was most likely buried alive. Alexa and Greta assumed the other nun had most likely suffered the same fate.

"I'm glad we weren't in their shoes," Greta said.

Finally, as satisfied as they could be that their friends were not casualties there, the two girls began looking for an exit and carefully tried to make their way back to the kitchen area, while continuing to search for their two friends. Alexa's ears were still ringing, but she couldn't hear any recognizable voices or cries for help; neither could Greta.

They made their way to the kitchen, which was at the rear of the building, only to find it had been totally destroyed and no longer existed as a room with any purpose inside the structure. It was now part of the outside, with its roof completely blown off and gaping holes in its walls. Greta said she'd take one side of the room and began searching.

Alexa climbed over some of the debris and looked around for any signs of life. She quickly realized the kitchen area had taken a direct hit so that was probably the location of most of the fatalities. Only a very short while ago that morning, she had left the breakfast table where all the nuns had been sitting, eating. There were fires burning in several places, and Alexa decided it was probably best for them to get as far away from the scene as possible.

As she turned to locate Greta to suggest they leave the kitchen area, she heard a faint voice cry out in pain from underneath the large pile of fallen stone. She turned back and tried to get close to where the source of the voice was coming from.

"Where are you? Let me hear your voice again, louder," Alexa shouted.

A few seconds later, the voice cried out again. Alexa couldn't clearly make out any of the words but could sense the direction where the sound was coming from and climbed over towards where she thought the person might be. She heard the voice again and this time could tell the injured person was lying below the large pile of stones and rubble where she now stood. She could see the shoes of one of the nuns sticking out and began lifting off the heavy stones, one by one.

"Greta, come over and help me, there's someone under here," she called. "Hold on, I'll get you freed," she added reassuringly as she continued to slowly and carefully remove some of the bricks. Finally, Alexa removed the last few bricks from around the trapped person's face and, to her surprise, discovered the nun's identity. It was the Mother Superior who had been so nasty to Alexa when she had first arrived at the convent. The nun opened her eyes and looked up at Alexa, staring back down at her.

"Oh, thank you, girl. Now hurry, get me out of here," the nun gasped.

There was a large wooden beam across the nun's chest area, with more heavy stones and bricks still piled high on top of it. When Greta joined Alexa and saw who was trapped under the rubble, her whole demeanor changed from rescuer to judge and jury.

"It's up to you, Alexa," she said, "but I wouldn't help her out if I was you. Not after all she's done to us and what she's put us through."

Alexa thought for a second and then leaned in, reaching down to the nun's neck. She felt around under the nun's white neck covering until she revealed her grandmother's silver necklace, which the old nun had taken from her so cruelly when she'd first arrived. The nun looked up at Alexa and again ordered her to get her out.

"You did take good care of my necklace and I did do a very good job here, but now I'm taking my necklace back and going home," Alexa announced. She undid the clasp and removed her necklace from around the nun's neck. Alexa estimated from the injuries the old woman had received, her chances of survival were slim to none. There was no way Alexa could lift the heavy wooden beam off her chest by herself and even with help, it would be a near impossible task.

From beneath the rubble, the nun drew her last breath and rattled death. Alexa knew there was nothing more she could do, so she slowly and carefully she made her way down off the pile of stones. Standing on firmer ground, she put her grandmother's necklace around her own neck.

Greta fastened the clasp for her friend. "Let's get out of here, Alexa," she said.

Once outside, it became apparent to Alexa and Greta that they were the only two survivors, out of about thirty nuns, the only ones who had made it out of the building alive and in one piece. In the distance, they heard the hum of a single returning airplane. The girls ran as fast as they could, away from the building structures and towards the surrounding trees. From behind them, they heard the now familiar whistling sound of a fast-falling bomb, and they quickly dived for cover in some nearby bushes.

The powerful bomb hit its intended target, landing right in the center of the third residential building of the convent, which was at the very rear of the property. Alexa later learned that the largest, newest residential building, which had several floors to it, was being used secretly by the Nazis, with the nuns' permission, as a makeshift hospital to care for and nurse wounded SS officers and German soldiers. From observed vehicle movements, Allied intelligence had identified this as a likely command headquarters, and decided that bombing the three buildings in one fell swoop would be the most effective way to bring it to its end.

Once again, Greta and Alexa were not seriously injured, bearing only a few scratches from the bushes they had taken cover in. They both felt enormously relieved; however, they were still worried and anxious over the whereabouts and well-being of their two friends. When they were sure the bombers were gone and the coast was relatively clear, they carefully made their way back towards the convent.

"Our clogs are gone and we both have no shoes on," Greta said. "We won't get very far barefoot."

She was right. They hadn't paid much attention up to that point but their work clogs were gone from their feet in the first explosion. The mix of adrenaline combined with their survival instincts had kept their minds focused on their moving to safety and not on the comfort of their own feet.

"You're right, Greta," agreed Alexa. "Let's head over to the other side of the convent. We can look for some shoes on our way. No one here will need them anymore."

The last building to be hit was badly damaged and engulfed in flames. The two girls headed towards the convent's kitchen area, and as they got closer, they heard some movement coming from inside its damaged walls. Then they heard muffled female voices and became filled with fear at the thought that maybe there were some nuns who had survived after all and would try to keep them enslaved again. They moved back slowly in the direction from where they had come, to watch from a distance. Out of the derelict structure appeared a woman; she was covered in grey dust from head to toe. She sat down on the ground and began putting on a pair of lace-up boots.

Alexa turned to Greta. "It's Henrietta, I think it's Henrietta."

Greta jumped up. "It is Henrietta, it's her, she's alive!" she shouted.

Greta ran out of their hiding place before Alexa could tell her to wait to make sure it was safe first. Henrietta looked up and saw Greta running towards her. She hadn't finish lacing up the boots but she jumped to her feet. The girls ran into each other's arms with Alexa joining them a few seconds later.

"Marta, get out here, look who's alive!" Henrietta shouted.

A few seconds later Marta emerged from the building's ruins, carrying a pair of boots, her eyes wide with disbelief at the sight before her. The four girls were alive. They had all survived and were relatively unharmed. They embraced for a moment or two then agreed they couldn't waste any more time; they had to get as far away from the convent as quickly as possible.

Alexa and Greta each began looking for a pair of the deceased nuns' boots in which they could make their escape. Henrietta disappeared around to the back courtyard and found two bicycles that were still in good working condition and decided they would be their best means of transportation out of there. Two girls on each bike—one would cycle while the other sat on the saddle, and then they could switch over, she suggested. The girls agreed with Henrietta's idea.

Alexa realized there was no way she could get back to their room where her things were, due to the extensively damaged building. So, she wouldn't be able to retrieve her blue shoes either. This saddened her immensely, as she wouldn't be able to take them back home to show her mother what good care she had taken of them—that same pair of shoes they had gone to buy together on the day they had both been taken. However, she had managed to get her grandmother's necklace back and she was still alive, which she reasoned were both far more valuable and irreplaceable than the blue shoes. Indeed, it was a miracle they were all still alive.

The girls tied up their boot laces, shook off some of the dust from their clothes and hair, and climbed onto the bicycles. They steered around the fallen masonry strewn all over the grounds and headed off downhill, out of that hellish place as fast as they could. They never looked back.

CHAPTER 14

The girls cycled for almost an hour, switching positions on the bikes, taking turns at steering, and stopping a few times for short rests along the roadway. Except for Alexa. She said she wasn't the best cyclist, so Greta pedaled their bike for them both. They weren't very sure of where they were heading to; after all, nothing was planned. The girls had had no idea when they woke up that morning that it would turn into the day they would regain their freedom. It could also have turned out very differently and indeed, so much worse for them all.

The four girls had come so close to being killed in the bombing raid that the day was a godsend, a real blessing, and each felt as though they had a protective force around them, keeping them safe and shielding them from harm. Alexa was convinced beyond any shadow of a doubt that her God had indeed heard her prayer the night before and had acted on their behalf. Her faith was already strong; however, this anchored it and made it even firmer.

As they cycled along the uneven roads, the four girls passed many damaged buildings, many of which had no doubt been intentionally bombed and targeted specifically by the Allied forces in air raids. However, it was obvious that many homes had been unintentionally caught up in the air strikes, with many structures left derelict and abandoned in a severe state of disrepair. There didn't appear to be many people around in the area they travelled through. It seemed more like a ghost town, totally deserted and deadly silent.

Henrietta and Marta's bicycle got a flat tire, so the four girls stopped on the open roadway and took the opportunity to rest a little. They had no supplies with them, nothing to eat or drink, and hadn't had anything since early that morning when they had eaten breakfast at the convent. Greta suggested they rummage around some of the abandoned damaged houses in the hope of finding some kind of nourishment. Although they weren't too enthusiastic at the prospect of searching through the dangerous structures, they agreed they had no other options.

About two hundred yards ahead of them, they saw a large house that had received extensive bomb damage. Part of its roof had been blown off, several windows were blown out, and part of the exterior wall on its right side had collapsed. The girls approached the house cautiously. Henrietta suggested she and Marta look around the back of the property towards the garden, while Greta and Alexa take the front side.

Alexa and Greta carefully began to climb up the mound of rubble where they thought there might have once been a doorway, to try and find a way inside the house. Greta was first to reach the top of the brick pile, with Alexa following close behind her. Greta turned around to extend a helping hand to her friend. Alexa, looking up at Greta, saw her eyes widen with shock. Alexa whirled around to see a large army truck, driving along the road, its driver staring directly at them.

As the truck came to an abrupt stop directly outside the house, four soldiers jumped out, their rifles pointed directly at the two girls. The soldiers yelled at them to stop in their tracks, exactly where they were, and then to slowly climb down.

Alexa's heart was in her mouth as she stood, rigid with fear, but Greta seemed to fancy her chances of escape and ran down the other side of the pile of rubble and into the house. Two soldiers chased her inside while Alexa began her descent to the ground below. Her hands held high, she walked over to the waiting soldiers who wasted no time in loading her into the back of the truck. She was surprised to see she wasn't alone; a number of miserable faces stared back at her until she turned away to peer out a gap in the canvas cover towards the house. Presently, the other two soldiers emerged from the building with Greta at gunpoint. They marched her over towards the rear of the truck and ordered her inside.

The two friends looked at each other wordlessly. In the blink of an eye, their freedom had been stolen from them once more. They were captured again. Alexa was vaguely comforted by the fact that in the soldiers' haste to guard her and chase after Greta, they had failed to search the rest of the property thoroughly and therefore hadn't discovered Marta or Henrietta. Alexa hoped they were both hiding at the rear of the house or in the trees at the bottom of the garden.

The military truck drove for a relatively short distance before coming to a stop, parking outside of what appeared to be an old school building. On the other side of the road was a schoolmaster's house and an old church, both of which had received some structural damage.

The other prisoners inside the truck, including Alexa and Greta, were ordered to get out of the vehicle and march single file across the schoolyard and into the large school building, under guard of the soldiers who kept their weapons aimed and at the ready. They were marched along the guarded corridors and guided into a large room where close to two hundred or more German men and women were being forced to sit on the wooden floor, all at least a body length apart.

The new prisoners were added to the group, the men at one side of the room and the women at the other. By the sounds of childish voices, it sounded to Alexa as though there was another room down the hallway where young children were being watched over, separate from the adults.

It gradually dawned on Alexa that the soldiers were actually Allied troops. They spoke with American, English, and French accents but seemed at first to be as stern and mean as the German soldiers had been. Alexa sat on the floor with all the others as directed; she could see Greta sitting three rows in front of her, to her left. She looked around for signs of Marta and Henrietta, but thankfully there was no trace of them in the large group. They had evaded capture.

Silence was maintained; no one was allowed to talk. It was made crystal clear to all the prisoners that they were not permitted to get up for any reason. Time passed by very slowly in the large room, with a growing sense of uncertainty.

They were not given any food to eat, and water was in short supply. Toilet breaks were not given very often, so sitting in quiet contemplation was all there was to do. The war was speedily coming to its end, but peace had not yet been declared. There were still bombs being dropped and rifles being fired on the front by both sides.

Alexa sat contemplating how happy she was that the war was finally going to be over, that she was still alive, and would now be a survivor. She hadn't let on to the soldiers that she was Polish, but then again, they hadn't asked. They had simply assumed she and Greta were German because they had answered them in German.

Time ticked by very slowly.

Every few hours, a group of ten German women were selected at random and taken out of the room at gunpoint. They were apparently being forced to work on extensive cleaning duties at the nearby damaged church and schoolhouse.

Alexa's thoughts gradually changed, turning into frustration as it dawned on her she was being held prisoner with the large group of Germans as if she were one of them. She was incensed at the injustice. It was the Germans who had kept her prisoner for over five years—first the Klauss family and then the nuns at the convent. Alexa, feeling a surge of courage and determination to no longer be victimized, suddenly jumped up to her feet.

"I won't sit here anymore. I am Polish. I'm not a German. Why do I have to sit here with all these German people?" Alexa exploded in her best Polish. "It's not fair!"

One of the senior-looking American officers walked over to her.

"Come with me," he said in Polish and led her out of the room. He then took her to his commanding officer and allowed Alexa to explain her situation. Alexa told them of her experience, of how she'd been taken by the Germans at age thirteen and kept as a slave for almost five years by the Klausses, after which—while trying to get back home—she'd been imprisoned by the nuns at the convent to work as a slave for another four months. The commander asked Alexa if she had been beaten or physically abused by her German captors, but Alexa told the truth: the family had been reasonably decent to her, apart from working her very hard as their unpaid slave and keeping her against her will for so long.

After she'd explained what she'd been through, the commander told Alexa he empathized with her and had decided she deserved freedom and empowerment. First, he took her to a smaller, quieter room where there was a Polish family of four and a young Ukrainian woman. He told Alexa to sit and ordered a soldier to bring her something to eat and drink; when she had finished, they gave her two bars of chocolate, which she placed in her pocket. After an hour or so had passed, the commander spoke privately to the soldier before telling Alexa to follow them back into the large hall filled with Germans but this time, not as a prisoner.

The soldier told Alexa to choose ten German women from the group, who were to be taken out for heavy manual labor duty across the road at the schoolmaster's house. It was to be used as the new officers' temporary barracks, and he said Alexa would be their boss and supervisor. She was to direct them—telling them what to do, where to do it, and to make sure they did it properly under her watchful eye.

Alexa felt uncomfortable with the whole idea and humbly told the commander she couldn't do it. He insisted she pick her ten workers from among the German women, march them out of the room, and put them to work. He wouldn't take no for an answer. He reminded her that these were the German civilians who had done nothing to help other young girls taken as slaves—like her—in homes all across Germany during the war years. Some of them had no doubt worked innocent girls as their own house slaves.

Realizing there was no point in arguing, Alexa obediently began her selection and couldn't help but feel slightly empowered as she chose them. The ten women stood up and formed a line; then, along with Alexa, they were marched out of the room under the guard of four armed soldiers.

When they reached the schoolhouse across the road, the extent of the building's damage became clear; it would take a huge amount of heavy clean-up work to make the premises livable for the officers. Alexa was told to give the order for the women to begin work—cleaning, washing, scrubbing, and sweeping—and to make sure they put real effort into the tasks. Alexa was no slave driver, but she made sure the women did as they were told, while she somewhat relaxed and supervised them.

After a while, two soldiers came to the schoolhouse looking for Alexa and ordered her to follow them. Alexa was apprehensive as they didn't explain why she had to go with them or say where they were taking her. However, Alexa followed them, and they led her down the street into the church.

"Have I done something wrong, officers?" Alexa asked.

"Please be quiet and follow us," one of the officers told her.

Inside, the church was deserted and a little dark; the sun was beginning to set and didn't allow much light in through the stained-glass windows, which were surprisingly still mostly intact. The soldiers led Alexa to the back of the church and down some stairs behind the altar towards a small door. They opened it and led Alexa into the room.

Alexa could not believe her eyes at the sight before her. She had never seen anything like it in her life. In front of her were several wooden trunks full of priceless treasure—gold necklaces, pearl bracelets, diamond rings, earrings, watches, decorative broaches, and precious stones of all kinds and colors. In one trunk were gold coins and solid gold bars. On the floor stood many pairs of silver, golden, and precious gem-encrusted candlesticks, along with ornate goblets, cups, frames, and statues. The loot of priceless treasures was mind-blowing and an awesome sight to behold.

One of the officers turned towards Alexa. "Take what you like. You were kept in Germany to work as a slave. Here, take as much as you want."

Alexa stared at the officer. "But this isn't mine. No, I can't. No, I don't want anything; I don't want any of it because it's not mine to take."

The two American officers looked at each other and burst out laughing at the young woman's response. They repeated she must take something, otherwise their commander would be angry with them. They explained it was his wish and order that Alexa be brought to the room and allowed to pick whatever she wanted for herself from the bounty, as some small kind of compensation for all she had gone through. Again, Alexa said she could not take anything from the trunks of treasures, for she knew in her heart it all belonged to many others, and her conscience wouldn't allow her to.

"Well, perhaps there is something else here in the room that you could have, something of lesser value. But please, you must take something because my commander won't be pleased with me if you don't," suggested one of the soldiers.

Alexa looked around the room again until she spotted over in the corner, leaning against the wall, several rolls of exquisite fabric, the likes of which she had never seen before. A beautifully delicate, pink-flowered patterned material with gold threads and embroidery on a green background particularly caught her eye. Alexa pointed to the roll of fabric and asked the soldiers if she could perhaps have some of it to make a dress. The soldiers were happy the young woman had finally chosen something and said she could have the entire roll. But Alexa suggested they give her no more than twenty-five or thirty meters, as that was all she would need.

After some more persuasion from Alexa, they measured out roughly how much she thought she would need, plus a little extra. One of the officers produced a knife and cut the material, folded it up and carried it back towards to the school building. They placed it for her in the quieter room, where the Polish family and the Ukrainian woman were.

Alexa spent the rest of her time there planning out and making a dress for herself. She saved an extra length for another dress and gave the remaining material to the other two women and their young daughters, so they too could make some new clothing for themselves.

Upon hearing Alexa hadn't chosen any of the jewels or valuable gold, the commander asked her later, "Why not?"

"It wasn't mine to take," Alexa answered.

The commander nodded slowly, looking at Alexa with an expression of great respect. Noticing this, she plucked up the courage to ask for one special favor. She explained to him her friend Greta from Denmark had been picked up with her that day after they had escaped from the convent and was still being held down the corridor in the large room with the other Germans. Alexa asked if she could give her one of her chocolate bars to eat, knowing she'd be hungry. The commander immediately sent one of his officers to the large hall of prisoners in search of Greta.

"Is there a girl named Greta from Denmark in here? A friend of Alexa's?" asked the soldier.

Greta raised her hand and stood up.

"Come with me please, you don't belong in here. There's been a mistake," he said.

Greta quickly followed him out of the large room, down the corridor, and into the smaller room where Alexa was. The girls embraced, and Greta thanked Alexa for not forgetting about her.

"How could I possibly forget about you? You're my friend," said Alexa.

For the next three days, the girls concentrated on making their new dresses out of the material Alexa had chosen. They were given pairs of scissors, needles, and threads to use from the school supplies and were allowed to relax, making themselves as comfortable as they could possibly be, with enough to eat and drink. Now, all they were missing were Marta and Henrietta. They both couldn't help but worry about where they now were.

CHAPTER 15

After the third day of being kept in the school, the soldiers told Alexa she and the others who were not German and who had been innocently taken against their will from other European countries, were to be moved out from the school the next day. A large army truck would be arriving to transport these casualties of war on the long drive to France. They would be safer there than they'd be in Germany and would be re-settled into a displacement camp until they could eventually return safely to their homes.

The group totaling close to twenty, mainly young women, were loaded onto the truck with Alexa and Greta. However, none of the others looked as pretty as they did in their newly made dresses, as basic as they were. The Commander decided to do one more favor for Alexa before she left on her journey, and that was to give her and Greta nicer pairs of shoes to wear than the ones they had on.

First, he asked them to remove their clumpy old lace-up boots, which they had taken from the dead nuns before leaving the convent. Then, he had one of the soldiers take the boots to the large room of Germans; from among the women sitting there, he selected two females who wore the same size of shoe as Alexa and Greta, to give up their pretty shoes.

The soldier took the two pairs of nicer shoes and handed them to Alexa and Greta to try on. The young women did as they were instructed and found they fit well enough; they really made their new dresses look even more elegant. The commander smiled his approval as both women thanked him for all he had done for them. Then they climbed up into the back of the open truck, to join the others.

"You're a beautiful young woman, Alexa, inside and out, and I hope you eventually get back to your home safely to reunite with your family. Godspeed," said the commander as he banged on the side of the truck, signaling the driver to move off.

"Thank you for everything," called Alexa, waving goodbye as the truck drove off.

It was far from a comfortable ride, sitting on the floor of the open top truck amongst a group of strangers, but the two friends took comfort from the fact they had each other. After the truck had been journeying for about two hours, it pulled off the road at an Allied military fuel-loading area. As the truck rolled in, it caught the attention of many of the military personnel and Allied soldiers there.

The passengers were allowed to get out of the truck and stretch their legs for a time, while the truck parked up next to the diesel pump to have its tank filled. Most of the young women were pretty Europeans in their late teens and early twenties, with trim figures and good-looking features. It became apparent to them they hadn't gone unnoticed and had attracted the attention of the young soldiers. But one girl in particular seemed to be attracting more attention than the others.

In a matter of minutes, Alexa and Greta had a small group of enamored Allied soldiers around them. It was clear that Alexa, with her natural beauty and strikingly good looks, was drawing the most attention.

Some of the American soldiers began offering them gifts of nylon stockings, and the French officers gave them bars of chocolate. By far the most impressive gesture came from a young Italian soldier who dropped to his knee and began playing his guitar, serenading Alexa with an Italian love song. Alexa blushed as all attention and eyes were focused directly on her and the crooning Italian soldier. When the song ended, there was a rapturous round of applause and whistles, while a blushing Alexa thanked the young soldier for his musical performance. Apparently smitten, the soldier stood up and kissed Alexa's hand before singing her another song in Italian.

Once their truck's tank was filled with diesel and ready to go, the driver told the group to climb back onboard. As Alexa was finding a space to sit, the Italian soldier ran over to the truck.

"For you, Bellissima!" he shouted, as he reached up and handed his guitar over to Alexa.

"But I don't know how to play it," Alexa protested.

"Don't say that," said one of the other women sitting near her on the truck. "Just take it, and maybe you can trade it for other things when we get to the camp in France."

The engine revved up and the truck pulled off back onto the road for the long drive towards France. Sitting in the back of the truck with all the others, Alexa's thoughts traveled back five years earlier when she was originally taken from Poland. She recalled being loaded onto that very first military truck with her friend Karolina, having both been torn away from their mothers in the Lublin square.

In the early days of her capture, she had thought a lot about that horrific day. In fact, she hadn't been able to rid her mind of the nightmare for the longest time, the whole ordeal replaying itself, over and over again, like a movie in her head, stuck on repeat. However, over time it had come less and less to mind, although it was never further than a thought away. Now, the journey in the back of the Allied truck triggered those memories once again, and they all came flooding back to her.

As she had done that very first day in the back of the Nazi truck, Alexa began to pray. She recited the 91st Psalm she knew so well silently to herself. This time, however, she prayed without the anxiety and terror she had felt on that first truck ride, helpless at the hands of the Nazi soldiers and their viciously snapping, snarling dogs.

The current truck ride was far more relaxed and Alexa felt much safer, knowing she was protected by the Allied troops and being taken to a place of sanctuary outside of Germany. However, there was still a great amount of uncertainty ahead of her. Alexa added her own personal petitions at the end of her prayer, asking to be kept safe from thereon and, as always, that she could go home one day soon to be reunited with her family. She left it in God's merciful hands.

After one more stop on the eight-hour journey, the truck finally reached its destination at Mourmelon in the Northeast of France, about ninety miles from Paris. An abandoned military airbase, it was now being used as a camp for displaced European civilians, run by the U.S. army and the Allied troops.

On arrival, the group was led over to a large grey canvas tent. Inside, soldiers sat at a desk with bundles of white forms and paperwork in front of them, waiting to register the new arrivals and record all their pertinent information. Greta and Alexa lined up to register together in the hope they would be placed together in the same barracks. They were near the front of the line of new arrivals and were processed fairly quickly, as there weren't many new arrivals that day.

Next, they were directed to a large, solid brick building, home to the camp's kitchen and cafeteria, run by the Red Cross. They were given some watered-down soup to eat, along with a piece of bread and a lukewarm cup of weak coffee while they waited to receive their assigned residence barracks where they would live temporarily. An hour went by before their names were called out by a French female soldier who then escorted them to their barracks.

There were two sections to the camp with about twenty long, solid brick buildings in each. Previously, these barracks had been used by the soldiers of the Air Force base when it had been operational. The larger, front section of the camp now worked reasonably well as a temporary shelter and sanctuary for the many displaced Europeans stuck in limbo while they waited to return to their homes. The rear section of barracks was used to house the American and Allied troops.

Once taken to their assigned building, which was for females only, Alexa and Greta were shown into a room with about twenty bunkbeds and told they would sleep in the second bunks from the end, at the very far corner of the room. They were metal army-issue bunkbeds, so were far from being comfortable. This was by no means a five-star hotel, nor could it even rank close to a one, but it did provide a place to lie down and rest in relative freedom and safety compared to what they had been used to. They were each given a set of clean white sheets, a pillow, and one grey blanket from the Red Cross, along with a clean towel to use, and told that every two weeks those would be refreshed and laundered.

Alexa and Greta made their way down the barracks to their assigned beds. Greta chose the top bunk, placing her bedding on top of it. They were both pleased they would be together for as long as they were to remain in the camp. Alexa placed her gifted guitar from the Italian soldier underneath her bunk.

The female officer handed them some ration cards with which they could get some minimal personal toiletries and clothing from the Red Cross supply store, and then pointed out the bathroom and wash area. Turning to leave, the officer hesitated.

"I wouldn't leave that there if I were you," she said, pointing to Alexa's guitar. "It'll disappear very quickly around here."

A large open room housing up to forty other women of various ages and backgrounds, the barracks provided almost no privacy. Trust and honesty could not be expected. The officer suggested Alexa might be able to trade or sell her guitar to one of the soldiers, although she wouldn't get much for it. She reasoned it would be better to at least get something for it, rather than having it stolen and be left with nothing to show for it. Alexa agreed the officer's suggestion would be a better idea, especially as she couldn't even play it. The officer took her to an American soldier whom she knew may be interested to make the trade. The soldier was happy to give Alexa a few American dollars for the instrument, and Alexa was happy to sell it.

After returning to her barracks, Alexa and Greta decided to explore the perimeter of the camp to familiarize themselves with their surroundings. There were many displaced people who, like them, were walking around the camp grounds. They were obviously trying to come to terms with having been liberated from the various hardships and imprisonments they'd had forced upon them, as well as now being relatively free again.

The looks on their faces told stories of torture, great suffering, and deep sorrow. Even though they were now relatively free, it was doubtful they would ever be entirely free from the memories etched into their minds—the ordeals they had endured and the horrific things they had witnessed and experienced during the war years.

As Alexa and Greta walked through the camp, they could feel the eyes of some of the other women staring at them intently. Alexa realized it must be due to their very different clothing. Everyone else was wearing old, dull clothes or plain army-issue work uniforms with worn-out old shoes, and looked far from attractive. In contrast, Alexa and Greta wore the dresses they had made out of the fancy colorful material Alexa had chosen, and the pretty pairs of relatively new shoes the American commander had sourced for them. They became more and more aware of the resentful stares and jealous mutterings as they passed by the women.

"Who do they think they are?"

"What do you think they had to do to get those dresses?"

"I wonder which Gestapo officer they slept with."

"I bet you they stole them."

Greta became increasingly upset by the unkind comments they overheard, while Alexa grew more irritated and angered by each one.

"Ignore them," said Alexa, linking her arm through Greta's. "They're only jealous."

Greta knew they were but she had less self-control than Alexa and was easily wound up. Suddenly, from behind them, they heard a woman's voice shout out. "Hey princesses, where's your castle?"

Alexa urged Greta to ignore her, but she couldn't. She stopped in her tracks and spun around to see who and where the offending woman was. As she did, she spotted who she thought was a familiar figure behind where the smirking woman was standing. She couldn't believe her eyes. Grabbing Alexa's arm, she pointed with her other hand.

"Look, Alexa! Is that who I think it is?"

Alexa looked in the direction of the figure and caught sight of a blonde walking into the Red Cross building. The jeering woman forgotten, the girls ran over to the building. To their amazement and joy, Greta's suspicion proved correct. There before them stood Henrietta, their dear friend whom they hadn't seen since the Allied soldiers had picked them up and taken them from the derelict house in Germany, four days prior.

"Henrietta!" they both shouted simultaneously.

Henrietta looked up, her eyes wide with surprise. Overcome with emotion, the three friends hugged each other tightly, laughing giddily like excited little girls. Marta entered the building, on her way to join Henrietta, and spotted her three friends locked in their ecstatic embrace. Running over to the girls, she threw her arms around them all.

"Marta!" exclaimed Alexa. "You're here too. Thank God you're both okay."

In an environment where there was little or nothing to celebrate or in which to find joy, the four friends were overjoyed they were reunited, all together in the same place.

"We are survivors, all of us," said Henrietta. "We survived being taken as children. We survived being worked as slaves by the SS. We survived that convent, those nasty nuns, and even the bombings, and here we are, together again."

They all agreed they had indeed been more than fortunate and took great comfort and strength from their survival.

"And we survived being captured by the Allied troops and brought here to France," added Greta.

"Yes, we did. God heard my prayers each time and made a way out for us and brought us all back together again," said Alexa.

"Well, whatever it was, I'm grateful. From here on, let's stay together until we all get home, no matter what," said Marta.

The four friends decided it would be best for them all to stay in the same barracks and to select bunks next to each other. Alexa suggested they quickly go back to the registration tent and explain the situation to the French female officer who had helped her sell her guitar, and request that Henrietta and Marta be allowed to take the empty bunkbed next to theirs.

The French officer agreed to their request and said she would change the records. She told them, however, that two women had been newly assigned to those beds, so they would have to ask them to move to another bunkbed at the end of the opposite side of the room. They thanked the officer and quickly made their way back to the barracks. The two women were already there but agreed to move when Henrietta insisted it was an order from the officer.

None of them had any belongings, except for Greta and Alexa. They both had their old clothes, rolled up and tied in a small bundle, which they had changed out of when they had put on their newly made dresses. Alexa no longer had the guitar but she did have a few U.S. dollars in its place.

Greta began telling Henrietta and Marta about everything that had happened to them since they had last been together at the derelict house. Marta and Henrietta were amazed at the schoolhouse story and about Alexa's bravery and boldness. They were shocked to hear about the priceless treasure Alexa had turned down and about the compassion and generosity the American commander had showed towards Alexa. They all laughed together over the Italian soldier instantly falling in love with Alexa and giving her his guitar; it wasn't hard to know why.

The hours passed and turned into days, then weeks and months, while they remained living in the camp. Everyone was given a job of some kind by the American troops and had daily duties to perform in return for food, clothing, shelter, and army protection.

Alexa and the three other young women were back doing laundry duties again on a large scale; they were very good at it, having had lots of practice while in German captivity. They could pretty much remove any stain or stubborn marks from a piece of fabric. Although they weren't being forced to work at hard manual labor, washing piles of laundry wasn't their prime ambition in life, nor was it an easy job. However, at least this time, working with the American and Allied soldiers, it was on a more voluntary basis, for the good of themselves and all the displaced people in the camp. They were relatively free for the first time in close to five years.

It was unclear to Alexa and her friends when they would be able to return home, as there was still much dangerous terrain throughout Europe. Many German soldiers and SS officers were running for cover and being chased and hunted down by the many Allied troops and the Russians, who were seeking revenge. So, the residents at the displacement camp stayed put, awaiting safer days ahead.

In return for their efforts, the workers were given smart American uniforms to wear as a form of identification, along with guaranteed food and shelter. They were also able to enjoy some time to relax and unwind when they weren't working or performing camp duties.

One warm Sunday evening, in the heat of the French July summer of 1945, Henrietta suggested that she, Alexa, and Greta try to borrow three bicycles from the French army and take a bike ride around the surrounding area, near to the camp. There was a little French village called Mourmelon-le-Petit close by, in which the American and Allied troops were made very welcome by the French locals. The three friends decided a cycle-ride together would be a welcome distraction and a great way to unwind a little.

Marta had caught a summer cold and would pass on the bike ride, choosing instead to stay and rest up in her bunk at the camp. Henrietta asked one of the young American soldiers whom she had gotten to know quite well if she and her two friends would be permitted to borrow some bicycles for a few hours to ride into town together. It wasn't something that was generally done, as the bicycles were primarily for the use of army personnel. But since the soldier had taken a real liking to Henrietta, he gave his permission. He said he would square it up with his commander if anyone asked and gave them special passes to leave the camp for a few hours.

As the three young women climbed onto the bikes, Alexa told her friends once again that she had only ridden a bicycle by herself once before, when she was a very young girl. She had been about seven years old at the time, and hadn't been very good at it. Undeterred, Alexa decided to try again. '*After all*,' she thought, '*how hard can it be?*'

She placed one foot on the ground and her other foot on the higher pedal; following Henrietta's lead, she pushed off and attempted to ride the bike. Her first try was unsuccessful, the bike toppling over and Alexa landing on the ground with a crash. Greta and Henrietta couldn't help but laugh and encouraged Alexa to try again.

Alexa rose to her feet, wiped herself down, and once again mounted the bicycle for a second attempt. This time, she was a little more successful, managing to get the wheels to move forward with both her feet on the pedals before losing her balance and falling off. She joined in her friends' laughter, finding it quite amusing herself. But she was determined to ride the bike and tried again, several times.

Her final attempt was successful and after a little more practice, she got the hang of it and rode along with her friends. The three of them headed off at a slow, steady pace, down the dirt road leading out of the camp and towards the village. The road was bumpy and full of potholes, but the young women managed to steer their way safely around them. They enjoyed the surrounding scenery of the beautiful French countryside as they rode past open fields, commenting on the breathtaking views—a welcome change of scenery to the displacement camp.

After cycling for about fifteen minutes, they arrived at the village of Mourmelon-le-Petit. They decided to use their ration cards to buy themselves a cold drink each. A little way ahead of them, at the bottom of a fairly steep hill, was a small restaurant with some tables and chairs set outside; a few American soldiers as well as some locals were sitting chatting together in the late summer sun. Henrietta suggested they stop there for a while; being in the lead, she steered her bicycle down the hill and over towards the restaurant, followed closely by Greta, with Alexa a little farther behind.

Henrietta and Greta came to a stop and pulled their bikes off the road, resting them against the side wall of the restaurant. They noticed they had caught the attention of the American soldiers, who were watching them approach with pleasure. Henrietta looked back towards Alexa, in time to see her whiz down the hill. For although Alexa had mastered riding a two-wheeled bicycle, she hadn't yet learned how to stop one. Alexa and her bike crashed into a giant bundle of hay positioned at the bottom of the hill. With a squeak, Alexa flew headfirst over the handlebars and disappeared into the middle of the giant haystack.

The American soldiers sitting outside the restaurant had a front row view of the live comedy show and erupted into laughter. Henrietta and Greta were also laughing hysterically at their friend's comical misfortune as they ran over to the pile of hay to help her.

"Are you alright Alexa?" Henrietta asked, trying to hold back her laughter.

"Yes, I'm fine," Alexa answered as she tried to climb out of the straw pile. Rather than a pretty, young woman neatly dressed in an American work uniform, what emerged was something resembling a disheveled old scarecrow with straw sticking out everywhere.

"What happened?" Greta asked.

"I didn't know how to stop the bike. I've never done it before," Alexa said.

Henrietta laughed even harder. "Are you serious?" she giggled. "All you needed to do was to pedal backwards to brake and the bike would have slowed down and stopped, you silly goose."

One of the American soldiers had got up from the table where he was sitting and made his way over to where Alexa was climbing out of the hay to see if he could be of assistance.

"Are you alright, young lady?" he asked.

Alexa flushed with embarrassment and quickly tried to brush the loose straw from her hair and clothing. She couldn't speak English but she guessed what he was saying.

"I no speak English," said Alexa. "*Sprechen Sie Deutsch?*"

The soldier then enquired in German if she was okay.

"Yes sir, I'm okay thank you."

"That was quite a trick you performed. Would you like me to recover your bicycle from inside the hay?"

"Yes, thank you, if it's not too much trouble."

The soldier began moving the straw apart, burrowing his way through in search of the bike. It didn't take him long to find it; pulling it out onto the road he shook off the straw. "There you go, it seems to be undamaged. What's your name?"

"I'm Alexa, and these are my two friends, Henrietta and Greta."

He shook their hands and greeted them politely before shifting his attention back to Alexa. "I've seen you around before, back at the camp, and hoped I'd get the chance to meet you in person one day."

Alexa blushed as she looked down at the ground. Her two friends turned and walked back towards the restaurant where they had left their bikes, leaving Alexa and the American soldier to chat alone.

"My name is Mark Austin, and I'm from Brooklyn, New York, in America. Where are you from originally?"

"I'm from Poland," Alexa answered, "but I have been away for five years now."

"That's a long time. You must really miss your family, and I'm sure they really miss you too."

"Yes, I can't wait to be reunited with them again."

"I'd like to buy you a drink—may I?" Mark asked.

"Yes, thank you. That would be nice; I'm rather thirsty after my bike ride."

"Yes, I'm sure, and it'll help get the taste of straw out of your mouth," said the soldier, grinning. Alexa smiled back at him.

Greta and Henrietta had sat down at a vacant table and were waiting for the waitress to come and take their order. They too had attracted the attention of a few soldiers. From time to time, they glanced over at their friend across the road, talking to the handsome American soldier, happy for the attention Alexa was receiving.

After a few minutes, Mark wheeled the bike over to the restaurant, rested it against the wall with the other bicycles, and invited Alexa over to a separate table to sit with him. The waitress went over to their table first and took their order.

"Two cokes please, unless the lady would like something stronger."

"No not for me; a coke would be nice, thank you."

"Has anyone ever told you how very beautiful you are?" Mark asked.

Alexa blushed again, not sure how to reply to his question. She hadn't received many compliments before and had never been alone with a man who was romantically interested in her. This was all new to her but his tall, dark, good looks hadn't escaped her attention.

"No," she answered, a small smile curving her lips, "but thank you."

The waitress returned with their drinks and placed the two icy-looking bottles of coke on the table, along with two glasses. She then proceeded to pour Mark's drink into his glass. Mark thanked her and told the waitress he'd take over, reaching for Alexa's bottle of coke. He poured it into her glass and placed it in front of her. Alexa thanked him, and the conversation began to flow naturally between them both. There was an obvious chemistry between them and a strong mutual attraction, obvious even to Henrietta and Greta sitting close by.

"I would love to see you again and perhaps take you out on a date," Mark said.

"I'll think about the date part but will also look forward to seeing you again," Alexa replied.

"Which department do you work in at the camp?"

"I'm assigned to the laundry department."

"Ah, good. Now I know where to find you."

They had chatted for about half an hour before Alexa thanked him for the coke and got up from the table. Mark said it had been his pleasure and he looked forward to seeing her again soon. Reaching for her hand, he gently kissed it as he stared adoringly into her eyes. Alexa felt her heart beat a little faster, a delighted smile illuminating her face. They said goodbye, and Alexa walked over to join Henrietta and Greta at their table. The women grinned at their friend, pleased she had received such attention from the handsome American soldier.

They finished their drinks and headed back to their bikes. As they wheeled them out onto the road, Alexa looked back towards the restaurant. Mark still had his eyes firmly fixed on her. He raised his hand and waved goodbye to her. Alexa waved back, then the three girls rode off on their bicycles, back in the direction of the displacement camp, as the sun began to set.

CHAPTER 16

Monday morning brought the start of a new work week to the camp. After eating their breakfast rations, the workers made their way to their various appointed workstations. Alexa and her three friends reported as usual to their positions in the camp's laundry department and began their duties with the other women assigned there, as they had done for the previous six months.

It was like being in a Turkish steam room. Intense heat rose from the vats of boiling water, filling the air like a heated fog or a train's released cloud of thick white steam. Despite the high temperatures, the workers had to manually beat the huge piles of never-ending laundry in the massive vats, stirring and thrashing them with large paddles, and scrubbing them on large metal scrubbing boards. Once rinsed of all traces of the laundering soap suds, the women had to feed the laundry manually through the heavy-duty jaws of the hand-wound mangles, to squeeze out the excess water before hanging up all the items to dry. Once hanging, the large number of white sheets resembled a sailing regatta.

The laundry building never shut down and its workers were rotated on twelve-hour shifts, so the mass piles of dirty laundry were always being cleaned around the clock. It was physically exhausting work. However, the women received a small wage for their efforts and were a vital and necessary part of the camp's functionality and hygiene.

That Monday, a little past mid-morning, two American soldiers entered the laundry department and began scanning the area, looking at the workers. Henrietta nudged Alexa, pointing them out to her friend who popped her head up from what she was doing to look over in their direction.

One of the soldiers spoke to the female supervisor, who was also an American soldier, and then handed her some paperwork. After reading the document, the supervisor looked down at a list on her desk and then pointed in the direction where Alexa and her friends were working. The three Americans spoke among themselves for a few more minutes before walking over to the young women. The supervisor stopped in front of Greta, told her to stop what she was doing, and asked her to please follow them. Next, she walked over to Alexa and told her to stop what she was doing.

"You have both been selected to work at the camp's supply store, so you will no longer be needed here in the laundry department as of today. You will go now with these two soldiers, and they will take you to your new positions," instructed the supervisor.

Henrietta was close by and overheard what had been said to her friends. As pleased as she was for her two friends to be leaving the hard and tedious work of the laundry department, she couldn't help but wish she too had been selected to go with them. Unfortunately, both she and Marta had not been picked to go to the new jobs and would have to remain where they were.

"See you later," said Alexa to her friends as she and Greta followed the two American officers outside, through the camp, and over to the supply store.

"How lucky are we?" said Greta, smiling.

"Well, just hold on a minute, we don't know what we'll be doing yet," Alexa cautioned.

"I know, but it's got to be better than doing laundry all day long. My hands will be glad of the rest and to be out of the water. That I do know."

They arrived at the Red Cross supply store where the soldiers took them inside and over to a main registration desk, where their names and details were written down in a large book. Then they were taken to the back of the main supply storage area where a female American officer took over and began showing Alexa and Greta where they would work and what their new duties would be.

"I hope you can both count and write," said the officer.

"Yes," they replied, "we can."

"Good, then you shouldn't have any problems here."

She directed them over to a large shipment of army blankets that had recently arrived and told them to start counting them. They then had to check the totals off against the shipping list and log the numbers into the ledger she'd given to them.

"See, I told you this job was going to be much better than doing laundry," said Greta, and Alexa had to agree with her.

The task of counting and recording all the army issue blankets took them a few hours to complete, and when they had finished, they began stacking them on storage shelves. Once their work was checked over by the supervisor, they were free to go for lunch. They made their way over to the large Red Cross building where the main canteen was and joined the line of other hungry workers waiting for food. Each person received a bowl of warm, watered-down vegetable soup and a buttered bread roll, which they ate wherever they could find a space at one of the many long wooden tables in the large dining room.

Alexa and Greta looked around the room for their two friends but, surprisingly, they couldn't see them. After they had finished their lunch, they made their way back to their new place of work. There, the supervisor gave them the details of their next job assignment and showed them to the area where they'd be working. A large crate of soap had been offloaded from one of the trucks, and Alexa and Greta were instructed to count and log them all into the ledger; they then had to place them into smaller boxes, one hundred bars in each box. They started working right away, both quite enjoying their new task.

A little while later, the supervisor escorted two young men dressed in plain American workers' uniforms and carrying a toolbox and stepladders to an area close to where Alexa was working. There was an electrical problem in the building, and several of the overhead lights weren't working. The two men were electricians and immediately began investigating the root of the problem. One of the men was particularly handsome—tall, blond and blue eyed—which both women hadn't failed to notice as he had first walked past them.

"Hey Alexa, he could easily pass for your brother," joked Greta.

"Very funny, I don't have a brother."

"Well, if he was your brother, I'd be wanting you to introduce me to him."

From high up on a ladder, the handsome electrician glanced over to the two women from time to time. He seemed to be rather distracted by one of them in particular. Alexa's beauty hadn't escaped his notice and he seemed to do a double-take every now and again, as if to make sure his eyes weren't deceiving him. Alexa subtly kept an eye on him as well, while she continued working but made a conscious effort not to catch his eye or let him see her obvious interest in him.

After a while, he came down from the ladder and began searching through his toolbox. Seemingly unable to find what he was looking for, he told his assistant to go and fetch the parts he needed to complete the repairs. While he waited for the other man to return, he casually strolled over to where Alexa was working and confidently introduced himself.

"Bonjour, Mademoiselle, my name is Antoni. May I ask what your name is?" he asked.

"Hello, my name is Alexa."

"I haven't seen you here before, and believe me when I say I would definitely have remembered you if I had."

Alexa wanted to look away from his captivating stare, but her eyes were transfixed by his and she couldn't disconnect. She was amazed at how handsome he was up close and even more amazed at how her heart seemed to have skipped a beat when he spoke to her.

"So, how long have you been working here in the supply store?" Antoni asked.

"Today is my first day here. I was working in the laundry department until this morning."

"Then today must be my lucky day, Alexa," he replied with a flirtatious smile.

Alexa didn't voice it out loud but she was thinking the very same thought. She glanced at Greta who continued counting the soap boxes nearby, while Antoni flirted with her friend. Alexa thought he came across as very confident and rather sure of himself, which no doubt stemmed from his handsome good looks. He was probably used to having women fall at his feet, hanging on his every word and doing exactly what he wanted, with minimal effort on his part. Well, with her he'd have to put in some extra effort if he wanted to win her favor.

"You smell like a garden full of fresh roses," he complimented her.

"It's probably all the soap you can smell."

"Would you like me to lift up those boxes of soap for you? They look far too heavy for the likes of someone as pretty and delicate as you to be handling."

"Thanks for asking, but it's okay; we don't have to move them ourselves. We only have to leave them packed and stacked."

"Okay, if you're sure," he said as his assistant reappeared with the parts he had sent him to fetch.

"I have to get back up the ladder now, Alexa, and fix the lighting, but why don't I meet you outside after you've finished work and we can chat some more and get to know each other a bit better?"

Alexa wanted to say yes but at the same time didn't want to appear too eager. So, she made up the excuse that she had to meet her two other girlfriends straight after work.

"Well, what about tomorrow then?"

"Maybe."

"No maybes; say yes for definite. I will wait for you outside of here after work ends tomorrow. Okay?" Antoni insisted.

"Yes, okay then," agreed Alexa.

"Good, I look forward to getting to know more about you."

Antoni smiled and winked at her as he made his way back up the stepladder to complete the electrical repairs. Alexa got back to the job assigned to her but couldn't take the grin off her face.

"Well look at you," said Greta. "Two men swooning over you in two days. It's like you put them in a trance or something," she grinned. "And let's not forget the poor young Italian soldier who serenaded you and gave you his guitar. He's probably still pining over you. What is it with you, Alexa?"

"They all came to me, let me remind you. I didn't go looking for them, nor did I give out invitations," she replied. "I can't help it if they like me."

Greta knew what her friend was saying was true, and even she couldn't deny Alexa's natural beauty. She knew Alexa hadn't in any way instigated the attention she was receiving, but still, deep down, Greta was a little envious that such interest hadn't been aimed in her direction.

As the afternoon ticked away, the two women concentrated on completing the tasks assigned to them in their new job and did so with relative ease and little further distraction. As the clock approached 4 pm, about an hour before they would finish their workday, a familiar face appeared in the supply store and made his way over to where Alexa was working.

"Good afternoon, pretty lady," said the tall, dark, and handsome man as he stood behind Alexa.

"Good afternoon, sir," said Alexa, turning quickly.

"Please don't call me sir. Mark will do just fine. So, how do you like your new job?"

"I like it very much, it's a nice change from being in the laundry department."

"Oh good, I'm so glad. I heard they were looking for two new female workers here, so I thought of you and your friend after meeting you both yesterday. I was able to pull some strings . . . and here you both are."

Suddenly, there was a loud crash of clanging metal, distracting their attention and bringing their conversation to an abrupt halt. Antoni had dropped one of his tools from up on the stepladder, shifting their attention away from each other and onto him. Antoni seemed quite pleased he had caused the distraction and waved to Alexa as he waited for his assistant to hand the wrench back up to him—perhaps the dropped tool wasn't entirely accidental. However, it only caused a brief pause between Alexa and Mark who quickly resumed their conversation.

"So, it was you who suggested us for this job," exclaimed Alexa. "Thank you very much, Mark; that was very thoughtful of you."

"You're very welcome. I thought this work would be easier on you both and that you'd be good at it too. I also knew it'd

IN ALEXA'S SHOES

be a good way for me to see you more often, as I regularly stop by here on a daily basis," Mark said, smiling at Alexa. "So, did you think any more about going out on a date with me?" he asked.

Alexa could see Antoni staring at her intently from the top of the stepladder while Mark, standing right in front of her, awaited her reply.

"No, I'm sorry but I haven't really had the time; I've been too busy today with my new job."

"No problem. I'll let you think it over some more, then I will ask you again tomorrow."

Greta came to Alexa's aid with the excuse she needed her help to check over her numbers. Alexa, relieved, politely excused herself. They said goodbye and Alexa hurriedly joined Greta.

"Thanks for that."

"No problem, but what are you going to do now? You can't go out with both of them."

"I know," said Alexa. "Now I have a real dilemma on my hands. They are both good looking and both seem really nice."

"Well, here comes the tall blond one again, so you better think fast," whispered Greta.

All the main overhead lights were now working, and Antoni's assistant was packing up their tools. Antoni wasted no time and quickly walked over to Alexa. He asked her once again if she would be able to meet him after she finished work that day instead of the next. Alexa sensed he was being somewhat more determined with her this time, which she put down to his seeing her chat with Mark. She stuck to her excuse of having to meet her friends after work but agreed she'd still meet him the next day.

Alexa felt butterflies in her stomach when she spoke with him and seemed very smitten with the handsome young man, much more so than she did when speaking with Mark.

Antoni said goodbye, and he and his assistant left the supply store. The two young women returned to completing their work for the day.

Alexa and Greta headed back to their barracks and waited there until Marta and Henrietta returned. They all made their way to the cafeteria building for their main meal. The conversation centered around Alexa and Greta's new jobs and why it was they had been selected for the two new positions over everyone else at the laundry station. It was Greta who filled her two friends in on the reason behind it.

"Well, it seems that getting our new jobs today was all thanks to the American soldier Alexa met yesterday after her bicycle acrobatics. It was he who suggested us for the jobs as he probably wanted to get in Alexa's favor and also be able to see her more easily and more often," explained Greta.

"Well, aren't you two the lucky ones? But hey, didn't he see you had another friend with you yesterday?" Henrietta asked Alexa.

"I'm sure he did, but I think they only needed two new people at the supply store."

Maybe tomorrow Alexa will be moved once again to another, even easier job," said Greta sarcastically. "Today she got another handsome new admirer—tall, blond, and even better-looking than the American one yesterday."

"Really, another one?" said Marta.

"And she has a date to meet with him tomorrow after she finishes work," added Greta.

"But aren't you supposed to be going on a date with the American?" asked Henrietta. "You better be careful, else you'll start another war!"

"Well I never! Never before been on a date and now she's got two dates in twenty-four hours with two good looking young men. You're so lucky, Alexa," Marta said.

"Okay, enough already. Let's change the subject," Alexa said.

"No, let's not, we're all actually quite enjoying this one," said Greta, laughing.

They finished their food while continuing to tease and quiz Alexa about her two suitors.

"So, who is this latest man?" Henrietta asked. "Tell us more about him."

"His name is Antoni and he's an electrician," answered Alexa.

"Where is he from?"

"I don't know. I never asked him, but I think he's also displaced, like us. He spoke to me in German."

"So, who do you like more out of the two of them?" Greta asked.

"If it was up to me, I'd pick the American. Then you could marry him and go live in Brooklyn, and start a whole new, safe and easy life with him away from Europe," said Henrietta.

"Well, they are both very handsome and seem really nice, but I did feel my heart beat a little faster when I spoke to Antoni," said Alexa.

"Ooh, was it love at first sight? Did you get butterflies in your belly?" Marta asked jokingly.

"I think I did actually, only I didn't know what they were at the time."

They giggled like giddy little schoolgirls as they left the building. They set off on a leisurely walk around the camp before retiring for the evening, all the while giving Alexa advice for her date with Antoni.

Sunrise brought the dawn of a brand-new day and while the majority of the workers in the camp were preparing themselves for another boring workday, no different from all those prior to it, for Alexa, this day held great excitement. Although she felt nervous and apprehensive about her first ever date at the end of her work shift, she was also very much looking forward to it and could think of little else the whole day.

Finally, the last hour of her work shift arrived. She found an old mirror in front of which she spent a little time straightening her clothes and fixing her hair in order to look her very best for Antoni. However, being such a natural beauty, very little effort was needed; just as well as there were no cosmetics, makeup, or fancy beauty products available to assist any of the women in the camp. Greta looked her friend over from head to toe and gave her a nod of approval. After her own final inspection Alexa said, "Wish me luck."

"You don't need any luck, my beautiful friend. Any man would be lucky to have a date with you."

"Thanks, Greta, but I don't feel so beautiful."

Alexa took a final look at the clock as the hour hand reached five. The two friends left their workstation together and headed towards the exit. Walking out into the daylight they saw Antoni across the way, leaning against a tree and smoking a cigarette as he waited patiently for his date. Alexa said goodbye to Greta and walked over to Antoni.

"Hello, beautiful, how are you today?" Antoni asked her.

Alexa immediately felt a flurry of butterflies fluttering inside her stomach and her heart again skipped a beat. Antoni dropped his cigarette to the ground and ground it under his boot. From behind his back, he produced a single yellow rose surrounded by a bunch of wildflowers he had hand-picked from a nearby field. He offered them to Alexa who excitedly reached out to take them. Their hands touched briefly for the first time, and their eyes locked. The thrill was palpably electric and Alexa felt as though she could hardly breathe as they stared at each other for a moment.

"Thank you so much, they're lovely," Alexa said eventually, a delighted expression on her face.

"Lovely flowers for a lovely young lady. Come on, let's get away from here."

They began walking away from the buildings of the busy camp and headed off towards the surrounding fields. The picturesque French countryside surrounded them, making the perfect backdrop for their first date. After walking together for a while, Antoni led them through a meadow to a nearby stream, and suggested they sit by large oak tree under its canopy of huge leafy branches. Anthony took off his uniform jacket; placing it inside out and face downward on the grass, he invited Alexa to sit. Alexa sat down, still holding her bunch of flowers in her hand.

"I wish I had some fresh baguettes, French cheese and some fine red wine to serve you, Mademoiselle, but alas I do not."

"Oh, don't worry about that," said Alexa. "I'm happy just to be here with you and you've picked a most charming spot for us to enjoy."

Antoni reached into his pocket and retrieved a bar of dark chocolate. "Well, I do have something nice for you to eat." He opened the paper wrapping and placed the bar of chocolate on top of his jacket, next to Alexa. He broke it up into small pieces and invited Alexa to help herself. Alexa appreciated that he had obviously put some thought into their date, even though he had very few resources.

"Thank you, I love chocolate."

Her mind immediately travelled back to the last time she had eaten some. She remembered being held in the old schoolhouse with all the Germans, and how she had boldly stood up for herself, declaring she was in fact a Polish citizen and had been taken prisoner by the Nazis, years prior. The kind American commander had sympathized and given her several bars of chocolate.

Then in an instant, her memories shifted to the old man who had appeared on the dark road on that cold winter's night when she was lost and trying to find her way to the convent. He had appeared like a guardian angel out of nowhere, an answer to her prayers; keeping her company, he had showed her the way and shared his bar of chocolate with her.

"What are you thinking about?" Antoni asked.

"Oh, only about the last times I had chocolate to eat."

"Tell me about it."

So, Alexa began telling him of the last two times she had had chocolate. She then rewound her story back to its nightmare beginning, telling Antoni of how she was originally taken from her mother in Poland, almost five years earlier. Antoni listened intently to every word of her story; several times he seemed visibly uncomfortable and smoked two cigarettes while she spoke. Alexa put it down to the stressful nature of her story.

". . . and then I was moved to the job in the supply store on Monday, met you, and here we are on our first date," she finished with a smile.

"That's quite a story, Alexa. You have been through a lot."

"Yes, but I always tell myself it could have been much worse. There are so many people who have suffered horrifically during the war and have perished. Me, I've always had God on my side, and he's kept me safe. I'm still alive, and soon I will make it back home and hopefully find my mother and sister there waiting for me."

"You have a very positive attitude despite what you've been through. That's good. You also don't seem to hold hatred or malice towards the Germans."

"Well, I suppose I don't really. Don't get me wrong, I despise what the Nazis have done to millions of people under Hitler's direction, but I don't hate all German people because of it. I believe that when hate is encouraged, supported, and allowed to run loose in society, the stronger it becomes. Hate is like a poison that can infect and quickly spread, becoming pandemic. Look at the influence Hitler's hatred of the Jews has had on such a mass scale. His toxic hatred became divisive, destructive, and deadly."

"You are right, Alexa. What you're saying is so true."

"Just look at how the Jewish race has been mistreated, terrorized, tortured, and almost totally annihilated across Europe, and for what? What did they ever do that was so terrible? They raised families, worked hard, and worshipped their God. Isn't that what we all should have the right to do?"

"You're right, Alexa," he said again. "I agree with you."

"I'm glad you do because it's very clear that through peoples' indifference and intolerance, hate spreads like wildfire. Look how it spread throughout Europe to non-Jews. Look at my life and that of my mother's. We were Catholic and yet our lives and the lives of so many others have been forever changed, all because of the spread of Hitler's hatred. So no, Antoni, I will not allow a breeding ground for hatred in my life. Love is the answer, only love. And I place my trust in God, the true source of love. He promises everyone will answer to him on judgement day and he will repay the wicked for their evil deeds."

"You have very strong faith for a woman so young. I wish I had such faith."

"Now, tell me your story, Antoni. Where are you and your family from?" Alexa asked, reaching for another piece of chocolate. How did you end up here in France at the displacement camp?"

CHAPTER 17

Antoni took out another cigarette and lit it, exhaling a cloud of grey smoke before answering. "My family are from Gryfów Śląski in Poland. I was born there."

"Does that make you Polish or German?"

"It was originally Polish land, and then in the 1740's, Prussia ruled over it. Years later it reverted back to Polish territory, and now it is back under German jurisdiction, but I don't think it will remain that way now the war is over. It was German land when I was born there, so technically and geographically I'm German, but I tell people I'm Polish. My family moved to Łódź when I was a small boy, and I went to school there. I grew up in Poland, speaking Polish and living Polish. I'm as good as Polish," Antoni said nervously.

"Oh, I see," said Alexa, somewhat surprised.

"Please, you must keep this between us. No one here can know I am geographically German. Please promise me, Alexa; you're the only person I've told."

Alexa admired his honesty; she knew how easy it would have been for him to lie about that fact to her and she would have been none the wiser. But she wanted to know more about him before committing to keep his secret.

"What have you been doing during the war?"

"My family used to be very wealthy. My grandfather owned five large and very successful fabric factories in Poland. Unfortunately, he was killed in a tragic car accident, and my

197

father and his siblings had to take over the running of the businesses. We lived very well in our large family home in Łódź. We wanted for nothing and had the best of everything. My parents were very happy."

Antoni stood up. He lit another cigarette while he paced away from the oak tree towards the edge of the stream and back again, staring at the ground as he walked. "Then the Nazis came. They took our factories and all we owned from us. They took our stately home and threw us all out onto the street with nothing. My father was forced to go and work for the German army. They gave him the job of handing out minimal ration cards to those Polish citizens who qualified for them; they were starving and had very little to survive on."

Alexa was riveted by Antoni's story and hung on his every word. She could feel the deep emotion pouring out from the young man.

"My father was a good-hearted man and deeply distressed by the plight of the desperate Polish families whom he saw lining up in front of him for their ration cards. He was so determined to help the Polish people that he began stealing extra ration cards which he would secretly give to Polish families with small children. Until one day, someone—an informant—reported him to the Gestapo and he was immediately removed from his post. I've never seen him again since that day, and even though I tried to search for any trace of him, there was no further information. There were rumors he'd perhaps been sent as a prisoner to a concentration camp. I don't even know if he's still alive."

"That's awful. I'm so sorry, Antoni," said Alexa, her voice filled with compassion.

He moved closer to her, sitting down on the grass to her left. Alexa gently placed her left hand on his right forearm but Antoni abruptly pulled his arm away. Alexa was startled, thinking she had done something wrong.

"I'm..." she started to apologize but Antoni was unbuttoning his cuff. Rolling up his sleeve, he held out his exposed right arm.

"Look. Do you see this?" Antoni pointed at his arm. It was heavily scarred over a large section, from the tendon of his right thumb, all the way up through his wrist, a long his veins, and up past his elbow.

"What happened to you? Who did this to you?" Alexa asked, tears welling in her eyes at the thought of the physical pain she could only imagine he must have gone through.

"I did it!"

Alexa was shocked. "What do you mean you did it?"

"I knew the Nazis were going to force me to join the German army, and I was determined I would not be placed in the position to kill innocent people. So, I took a sharp knife and hacked away at my own right arm in the hope they would find me unfit for combat. It was the most painful physical experience I've ever endured and took a long time to heal. But it worked because I was trained as an electrician instead." He turned and stared into Alexa's deep blue eyes. "And that training brought me to work in the supply store yesterday, and brought me here to you today. Electricity brought me to you, Alexa."

Alexa's eyes were fixed firmly on his. There was a moment of silence and then Antoni leaned in and kissed her gently on the lips. It was Alexa's very first kiss and she wasn't quite sure what to do, but she didn't want to pull back. Secretly, she had wanted him to kiss her from the very first minute they had met. The kiss lasted a few seconds before Antoni pulled back.

"So, you see, you must keep my secret. No one can ever know I am German. They wouldn't understand."

"I will keep your secret. I'll tell no one, I promise."

Antoni had gained her trust and leaned in once again to kiss Alexa. This time he reached his arms around her, holding her closely to him in a tight embrace. The kiss lasted considerably longer than the first one, and Alexa hopelessly melted into Antoni's arms. She could have stayed there all day, absorbed in the comfort and safety she felt, wrapped in Antoni's arms—something she had never felt before. '*This must be love,*' she thought blissfully.

Eventually, Antoni peeled his lips from Alexa's. Releasing her, he reached for her hand. "I want you to be my girlfriend. Will you be my girl?"

Alexa was still trying to catch her breath and felt quite light-headed after their second kiss, but she didn't need much time to think about the question or to give him her answer. "Yes, I'll be your girl, Antoni."

The warm July evening drew to a close as the sun gradually sank down from the deep crimson sky towards the horizon. Antoni suggested they start heading back to the camp, realizing it was getting quite late and they had missed dinner already. Neither of them seemed too bothered by that fact, nor were they very hungry, which was just as well.

Antoni stood up and helped Alexa to her feet. Handing her the remainder of the chocolate bar, he picked up his jacket and shook off the loose grass. He took another cigarette out of his pocket and raised it towards his mouth, but instead he stopped and pulled Alexa close to him, laying another kiss on her soft lips. By now she was getting the hang of it and kissed him right back.

Antoni lit his cigarette; holding it in one hand he took Alexa's hand in the other and led her through the tall grass and out of the meadow. Alexa felt like she was walking on clouds. '*Yes, this must indeed be what love feels like,*' she thought and happily held on to Antoni's hand.

When they arrived back at the camp, Antoni said he'd meet her again the next day after work outside the supply store. Alexa agreed and they shared one final lingering kiss goodnight before leaving each other's company.

"Don't forget your promise, Alexa. Tell no one I'm German. Okay, my beautiful girlfriend?"

"Okay, I won't forget, I promise. It's our secret."

"Goodnight."

Alexa turned and walked towards her barracks where she knew her friends would be waiting for her return and anxious to hear all about her date. She'd tell them about most of it, except about Antoni's history or where he was born. She'd keep his secret as she'd promised.

As she entered their room, Greta was the first to notice her and announced her arrival to Marta and Henrietta. They all noticed the glow radiating from her and how ecstatically happy she appeared to be.

"Alexa's in love," chanted Marta. "Alexa's in love."

"So, and what if I am?" Alexa replied with a large smile on her face, not denying it.

"Tell us all about it," said Henrietta. "How did your date go with the electrician?"

"It was great and he's now my boyfriend," announced Alexa as she plopped down onto her bed.

"Does that mean you kissed?" Marta asked, sitting down next to Alexa.

"Maybe it does. We sat by a stream and talked for a while. He brought me a bar of dark chocolate and even gave me flowers. Oh no!" Alexa exclaimed.

"What is it?" Greta asked.

"I forgot to pick up my flowers. I left them behind where we were sitting."

"You must have had your mind on other things," jibed Marta.

"Don't worry; if you're his girlfriend now, I'm sure he will be giving you plenty more flowers," said Greta.

"Does this mean you'll not be interested in a date with the American soldier now?" Henrietta asked.

"That's right, I'll have to tell him I'm not interested in going out with him. But you three are very welcome to go on a date with him if you wish," said Alexa with a wink. They all laughed, except for Greta.

"Poor Mark, he looked miserable. He came by and asked where you were and I told him you were out with Antoni. You've broken his heart, you know, Alexa," said Greta.

"I haven't," said Alexa with a toss of her head. "It's not as if we'd started going out or anything. Oh, please don't say he's miserable Greta. I couldn't bear that."

Greta gave her friend's shoulder a squeeze. "He'll be fine," she said. "In any case, there are plenty of girls who'd give their eye teeth to go out with Mark. He'll get over it."

"Yes, he'll be fine," said Alexa with determination.

It was getting late and Alexa was tired from her long day and all its excitement. All she wanted to do was to climb into her bed by herself, reflect on her date with Antoni, and drift off to sleep daydreaming about him, but she knew her friends wouldn't be able to leave her in peace. Not until their curiosity was satisfied. So, like the good friend she was, Alexa answered all their questions as best as she could, all the while remaining conscious of her promise to Antoni to keep his secret.

The following morning, the girls headed off to work after they had finished breakfast. Alexa was especially hungry as she had missed dinner the night before and ate two helpings of watery scrambled eggs. Soon after Marta and Henrietta arrived at work in the laundry department, an American and a French officer appeared, asking to speak to Henrietta. She went with them then returned to her workstation about half an hour later.

"What did they want with you?" Marta asked.

"Apparently, an Allied truck is going to transport some people from here back to the Netherlands. They say it should be safe to return now and, since I'm Dutch, I've been selected to go home."

"When?"

"Tomorrow!"

The two friends stared at each other for a moment, as the reality of her words sank in, and then began hugging one another. As much as Henrietta had wanted to go home for so long and this had remained her ultimate goal, knowing she'd be setting off the next day was rather overwhelming.

For Marta, it was also a shock and hard to process. She was happy for her friend to be finally returning home to find her family, but her heart ached at the thought they'd soon be parted, after being so close, like sisters, for so long.

"I'm going to miss you more than you know, Henrietta. My days will be empty without you," said Marta, trying desperately to fight back her tears but some escaped and trickled down her cheeks.

"Please don't cry, Marta, I'm trying to be strong right now. Anyway, you'll probably be next. We'll all be going home soon. We knew the day would eventually come."

"What about Greta? Is there a transportation to Denmark, too?" Marta asked.

"Oh, I never thought. I don't know. They never mentioned that to me. We'll have to find Greta and ask."

The girls finished working their morning shift and when lunchtime arrived, went off in search of Greta and Alexa to tell them the news. Filled with sadness, they all seemed to lose their appetites. Henrietta tried to be strong, and insisted she needed a sweet black coffee for the shock. They all got themselves a cup and sat drinking them together. Greta had heard nothing about the transportation arrangement that morning, so they assumed she wouldn't be included in it.

"Let's not go back to work this afternoon," suggested Greta. "Let's spend our last afternoon together."

The four friends looked at each other and nodded in agreement. It seemed to be the best idea, and even the thought of it made them all feel a little bit happier under the circumstances. They'd take advantage of the situation and make the most of the limited time they had left together. They finished drinking their coffee, then grabbing a fresh apple each to take with them, they headed off together out of the displacement camp.

They made their way towards the nearby French countryside and into an open field. The four friends spent several hours relaxing in the tall grass, chatting and laughing as they spent their last afternoon together in each other's company, lying in the hot July sun. They all agreed that no matter where they ended up, or whatever paths their lives took them down, they would always remain good friends. They vowed they'd all find each other again somehow and that they'd keep in touch until they were old and grey.

The hours went by very quickly, and soon it was time for them to make their way back to the camp in time for dinner. They decided to return to their barracks to clean up first before going to eat. On Greta's bed there was a note which had been left for her attention, ordering her to report to the main army office as soon as possible. The four friends looked at each other in silence, as if they already knew the reason for the note. They all went together to the main army office and, as they had suspected, Greta was informed she too had been selected to travel to Holland on the same truck as Henrietta, as a first step on her journey home to Denmark. They would be leaving first thing in the morning.

The four friends made their way to dinner for their last meal together. While they were sitting eating, Antoni came to their table to speak to Alexa. She introduced him to Henrietta and Marta, whom he hadn't yet met. They were both glad to meet him, noticing how handsome he was in person. Alexa and Greta hadn't exaggerated about his good looks. Antoni asked Alexa to come and speak with him alone, so she got up from the table and walked outside with him.

"I waited for you after work today. Why didn't you meet me as we had agreed?" Antoni enquired.

"I'm so sorry, Antoni, but at lunch we discovered that Henrietta has been selected to be transported back to Holland tomorrow morning. We all skipped work this afternoon so that we could spend our last day together. Now we've just found out that Greta is leaving with her too."

"Oh, I see, but that's good news, right? That they are finally going home?"

"They are my best friends and we've all been together every day since the convent. We are family now. We are all going to miss each other so much, and who knows what they will find when they return home?"

"I don't suppose you want to spend some time with me after dinner, do you?" Antoni asked.

"I'm sorry, but I want to spend this last evening with my friends."

Antoni looked disappointed but nodded his understanding. "Can I see you tomorrow after work then?"

"Yes, I'll meet you outside the supply store when I finish work."

Antoni leaned over and kissed her cheek. Alexa said goodbye and headed back to her friends.

"So that's your handsome boyfriend," said Henrietta, grinning. "He's a good looker alright. I'm glad I got to meet him before I left here."

"Are you going to marry him, Alexa?" Marta asked her.

"Well, he's not asked me yet."

"Don't let that stop you," said Greta, and they all laughed.

After dinner, they made their way back to their room in their barracks for their final night together. They tried to write down a reliable address where they could be contacted when they got back home—a difficult task since they didn't know the situation at their homes. They were full of mixed emotions. Alexa suggested she say her prayer for them all out loud, and her three friends agreed.

They knelt together, closed their eyes, and clasped their hands. As she recited Psalm 91, Alexa changed some words from singular to plural, using "us" and "we" instead of "me" and "I." Once she reached the end of the psalm, she said a firm "Amen," echoed by Henrietta, Greta, and Marta. This time, the three of them said it with more conviction and hope than they ever had before. And then they slept.

The morning arrived all too soon and the young women awoke to grey, overcast skies and a light rainfall. Washed and dressed, Henrietta and Greta bundled their meager belongings together before they all made their way to one last breakfast together. Their mood was somber, and the girls were visibly saddened.

Soon, it was time for Greta and Henrietta to board the truck, bid their friends *au revoir* and begin their journey home. There was a small group of people gathered around the truck.

Reluctantly, the girls started saying their final goodbyes and hugged each other tightly.

One of the French soldiers asked loudly, "Okay, so who's traveling to Belgium and Holland on this truck?"

His question caught Marta's attention as she was, after all, from Belgium but she hadn't been told she was to go on the truck with the others.

"Ask if you are meant to go with us," said Henrietta.

Marta told the soldier she was from Belgium and asked if she should be getting on the truck. The soldier checked his list for her name and said yes, she was indeed on it and was supposed to be traveling on the same transport. Marta panicked; no one had informed her and she didn't have her belongings ready to leave. The soldier told her to go and get them quickly; she was to hurry up as the truck would wait for her for ten minutes only.

Alexa went back to the barracks with Marta, running all the way there and back. They hardly had time to process the reality of the situation. Alexa, however, understood clearly what it meant for her. She was going to be left alone. Her three friends were all leaving together on the truck to return to their homes, but she was staying behind. Alone again.

The truck engine revved loudly. All the passengers were on board except for Greta, Henrietta, and Marta. They all hugged Alexa one last time as they tried to fight back their tears. They climbed into the back of the truck and it pulled off as they waved and blew kisses to Alexa, tears rolling down their faces. Alexa was left standing alone in the rain, watching the vehicle as it rumbled out the camp gates and disappeared into the distance. Her friends were gone, gone too soon.

Alexa made her way to the supply store where she was due to start work. She hadn't had to work alone since she was at the Klausses' farmhouse. Her American supervisor came over and inquired as to where Greta was and why they both hadn't showed up for work the previous afternoon. Alexa began to explain what had happened with her friends the previous day; she tried hard to keep her emotions in check but failed miserably. She couldn't hold back the tears that streamed from her eyes as she told her story.

Thankfully, the female supervisor was empathetic to Alexa's version of events and sympathized with her as best as she could. "Look, I'm sure you'll be going home soon too, Alexa, back to Poland. I hear it's safer there now. You'll probably be reunited with your family and friends too, whom you haven't seen for so long. Then you can get in touch with Greta and your other two friends again when you're settled. How you're feeling now is only temporary, believe me," she tried to reason.

The woman's positive words helped to calm Alexa somewhat. She dried her tears, composed herself and prepared to start her day's work. *I've gotten through tougher days than this,'* Alexa thought as she shifted her focus onto her work.

CHAPTER 18

Alexa's workday finally came to an end and she headed outside the supply store. Antoni was waiting there for her, as he said he would be.

"Hello, beautiful! How are you today?" Antoni asked as she walked over towards him.

"I'm glad to see you, but it's been a really tough day. All three of my best friends left the camp this morning, and I'm all alone again."

"You're not alone, Alexa. You've got me, and I'm not planning to leave you anytime soon." He reached out his hand and pulled her close, holding her in his arms. She felt comforted and reassured by his words as she nuzzled her head into his chest. Antoni held her tightly and stroked her hair. "Don't worry. You've got me, I'll look after you, darling."

They headed off towards the canteen building and ate their first meal together, which would prove to be the first of many. Eating together became the young couple's new routine and from then on, they spent almost every spare moment in each other's company when they weren't working. They were inseparable.

In their conversations, Antoni regularly brought up the subject of leaving the displacement camp and of finally returning home to Poland with Alexa. Even before the official end of the Second World War on 2 September, 1945, many of the displaced Europeans had gradually begun to try and make the long and difficult journey back to their homes by any means possible. They were searching for what they had lost, for what had been left behind, and for what was violently and horrifically stolen from them, as well as for the familiar—their families, their friends, their homes, their belongings . . . their lives.

Antoni had managed to save up a small amount of money by doing some private electrical repair jobs in a few of the local French homes and businesses. It wasn't much, but it was something. He had also won some money from gambling in occasional card games with both the American and Allied troops. He was deceptively good at poker and had a great poker face. He started making plans for them to leave France and make the long journey back to Poland together. Alexa told him she didn't have any money, nor did she really own anything of value besides her grandmother's necklace with the cross. It probably wasn't worth much beyond sentimental value, but to her it was priceless.

Antoni explained to Alexa that when they were ready to leave, it would be best for them to get a ride into Paris on one of the Allied trucks and from there to catch a train to Berlin. They'd have to change trains in Berlin, but from there they could board a train that would take them to Warsaw, in the center of Poland. Once there, they could travel relatively easily by train or bus to Łódź, where Antoni's mother and father lived and where he had grown up. Hopefully once there, he would locate his father, Fritz, or at least be able to begin the search for him. Next in their plans would be to travel to Alexa's hometown of Lublin, in search of her mother, Sophia, and her sister, Asha. After that, there was no plan. They would go day by day and try to rebuild a new life for themselves.

It was now nearing the end of September. Alexa and Antoni had been dating for a relatively short time. Although they'd only been together for almost two months, they were completely in love with each other. It wasn't uncommon in the displacement camp for marriages to take place, since many people were alone, abandoned, and stripped of their families. They were desperate for love, for a feeling of closeness with another human being who understood their trauma, for a connection with someone of the opposite sex, a partner. When they found someone to share intimacy with, they'd fall into each other's arms quickly; marriage was entered into lightly with big expectations.

A priest from the Red Cross performed simple ceremonies for young couples who had met each other in the camp and fallen in love, or "in like." The celebrations were by no means elaborate but they were happy occasions during which vows and rings were legally exchanged. The brides would often wear a simple, second-hand white lace dress, which the Red Cross would loan out for such occasions, and hold a small bunch of fresh flowers. Beyond that, depending on how popular the couple were, there was not much else. Their friends would throw them a small party with whatever supplies they could gather together.

Antoni decided to ask Alexa to marry him. Provided Alexa said yes, which he was sure she would, he'd waste no time in arranging the nuptials. Then he'd put the plans in motion for their journey back to Poland together as soon as possible.

The last Friday of September arrived. At the end of the workday, Antoni waited outside of the supply store for Alexa to finish her shift. When she came out, Antoni suggested that after dinner, they take a leisurely walk to the meadow where they'd gone on their first date. It was a beautiful, balmy evening out, and he thought they could go and watch the sunset together.

Alexa loved his romantic idea, so after they finished eating, they made their way out of the gates and away from the camp, arm in arm. They walked back to the same oak tree by the little stream where Antoni had first taken her, almost two months earlier. Alexa began looking around the base of the tree, as if she had lost something, until she exclaimed in surprise. Lying scattered on the ground where she had left them, albeit very withered and far from how they had looked when she'd first received them, were the remains of the bunch of wildflowers Antoni had first given her.

"What are you looking for?" Antoni asked her.

"Look, do you remember these?" Alexa pointed down to the remains on the ground.

"No, what are they?"

"Those were the flowers you gave me on our first date. I was so upset when I got back to the barracks that night and realized I had forgotten them."

Antoni laid his jacket inside out on the grass and told Alexa to sit down.

"Don't move. I'll be back in a few minutes," he said.

"Where are you going?"

"It's a surprise! Just sit here until I get back, okay?"

"Okay."

Antoni lit a cigarette and walked off into the tall grasses of the meadow. When he returned a few minutes later, he had a large bunch of pretty wildflowers in his hand with a red rose in the center. He appeared from behind the tree and sat down next to Alexa.

"Oh Antoni, they're beautiful."

"I wish I could give you something even more beautiful right now, but I'm afraid this is all I have." He handed her the flowers and took hold of her right hand, "Alexa, I want to marry you. Will you be my wife?" Antoni reached his hand into his shirt pocket and from it pulled out a white cotton handkerchief. He opened it up and from its center lifted out a round-shaped piece of metal.

"I know it's not much, but it's the best I could do for now."

Alexa looked down at the simple ring, handmade from a piece of wire that had been bent around twice. Threaded through the wire were two glass beads, one clear smaller one and a red-colored one next to it. She realized Antoni had made it himself. Looking up into his eyes, she spoke the words he wanted to hear.

"Yes, I will. I will marry you, Antoni." Those were also the words she had long wanted to say to him. She was head over heels in love with Antoni and had dreamed about sharing her life with him since soon after the day she'd met him.

Leaning over, Antoni pulled her close. They locked lips and shared a long and passionate kiss.

"I love you, Antoni," she whispered eventually.

"And I love you too, Alexa, and when we get back to Poland, I promise you I will buy you a beautiful, more precious ring you can be proud of."

He placed the ring on her finger, then tightened it to make it secure. They leaned back against the tree and watched the setting sun as it filled the sky with deep reds on its descent. Overhead passed a flock of geese in flight, a beautiful sight against the sunset. The geese let out their collective cries as if publicly declaring their approval for the young couple.

Antoni began telling Alexa the plans he had made for them about getting married as soon as possible so they could then leave the displacement camp at Mourmelon and begin their long journey home. Alexa didn't need much persuasion. She was in total agreement with his plans.

"Okay," said Antoni with a wide grin. "I'll go into town to see the jeweler who I did some electrical work for, and buy our wedding rings. Then I'll speak with the priest at the camp to see how soon he can marry us. After we do that, we can get set to leave, and I'll buy us tickets for the train to Berlin from Paris."

"Wow! It's really happening."

"Yes, beautiful," he murmured, touching his lips to her forehead. "We're getting married and we're going home."

Antoni sat with his arm around Alexa, her head against his chest, as they watched the sun disappear below the horizon. As darkness filled the sky, the newly-engaged young couple slowly made their way back to the camp, walking hand in hand. The stars sparkled in the sky above, like diamonds against a blanket of black velvet.

Antoni walked Alexa back to her barracks and kissed her goodnight. Alexa felt as though her heart would burst with happiness. She wished more than anything that she could go inside and share her wonderful news with her three best friends . . . but they were gone.

On Saturday morning, Antoni rose early and went in search of the Catholic priest to discuss the possibility of his performing their marriage ceremony. The priest was willing and said he could marry them the following Saturday morning, in the small chapel inside the camp.

Next, Antoni hitched a ride into the nearby town of Mourmelon-le-Petit and visited the local jewelry shop. He greeted the owner, Robert, for whom he had completed some electrical repairs the previous month, and told him of his plans to marry his beautiful Polish girlfriend. He selected two plain gold wedding bands from the array, which Robert gave him at a reduced price. Robert told Antoni that his wife, Sonia, was a hairdresser. If Alexa wished, he could arrange for his wife to give her a new hairstyle for free, the day before the wedding. Antoni said he'd tell Alexa about the kind offer and hopefully he could arrange for her to come back on Friday if she was interested.

His next stop was the local train station, where he enquired about the schedule from Mourmelon-le-Petit to Paris, and from Paris to Berlin. It was only an eighty-minute train ride into Paris, so if he didn't manage to organize them a ride directly into Paris on one of the army trucks, the train from Mourmelon-le-Petit would work out fine. Satisfied, he made his way back to the camp to share the good news with Alexa.

On hearing Antoni's updates, Alexa was ecstatic and told him she couldn't wait to become his wife. But she did wish her three friends were still around to witness their vows on their wedding day. Neither of them would have any family members there, nor would they have any really close friends attending to help them celebrate the occasion. It didn't bother Antoni too much, but he could see it made Alexa sad. She never imagined her wedding day would play out in such a non-eventful, no frills way. Antoni reassured her that when they got back to Poland and reunited with their families and friends, they would have a proper wedding celebration. Alexa cheered up, telling him she would view their upcoming nuptials as more of a formality and as sort of "part one" of their union.

The following week sped by quickly, and Alexa counted the days until she would marry the handsome young man with whom she was so in love. She agreed to go and have her hair done by the jeweler's wife so walked into town, accompanied by Antoni. The women were introduced, happy to make each other's acquaintance.

Sonia, an elegant and very pretty blonde woman, seemed genuinely excited and happy for the young couple. She welcomed Alexa warmly, and the first thing she did was make a fresh pot of coffee for them both at the back of the shop. Antoni and Robert made themselves scarce, leaving the shop together and saying they'd return in a few hours' time. That suited the women just fine as they were already getting to know one another better, chatting and discussing various hair styles.

Sonia mentioned she had some brand-new hair dyes to try out, which were all the rage in Paris. Alexa decided she'd like to try a new hair color—it would be a welcome change from looking like a perfect, blonde German woman. After all, the war was over now, she reasoned, and so being blonde and Arian-looking wouldn't have to be her saving grace anymore. From the three available colors, she chose the dark brown dye and the jeweler's wife seemed only too happy to oblige her.

When the process was complete, she looked in the mirror at her new hairstyle. Alexa was happy with her new image, even though it was only temporary. The blonde Alexa was gone. A little over two hours later, Antoni and Robert returned to the shop, and had their first look at Alexa's new hair style.

"Wow! What have you done?" Antoni asked her, his eyes wide with shock.

"I decided I needed a change, so I got rid of the blonde. Don't you like it?" Alexa's face fell, her happy smile fading with disappointment.

"I'm just surprised, that's all," said Antoni. "I love blondes."

Robert nudged his arm and said quickly, "He meant to say he loved *your* hair blonde, didn't you Antoni?"

"Yes, of course I did. I loved your hair blonde, Alexa. That's who I fell in love with."

"So what? Now you don't love me with dark hair?"

"Don't panic. It's only a temporary dye," said Sonia. "It will wash out in a few weeks and she'll be back to blonde again."

"Of course I still love you, Alexa. We're getting married tomorrow, aren't we?"

"Yes, but . . ."

"But nothing. Tomorrow you'll be my wife and when the dye washes out, you'll be blonde again."

Alexa thanked Sonia for doing her hair for free and for the pleasant few hours they had spent together in each other's company. Robert and Sonia wished them all the very best and congratulated them in advance for their wedding day. Antoni and Alexa left the shop and headed back to the camp.

"Are you sure you still love me, Antoni?" Alexa asked, searching his face for reassurance.

"Of course I do, I love both of you," he laughed.

"That's not funny."

"Sure it is; it's like getting two wives for the price of one. What more could a man ask for?" He laughed even louder.

"You better behave, Antoni, or you'll end up with none." Then Alexa laughed.

"You're more than enough for me, Alexa. I'll be so happy to have you as my wife," said Antoni, kissing her on the cheek. Then he took a second look at the new Alexa and cracked a half-smile. "But please don't ever dye your hair dark again. For our second wedding in Poland, I want you blonde again, okay?"

"Okay," she replied, and they continued on, walking hand in hand back to the camp.

Alexa opted not to wear the basic Red Cross white lace dress, loaned to all the young brides in the displacement camp. Instead, she wore her smart army-issue uniform which matched Antoni's attire. She had decided to wait for their second wedding, their proper celebration, to dress as she'd really like.

The ceremony was over very quickly. After they exchanged their vows and placed the wedding rings on each other's fingers, the priest pronounced them husband and wife. They sealed the proceedings with a kiss, and both signed the necessary official documents. One of the Allied army soldier photographers in the camp took a photograph of the newly-married couple, and once he developed it, gave it to the newlyweds as a souvenir. It was their first photograph together.

Antoni had informed the Mourmelon camp army office that he and his new wife would be leaving the displacement camp that weekend, to make their own long journey back to Poland together. The camp commander arranged for them to be driven on the Sunday morning into the center of Paris to the main railway station and authorized for them to be given some supplies for their journey, as well as some extra ration cards. The commander also gifted them a bottle of French wine to celebrate the beginning of the young couple's new life together.

They spent their wedding day in the camp and were congratulated by several of their fellow campmates and a few of Antoni's friends. They ate in the Red Cross building as they did every day, but word had spread about their marriage and halfway through their meal, a few of the Allied troops came over to their table. They brought a bottle of vodka with them to celebrate, and the soldier who had bought Alexa's guitar from her played some songs, serenading the happy couple.

The impromptu party, with singing and dancing, went on for a few hours. Antoni and Alexa had their first dance together, and one of the French cooks brought out a small cake she had made for them. It all helped to make their wedding day that little bit more special.

As 9 pm approached, the newlyweds thanked everyone for celebrating with them and for all their good wishes for their journey the next morning. Since Alexa's three girlfriends had left the camp, no new women had been assigned to share her bunk. The camp at Mourmelon had served its purpose for over a year as a safe haven for many displaced people. Quite a number of people had started leaving the camp over the previous month to return to their homes, and there hadn't been any new arrivals. The camp had recently notified all its inhabitants that it was going to close as a refuge for the displaced, so those who were still there were already making plans with the Red Cross to finally leave.

Antoni gathered the few belongings from his barracks that he'd be taking on their journey and brought them over to Alexa's room. He packed them, along with Alexa's things, into an army issue duffel bag, ready for their morning departure. He then carried their packed bag to a room where he had been granted permission for them both to sleep. It was to be their last night in the camp and their first night together as a married couple. They spent the night close together, sleeping in each other's arms.

The morning was a beautiful one, bright and sunny with clear blue skies. Antoni and Alexa ate their breakfast together, collected their belongings, and made their way to the army truck on which they would travel to the train station in Paris. They both took a last look behind them at the place that had been their home for the past six months. They gladly said their goodbyes and climbed on board the truck. For the first time, they sat up front, next to the driver.

CHAPTER 19

About an hour and a half later, the truck arrived on the outskirts of Paris. As it drove through the suburbs en route to the capital, it was clear that many of the outlying areas of Paris had suffered from several bombing raids. At the start of the war, parts of the outskirts of Paris were bombed by the Germans, but towards the end of the war, the Allied troops caused much of the structural damage as they targeted French factories taken over by the Nazis during the German occupation.

Although Paris was not as heavily bombed as many of the other major European cities, the scars were still very visible. It was said that due to Hitler's fascination with Paris, his desire was to keep the city in its state of architectural beauty, so it had pretty much remained intact.

The truck driver was a French soldier who knew his way around the city. So, he treated the newlyweds to a scenic route, driving them around the Arc de Triomphe, down the Champs Elysées, and south towards the Eiffel Tower. Alexa was in awe of the world-famous landmark, getting a sense of its tremendous height even though they were on the opposite side of the river. They drove along the banks of the river Seine where the beautiful architecture of Paris was unspoiled. They passed by the ornate Louvre Museum and the majestic Notre Dame Cathedral, both of which had remained untouched.

The driver then turned left, heading north towards the Gare Du Nord, Paris's main train station, another architectural gem in its own right. He brought the truck to a stop outside the station and wished Antoni and Alexa *bon voyage* as they jumped down onto the street, Antoni shouldering their duffel bag of belongings. The couple thanked the soldier for the drive and the scenic tour, and headed into the station to find out the departure times of trains to Berlin.

The rather disinterested-looking clerk in the information booth told them the next direct train bound for Berlin was due to leave at 1 pm from platform five, jabbing his finger in the direction of the ticket counter from where Antoni could purchase their tickets. With two second-class tickets in his pocket, Antoni took Alexa's hand.

"Let's go find platform five," he said.

Alexa looked around her as they walked through the station. It was a tall structure with large arched windows reaching high up on either side, and a massive, glass roof supported by long, ornate, cast iron beams and pillars. It was a bustling hub of constant activity with people coming and going in all directions. It was a real tapestry of humanity, Alexa thought. There were French, American, and Allied soldiers carrying duffel bags disembarking here and boarding trains there. There were many civilians too, a mix of young and old; some were rich-looking, neatly-dressed Parisians—businessmen in tailored suits and elegant ladies in fine French fashions, complete with matching heels, hats and handbags.

There were many poor people too, Alexa noticed, in rough-looking, raggedy old clothes. Some were injured and wounded while others were gaunt-looking shells with protruding bones, hollow faces with sunken eyes, blank stares and empty expressions, no doubt shadows of their former selves. Perhaps they were refugees—liberated prisoners from labor and concentration camps, or men and women from various displacement camps. Each face told its own heartbreaking story; for now, they were silent, unable to form the words that would describe the horrific experiences they had endured. Whatever they looked like and whoever they were, they were all struggling to return home, wherever that might be.

It was almost 10 am, and since they had a few hours to spare before boarding their train, Antoni suggested they pass the time in a Parisian café. They walked back out of the main entrance and onto the streets of Paris. Alexa had never been in such a large and beautiful city before and was delighted by the experience. There was so much to see and take in. She scanned the sights around her, soaking it all up.

The streets were lined with blocks of elegant five- and six-story residential buildings, some with ornate balconies overlooking the streets below, painted wooden window shutters and flower boxes full of color. Even the tall street lamps were elegant, with two or three large, white, round glass shades on each pole; Alexa could imagine them illuminating the streets at night with a magical glow.

They passed by the shop windows with their colorful and artistic displays and fancy, hand-painted signage. Freshly-potted floral arrangements and hanging baskets decorated the doorways. A number of Parisian cafés had strategically placed small tables and matching chairs on the pavements to entice their patrons, offering them promise of a comfortable seat and rich, freshly-brewed coffee and pastries, while reading their newspapers or chatting with a friend. Life in Paris seemed vibrant and most definitely worth living.

While she walked arm in arm with her new husband, Alexa glanced down at her wedding ring. It suddenly dawned on her they were in the City of Love and technically, they were on their honeymoon. Antoni steered her in the direction of a quaint little café across the street, suggesting they stop for a while. The morning sun was still shining brightly as they sat down at their selected table.

Antoni lit a cigarette and waited for the waitress to bring them a menu. He told Alexa he had enough money for them to order a hot drink and small snack each. Once the waitress arrived, Antoni ordered two strong, black coffees in his best French. Then he asked for a croissant with jam for himself; Alexa would select a fresh pastry from the selection on display inside.

For the first time in her adult life, Alexa felt truly free—a free citizen of the world. She felt safe in the protection and love of her handsome new husband. This was a fresh chapter in her life. She wasn't just an actor in this romantic movie that was unfolding; she was the leading lady in it. Excited and ready to embrace life, Alexa felt happier than she had ever felt before.

As noon approached, Antoni said it was time for them to leave the café and head back to the train station. He paid their bill to the waitress, shouldered the duffel bag, and took Alexa's hand as they began walking back to the Gare du Nord along the same way they had come. Presently, Antoni stopped at one of the bakers and purchased some fresh baguettes with the French ration cards he had been given by the Mourmelon camp commander. At another shop, he bought some smoked sausages, sliced ham, and two local cheeses for their journey. Using up the majority of the remaining French ration cards, Antoni bought two bottles of milk, some butter, a small pot of jam, and some chocolate.

As they continued walking through the streets, Alexa caught sight of a book shop and stopped to take a look in the window. She noticed an old Polish Bible on display, which was exactly like the one she had when she was a child, and pointed it out to Antoni. Antoni was not religious himself but he could see how interested Alexa seemed to be in the small black book.

"Oh Antoni, could we buy it, please?"

"It depends how much it costs, darling."

"My German Bible was lost when the convent was bombed, and I haven't had one since. This Bible is the very same kind as the one I had growing up in Poland."

"Okay, let's go inside and ask how much it is."

Inside the shop, they found an elderly French gentleman sitting behind the counter. Alexa lifted the Bible from out of the window display and flicked its pages backwards and forwards a few times, and then brought it over to the counter. While Antoni asked the old man how much he wanted for it, Alexa opened the Bible to Psalm 91 and began quietly reading the chapter she knew so well. The shopkeeper encouraged her to read it louder so he could hear her too. She obliged, and noticed the old man's eyes light up.

"Are you Polish?" he asked. "My grandmother was Polish."

"Yes, we both are," said Alexa, "and we are returning home to Poland today for the first time in five years since the start of the war."

"My wife and I are heading to the train station to catch the one o'clock train to Berlin. How much do you want for the Bible, sir?" asked Antoni.

"Since your wife reads it so beautifully, she should have it."

"I had the very same Bible when I was a young child in Poland," Alexa explained with a smile. "My grandmother and my mother would always read it to me."

"Well, now it is yours again. Please take it as a small gift from me. Take it back to Poland with you on your journey home and read it often."

Overcome with emotion at the old gentleman's kind gesture, Alexa leaned over the counter and kissed his cheek.

"Thank you so much, sir. This means more to me than you could ever know."

"You're very welcome. Bon voyage and may God be with you, Madame."

Antoni thanked the old man and shook his hand. The young couple walked out of the book shop, Alexa carrying her new Bible in her hand. She was delighted with it, as well as being touched by the gentle kindness of yet another stranger towards her.

When they arrived back at platform five, the time was 12:40 pm. The whistle blew as the inbound Berlin train pulled into the station, its brakes screeching as it slowed to a complete stop with a large blast of steam billowing out from the front engine. Once all the passengers had disembarked, Antoni located an empty second-class carriage and climbed on board. Helping Alexa up the few steps, he led her to their compartment.

The train compartment had room for six people, but they were the first to arrive. Antoni lifted their duffel bag up onto the overhead storage shelf above them, placed their food on the seat next to him, and pointed for Alexa to sit nearest to the window. Antoni returned to the platform for a smoke before the train left, which was alright with Alexa since she really didn't like the smell of cigarettes; she secretly hoped he would stop one day. Once he had finished smoking, he climbed back on board and joined Alexa in the compartment, closing the sliding door to give them some privacy. The station master blew his whistle and the train released a blast of hot steam before gradually moving off along the platform and out of the station, rolling down the tracks as it slowly picked up speed. Antoni put his arm around his wife's shoulder, drawing her close as the train pulled out of the Paris station and began its long journey to Berlin.

"We're finally going home, darling," Antoni said as he kissed her cheek.

"At long last," she sighed and kissed him back.

After about twenty minutes into their journey, the sliding door of the compartment opened and the train conductor appeared, asking to see their tickets. Antoni handed them to him for his inspection. The conductor tore the corner of the tickets and gave them back to Antoni with a curt "thank you" before exiting, sliding the door closed behind him.

Seeing the conductor triggered Alexa's memory of her last train journey, after leaving the Klausses. She recalled the fear she had felt that day as the conductor had yelled at her, telling her she didn't have a first-class ticket and shouldn't be there in the first-class carriage. The terror and anxiety she felt, in case her true identity was discovered by the Nazi soldiers and SS officers who filled the entire train carriage, had almost paralyzed her with fear.

"You look very serious," Antoni said. "What are you thinking about?" he asked, kissing her furrowed brow. Alexa shared the story of her last train journey with him.

"That must have been terrifying for you," said Antoni. He told her he was proud of her for fooling the Germans and keeping her Polish identity concealed, and laughed at how she had managed to make the SS officer feel bad for her predicament and pay the balance of her ticket to make it a first class one.

Alexa also laughed at that part of the story for the very first time. She had never looked at it that way before. Having Antoni by her side seemed to make everything much better and more bearable. She pointed out to him that her belief in the power of prayer and her unshakable faith in Psalm 91 had gotten her through many difficult times since she was taken from Poland. Antoni had never been convinced by the idea of prayer and God's saving power, but he listened, nodding his head, respecting her belief in them.

Antoni suggested they get comfortable and take a nap; they'd had a very early start that morning and still had a long train journey ahead of them before arriving in Berlin. Alexa agreed and stretched out on the seat, snuggling her head into Antoni's chest. The repetitive sound of the train speeding along the steel tracks made a relaxing melody of four beats to the bar, which soon soothed the couple into a deep sleep.

After roughly five hours into their journey, the train crossed the border at Strasbourg, leaving France and traveling north through Western Germany towards Frankfurt. Alexa was first to awaken and opened her eyes. As she sat up, Antoni also woke up. She reached for the bag of food supplies they had bought and began preparing something for them to eat. Antoni used the pen knife he always kept in his pocket to cut open the baguettes, slice the cheese and sausage, and spread some butter. They opened one of the bottles of milk and shared it between them.

Soon after they had finished eating, the train pulled into Frankfurt station. Antoni took the opportunity to stretch his legs on the platform for a few minutes and smoke a quick cigarette. Alexa stepped out of their compartment into the corridor of the carriage, lowered one of the windows near to where her husband was smoking, and leaned out of it, taking in the view. A few minutes later, after all the new passengers had gotten on board, the station master blew his whistle and waved his flag, signaling the train driver to depart. Antoni climbed back onto the train and it was soon speeding up again, continuing on its journey to Berlin.

They walked back towards their compartment and, once there, discovered they weren't alone anymore. A young woman had boarded the train at Frankfurt and had chosen their compartment to sit in; perhaps she'd thought it was an empty one. Alexa and Antoni were surprised to see her there, but they said hello to her and sat in their seats across from her. The woman seemed withdrawn and not wanting to engage in a conversation. Her head was turned all the way to the right, her face almost touching the window as she stared out of it, avoiding direct eye contact with the young couple. She sat very still and quiet, tightly clutching a brown paper bag on her lap.

It was obvious to Alexa the woman was filled with fear. She recognized that look and knew it all too well. She estimated the woman was roughly twenty-five years of age. She had what looked like dark hair, but it was hard to tell its length or style, as she wore a head scarf that covered most of her hairline. Her clothes looked well-worn and very shabby, almost as though they belonged to someone else.

Alexa glanced down at the woman's shoes, noticing they were slightly too big for the woman's feet and better suited to an elderly woman. She raised her eyes to the woman's face, noticing her protruding bone structure, indicative of how thin she actually was. Alexa surmised this woman was a poor soul who must have gone through a horrendous ordeal.

About half an hour after leaving Frankfurt, Alexa began reading her new Bible to herself. It gave her such comfort to be able to browse through its pages and read it in Polish once again. She revisited some of her favorite scriptures and re-read them, losing herself in the verses. After a while, Antoni told Alexa he was going to the toilet and asked if she minded if he took a walk to the restaurant carriage to see what was going on there. Alexa said it was okay with her; she'd be happy reading until he returned. Pocketing his cigarettes, he kissed her cheek and said he'd be back in a little while. Alexa continued reading, and the woman continued staring out of the train window, as if in a trance.

Antoni walked along the narrow corridor of the moving train, passing through two more carriages before reaching the restaurant car. There were a few tables occupied by people, eating and drinking; at one table, a group of American soldiers were playing poker.

Antoni sat on a stool at the small restaurant bar and asked the bartender how much it would cost for a beer; he figured he may as well use up his few remaining Francs. He lit a cigarette as the bartender served him his beer. Once he had finished smoking, he took his beer over to sit at the empty table next to the American soldiers, in hope of striking up a conversation with them.

Antoni wasn't shy and before long, he'd wangled his way into their poker game. They dealt him a hand of cards and he started putting his plan into action. He bluffed he was a relative beginner at the game and fancied his chances with his last few Francs. He told them he had gotten married the day before and was feeling lucky.

The Yanks were more than willing to win his money from him, so Antoni deliberately lost his first two hands, casting his hook. On his third hand, he slowly began reeling them in. He put on his familiar, winning poker face and the next few hands were his.

Reaching for his winnings from the center of the table, he thanked the soldiers for letting him play and announced he had to get back to his wife. But the soldiers were far from happy and wanted Antoni to continue playing, giving them the chance to win their money back. Hoping to calm them down, Antoni promised he'd go check on his wife, tell her where he was, and then return to their poker game. Eventually the soldiers agreed but told him to hurry back.

Antoni had them right where he wanted them. They had no idea they had fallen into his trap and that he'd soon return for the "sting" to clean them out.

Pleased with himself, Antoni made his way back to the train compartment where Alexa was. The scene hadn't changed at all since he had left. Alexa was still reading her Bible and the woman sitting across from her was still clutching her paper bag and staring out the window. Antoni sat down and explained to Alexa about the poker game he had gotten into with the American soldiers in the restaurant car, and how he was winning money they would need to continue on with the next part of their journey. Alexa understood and agreed he go back and play for another hour, assuring him she'd be okay reading her Bible until he returned.

Antoni said he'd wait another ten minutes as part of his plan, so the soldiers wouldn't think he was too eager. Alexa took the opportunity to go to the toilet while Antoni kept an eye on their belongings. When she returned, Antoni kissed her again and left the compartment, sliding the door closed behind him, and made his way back to the restaurant car.

Before Alexa continued reading her Bible, she reached for their bag of food and took out a bar of chocolate as well as the bottle of milk which she and Antoni had started drinking earlier. She tore open the outer wrapping of the chocolate and broke a few pieces off. Alexa looked over at the young woman sympathetically and asked her if she would like some, but the woman didn't respond. Alexa figured the woman must not understand Polish and asked her again in German but still she didn't respond. So, Alexa moved to sit beside her, placing her hand on the woman's shoulder. This time, she got a reaction. The woman flinched nervously and then burst into tears, taking Alexa by surprise.

"Please don't cry. I was only trying to be kind and give you some of my chocolate."

The woman turned and looked at Alexa directly for the first time, with her sad eyes full of tears.

"It's okay," Alexa said reassuringly. "I won't hurt you. Look, I'll go back over to my own seat." Alexa placed the chocolate down next to her and moved back over to where she had been sitting.

"No one's been that kind to me in such a very long time," said the tearful young woman in a Polish accent.

"Look, it really is okay. You are more than welcome to share my chocolate with me, and I have some milk too. Would you like some?" Alexa reached for the bottle of milk and held it out to the young woman.

"Wait," said the woman as she reached her hand into the paper bag on her lap. Out of it she pulled an old metal cup which was dented in several places with most of its outer enamel coating chipped off. "I have my own cup," she said, very matter-of-factly. She held it out towards Alexa with both hands, who filled it up halfway with milk. The woman's hands shook as she quickly raised the metal cup up to her mouth and began drinking.

Alexa held out the bar of chocolate to the woman. "Please, take as much as you'd like."

The woman carefully rested her cup on her lap with her right hand, and with her left hand reached over and took a piece of chocolate from Alexa, then slowly lifted it up to her mouth.

"You are Polish?" Alexa asked.

The woman swallowed her mouthful of chocolate. "Yes," she replied.

"We are too. My husband and I are returning home for the first time since the start of the war."

The woman finished the remaining milk in her cup, wiped it clean with her sleeve, and put it back in her bag.

"Wait, you can have some more if you'd like."

The young woman began to cry, tears trickling down her face. Alexa was moved with pity for her. She moved to sit next to the woman again, putting her arm around her shoulder. At first, the young woman pulled back, but then reluctantly fell into Alexa's arms sobbing, in real need of some human affection.

"There, there, it's okay; you're safe now," Alexa tried to reassure her.

After a few minutes, the woman composed herself, visibly trying to rein in her emotions.

"My name is Alexa, what's yours?"

"Teressa," she answered, and slowly the two young women began talking candidly to one another.

For the next half-hour, the two strangers spoke to each other honestly, as if in a confessional. The young woman confided in Alexa about the nightmare she had survived, hesitantly at first. But Alexa was a good listener and displayed real compassion and empathy as the woman spoke.

So, Teressa told her the harrowing story of how, when she was twenty-three years of age, she was taken by the Nazis from the ghetto in Kraków along with her two small children, her husband, and her parents, and sent to Auschwitz concentration camp. She told how at gunpoint, they were all crammed into boxcars like animals, huddled together with strangers and transported to hell on earth. She told of how she was separated from her family on that first day when they arrived at the concentration camp, and that she had never seen her son or daughter ever again after they were torn from her arms. Nor had she ever seen her parents or her husband again, either.

Teressa spoke of how she believed she was the only one still alive in her family, but she couldn't understand why.

"Why didn't I die?" she kept asking, over and over again.

She related how all humanity was stripped from her on that first day. "They took my belongings. They took my clothes. They took my shoes. They took my wedding ring. They took my hair, shaving it all off of my head. They took my dignity and my identity."

She told Alexa her name was also stolen that day. Lifting up her sleeve, she showed Alexa the number on her left forearm. The ink tattoo had been etched into her skin on the first day she arrived at the camp by the tattooist, a fellow Jewish prisoner. It was her only means of identity in the camp from that day onwards.

Teressa spoke of how desperate and demoralizing the living conditions were for all of the prisoners in Auschwitz-Birkenau. How they had been crammed together to exist in dismal, unsanitary barracks, each one packed beyond capacity with hundreds of desperate prisoners, six or more people lying on each bunk. They had no bedding or blankets, no heat in the winter, and no food or drink. They had been starved and beaten and worked like dogs, even less than dogs. The Nazis' Alsatian dogs lived a far superior life than the prisoners.

Teressa explained how worthless human life was inside the camp and how insignificant a prisoner with a tattooed number actually was. She told of how quickly someone could become a target for death, and of how a bullet could find its next random target within a split second for any reason or no reason at all.

"An unexpected bullet was the best way to go," she said in her opinion. That's the way she had wanted to go. "Much better than being piled naked into the gas chambers with a group of desperate people all clambering on top of you, trying to get their very last breath of air." Teressa paused and shook her head, as if to dislodge the horrible images. "In the end it made no difference how a person expired because once they were dead, by gas or by bullet, they were thrown into the ovens anyway, and up through the chimneys they'd go."

She spoke of how she'd prayed and prayed so hard to God so many times to help her and her family, but God didn't listen to her so she eventually gave up. There was no God, she had decided, only living hell in Auschwitz. She said if you were really lucky, you'd die in your sleep and not see the next morning, but she had never been that lucky.

And then she spoke of how one morning, she had been selected and put on a transport out of Auschwitz. She had journeyed by train to Germany where she was forced to slave in a labor camp. Once the war ended and the camp was liberated, she was too ill and too weak to travel home. Besides, she had no family to return to, nor anywhere really to go.

The tears trickled down Alexa's face as Teressa related her horrific experiences. Now it made complete sense as to why the woman was so withdrawn and nervous. '*How could someone be anything different after going through all that?*' she thought.

Alexa decided to tell Teressa her own story, in the hope it might take her mind off her own nightmare for a little while. Teressa listened to Alexa's personal experience with compassion in her eyes.

"I hope you will find your mother and sister and that they are still alive," she said when Alexa had finished.

Alexa hadn't ever allowed herself to think Sophia and Asha wouldn't be alive. She had always held onto the idea that she'd return to Lublin one day and find her mother and sister there, waiting for her at home. Teressa's words made her think realistically; there was a real possibility it might not actually be the case. '*Well, I'm almost home now and I'll soon find out the truth',* she told herself, refusing to give any more fuel to that fire.

Once the two women had shared their stories, enabling for a little while a flood of emotions, they were quite exhausted by it all and sunk back into silence once more. Teressa turned her head to stare blankly out of the train window as she had done before, and Alexa immersed herself in the comforting verses of her Bible.

After a little while, Teressa suddenly stood up and said she had to go. Alexa looked up from the pages of her Bible and said, "Okay," thinking she was going to the toilet. But Teressa never returned to the compartment.

Antoni's plan worked exactly as he had wanted it to and he left the American soldiers' poker game as the big winner, taking the large portion of the winnings. Grinning, he made his way back towards their compartment, fingering the bundle of U.S. dollars in his pocket. It was more than enough to get him and Alexa back to Poland, and even enough for them to live off for at least a month.

He opened the sliding door of the compartment, eager to tell Alexa the good news. Alexa closed her Bible and cuddled with Antoni for the rest of the journey to Berlin.

Presently, his story told, he noticed they were alone. "What's the chocolate doing over there, and where's that woman gone?" he asked.

"Don't ask," replied Alexa, tightening her hold on him.

CHAPTER 20

It was late at night when the train finally arrived in Berlin. Wanting to spend as little time in Germany as possible, Antoni wasted no time in finding out the departure time for the next train to Warsaw. He found the station master who told him the train would not go all the way into Warsaw's main station, due to extensive bombing and damage on the train line. He inquired as to where he should depart from the train, pointing out that he wished to travel to Łódź. The station master told him where to get off the train, but couldn't suggest alternative transportation to Łódź at that time.

So, Antoni bought two tickets for the overnight train due to leave at midnight. The young couple sat in the station until it was time to board. Alexa made them another baguette with some of the remaining sliced ham and cheese. There was nothing to buy in the station at that time of night. Antoni promised Alexa that once they boarded the train, he would take her to the restaurant car for a hot drink.

Midnight fast approached. They climbed onto the Warsaw train and as promised, Antoni took his wife to the restaurant car, where they sat down at a vacant table. Once the train had pulled out of the station, Antoni ordered them some hot coffee from the restaurant bar.

The journey to Warsaw was uneventful. It was peaceful and quiet, and the train didn't seem to be too full of passengers. Antoni found them an empty compartment in one of the carriages, which they had all to themselves. They settled down comfortably into their seats and slept through the night, with Alexa nestled in Antoni's arms.

They spent two nights on the train to Warsaw, and as daylight broke, they got their first look at their native Poland. They both had mixed emotions. While they were glad to be almost home, they were also filled with anxiety as they began to see the massive destruction that was everywhere.

As the sun began to rise, it illuminated the view outside the train window. But it did not shine on or reflect any fresh, vibrant colors. Rather, it poured light onto row upon row of ruins—dull, grey, burnt-out skeletons of derelict buildings. They were seeing for the first time the large-scale destruction and extensive damage the city of Warsaw had suffered.

Half-standing, bomb-blasted buildings remained, empty shells with windows, walls, and roofs blown out. There were great piles of debris everywhere. High mounds of bricks and concrete, mangled together with twisted metals and splintered wood, filled the landscape as far as the eye could see. It resembled a Biblical apocalypse of catastrophic proportions. Hitler's original plan to totally annihilate the city by bombing it along with everyone in it had almost completely succeeded.

The Nazis and the German Luftwaffe had demolished about eighty-five to ninety percent of Warsaw, almost razing it to the ground. Very few buildings were left intact. All significant buildings of importance were first plundered, then set alight with flamethrowers, and finally blown up by specialized German troops. Warsaw's historic old town with its beautiful architecture, its castle, museums, government buildings, churches, schools and libraries, homes and residential buildings, were all destroyed. The Nazis had even demolished Warsaw's main train station in January that year, before their retreat, so trains could no longer go all the way into the center of the city.

Alexa and Antoni had read a few newspaper articles and had heard some radio reports about the damage Warsaw had suffered at the hands of Hitler's army, but they never imagined it would be as devastated as it was. Alexa was beyond shocked by what she saw out the window; she hadn't been prepared to see such large-scale destruction. She began to pray silently over the desolation and obvious loss of life she knew must have occurred, but she also prayed the rest of their journey would be a safe one.

The train began to slow down, and the conductor came along the carriages, telling all the passengers that the train would come to a complete stop in roughly fifteen minutes, its journey terminating at the Zachodnia Station, on the outskirts of Warsaw. Antoni and Alexa gathered their belongings together and made their way out into the corridor.

When the train finally stopped, unable to go on any farther, everyone exited the carriages and climbed down onto the platform. Antoni scanned the area to get his bearings. The station was roughly eighty-five miles from Łódź, the town where Antoni's family lived and their first destination. They headed out of the small station and made their way onto the streets of Warsaw, where the true scale of the devastation and destruction was clear to see.

Walking along the main roadway, they headed west out of the city. On their journey they passed several civilians also walking along the roadside in one direction or the other. Many were pulling small carts or pushing old, damaged prams, loaded with their few belongings or some salvaged furniture they had perhaps picked up on their journey. Most walked alone, although some were in groups of twos or threes. Each seemed to have a definite destination to which they were headed, no matter how long it would take them to get there.

On either side of the roads were groups of Polish work crews, made up of both civilians and army soldiers, who were attempting to clear the piles of rubble and debris from the bombed-out buildings. The Varsovian men and women from all walks of life and backgrounds rolled up their sleeves and got stuck into the mammoth clean-up task before them. People from other towns and cities across Poland had also volunteered and come to help. They formed long human chains, passing buckets full of rubble from one to another, brick by brick, from hand to hand, moving the chunks of concrete down the line to fill up the waiting trucks.

"The entire nation builds its capital!" became the city's rallying cry.

It was obvious the clean-up task would take a great deal of effort, but it seemed well on its way. Warsaw's people were determined to rebuild their beloved capital. Firstly, for life to be lived there once again by the living and the future generations; secondly, as a tribute and a mark of respect to the hundreds of thousands of Poles who had been murdered there at the hands of Hitler's henchmen.

After walking for roughly half an hour, Alexa suggested they sit down and eat something; it would also mean they'd have one less thing to carry. They found a small patch of grass nearby and sat down under the morning sun to finish off the rest of their food. They didn't rest for very long before continuing on their journey once again. Antoni carried their duffel bag on his back and lit up one of his cigarettes.

Not long after they began walking again, an Allied truck pulled up alongside and asked where they were going. The soldiers had recognized Antoni and Alexa's American army issue uniforms and offered them a ride to Łódź, as they were heading in the same direction. The couple gratefully jumped up into the rear of the truck and settled down for the bumpy ride.

Hours later, the truck finally reached the center of Łódź. Alexa had never been there before, but for Antoni, he was home at last. His first thought was to make his way back to the home where he had lived and grown up in with his parents. It was the last place he had lived before being taken to Germany to work. He hoped he would find them there, waiting for him. Antoni led the way, and after a twenty-minute walk they arrived at his home.

Sadly, there were no visible signs of life. The front door was locked, and no one was home. Antoni knocked on the door of the neighbors' house, but the people he used to know who once lived there were gone. The new occupants didn't seem to know who his parents were, or anything about them at all.

Antoni decided they would make their way to his grandfather's villa to see if there were any other family members still living there. He knew the SS had taken over his deceased grandfather's five fabric factories and mills in Łódź at the beginning of the war while Antoni was still living in the city as a teenager. However, he now prayed his family had repossessed their businesses and villa now the war was over, and that perhaps he'd find his mother and father safely living there together.

As they approached the road where the villa was located, Antoni tried to catch his breath. The location looked far different from the way he remembered it. The villa had been bombed and lay in complete ruin. He hardly recognized the remains of his grandfather's once stately home. This was the place where he had spent many hours as a young child, playing and enjoying life. He had many happy memories there, but now it was destroyed. Like the buildings they'd seen in Warsaw, there was no roof, no walls, no windows. Only large piles of rubble remained—bricks and mortar, broken glass, and twisted metal, mangled with broken wooden, burnt-out and charred beams.

Antoni was unable to believe his eyes. He lit a cigarette with trembling hands as he stared at the sad, derelict state of his family's villa before him, shaking his head. Then he dropped their duffel bag and sat down on the ground in shock. Alexa tried to comfort him but couldn't find anything reassuring to say. She was at a loss for words.

After a little while, Antoni took a final look at the destroyed villa before getting to his feet and heading back towards town with Alexa, trying to figure out what to do next. They found a café on their way and decided to stop. Inside, they sat at an empty table and ordered two coffees. Things hadn't gone the way Antoni had expected. He had been so sure that his mother would have been waiting for him at home. He had only been gone for three years since he had been forced to join the German army. But, in reality, three years was a whole lifetime for some people.

"Antoni, is that you?" asked a female voice. Antoni quickly looked over in the direction of the voice and found a pretty, blonde young woman staring back at him.

"Elena!"

The girl ran over to Antoni and hugged him, obviously delighted to see him.

"I knew you'd make it back here safely one day, I just knew it," she beamed.

He turned to Alexa. "This is my cousin, Elena. Elena, this is my wife, Alexa."

"Your wife. Wow, she's pretty and you are all grown up, my little cousin."

"Where is my mother?" asked Antoni. "Is she still alive? We went to the house but the people living next door said she doesn't live there."

"No, she doesn't live in that house anymore, but yes, Auntie Stephanie is still alive. She'll be so happy to see you and meet your new wife. I'll write down her new address for you," she offered.

Antoni was relieved to hear his mother was still alive, but he also wanted to know about his father. "What about my father? Where's Fritz?"

Elena sat down on one of the chairs at their table, the happy smile disappearing from her face. "You remember he was arrested for giving out extra ration cards to the Polish families? Well, they also accused him of giving them to the Jews in the Łódź ghetto. Two of Grandfather's factories were within the ghetto's walled area, and the Nazis claimed your father used them to smuggle in ration cards to the Polish and Jewish families with children. They transported him to the Stutthof labor camp, and no one has ever seen him again."

Antoni said nothing but was obviously overwhelmed with emotions. Pushing his chair back, he walked outside the café and lit up another cigarette.

"I'm sorry to have to share this awful news with him now, but what else could I say?" Elena turned to Alexa with a hopeless expression on her face.

A little while later, Antoni came back into the café and said he must go find his mother. Elena wrote down her address and said she'd pay for their coffees. They said their goodbyes and the young couple left the café, promising to see Elena again soon. Antoni and Alexa found their way to the address Elena had written on the piece of paper and knocked on the door. A few seconds later a woman opened the door.

"Hello, Mama," said Antoni.

The woman stared in amazement at the tall, handsome young man standing before her. "Antoni, is it you, my son?"

"Yes, Mama, I'm home," said Antoni, throwing his arms around his mother and embracing her tightly.

"Oh, thank you, God," she cried out loud as she wept tears of joy. After a few precious moments in each other's arms, Antoni pulled back and introduced Alexa as his new wife. His mother was surprised but greeted Alexa warmly and brought them into her home. She repeated again and again how she couldn't believe the wonderful sight before her eyes. Her boy had finally come home.

Mother and son spent the next few hours catching up on each other's lives, their personal experiences during the war, and those of Antoni's friends and family members. Antoni's mother filled them in on the events that caused the loss of the family business and the destruction of his grandfather's villa. As they spoke of Antoni's father's imprisonment by the Gestapo and his transportation to Stutthof, his mother began sobbing.

Once she had composed herself, the woman turned to Alexa. She wanted to get to know her and insisted they stay with her at her home. She had no desire to let her newly returned son out of her sight anytime soon.

The couple stayed with Antoni's mother, and she took great pleasure in fussing over them and making them as comfortable as she possibly could. She gave Alexa some of her nice clothes and shoes to wear, instead of the army issue uniforms they had on. She opened a trunk in her bedroom where she had stored some of her husband's clothes and gave Antoni his father's clothing to wear, as it was almost a certainty that Fritz would never return home now.

Three weeks went by, and as much as Alexa was enjoying living with her mother-in-law and getting to know the other members of Antoni's family nearby, she longed to see her own mother and sister again. After she and Antoni discussed the matter privately, they told Stephanie they would be making the journey to Lublin to track down Alexa's immediate family; from there they would decide their next move.

Stephanie wasn't thrilled at the thought of them leaving her, but she understood their reasons and hoped Alexa would also be successfully reunited with her family. She gave them a generous amount of money which she had saved and hidden, packed their clothing into a small suitcase each, and prepared some food for them to take on their journey.

The next day they headed for the main train station in Łódź and bought tickets to take them to Lublin, Alexa's hometown. The train ride took them seven hours and finally by late afternoon, Alexa was back in Lublin. Although this was her hometown, it didn't look quite like she had remembered it. Like Warsaw, Lublin had suffered severe structural damage—from the Nazi army during the war and then at the end of the war, from the Russian army as they marched in to liberate Poland. Lublin had suffered at least seventy percent destruction of its city and, although not as severe as in Warsaw, the death toll of its Jewish population was extremely high, with many Polish Christians losing their lives too.

Alexa wasted no time in making her way back to the home where she had lived with her family as a child. Antoni told her to slow down, but as she drew nearer to her neighborhood, she felt a strong desire to start running, as though she couldn't wait a minute longer. She wanted to throw open the front door of her house and run into her mother's arms as she had done as a child. She longed for her mother to embrace her tightly, the way that Antoni's mother had greeted him, with tears of joy. She wanted to hear her mother's voice say her name again after all these years, and tell her she was finally home and safe. She wanted to be reunited with her adoring little sister, Asha; she wouldn't be so little anymore but Alexa was sure their love for one another would be as strong as it used to be. All these thoughts raced through her mind as she hurried to reach her house. Finally, they arrived and stood outside her childhood home.

Alexa straightened her clothes and fixed her hair, then walked up to the door and reached for the door handle. Antoni caught her hand and told her it would be better if she knocked first. Hardly breathing, Alexa knocked on the front door and took a small step backwards, readying herself for her family reunion. A few seconds later the door opened, and there before her stood a middle-aged man whom she'd never seen before. This took her by complete surprise.

"Is . . . is my mother home?" she stammered.

"Who is your mother?" asked the man, rather sternly.

"Sophia! Sophia is my mother and this was our family home where we lived with my little sister, Asha. Where are they?" she asked, an edge of panic creeping into her voice.

The man stared at Alexa and then at Antoni standing next to her. "Look I don't want any trouble. I don't know where your family are, but they don't live in this house. I live here and have done so for almost four years. I'm sorry but I can't help you." The man went back into the house and closed the door firmly behind him.

Alexa's heart sank and tears began to well up in her eyes. She turned to Antoni, who took her in his arms and told her to be strong; they'd keep looking, as he had done to find his mother back in Łódź. Alexa suddenly had a thought, pulling away from Antoni.

"Our neighbors . . ." she said, hurrying over to the house next door. Magda and Michael, and their twins, Eva and Peter—they would know where her mother and sister were. Alexa knocked on the door, which was opened by a woman who was clearly not Magda. Alexa asked if she knew the family or where they were. The woman eyed the young couple suspiciously.

"Well, they're definitely not in my house. I'm sure they are back in Germany somewhere with all the other murderers, from what I've heard."

Alexa had forgotten Magda and her family were German and had moved to Lublin from Berlin when she was eight. Their German heritage had never been a problem before the war, but Alexa could understand why it would have become one during the war and definitely after it had ended.

"Are you Germans too? Because if you are, you're not welcome around here," snapped the woman as she stared at them through narrowed eyes.

"No, no," Alexa said hurriedly. "We are Polish. I used to live next door with my family but my mother and I were captured in the market square by the German soldiers over five years ago. My mother and I were transported to work in the forced-labor camp in Dachau, Germany, and that was the last place I saw my mother. I was taken as slave labor for five years, and today I've returned home for the first time. My little sister was left in this house with our neighbors the day my mother and I were captured, and I'm trying to find her too."

The woman's stern expression softened upon hearing Alexa's situation and that she was Polish.

"Well, I have no idea where your mother and sister are. I'm sorry for what you went through, but I can't help you. I'm glad you're not German, but I'm glad the German family are gone from this house. People in this town won't tolerate Germans here, you know," she said.

Antoni thanked the woman for her time and said they'd continue their search elsewhere. Gently taking Alexa's hand, he led his wife away from that place and all its memories. Alexa was crushed; Magda and her family were gone and she was no closer to finding out what had happened to her mother or the whereabouts of her sister.

Alexa shook her head, trying to clear her thoughts and think of her next move, of what she could try next to help her get closer to finding her family. She suddenly thought of her best friend, Helena, whom she had last seen five years earlier, on the day before Alexa and her mother were captured. She remembered that last Friday afternoon when they had walked back from school together, after the Germans had ordered all the pupils and teachers to leave the premises and march on the long roadway back into the town. In her mind's eye, Alexa could see the final image of Helena who, once they had parted, had turned back before reaching the street where her home was and waved goodbye to her. Alexa recalled vividly how she had responded by waving back and blowing a kiss in the wind to her, and then all too quickly she was gone from her sight.

Alexa told Antoni she wanted them to go to Helena's house next. They didn't have too far to walk, only a few streets. Alexa approached the front door of her friend's home, took a deep breath, and knocked. The door opened and there before her eyes stood her best friend.

"Helena!"

"Alexa? Oh, thank God, you're alive!"

The two girls, now young women, hugged each other tightly as though they were those two little girls again. They hugged and cried and laughed, completely overjoyed to see one another.

"Helena, what's going on? Who is that?" said a voice and then Helena's mother appeared at the door behind her daughter. "Alexa, oh how wonderful," she exclaimed, flinging her arms around them both in a warm embrace.

Alexa introduced Antoni to them as her new husband and the excitement levels grew. There had been very few occasions over the past five years of war for them all to experience such joy and happiness, but this was truly a time for them to celebrate.

"Where are my mother and Asha?" Alexa asked presently. "Do you know where they are?"

"You better come inside, dear," Helena's mother said.

Helena's mother began preparing a tray of coffee for them and brought it into the lounge. Alexa braced herself and asked again if they knew what had happened to her mother and sister. Helena and her mother looked at each other apprehensively as they sat, one on either side of Alexa; both the women took one of Alexa's trembling hands in her own. Alexa could sense their tension and dreaded their next words.

"We are sorry to say we have never seen your dear mother again and she has never come home," Helena's mother told her.

Alexa burst into tears, broken by this news of her dear mother. After a few minutes of sobbing, she enquired through her tears about her little sister, Asha. Helena and her mother related how, when she and her mother never returned home that day, their neighbor Magda continued to look after Asha. They told Alexa that Magda and her family had taken her in and raised her as one of their own.

Alexa seemed happy and comforted to hear that, but their story continued. About a year after Sophia and Alexa still hadn't returned home, her mother's sister-in-law had come to visit from Katowice. Upon hearing the situation, she had made arrangements for Asha to go back and live with her. They said they hadn't seen Asha in almost four years.

Helena left the room and after a few minutes returned, carrying an unopened parcel wrapped in brown paper and tied with string. She handed it to her friend and told her that Asha had left it in her safekeeping, with instructions for her to give it to Alexa whenever she returned home.

Alexa's eyes filled with tears again as she held the parcel in her hands. Written on the outside, in her little sister's handwriting, were the words "For my sister Alexa." She ran her finger slowly over her sister's words as if, somehow, she could touch a tiny part of her. She turned it over and over in her hands, stroking it gently, but she didn't open it yet.

Helena asked Alexa what had happened to her the day she had been taken away with her mother. Alexa started at the beginning, when she was trying on the blue pair of shoes.

She filled in all the facts she could, finally telling them of how she'd worked in the displacement camp in France for six months, where she'd met Antoni and married him the previous month.

Helena and her mother hung on every word of her story and were moved to tears several times during Alexa's account of her ordeal. When Alexa stopped talking, they both hugged her, holding her close. Alexa was comforted by their love for her and real empathy for all she had gone through.

CHAPTER 21

Alexa carefully opened up the parcel to reveal its contents. Inside, her little sister had enclosed a change of clothing for her, along with their family Bible. Alexa was touched by her little sister's thoughtfulness. The clothes wouldn't fit her now, obviously, but she was moved by the gesture.

Opening the Bible, she discovered a few family photographs of them all. She hadn't seen her family in person, or even a picture of her mother and sister in so long. They had existed only in her mind's eye and in her precious memories. Looking at the photographs was like holding a carbon copy of her memory. They were both exactly as she remembered them to be. Looking at the photos warmed her heart but broke it at the same time. There were photos of her father and grandmother too, and she took pleasure and comfort in seeing their faces once again.

In amongst the photographs, there was also a piece of paper on which Asha had written the address of where she was being taken to live with her uncle's wife, Isabella. Alexa's uncle had died when the girls were young, so neither of them had known him or his wife very well at all. The address was somewhere in Rzeszów, which was almost a three-hour journey away from Lublin by train. Alexa was determined to find her sister again, so the following morning, she and Antoni boarded a train bound for Rzeszów and made their way to the home of Alexa's aunt, in the hope of finding Asha there.

Arriving at the address, Alexa knocked at the front door. After a short pause, a woman answered and asked what they wanted. Alexa began explaining who she was and that she was searching for her younger sister. She asked if Isabella was home, at which point the woman said that she was Isabella, her uncle's wife, and invited them inside.

As she led them into the lounge, it was obvious Alexa's aunt had a taste for the finer things in life. The room was spacious and looked very grand with expensive decor, antique furniture, and a collection of elegant ornaments. The woman obviously had money or had been left a significant amount of wealth from her deceased husband. Alexa recalled her mother had once told her he'd been a rich man.

"I have just returned from visiting my childhood home in Lublin yesterday, where I went to try and find my mother and sister. I haven't seen them since the day my mother and I were rounded up by the SS, over five years ago." Alexa began explaining her dilemma to her aunt as best as she could, in the hope she would be empathetic and give her the answers she was desperately seeking. "There was no sign of my mother or sister in Lublin. Not at our old home and not at our neighbor's home either. I did find my best friend from school, and she gave me a small package which she told me Asha had left behind for me. In that package, Asha had left a note with your address, telling me she was being taken to live with you. So, we came straight here to find her."

The woman's whole demeanor suddenly changed completely, and a look of agitation and uneasiness seemed to come over her face. "Well, yes, I did bring her here to live with me," she said, fidgeting slightly on the edge of her chair, "but she's not living here now."

"Where is she? Is she okay? Please, I need to find her," pleaded Alexa. "It's been so long since I last saw her, when I was taken away to slave in Germany."

Isabella looked extremely uncomfortable as she prepared to deliver her next words. "Well, your sister Asha didn't like living here in my fine house in Rzeszów. It seems it wasn't good enough for her, and she kept crying and begging to go back home to Lublin, to wait for you and your mother to return. So, I eventually arranged for her to go and live at the home of a wealthy Polish woman in Lublin, where she was offered room and board in exchange for some help with the lady's four young children."

Alexa couldn't believe what she was hearing. Not only was Asha not being cared for by her own family, but it now seemed as though she was working in return for a roof over her head. Alexa couldn't help but draw the parallels with her own situation, having been worked like a slave in Germany for all those years, and now finding out her young sister had perhaps been forced to do something similar, but in their very own hometown.

Alexa couldn't understand why Helena and her mother hadn't seemed to have known anything about Asha living and working in Lublin. Something didn't seem right to her.

"Do you have the address where she is?" she asked.

"Maybe; I think it's written down somewhere in my bureau. Wait here. I will go and look for it," Isabella said, leaving the room.

Alexa turned to Antoni in hope of some comfort and reassurance, but even to him, things didn't sound very good. Alexa's aunt returned a few minutes later with a piece of paper on which she had scribbled down an address and handed it to her.

"How long has my little sister been living there at this woman's house in Lublin?"

"I don't know; I haven't been keeping count," said Isabella shortly.

Alexa was taken aback by her response and impolite manner but decided it was best not to push her on the matter. However, there was one more question she had to ask before they left. "Do you know where my mother is?"

"No, I have no idea. Nor do I have any interest in finding out. I never really liked your mother anyway," she declared.

Alexa, who was always calm, was incensed, and inwardly her blood began to boil. *'How dare this woman say such things about my lovely mother,'* she fumed to herself. She tried to keep her emotions in check but it was no good.

"How dare you speak about my mother that way. She never really liked you either, but at least she had manners enough to give you respect," said Alexa, her face turning red with anger.

"Get out of my house you ungrateful child, you. You're no better than that nasty little sister of yours. Your mother was probably glad to be rid of you both. No wonder she's never come back!" shouted Isabella, her voice shrill.

"Don't talk to my wife that way," said Antoni, stepping between the two women. "There is no need for you to be so cruel and hurtful."

Alexa was proud of her man for standing up for her and coming to her defense, but as mild-tempered and peaceful a person as she usually was, she wanted to lunge at the mean old woman.

"Get out. Leave my house, I said. Immediately!" barked Isabella.

"Don't worry, we are going," said Alexa. She and Antoni headed out the room and along the hallway towards the front door, with the irate woman following close behind as she continued to hurl abuse at them. Antoni reached to open the door and they stepped outside.

"And don't come back!" shrieked Isabella.

Alexa had no intention of ever going back and hoped she'd never set eyes on her nasty aunt again for as long as she lived. As she stepped over the doorstep and onto the garden path, she became overwhelmed with a desire to throw one more deserved, unkind comment back at the woman. "You would have made a very good Nazi," she yelled at her.

"Or a Gestapo wife," Antoni added. Grabbing Alexa's hand, they ran down the path and away from that awful place.

As they headed back to the train station, Antoni voiced his surprise over how unexpectedly nasty Alexa's aunt had been. Alexa told him she vaguely remembered overhearing a conversation between her mother and grandmother when she was young, about her aunt Isabella being an unpleasant woman who was sore and bitter over the fact that, in her opinion, she had married the wrong brother. Seemingly, she had really wanted to marry Alexa's father and had only settled for his brother after he had married Sophia, Alexa's mother. They agreed it was no wonder she was so bitter and cruel, even though it didn't excuse her poor behavior.

They redirected their thoughts to the more pertinent issue of Asha's whereabouts. Neither of them could understand why Helena hadn't known Asha had come back to live in Lublin. Surely, Asha would have gone to visit them and to enquire if there was any word about Alexa and her mother. It made no sense to them. It didn't add up.

They stopped first at a small café for some refreshments before beginning their long return journey, then they boarded yet another train in Rzeszów and headed back to Lublin, determined to on locate Asha.

When the train arrived in Lublin's main station, the fatigued young couple asked some locals for directions to the address Isabella had given them. After a long walk in the chill of the late October evening, they arrived at the large property where Asha was supposedly staying. Alexa was anxious and more than a little apprehensive, but it was the only possible lead she had left to try.

Taking a deep breath, she walked towards the front door, Antoni close behind her. Before she could raise her hand, Antoni knocked firmly on the black wooden door and stood back with his wife as they waited for a reply. Eventually, a short, slender brunette opened the door.

"Can I help . . .?" she started before the words faded on her lips, her eyes widening with surprise.

Alexa hadn't seen her little sister for over five years but she would have known her anywhere. She could have picked her out from amongst a crowd of a thousand young girls and from a mile away. Before she could form the words herself, her little sister beat her to it.

"Alexa! Oh my God, is that you?" shrieked Asha.

"Yes, my darling little sister, it's me. At last, I've found you," cried Alexa.

"Thank God, you've finally come for me. I've prayed and prayed for the day you'd come for me."

The two sisters threw themselves into each other's arms and hugged one another tighter than they had ever hugged or been hugged by anyone ever before. They laughed, and cried, and hugged, and cried again. The tenderness of their reunion was abruptly cut short by the appearance of a tall woman at the door, behind Asha.

"What is going on here? Who are you people?" asked the woman. A small child appeared at her side, wrapping itself around her leg.

"I am Alexa, and this is my little sister. I have come to take her home," said Alexa, beaming.

Asha moved to stand by Alexa's side, as they both faced the woman in front of them. Asha's tears continued to roll down her cheeks while she clung on to Alexa's arm.

"Well, you can't just take her away," said the woman. "She works for me."

"Not anymore, she doesn't," said Alexa, straightening her shoulders.

"The war is over, haven't you heard?" Antoni added, stepping closer to Alexa.

"The war may well be over, young man, but money is money, and I paid good money to this girl's aunt for her."

"She's not an object, she's a human being and she's my little sister. My aunt had no right to trade her to you for any amount of money. How would you like it if someone did that to your children?" Alexa glared at her, her words dripping with disgust. "My sister has worked her very last day for you. Now, we are going to collect her things and she is leaving your house with us this very hour."

"You'll have to wait until my husband gets home," said the woman with a disdainful sniff.

"Actually, we won't," Antoni replied firmly.

"Come on, Asha, show me where your things are," said Alexa. She held Asha's hand and they pushed past the woman into the house. Antoni followed close behind them and stood guard in the hallway. The woman of the house continued her protests but after a short while, realizing she was wasting her breath, finally went quiet.

It didn't take long for Asha to gather all her things together; she didn't have very much. Then she and Alexa quickly made their way back down the long hallway with her belongings, trailed by the woman who once again began to air her grievances. But it was no use—a few more steps and Asha was finally out of the house and free.

Antoni took her bag and introduced himself as her sister's husband. The tears continued to stream down Asha's face and her whole body shook. She was in shock by the events of the last few minutes; her big sister had finally come for her. She told them through her sobs that she had always hoped and prayed that one day, she and Alexa would be reunited but she'd almost given up hope it would ever happen.

Now, she couldn't take her tear-filled eyes off her big sister. Alexa walked with her arm around Asha, holding her close; she was also in a state of disbelief. It was a dream come true for them both. Well, part of their dream at least.

Alexa suggested they go to Helena's house. There weren't too many people or places in Lublin known to Alexa where they could still go, but she was sure they'd be made welcome by Helena and her mother.

As they approached Helena's home, they were relieved to see lights shining warmly from their front room. Antoni knocked on the door and before long, Helena's mother appeared. She was delighted to see the young couple again and even more excited to see Asha with them.

"Oh, dear girl, you're safe," she exclaimed and then, turning to Alexa, "Where did you find her?"

"We've only just found her in the last hour," said Alexa. "It's a long story."

Helena's mother invited them inside. Settled in the lounge with a tray of refreshments, they tried to catch up as best they could on each other's lives over the previous five years. Asha told them of how her aunt Isabella had been very mean to her from the start and had never let her leave the house alone. She told of episodes when Isabella would beat her and how eventually she announced one day that she was tired of her presence; soon after, she sold her to the rich woman in Lublin.

Asha related how she had a long list of heavy chores to carry out daily, taking care of all the household duties as well as looking after the woman's four young children. She hadn't been allowed out of the house alone and was locked in a room at night and whenever the family went out. She too had been a prisoner of forced labor.

Alexa was stunned by the parallel course of their lives. At least she had been five years older than Asha when she was forced to work for the Klausses; Asha had been nothing more than a little girl. It was so unfair, and almost too much pain to bear. But they were together again and the important thing was to try and console Asha, who became more and more upset as she related her story, her sobs continuing long after her words had stopped. Alexa held her hands as Helena enveloped her in a comforting hug. Asha had always been a gentle and emotional little girl, but now she was a broken soul.

As her sobs became quieter, Asha lifted her tear-streaked face to Alexa. "What happened to Mama?" she asked.

"I wish I had the answer to that question," replied Alexa gently. "All I know is the last time I saw her was the day after we left you with Magda. Remember, it was when we went into town to buy my new shoes. Well, while I was trying on the blue shoes I wanted inside the shop, the Nazi troops pulled up outside in the street and started rounding everyone up. They took us, and the shopkeeper, too."

"Where did they take her to? Where did they take you?" Asha's brow was furrowed, her eyes red and swollen. Alexa brushed a stray strand of hair, damp with tears, from her sister's cheek before answering, her voice low and matter-of-fact. She tried to spare Asha the more horrible details.

"Mama and I were transported to a work camp called Dachau in Germany. There we were separated and I never saw Mama again after that. I was sent to Frankfurt, where I was lined up in front of SS officers and their wives and finally selected by one of them because I was wearing grandma's necklace with the cross on it. One of the SS wives saw it, pointed to it and asked if I was Catholic. When I said yes, they selected me to be their unpaid slave. They took me to their farmhouse, and I worked all day from four in the morning until eleven at night, seven days a week, taking care of the house, their farm, all the chores, and their three children. I did that for five years."

Asha started to wail uncontrollable tears again, and hugged her big sister tightly.

"Don't cry Asha," said Alexa, holding Asha's face in her hands. "It wasn't as bad as what you went through. I was never beaten."

Alexa skipped forward in her story to tell them about the displacement camp in France, about Antoni and of how they had been married there, a little over a month before. That part of her story seemed to lighten up the mood a bit, and Asha finally stopped crying.

Asha asked to see her wedding rings whereupon Alexa sheepishly held out her hand to show her unpretentious rings. Silent up to that point, Antoni explained how he had made the engagement ring himself from some old wire and glass beads as a temporary substitute until he could afford to replace it with something more valuable in the future. He proudly pointed out that Alexa's gold wedding band was real and that he had purchased it, along with his own, in France. Helena, her mother, and Asha all agreed it was very thoughtful and meaningful of Antoni to have made the token engagement ring, Asha adding with a shy smile she thought it very romantic.

Asha then stood up and walked over to where she had dropped her bag of belongings on the floor. Opening the bag, she pulled out a pair of well-worn, lace-up brown shoes. She reached into one of the shoes and pulled out a pair of rolled-up white socks from the toe section. Sitting next to Alexa, she began to unfold them and then pushed one small hand inside one of the socks. Alexa watched her curiously.

"What are you doing, Asha?"

Pulling her fist out of the sock, Asha opened it to show what lay in the palm of her hand. "Here Alexa, this is perfect. You can use one of these as your engagement ring."

"Oh, my goodness," Alexa gasped. "Those are Mama's rings. But how did you get them?"

"Don't you remember? The day you and Mama went to buy the shoes and I was lying ill in bed, she let me wear her rings until she came back. But you both never came back, so I've kept them safe all this time."

Alexa's eyes filled with tears, which rolled unchecked down her cheeks. She took the rings and examined them closely, then held them tightly in her hand and placed them firmly against her chest close to her heart.

"My fingers are too small to wear them and I've always been afraid of losing them, so that's why I've kept them hidden in my shoes. But you're married now, so you should have them, Alexa."

"Thank you so much, Asha," she whispered. "I can't tell you what this means to me."

"You don't have to," said Asha. "I know what it means to you."

Alexa worked Antoni's wire ring off her finger and placed it on the table in front of her. She then slid her mother's engagement ring onto her wedding finger, on top of her own gold wedding band. She stretched her fingers out straight and looked down at her hand, a small smile of contentment curling the corners of her mouth.

The ring was made of yellow gold with four claws holding a raised, rectangular cut amethyst in place. Alexa vividly remembered her mother wearing it proudly, and now *she* would wear it with even more pride. This was indeed the most perfect ring she could have wished for. Sentimentally, it was priceless, and Alexa was delighted to now have it as her own. Reaching for Asha, she threw her arms around her little sister, kissing her cheeks and forehead repeatedly.

"I have something for you in return, darling," said Alexa as she reached both of her hands up towards the back of her neck. Unclipping the necklace clasp, she took off her cross. "Do you remember this?"

"Of course," said Asha. "It's Grandma's cross. And you still have it."

"I've worn it all these years, and it's kept me safe all these years, from when I was thirteen and taken away from home until now, and it's brought me back home again safely. Now you are thirteen years old it will be yours, and it will protect and keep you safe." said Alexa as she reached over and fastened the delicate chain securely around her sister's neck.

Asha reached up and grasped the cross, looking at it with an expression of pure delight and disbelief, at the same time. It was her turn to hug her sister tightly. "Thank you so much, Alexa," she said. "I'll wear it always. I'll never take it off."

"I'll wear Mama's wedding ring on my other hand and keep it safe until you get married one day, and then it will be your wedding ring. In that way, Mama will always be with both of us in a small, symbolic way."

Asha nodded agreement and hugged her sister again. "Thank you," she said, smiling up at Alexa.

It was too late for them to go anywhere else for the night, and in any case, they had nowhere else to go. Helena and her mother insisted on them all staying the night, making up beds for the three of them.

Early the next morning, Alexa and Antoni started discussing their best options for the future. They were now a family of three. Antoni said he'd start looking for electrical work and, as the town of Lublin was rebuilding, he didn't think it would be too hard for him to find employment of some kind.

After breakfast, Antoni headed off in search of work. As he asked around, he was told he'd have to register his name and skills at the town hall. When he got there, the Polish clerk asked his full name, town of birth, and work history. As he wrote down Antoni's details, he looked up at him suspiciously and started asking him more probing questions.

"What kind of name is *Metzinger*? It's not Polish. In fact, it sounds German to me. Are you German?"

"No, I'm not German," said Antoni. "I'm Polish. I grew up in Łódź."

"You may well have grown up there, but you were born in a German town with a German surname. That's the kind of people we don't want here in Lublin. Don't you know what your people did here and throughout Poland?"

"They are not my people," said Antoni through gritted teeth. "I am not German."

"Tell that to your parents," sneered the clerk. "You even look German. There is no work for you here. I suggest you leave Lublin immediately because I'm going to spread the word about you, and that kind of word travels fast."

"Look," said Antoni, trying to be patient. "You've got it wrong."

"No, you've got it wrong. Clear off out of this office and go back to Germany, before I call the police on you!"

Antoni had no choice but to leave the office. Even though he didn't feel like he was German and had grown up in Łódź, the truth was his birthplace was Gryfów Śląski, a part of Poland that had been under German occupation at the time. So technically, whether he liked it or not, he was German, and his surname was definitely German.

He quickly made his way back to Helena's home to tell Alexa what had happened. They might have to rethink living in Lublin because it looked like it was going to prove very problematic for them there.

They didn't have too many options to choose from, so Antoni decided it would be best for them to make their way to his birthplace, Gryfów Śląski. Polish newspapers had begun to report an abundance of vacant apartments for rent there, as well as plenty of work available. Due to its proximity to the German border, not a lot of native Poles wanted to live there and all the remaining German soldiers living there had been chased back over the border by the Russian troops. After some long deliberations, Antoni and Alexa decided it would be a good place for them to try and start a new life, at least for a few years, until the raw wounds of the war began to heal and they were back on their feet.

They planned to leave Lublin and journey to Gryfów Śląski with Asha, in search of a new beginning. Helena's mother was happy for them to stay with her until they were ready to leave. She went into town and bought three one-way train tickets for them, as well as some fresh loaves of bread, meats, cheeses, and drinks for their journey. She wouldn't let Antoni reimburse her for what she had spent. It was her way of doing a little to help them out.

She had great empathy and imagined how it could easily have been her daughter, Helena, who'd been taken by the Nazis in 1940 and separated from her. Helena could be the motherless one, with no family, no home, no employment, and the daunting task of trying to rebuild an entirely new life from scratch. So, she refused Antoni's offer of money, insisting it was the very least she could do; besides, she knew beyond a shadow of a doubt that Alexa's mother would have done the very same for her child, had she been in her shoes.

It was decided that early the following morning, Antoni, Alexa, and Asha would make their own way to the train station. Alexa knew the way and Antoni didn't want anyone to connect him to Helena and her mother, on account of his being considered German, in case anyone gave them any trouble. The day dawned; they packed their belongings, took the food which was prepared for them, said their heartfelt goodbyes, and began the walk to the station.

They reached the station in time to catch the 7 am train. The train ride would take about fifteen hours as it journeyed from Lublin in the East of Poland to Gryfów Śląski in the West of the country. They were all relieved to be leaving Lublin. Alexa had the horrific memories of being taken by force with her mother from there and never seeing her again after Dachau. Asha had heartbreaking memories of being abandoned there, of losing her mother and sister, and then being sold by her evil aunt to return there as a house slave. As for Antoni, his run-in with the man at the employment office gave him an idea of the levels of hatred now felt towards Germans by the Poles. They all hoped life would improve for them in a new town.

CHAPTER 22

A rriving in Gryfów Śląski, they found it was as Antoni had heard. There was plenty of work and an abundance of vacant places to live. Antoni quickly found a job as a full-time electrician and rented a furnished apartment for them all in the center of town. It had two rooms, a spacious kitchen, and a small bathroom.

Before long, Alexa found employment as a cook in a local restaurant, and she also managed to get Asha some afternoon shifts in the same establishment, clearing tables and washing dishes. They all pooled their wages to pay the rent, food and bills; any left-over money each week was saved in a jar. This was the first time both Alexa and Asha received payment for their hard work, and they took tremendous pride and satisfaction from it.

Almost a year had gone by when in the August of 1946, Alexa gave birth to her first child, a baby girl whom they named Stasha. The following year in September, Alexa gave birth to a baby boy, her first son whom they called Henry. Alexa was a wonderful and very loving mother and was delighted to be raising a family of her own. Antoni continued to work hard and was the main source of income for his family. He worked long hours and earned a good wage from an electrical company installing street lighting, for which there was a great need after the war. Alexa stayed home to look after her children, which was a full-time job in itself, while Asha continued to work at the restaurant, eventually being promoted to a full-time waitress.

At the end of her third pregnancy in the September of 1948, Alexa gave birth to another son, whom she named Richard. Tragically however, the baby boy only lived for three short weeks before he died suddenly in his sleep. Alexa was devastated, heartbroken over the loss of her tiny infant as deep sorrow once again touched her life. She was only twenty-two years old at the time and couldn't understand why such a tragedy had befallen her. Fortunately, she had her other two children who still needed her care and full attention. Her sadness was often interrupted by her son and daughter's needs; they brought her great joy and reminded her of happiness.

After Richard's death, Alexa, disliked living in the same apartment. It reminded her far too much of discovering his tiny cold and lifeless body in his crib. So, Antoni eventually found them a bigger home to live in, with three bedrooms, outside the center of town. The change of location was very beneficial for Alexa; although it didn't take away all of her pain and heartbreak, the new surroundings were a welcome distraction.

Since the bigger apartment was more expensive, Antoni had to work even longer hours, which often meant his having to work away from home. Sometimes, he was gone for a few days at a time. Asha moved with them to their new home and continued to help Alexa with the children, but she had met a young Polish man and their romance blossomed. They had started dating seriously, so her attention lay elsewhere.

Four days after Christmas in 1949, Alexa gave birth to her second daughter, Sofia. She was blonde-haired, blue-eyed, and beautiful like her mother; more importantly, she was healthy and lived past her first year.

In the summer of 1950, Asha married and moved out of Alexa and Antoni's home and into her own apartment with her new husband. As promised, Alexa gave her younger sister their mother's wedding ring, which she had looked after since Asha had given it to her for safekeeping.

Asha was delighted to wear her mother's wedding ring as her own; she told Alexa it gave her the sense that a part of their mother was always close to her. Asha still lived close to her sister and visited Alexa several days a week. She also helped her out regularly with caring for her nieces and nephew, until her husband was offered a better job in the town of Kraków, and they moved away. Alexa went on to have two more children with Antoni over the next four years, a boy she named Stefan and a girl she called Krystina.

Alexa had a full house with her five small children to look after, which was like having several full-time jobs at once. Her hands were always busy, and there was little or no time for anything else besides childcare, cooking, laundry, and housework. But she was young and healthy, and happy to be working to raise and nurture her own young family while her husband provided for them. To her, it was never a chore but rather something she took great joy in—caring for the needs of her own family.

Stasha was seven years old, Henry was six, Sofia four, Stefan two, and Krystina only a few months old, when Antoni began working away from home more and more. Alexa was still very much in love with Antoni and appreciated his working so hard to put a roof over their heads, food on their table, and clothes on their backs. She was a loyal wife and an adoring mother; she had good morals and was still a beautiful young woman who took pride in her appearance. She never smoked or drank as some of the young women did after the war, and she was always well-spoken, polite, and very well-mannered.

Antoni was very good at his job, and after a relatively short period of time, he was promoted to senior electrician. He had learned to drive and was given a company work truck to get around from job to job. One day, Antoni told Alexa he had a big installation job in Jelenia Góra, about thirty kilometers away from where they lived, so he'd be gone for at least three days. Alexa was used to being left at home alone with the children while he worked away. She always looked forward to his return.

On the second day Antoni was out of town on this particular job, one of his colleagues arrived at their home. When Alexa answered the door she panicked, immediately thinking the worst, that Antoni had been in a serious accident at work. However, Antoni wasn't hurt at all.

His colleague seemed to be a decent man. He explained to Alexa that his conscience had forced him to come and tell her what he was about to divulge to her. Alexa never expected for one moment what she was about to hear.

"I'm so sorry to tell you this," said the man, "but your husband is not working far away from home on a long installation job as he told you. He is actually only ten kilometers away, near Lubań."

"What do you mean?" asked Alexa.

"He's met an attractive, eighteen-year-old woman and is with her now, at her home. He's been having an affair with her for months and has told her he'll marry her. There have also been other women he's been involved with over the past few years, way before her. I'm sorry to be the one to tell you, but I couldn't stay quiet about it anymore. You are a beautiful young woman, and Antoni is crazy to even look at anyone else. He's so lucky to have you as his wife and the mother of his children. I felt you should know."

Alexa stared at the man. She felt dizzy as the blood drained from her face, and sick to her stomach, as though the bottom had been ripped out of her world. She couldn't believe the words she was hearing. She felt a stabbing pain in her heart as the man spoke, and her mind began to race back through the recesses of her memory, searching for dates, times, discrepancies, and holes in Antoni's stories that hadn't added up or might have sounded suspicious at the time.

Now she doubted everything. The trust she had had in her husband was now shattered, and everything was tainted by the liar's brush. Thoughts raced through her head. The boisterous children were running around or playing inside the house, making a noise as usual. Alexa suddenly screamed at the top of her lungs for them to be quiet, something she had never done before and which was so out of character for her. The startled children stopped in their tracks. Alexa didn't know what to say to the man after his delivery of the devastating news, but she thanked him for confiding in her and told him that, as hard as it was to hear, it was better she knew the truth.

On the third day, Alexa awaited Antoni's return home, ready to confront him face-to-face with the information she had received. She had rehearsed over and over again what she was going to say to him when she saw him, but she worried her emotions and anger would take over. She had always been a peaceful person, but this news about Antoni's infidelity and betrayal not only broke her heart, but it infuriated her and made her blood boil.

Antoni eventually arrived home and when he walked through the door, he approached his wife to kiss her, as always. As he leaned forward towards Alexa, she pulled away from him and told him not to kiss her with his cheating lips. Antoni wasn't expecting such a response from her and it caught him off guard, but he quickly put on his poker face and asked her what she was talking about. Alexa informed him she knew he had been with another woman for the past three days, and she also knew there had been others before her, too. He kept a straight face and accused her of being crazy while trying to laugh it off. Then he became defensive and protested his innocence, which he tried to back up with the excuse of his having to work so hard to provide for their large family.

Alexa didn't back down but instead asked him how he planned to marry the young eighteen-year-old girl when he was already married to her with five small children. She suggested he take their children over to the young girl's house and see how long she would remain interested in him, knowing he was already a husband and a father.

Alexa raised her voice, shouting out her accusations, which she had never done before. Antoni lost his temper and for the very first time, lifted his hand to Alexa, slapping her hard across her face. The older children saw him hit their mother and began to cry. It was as though a flame had been lit, igniting Antoni's temper, and he completely lost control. He continued to strike Alexa a few more times with his hands and finally pushed her down to the floor. Uncaringly, he stepped over her and headed back out of the front door, slamming it behind him, and drove off in his truck.

Alexa was in shock; the tears running down her face stung as they reached the open cut on her right cheek. She was shaking in fear, and she was hurting. The children were scared, her oldest three visibly upset. Alexa got to her feet and went to the bathroom to tend her wound. Looking in the mirror, she made up her mind. She would not tolerate such treatment and certainly not from someone who supposedly loved her.

She began packing a suitcase with a few changes of clothes for her three youngest children and herself. She then began to explain to Stasha and Henry that when their father came back home, she would be going to visit their aunt Asha in Kraków overnight and they would stay with their father. But the children were not happy with that arrangement and Alexa realized she couldn't leave without them.

Antoni arrived back home a few hours later with a bunch of flowers in his hands; he apologized profusely for his behavior and begged Alexa to forgive him. Alexa reverted to her old defense mechanism and became who she needed to be in the current situation: the wounded but forgiving wife. But internally, she refused to be treated that way or to live with someone who was unfaithful as well as violent towards her.

The following day when Antoni left for work, Alexa finished packing her suitcase and took all the money from the savings jar. Then, with all five of her children, she left the apartment and headed for the railway station, boarding a train to Kraków where they would visit Asha.

Alexa stayed at her sister's home for five days before returning home to Antoni. The break had done her good but she missed her husband, despite what he had done to her. She still loved him. Antoni seemed to have learned his lesson and was on best behavior for a while. Unfortunately, he didn't have a complete change of character or habits, and before long he was back to his womanizing and cheating. However, he never lifted his hand to Alexa again.

Alexa tried to handle her husband's unfaithfulness as best as she could, but it wasn't her idea of a happy marriage; she knew deep down she deserved much better. By the time Stasha, her oldest daughter, finished attending her first school at age eleven, Alexa had finally built up enough courage and strength to leave Antoni, determined to provide for and raise her family on her own. However, Antoni had other plans.

He told Alexa she was only allowed to take the three girls with her and he would be keeping his two sons, Henry and Stefan, with him. Alexa refused but Antoni insisted she would not take his sons away from him. So, Alexa left, taking her three daughters, with the full intention of returning for her boys once she had settled down in a new apartment and had her own income, which she eventually did.

CHAPTER 23

Many years had passed since the days of Alexa's servitude, when she was first taken and enslaved by the German SS family at the tender age of thirteen. Alexa continued to be a hard worker throughout her life, as she had been in her youthful years.

At one point, as a single parent, she held down four part-time jobs at once, in order to support and provide for her young family. Her day would start by baking fresh bread at the local bakery. When that shift ended, she'd work a full shift in a laundry house where she'd wash, hang, iron, and fold large piles of laundry. Next, she would work in a nearby cafeteria, preparing and cooking large meals to be served to a steady stream of hungry customers. Finally at night, she'd collect large buckets of coal and carry them on foot for five kilometers for delivery to customers near where she lived.

During her workday her older son, Henry, would stop by the bakery and she'd give him fresh bread to take back home for all her children to eat for breakfast. While she worked in the laundry house, she would take care of her own family's laundry needs as well, so her children always had clean clothes to wear. Every day after school, Stasha and Henry would do their bit to help. Stasha would bring her siblings round to the back of the cafeteria, where Alexa would give them some food to eat. Stasha would then take the children back home and look after them until their mother came home at night.

Henry would fetch and carry home the clean clothing for the family. Finally, after her long day of hard work, Alexa would eat before leaving the cafeteria, then collect the two heavy buckets of coal for delivery, and walk the long trek back home. This was her daily routine for the years while her children were still young, and her only means of providing for them all.

But she didn't stop there. To better herself and her income, she studied hard at night while her children slept, with a view to qualify as a crane operator at the large ship-builder's yard and port in Gdańsk. She had faith and determination that she could achieve the goal she'd set herself so she was delighted when her hard efforts and sacrifices paid off and she passed the exams with flying colors.

Alexa became the very first fully qualified female crane operator in Gdańsk, a job usually carried out by men only. This great achievement allowed her to earn a higher wage and a whole new level of respect. She was eventually moved to a management position and offered a larger apartment with extra bedrooms to live in with her family.

Throughout the years of her hard work, Alexa remained the proud mother of six beautiful, growing children. She loved having a vibrant family of her own to love and care for, but she had chosen badly when it came to love. She and Antoni were finally divorced and several years later, Alexa met the man who would become her second husband.

Once again, she loved him very much, although not as much as she had loved Antoni. They built a life and a future together and had a daughter, whom they named Violetta. Unfortunately, however, as time went by in their relationship, it became apparent to Alexa that her husband had more of a love for alcohol than he did for her and their daughter. One day he went out drinking and never came home again.

Alexa found herself single once more, looking after her young children alone.

As the years went by in Poland, Alexa regained contact with and maintained her friendships with her three dear European girlfriends, Henrietta, Marta, and Greta, long after the war had ended. They kept in touch by writing to each other and making regular phone calls to one another, updating each other on their young families' progress and the various paths their lives were taking. They had all individually visited Alexa in Poland with their children, at some time or other, and their friendships grew ever stronger with the passage of time.

Alexa had also kept in touch with the Klauss family. A few years after the war ended, she wrote to the family, thanking them for freeing her and informing them she had been successfully reunited with her younger sister, but sadly not her mother. She asked after their children, for whom she still had a genuine fondness after caring for them full-time for five years of her life. Alexa was delighted to receive a warm reply back from the family in the form of a letter, which was then followed soon after by some gifts.

From then on, every few months, the Klausses began sending Alexa large cardboard-boxed parcels, packed full of goods for her and her family. Alexa was surprised to receive these large parcels full of coffee, tea, chocolate, sweets, biscuits, cheese, tinned meats, medicines, shoes, leather jackets, all kinds of clothing for both adults and children, and small ornaments. And there was always a couple of hundred Deutsche marks safely hidden inside one of the items.

Poland had taken a long time to recover after the war had ended, and poverty there was widespread. Life wasn't easy in Poland, and times were indeed hard. The rebuilding of life took great effort and inner strength and it was a very long and painful journey of recovery for most.

Alexa greatly appreciated the packages that came from Germany for her and her family and enjoyed sharing them. She was a giver and kept very little for herself. In some small way, the packages were a form of compensation, a way of making up for all the years she had slaved and worked so hard for the Klausses in Germany, without ever being paid.

The packages continued to arrive at her home for many years; Alexa saved all the German marks enclosed within, depositing them in her bank account. Alexa eventually received some reparation payments from the German government as well, for the five years during the war she had been kept to work against her will. This was part of the German government's restitution program by which they made monetary payments to many Europeans who had been taken from their homes by the Nazis, lost all their belongings, and imprisoned or used as forced German labor.

The reparation payments to Alexa were a minimal amount and they continued sporadically, every six months for a couple of years as a form of compensation for all the time she had been worked by the Klausses. Of course, these payments could never make up for what Alexa had lost and sacrificed during the war years, and although it wasn't a small fortune, it did allow Alexa to buy some larger household items and a few extras. Issued only for a limited time, the reparation payments eventually came to an end. However, the parcels from the Klauss family continued to arrive for decades.

During the years leading up to and especially through the "Solidarity" movement in the 1980's, life became even harder in Poland and many basic general items became unavailable to buy in the shops. Such items that were once taken for granted became highly sought after. Whenever news of an incoming shipment or delivery was due to arrive at a local store, word travelled quickly, and a mass of people would stand in long lines in the street outside the shop for hours in advance, in the hope of making a successful purchase.

During these tough times, several of Alexa's good friends who were living in wealthier parts of Europe and were better off than she, also began helping out by kindly sending parcels of goods to her and her family. In the spring of 1978, Alexa received a letter from the Klauss family inviting her to travel back to Germany, but this time on vacation as their guest. Since her children were all grown up, Alexa decided to take them up on their offer and to bring her oldest daughter along with her on the journey. Plans were set in motion for the trip and flights were booked and paid for by the Klausses.

Alexa was a little anxious about returning to Bitburg, the old town in Germany where she had been forced to live and work during the Second World War. Although she had been terrified as a young girl when she was first taken and was initially very scared when she had first arrived at their home, once she became familiar with and used to the Klausses, she wasn't afraid of them anymore. Although they had demanded hard labor from her on a daily basis and had given her a full list of chores to carry out, they weren't overly mean to her or physically abusive.

The family had grown fond of Alexa over a relatively short period of time and so had not been wicked to her–as was the case with many other SS-run households, with their cruel treatment of innocent young teenagers who had also been taken from European countries against their will. The Klausses had trusted Alexa, even to the point of allowing her to cross the border each Sunday into Luxembourg during her last year with them, to spend the day alone at the shoemaker's home. Now, Alexa, although naturally a little apprehensive to revisit her past, found herself quite looking forward to seeing some of the people she'd grown fond of, as well as the place where she had spent those years of her life as a captive.

Alexa and her daughter boarded the plane in Gdańsk. It was their very first time on an airplane, and the excitement of the flying experience was a good distraction for Alexa. The flight was short and in less than two hours they landed safely in Frankfurt. From the airport, they took a bus into the city's main station and boarded a train for the journey to Bitburg.

Alexa couldn't help but reminisce about her past train rides. On the very first one, after being captured by the Nazis, she had been forced at gunpoint into a train wagon as a young teenager. Not knowing what or where she and the other boys and girls were destined for, they were crammed together in the dark and dingy boxcar with the foul smells that made her nauseous and others vomit.

Her second train journey was the one towards her freedom. She had unwittingly entered the first-class carriage full of SS officers and soldiers, only to discover she didn't actually have a first-class ticket and shouldn't be there. She recalled the scene vividly, along with the mixed emotions of panic and fear she had felt as she concealed her true identity and pretended to be an eighteen-year-old German civilian. She thought of the SS officer who came to her aid by paying the train conductor the rest of the money needed in order to convert her ticket into a valid first-class one.

Alexa couldn't help but be convinced by the power of her prayers. She had lost count of how many times she had petitioned God on her own behalf for his protection and help, but she was very aware of the many times God had heard her petitions and had answered her prayers. Alexa's faith had been strengthened by what she felt was God figuratively taking hold of her right hand and guiding her through the dangers she had faced through the years. So, no matter what situation she found herself in, she never felt truly alone and never became completely overcome or paralyzed by fear.

Alexa's daughter interrupted her mother's thoughts, asking if she could go and buy something from the restaurant car.

"Of course, darling," said Alexa, giving Stasha some money. "But don't be too long."

Stasha left their compartment and slid the door closed behind her, which triggered Alexa's memories of her train journey from Paris to Berlin with Antoni, soon after they had married and left the displacement camp. She smiled as she recalled the few hours they had shared in Paris—their honeymoon—before boarding the train. She remembered how they'd walked through the Parisian streets hand in hand, the café they had sat in, drinking coffee, and the Polish Bible the elderly French man had given her in the old bookstore. And then, they'd caught the train to leave France as they began their long journey home.

She remembered how good it had felt to snuggle into her husband's chest as they slept on the train. She also remembered how Antoni had wangled himself an invite to join the poker game with the American soldiers; he had even won a nice sum of money off them there in the restaurant carriage.

Antoni had been the true love of her life, and those earliest years spent with him had been amongst her happiest. It had broken her heart to find out he was unfaithful. Even though she had chosen to leave him and eventually obtained a divorce, deep down in her heart she still held a torch for him and knew she always would.

A little while later, Stasha returned to the train compartment, and about five hours later, their train finally approached Bitburg.

As they disembarked, Alexa looked around, scanning the faces of the people on the platform for a familiar face. Then she spotted a tall blond man in his forties, whom she recognized as Richard, the Klausses' oldest son. He was no longer the young teenager he'd been when she had last seen him, but she couldn't mistake his facial features. He was the spitting image of his father.

Alexa waved to him, catching his attention. He walked over to them and re-introduced himself to her, kissing her on each cheek and welcoming her before introducing himself to Stasha. Taking their suitcases from them, he led them out of the station towards his car. Alexa was surprised at how much he looked like his father. Herr Klauss had been in his early forties when Alexa had first met him, and to her, Richard was now his double. She hadn't seen the family for over thirty years, and realized everyone would have changed and aged.

Herr and Frau Klauss still lived in their same farmhouse, and as Richard drove through the town towards it, Alexa began to recognize the once-familiar surroundings. Richard turned into the gates, drove up the long driveway, and stopped outside the Klauss family's home. The outside of the property didn't look as well kept as she remembered it used to be. As they all got out of the car, Herr and Frau Klauss came out of the house to greet them.

"Alexa, it is so good to see you again. Welcome," said Herr Klauss. "And this must be your daughter."

"Hello, Herr Klauss, it's good to see you again."

"Please, Alexa, call me Fredrick." He shook her hand and kissed her on both cheeks, as was the German custom. "And please, my wife is Emilie."

Alexa had never been permitted to call them by their first names when she was a teenager working for them, so it seemed a little odd and unnatural to her at first. But these were different times and she was no longer a young girl; nor was she their slave. She was a woman to be respected in her own right.

"Alexa, welcome," said Frau Klauss. "It's wonderful to see you again. How was your journey?" she asked as she greeted Alexa without the handshake, hugging her warmly and kissing her cheeks.

"Thank you, our journey was fine, Emilie. This is my oldest daughter, Stasha."

Frederick and Emilie Klauss greeted Stasha, acknowledging what a pretty young girl she was They then invited them both into the house, followed by Richard who carried in their suitcases.

Frau Klauss served coffee, sandwiches, cakes, and pastries in the lounge for everyone to enjoy while they all caught up on each other's lives and news. All of the Klausses' three children were married with children of their own and no longer lived at their parent's farmhouse. They didn't live too far away, though, and Alexa was assured she would see them all during her visit.

After over an hour of chatting together, Richard excused himself, saying he had to be going. He promised he'd come by soon to take Alexa and Stasha out in his car, to visit some of the sights and some of the other local people who remembered Alexa and were looking forward to seeing her again.

Alexa began to clear the table, gathering the used plates and cups together, but Frau Klauss said there was no need— she was their guest. However, Alexa insisted it was no bother and carried the tray full of dishes into the kitchen. It was all very surreal, and as she walked through the kitchen door, her mind flashed back like a time machine to when she was a teenager, slaving for the Klausses.

The kitchen hadn't changed much. It still had the same layout and even the kitchen furniture was the same. Only the color of the walls had changed, a cosmetic change. Alexa placed the tray on the large kitchen table. Instead of washing all the dishes and cleaning up as she had always had to do all those years before, she left the full tray sitting on the table and turned to leave the kitchen behind her. That wasn't her job anymore.

It was getting late, and both Alexa and Stasha were tired from their journey, so Herr Klauss carried their bags upstairs, while Frau Klauss showed them to their bedrooms. They took Alexa to Richard's old bedroom, which had been redecorated since he was a child, and told her to make herself at home. Alexa was relieved they hadn't expected her to sleep in her old room; she felt that might have been too much emotionally for her to handle. They showed Stasha to their daughter Anna's old room, which had also been redecorated and looked warm, comfortable, and inviting.

The Klausses told them to make themselves at home and to help themselves to anything they needed. Alexa was grateful for the kindness they were showing her but couldn't help but compare how very different things had been some thirty plus years before to how they were now.

Alexa didn't hold any malice towards the Klausses, nor was she a person who was filled with hatred or one to harbor resentment. However, she was human and remembered all too well how hard and long she had worked on a daily basis, all year round, for five long years. She remembered how depressed and alone she had felt back then, with no family of her own around her, and how desperate she had been to be reunited with her own family in Poland.

There had also been the fear factor that had haunted her daily: she was an undesirable Polish girl in the eyes of the Germans and could easily be taken off to a concentration camp or killed at any time. These feelings had been prominent every day of her captured life from the age of thirteen.

However, she was also well aware her experiences could have been so much worse for her and even more horrific than they actually were, living with the Klausses. She remembered how she had made certain choices—conscious decisions to keep herself and her frame of mind positive, as difficult as it was at times. She'd kept her faith strong and her hope fueled and alive, in the firm belief that her situation was only temporary and one day she would be free.

As Alexa reflected, she realized this had been her blueprint for survival, her escape from tragedy to triumph. It was how she had chosen to live her life rather than just merely survive it.

Alexa made sure Stasha was comfortable in the guest bedroom. As she left the room and turned out the light, she reflected again on how ironic the current scenario was. There she was, wishing her own daughter goodnight, some thirty plus years later in the Klausses' daughter's bedroom, where she had once looked after young Anna. She could never have imagined this scene ever happening, way back then.

Alexa said goodnight to the Klausses and retired for the evening. She closed the door to Richard's old bedroom and leant against it for a moment, letting her mixed emotions wash over her. As had been her unbroken routine since she was a young child, Alexa prayed, reciting Psalm 91 as she did every night before going to sleep. That was the one constant in her life, the one thing that had never changed. Her belief and faith in God had never faltered, and she trusted without a shadow of a doubt that God had indeed protected her throughout her life and trials, ultimately delivering her to safety.

The following day, their first in Bitburg, Alexa took Stasha for a walk into the old part of town. It all seemed very familiar to her, even though it had been so long since she had last walked those very streets. She recognized some of the old buildings but there were many that were no longer standing in their original places. New taller and more modern buildings now replaced them.

Alexa recognized the home where her friend Elizabeth had lived and worked all those years ago and decided to knock on the door to see if it was still owned by the same family. The home looked old and uncared for, its neglected front garden overgrown with weeds and its fencing broken with missing pieces. Alexa approached the front door and knocked upon it. There was no immediate answer and she and Stasha were about to walk away when the door slowly opened to reveal a short, elderly, white haired woman. As Alexa looked into her eyes, she recognized her as the wife of the family for whom her friend Elizabeth had worked long ago.

The woman clearly didn't recognize Alexa at first, so she told her who she was, triggering the old woman's memory, whereupon she greeted her warmly. The woman told Alexa she now lived in the large house all by herself; her husband had died many years prior and her children were all married with their own children and living in East Germany.

She seemed very happy to have visitors and warmly invited Alexa and Stasha to join her for coffee. Alexa asked after Elizabeth; perhaps she knew where she might be living now. But the woman said she had no idea, and she didn't have a contact address for her. That was the only reason Alexa had stopped at the house in the first place—to ask what had happened to Elizabeth after the war had ended. However, being polite, she drank her cup of coffee before making her excuses, telling the woman they had to leave as they had somewhere else they needed to be. The woman told them to come back again anytime they were passing, but Alexa had no intention of returning there.

Alexa and Stasha stayed in Bitburg at the Klausses' home for a week. On the morning of their second day there, Richard returned to the farmhouse as promised to take them on a tour of some of the local places of attraction and interest. Around noontime, he drove them to visit an old family friend and neighbor of the Klausses, the Kleins.

They remembered Alexa very well as a lovely young teenager and were genuinely delighted to see her again. They insisted Alexa, Stasha, and Richard join them for lunch and prepared a feast for them all to enjoy. Over food and drink, they shared their various memories and stories from the past together, from when Alexa was a young girl and through her teenage years when she had worked for the Klausses. Then they caught up on events from when she had left the town of Bitburg in 1945, right up to the present day.

The Kleins also showed a sincere interest in Stasha, asking her questions about her life in Poland, her siblings, her likes, her hobbies, and her ambitions for the future. They made Stasha feel very welcome, and she saw for herself how well-respected and liked her mother was. The fondness the family felt for Alexa was obvious and most endearing, even after the passage of such a long period of time and no contact for decades.

Stasha loved her mother very much, but they were mother and child so it was natural; they were blood relatives. But these German people, as nice as they seemed, were all strangers in Stasha's eyes. She had never heard of them before and couldn't understand the real affection these people seemed to have for her mother. Weeks later, when back in Poland, Stasha shared all these experiences with her brother Henry. She told him how she couldn't quite understand what made their mother so special to these people.

After they had spent a few hours at the Kleins's home, enjoying their hospitality, Richard said it was time they left, as they had another few stops to make that day around town. The Kleins gave both Alexa and Stasha some small gifts and souvenirs to take home with them and hugged them goodbye before they got into Richard's car.

Richard drove them for a further fifteen minutes to another house where they were expected. Alexa didn't recognize this house but as they walked towards its front door, she noticed it was pretty and well cared for. Its gardens were full of vibrantly colorful flowers, which filled the air with their sweet fragrance. Alexa asked who lived in the house but Richard only gave a mischievous smile and told her it was a surprise.

He knocked on the door, which was quickly opened by a neatly-dressed, older woman who smiled at Alexa with delight. Alexa recognized the woman immediately, and was equally delighted to see her too.

"Oh, my goodness, is it really you, Alice?" exclaimed Alexa. Without waiting for a reply, she wrapped her arms around the now elderly woman. They hugged tenderly before pulling back to look at each other.

"Oh, Alexa, how wonderful it is to see you again. I've prayed and prayed for your safety all these years," she said, her voice cracked with emotion, "and here you are standing in front of me."

They embraced again, and Alexa's eyes were filled with tears of joy. For the woman standing before her was the shoemaker who had once lived over the border in Luxembourg. It was she who had realized Alexa was being kept and worked as a Polish slave by the German SS officer and his family, when she had come to collect their custom-made shoes. All those years ago, she had gone out of her way to make seventeen-year-old Alexa feel welcome, wanted, and cared about, inviting her into their family home as their special guest.

Alice and her husband, a high-ranking town official, had challenged Herr Klauss when he came looking for Alexa, and demanded Alexa be allowed to come over the border to visit with them in Luxembourg every Sunday; she would have a day off to relax and spend with their family. Alexa had never forgotten the generosity and kindness extended to her by Alice and her family, even though they had lost touch after the war's end. They had restored her faith in humanity and had reminded her that not all people were bad and abusive;

not all people should be labeled the same or painted with the same brush. Beyond that, she was indeed worthy, of value, and very likable. They had even made her a pair of her very own shoes as a gift.

Pushing the memories aside, Alexa introduced Stasha to Alice, who was delighted to meet her. She kissed her on both cheeks and then invited them all into her home. Alice prepared fresh coffee for them all, served in her finest set of bone china. She brought out a tray of fresh cream cakes and a selection of pastries for them all to enjoy. There was also a plate of fine Belgian chocolates and biscuits, which she placed on the table before them, and invited them all to help themselves.

Alice and Alexa began to catch up on the void of years passed since they'd last seen each other. Alice updated Alexa on her family, telling of her two grown children and their individual lives, and proudly showing photographs of her grandchildren and shared stories of their achievements. Alice had left Luxembourg a year after the war had ended and made the move to live in Bitburg with her husband and family, after their home had been destroyed by an accidental fire.

Alice then asked Alexa about her journey back to Poland when she was eighteen and had left the Klausses' farmhouse near the end of the war. Alexa hadn't talked much about her own story since the end of the war years. She knew what she had gone through, but she also knew many others had suffered far worse experiences. So, she had kept her experiences privately to herself, concentrating on raising her children and working hard to support them. However, back in Germany again after all this time, she had told her personal story of the long journey she had made to get home to Poland, three times already. Telling Alice would be her fourth time, but these were people who genuinely cared about what she had gone through and what she had returned to find, so it seemed easier to share it with them.

She told them a detailed account of her boarding the first-class train carriage and almost fainting in fear as she found it full of Nazi soldiers and SS officers. She related her long walk at night through the snow-covered forest, her arrival at the convent, and how she had been kept there against her will, worked by the nuns for a further four months until the bombing by the Allied forces.

She told them how she had escaped with her three friends until she had been picked up by the Allied troops and taken to the abandoned school with the local German civilians. She described how she had stood up for herself, declaring she was Polish and that there had been a case of mistaken identity. She told them about the sympathetic US commander who had her select ten German women to supervise, and then offered her treasures beyond her wildest dreams.

Alice hung on every word of Alexa's story, listening intently as it progressed onward with her journey to the displacement camp in France and her time spent there, reunited with her three girlfriends. Then, she spoke of her first love and of marrying Antoni and their journey back to Poland together to find their families.

Alexa shared about the heartbreak she felt of never finding her mother alive; she had eventually learned Sophia had been hospitalized after serious beatings and either killed there or marched to a concentration camp. Even at the age of fifty-one, Alexa still became emotional when she thought of the senseless murder of her beautiful mother, and of the last time she had ever seen her in Dachau, where they were separated forever by the Nazis. She then talked about the joy she had upon finding and being reunited with her little sister, Asha, and how inseparable they had become.

Alice went to her drinks cabinet and returned with a crystal decanter filled with cognac from which she asked Richard to pour them each a glass. Alexa's story obviously evoked deep emotions in her listeners as she spoke, especially Alice, who had been visibly moved. In some way, Alexa found it to be therapeutic and somewhat of a release and healing process for her, as she talked about her personal experiences.

There was a knock at the door and Alice excused herself to get up and answer it. She returned to the lounge accompanied by another older woman, who had heard Alexa was visiting with her friend Alice. The woman had never known Alexa personally but she was anxious to meet her. Alice introduced her to Alexa and Stasha. Richard seemed to know her already, and they greeted each other warmly.

Once the introductions were over, the woman invited Alexa to come to her home for some refreshments and said her husband and family really wanted to meet her too. Alexa thanked the woman but politely declined her invitation. She explained they had already been shown so much German hospitality that day, they couldn't possibly eat or drink anymore.

The woman seemed very disappointed and begged Alexa to reconsider. Alexa could see the woman was very anxious and that it seemed very important to her for some reason. Alice even began to join in, encouraging Alexa to go to her friend's home, which was close by, even if for a short visit. Eventually, they managed to persuade Alexa to go to the woman's home, although she made it clear she wouldn't be able to stay for very long.

Richard went out to start the car while Alexa said her goodbyes to Alice, promising to return to see her again two days later, when the rest of her family had arranged to visit. Alice promised them a hearty home-cooked German meal together. Alexa and Stasha headed out of the house and into the car with the woman and Richard. Alexa and Alice waved to one another as they drove off.

CHAPTER 24

After driving a short distance, Richard pulled his car over off the road and parked it outside a small white cottage, which was where the old woman apparently lived. They all got out of the vehicle and made their way into the woman's home. There, a man sat in a high-backed, comfy-looking leather chair, whom Richard greeted first by calling him "Uncle Hans" and hugging him in a manly way.

The man stood up from his chair, and Alexa became aware of his height. Although he was well into his seventies, he had retained his height and was a rather elegant, good-looking gentleman with a full head of grey, almost silver hair.

"Hello, Alexa," he said, looking straight into her blue eyes.

"This is my husband, Hans," said the woman, introducing him to Alexa.

Alexa looked back at him but she didn't recognize him as someone whom she had ever known from her past. Hans extended his hand to shake Alexa's.

"Do you remember me?" he asked.

Alexa felt embarrassed as she had no idea who he was. "I'm sorry, sir, but it's been so long since I was in Germany. Please forgive me, but I'm afraid I don't remember you." She reached out her hand to shake his.

"Do you remember our train ride together?"

Alexa looked puzzled and somewhat confused as she began to search her memory for a match.

"I'm the officer who paid your ticket on the train," he said with a broad smile.

Alexa couldn't believe her ears. However, hearing his words, she immediately made the connection, recognizing him clearly from that day in the first-class train carriage, all those years before. He was the tall, blond SS officer who had smiled pleasantly at her and been so kind. It had always puzzled her; she had never been able to figure out exactly why he did what he did. He was the one who had come to her aid when the train conductor was giving her such a hard time over her ticket discrepancy. He was the one who asked the train conductor how much it was to upgrade her incorrect train ticket to a first class one and had then kindly paid the amount, so she could remain seated in that carriage. Now after all those years, the pieces of the puzzle were slowly beginning to fall into place.

"Wow, I remember you now," said Alexa.

Hans gave Alexa a gentle hug, but she hugged him back tighter, now she knew and remembered who he was. Immense gratitude for his kind gesture all those years ago overwhelmed her. She was amazed by this unexpected revelation, her surprised expression continued to show upon her face as the others looked on with excitement.

"Oh, sir, thank you ever so much. I don't know what would have happened to me that day if you hadn't paid for the rest of my ticket. Herr Klauss told me he had bought me a first-class ticket and said specifically I was only to sit in the first-class carriage."

"I know he did," said Hans. "Frederick is my cousin and I told him it would be better if we set things up that way for you. We knew I'd be traveling on that very train in the first-class carriage that day, and I agreed to look out for you and make sure no one hassled you and that you'd come to no harm under my watch."

Alexa stared at Hans; it was hard to believe Herr Klauss and he had gone to all that bother to ensure her safety.

"We decided it was better you didn't know about our plan, so there was no way you could give the game away or blow my cover. As you know, at that time you, being Polish, could very easily have been killed. Believe me when I tell you, there were plenty of blood-hungry soldiers in that carriage who wouldn't have thought twice about shooting you."

Alexa was very well aware of the dangerous situation she had been in back then in the train carriage, and now it all made complete sense to her. She began thanking Hans profusely, over and over again, for having made sure she was safe.

Hans's wife brought a tray of fresh coffee into the room and placed it down on the table in front of them. Hans asked Richard to bring over his crystal decanter and some brandy glasses from the sideboard and poured them all a drink.

"How did you get on, once you finally got off of the train? Hans asked her. "I remember watching you from the window as you walked away with your little suitcase. Did you reach the convent safely that night?"

Alexa told him she had walked through the snow-covered forest in the dark for several hours but didn't go into great detail about how difficult a journey it had been for her on foot. She told how she had eventually reached the convent very late at night but the nun wasn't pleased to receive her, nor was she very nice to her. Alexa described how she was placed in a locked, brick, cell-type room in the basement and then kept in the convent for four months, forced to work hard labor with three other European girls who were also being held against their will.

"That was not the plan," said Hans, frowning. "You were only supposed to stay there for two or three nights. That nun was another cousin of ours, and it was Frederick who arranged that part of your journey with her. I never liked her, not even when I was a young boy. I knew she was mean, but that was wicked of her to do what she did. What happened in the end? How did she eventually let you go?"

"Well, she didn't really let me go. The convent was targeted by the Allies in several bombing raids, and unfortunately she was killed with most of the other nuns who were there."

"Good, serves her right," said Hans. "At least you weren't killed and got away alright."

"We were very lucky. My three friends and I all made it out of the convent ruins together uninjured, with only a few scrapes and cuts. We were finally free from that nightmare and able to escape, after all those months."

Alexa didn't go into all of the details of her long journey back home, but at least now she knew the important part the Klauss family had played in planning her escape journey. Now Hans also knew the missing details of his and Frederick's attempts to assist Alexa to get away safely. The risks they had taken had definitely been worth it.

Hans raised his glass and made a toast. Everyone else joined him, reaching for their glasses as he said out loud, "Here's to surviving!" Then he knocked back his cognac in one go and placed his empty glass down on the table. Standing up, he said, "Wait here," and walked out of the room.

He was gone for about ten minutes before returning with an empty, medium-sized, black suitcase. Walking over to Alexa, he handed it to her. "Here, this is for you," he said. "It's the same suitcase I had with me in the first-class train carriage that day, all those years ago. I want you to have it as a souvenir from my family to yours."

Alexa was surprised at his kind gesture. "Thank you very much, Hans, that's very kind of you, but it's okay; you keep it," she said humbly.

Hans wouldn't take no for an answer and insisted Alexa keep the suitcase to carry her belongings and take back home to Poland with her. Realizing how insistent Hans was that she accept his gift, Alexa finally agreed to take it, thanking him for his generosity. Hans said she was very welcome; he was sure she'd need the extra luggage to carry all the gifts and souvenirs she was no doubt accumulating during her visit.

"It seems like a very good, strong suitcase that will carry all of our things safely and keep them nicely protected. Thanks again, I'll take good care of it," she promised.

"It's getting late," said Richard, "and it's time I drove you both back to my parents' house. I still have another two hours' drive home after I drop you both off."

Alexa agreed it was time they left. She thanked Hans's wife for her hospitality and for insisting Alexa come to meet her husband. Turning to Hans, she thanked him again for what she now knew he had done for her all those years ago on the train. "I will never forget what you did for me. Thank you," she said.

"I'm glad you were safe and that you survived. I'm also really happy I could help you in some small way to get you back home," Hans said, holding both her hands in his.

Alexa picked up the suitcase and handed it to Richard to put into his car before hugging Hans goodbye. She knew she'd probably never see him again but was so grateful she'd had the chance to meet him once more, and to thank him in person for his kindness. Stasha climbed into the back seat of the car as Richard started up the car engine. Alexa sat in the passenger seat next to Richard who swung the car back onto the road. Alexa looked back to see Hans and his wife waving until they were out of sight.

Turning to face the road ahead of them, Alexa shook her head slowly, still overwhelmed by the new revelation she had just learned. "That was quite an unexpected surprise," she said.

"Yes," said Richard, "we knew you'd be surprised as you would never expect it."

"But I don't remember your Uncle Hans living in the village when I was here, all those years ago."

"Well, no, you wouldn't because he didn't live here back then. He lived in Berlin."

"Ah, that's why I wouldn't have known him. When did he move here?"

Richard paused, not answering right away. Then he began to explain.

"Well, sometime after you left our farmhouse and the war finally came to an end, the Allied troops began hunting down . . . how can I say? Well, anyone who served as an SS officer was hunted down and arrested. They started conducting extensive investigations to discover who had played which roles during the war." Richard appeared to be visibly uncomfortable as he spoke.

"So, what happened?" asked Alexa. "Can you tell me?"

"One day, some British soldiers arrived at our farmhouse and searched it thoroughly. Father was arrested and taken away that day, and he didn't come back home for a very long time. At about the same time, Uncle Hans was also arrested in Berlin. So, his wife, my aunt Danka, packed up all their personal belongings and came to live with us."

"I had no idea," said Alexa.

"No, of course you wouldn't. My parents don't talk about it ever, so please don't mention to them that you know, or that I have told you."

"No, don't worry, I won't," said Alexa quickly.

"My father was tried at Nuremberg," Richard continued, "where they sentenced him and sent him to prison. They found him guilty of war crimes—they called it that, but my father didn't kill anyone. He didn't work at any of the concentration camps. He was a good man, a good father, and a good husband to my mother."

"I never knew what he did, or what his job was—never in all those years, and I never asked," Alexa said.

"He had an office job, keeping records to protect Germany's precious art collections during the war so they wouldn't all be destroyed. He didn't visit concentration camps and he certainly didn't kill anyone. He wasn't responsible for prisoners, nor was he involved with anything bad that happened to the Jews, or the Poles, or any other Europeans."

Alexa heard Richard's words; turning to look out the window she thought, '*But I was Polish, I was a European, and your parents selected me to be their unpaid slave for five years.*' Part of her wondered how Richard could say such a thoughtless, insensitive thing to her. After all, he was no longer a young boy. He was a grown German man who knew the facts about the atrocities perpetrated under the Nazi regime. The whole world knew how many millions had suffered and been killed, tortured and enslaved. And yet he seemed to be defending part of that very regime, at least the part his father was responsible for.

"My father had to spend five years in prison. It was very hard for my mother and our family, and I had to become the man of the house. Uncle Hans was sentenced to three years in prison It wasn't easy for him or for my father."

Alexa could no longer hold back her words. "Well, it wasn't very easy for me either," she said, "being rounded up and taken away from my home and family at thirteen years of age and imprisoned to work as a slave for your family for five years, let me tell you."

Richard opened his mouth as if to say something and then shut it again. He shook his head and rubbed his furrowed brow before dragging his fingers and thumb down the sides of his face. Alex watched him out the corner of her eye. Had the penny dropped finally? Had Richard grasped the reality of the situation Alexa had been forced into as a child at the hands of his own people? At the hands of his own parents? Had he realized how insensitive and selfish his words had been?

"Yes, I'm sure it was very difficult for you indeed. I'm sorry, Alexa; I didn't mean to be so insensitive. I didn't think; please forgive me. There is no comparison with what you went through."

"It's okay, apology accepted, Richard."

"Thank you, Alexa." Richard stopped talking. Instead, he twiddled the round knob of the car radio and turned it on. "God bless the child who's got his own, who's got his own . . ." A Billie Holiday song was playing on the local German radio station.

Stasha began to sing along to the chorus from the back seat of the car, while Alexa pondered on the irony of that very moment in time. *'Herr Klauss got five years in prison after he freed me from my five years as his prisoner. An eye for an eye. I wonder what he actually did . . .'* But she didn't ask.

Alexa stared out of the window, silently trying to process all the new information she had gained that day. Stasha didn't speak German so she hadn't understood her mother's conversation with Richard. She continued to hum along to the melody as Richard drove them back to the farmhouse.

Alexa spent the remainder of her week in Germany meeting a few more people from her past. Everyone remembered her fondly, and most gave her little gifts or souvenirs to take back to Poland with her to remember them by. As it turned out, the suitcase Hans had gifted to her came in very useful indeed.

When Alexa returned home, she had more than double the belongings she had originally taken with her. Once she unpacked the black suitcase, she placed it on top of her wardrobe. There it stayed as one of her most treasured possessions, at which she'd glance now and then. She never used it for anything other than as a permanent reminder of her harrowing journey back to freedom and to be grateful for each day of life she had lived since. She never forgot.

The trip back to Germany had been a very beneficial journey for Alexa on many levels. She had been warmly received by the Klausses who had treated her as though she was part of their own family. While they never discussed the fact they had chosen her out of a line-up of Aryan-looking teenagers who'd all been taken away from their families and forced to work as unpaid house slaves all those years ago, there was almost an unspoken apology, a silent remorsefulness which Alexa sensed from them. She didn't feel she needed to hear the words "I'm sorry," and the Klausses never said them to her. But through their actions, they showed they really had cared about her. That in itself gave her a sense of healing and closure.

The multiple large parcels of goods and money they sent for many years was the way they presumably chose to handle their feelings of guilt. Alexa was sure they knew they could never make up for the impossible situation Alexa had endured; at the same time, they all knew and understood that Alexa could have been treated much worse by another SS family, as many other young girls were. Some young European girls had been regularly and violently beaten by their captors and even raped, so in comparison to them, Alexa had been in a far better position.

After all, Alexa reasoned, it wasn't the Klausses' own doing or choice that these teenagers had been forcibly removed from their homes and made to work for German households. It's was simply the way it was during the war. Alexa was one of the many casualties of Hitler's war.

The Klausses continued to send parcels to Alexa and her family for the rest of their days. They also sent her letters and cards, and would telephone her from time to time. When the elderly couple finally passed away at a ripe old age, their children continued the tradition of sending parcels to Alexa. Although not quite as frequently, they still generously sent them and every few months made phone calls. They never forgot Alexa.

Throughout her long life, Alexa's home was a constant hub of activity. Her telephone—an important means of international contact for her—rang often. On a monthly basis, friends from her past across Europe would call her to enquire how she was and remind her they hadn't forgotten her. Their conversations— especially those with Marta, Greta, and Henrietta—were uplifting as they shared their news with each other, right up until their deaths. Alexa's family members were also regular callers, especially those in her family who lived abroad in various countries and who couldn't visit as much as they would have liked to.

Alexa's five children with Antoni had all married, and each couple had given birth to a girl; so, Alexa had five granddaughters, all of whom were a year apart in age. They were all born in Poland where they remained living, except for Stefan's daughter. He had married a pretty young Scottish woman named Rebecca, whom he had met while she was visiting her father's family in Poland. Stefan proposed, and within a short time they were married.

Alexa loved all her children but had always had a special unconditional love for Stefan, who was a handsome hooligan and the prodigal son of her family. He could do no wrong in her eyes. He took after his father in so many ways, including his looks. Alexa was so delighted when he decided to settle down with his Scottish lass that she gave Stefan her amethyst engagement ring, which had once belonged to her mother, and her gold wedding band from his father, Antoni, for him to give to his bride.

Stefan had no desire to remain living in Poland with his new wife and instead moved to Scotland to live with her there, seeking a new life with better opportunities for himself. However, within the first year of their daughter, Rochelle, being born, Stefan was unfaithful, following in his own father's footsteps.

Rebecca decided she had no other option but to divorce him and raise their young daughter alone. Although Stefan had never held his family in very high regard, nor kept in regular contact with them or his mother, his ex-wife did. Rebecca would call Alexa from time to time and update her on Rochelle's progress as her young daughter grew up. Unfortunately, she could never update Alexa on her son Stefan's life or his whereabouts, which saddened Alexa greatly. She always wondered where he was. Rebecca became like a daughter to Alexa, and their relationship became a very special one.

Rebecca took her daughter, Rochelle, to Poland to meet Alexa for the very first time when she was only two years old. In age, she was the middle child of Alexa's five granddaughters. Alexa fell in love with her granddaughter at first sight and was delighted to spend time with her.

From then on, Rebecca would take Rochelle to Poland every summer for four weeks' vacation during the school holidays. In this way, Rochelle came to know her grandmother from a very young age, and grew to love her very deeply. As a young child Rochelle learned quickly to speak Polish and so could communicate with her grandmother easily. Beyond words, they understood each other very well.

CHAPTER 25

In her later life, Alexa further developed the creative skills she had learned early on in her childhood and over the years, became a very talented artist. She had a special aptitude for painting flowers, especially poppies and sunflowers, and sold several original pieces in various art galleries in Poland. She also received many commissions throughout Germany and Europe over the years.

Alexa took pride in her art and of the fact her talent had come from her father and ran in the family genes. As Rochelle grew older, Alexa would spend time drawing pictures for her granddaughter when she'd come to visit her during the summer months.

When Rochelle was about seven years old and on vacation in Poland, her grandmother taught her how to paint; with practice and perseverance, the little girl became rather good at it. The artistic gene was a common one shared by five of Alexa's children. They were all very artistic, except for Stefan. The gene had seemed to skip him and instead passed on straight to his daughter. Rochelle was the only artistically talented one out of the five granddaughters, which gave her and Alexa an extra special bond.

When Rochelle turned thirteen years of age, her mother gifted her the amethyst engagement ring. She had been divorced from Stefan for a long time and seeing as it had once belonged to both Sophia and Alexa, it seemed appropriate for

Rochelle to have it next. From that day on, Rochelle never took it off her finger, and it became one of her most treasured possessions in life.

When Rochelle was eighteen years of age and working for a newspaper, she answered a call to place an American job vacancy in the sheet. After some deep thought and debate, she decided to take the job in New York herself, where she went and lived for twelve years. During those years living in America, Rochelle made long-distance calls to her grandmother every other month, and they continued to share a mutual and unconditional love. Alexa would always ask her granddaughter the same question: "When are you coming back to visit me in Poland?"

Alexa always made it known she wanted Rochelle to leave America; it was simply too far away from Europe and her. Their relationship remained very special to Rochelle, who showed her love for her grandmother by sending her cards and gifts, and keeping in regular contact with her. Finally, she made the long trip over to visit Alexa in Kraków.

Following the nightmare events of September 11th, 2001, in New York, Rochelle reluctantly decided to move back home to Scotland to live. Once there, she booked a long-overdue, seven-week vacation to visit with her grandmother in Poland and enjoy some quality time together and a much-needed catch up. Alexa still lived in Kraków at the time; it was a beautiful town and one which Rochelle loved very much, having visited there often during her teenage years when spending time with her grandmother and family.

They both made the most of their precious time together, and Alexa spoiled her granddaughter as she had always done when she was much younger. They spent most of their time in conversations lasting hours on end, all about the family, life in Poland, and art. Alexa would always begin a discussion on how important and great God still was in her life. Alexa read her Bible daily, and every morning when she woke up and every night before she fell asleep, she'd recite her life-long prayer of Psalm 91. She said it aloud every night while her granddaughter stayed with her, before they both went to sleep.

"Where did you learn this prayer, Babcia?" asked Rochelle.

"My grandmother taught it to me when I was a little girl. You know, the version I say is actually a Polish rhyme young children used to learn in school. An old Polish poet from the sixteenth century by the name of Jan Kochanowski wrote it based on the original verses of Psalm 91. But you know it was God who wrote the original, right?" Alexa smiled.

"Can you say it out loud for me now, Babcia?" Rochelle asked, smiling back at her grandmother. And Alexa would begin to recite her beloved 91st Psalm.

Rochelle shared many stories of her adventures during her twelve years of New York living with her grandmother who hung on her every word, as if she were walking in her shoes across America with her. Alexa asked if she had ever been to Brooklyn, New York. Rochelle told her she had and began explaining what it was like there, describing what it was like to cross the Brooklyn bridge and look back over the East River to Manhattan's amazing skyline. She described the ornate brownstone buildings with their metal fire escapes climbing up the outside and bright-colored fire hydrants on the streets below. She told her Babcia of the wide mix of cultures, the variety of international foods for sale available on most blocks, and the tempting aromas filling the air, especially in the warmer months. And she told her about the summers at Coney Island with its amusement park rides, boardwalk, and packed beach.

"Yes indeed, I have been there several times," said Rochelle. "Remember the tee-shirt I sent you, Babcia, a few years ago, the white one with *BKNY* on it? Well, that's where I bought it for you—in a store in Brooklyn."

"Ah yes, my darling, thank you," said Alexa. "I loved it and still have it. It's in my closet, tucked away safely to keep it good."

"I remembered you always had a thing for Brooklyn, and that's why I bought it for you. What's that all about anyway?"

Alexa paused for a moment and smiled, and then she began to tell the story of Mark, the American soldier she had met at the end of the war. Alexa told her granddaughter that life could have been so different if she had only chosen Mark from Brooklyn to marry, instead of Antoni. Then she remarked, "But if I didn't marry your grandfather, I wouldn't have had you as my granddaughter or all my beautiful children."

"Well then, thank goodness you did marry Antoni," said Rochelle. "I couldn't live without you in my life. You're my number one, my sunshine, my bright diamond, my heart, and I love you so much, Babcia."

"And I you, my darling. You're my brilliant, my balsam, my princess."

Rochelle directed her grandmother's attention to her left hand, and there on her middle finger, she proudly displayed her amethyst ring. "Do you remember this Babcia? I still wear it all the time; I never take it off."

"Oh my, how could I forget it? I haven't seen it in a very long time," Alexa said pensively as she stared down at the ring. "It looks good on you; it was my mother's, you know."

"I know, Babcia. It was your mother's, then yours, then my mother's, and now it's mine."

Alexa reached over and squeezed her granddaughter's hand fondly. Rochelle asked her grandmother if she'd like to try the ring on again.

"Yes, okay, it has been a very long time," she said. "My fingers are fatter now, so it might not even fit me."

Rochelle slid the amethyst ring off her middle finger and passed it to Alexa, who slipped it on to her wedding-ring finger. It would only go on so far, not past her knuckle, so she placed it on her little finger instead. Alexa raised her hand and looked closely at the invaluable ring with eyes full of emotion, and took a deep, trembling breath. "All so long ago," she whispered, as if to herself.

Rochelle asked her to share her war story with her.

"It's a very long story, my darling."

"Good," said her granddaughter with a gentle smile. "We've got plenty of time."

Alexa asked her to first make a fresh pot of tea and get them some cheesecake. Sitting next to her granddaughter on the couch, Alexa took a deep breath and began to tell her story from the very beginning, while she continued to wear the ring. Rochelle gave her grandmother her undivided attention.

Alexa first began talking about her parents, and gradually led up to that fateful day in the September of 1940, when she and her mother had left her younger sister behind with the neighbors, wearing her mother's rings. That day. The day her mother had taken her on a fun outing to buy a new pair of shoes but instead her world had suddenly been turned upside down and life as she knew it was wrenched from her, torn apart by the Nazis who had driven into the town square.

Rochelle was engrossed in her grandmother's story, caught up with and feeling Alexa's emotions as she narrated her story. As her grandmother related her traumatic experiences as a young teenage girl, Rochelle imagined herself in Alexa's shoes. Tears welled up in her eyes as Alexa recalled the last time she had ever seen her mother, when Sophia had been struck on the head in Dachau and knocked unconscious to the ground.

Tears trickled down Rochelle's cheeks. "Oh Babcia, that's awful; I'm so sorry," she said, fighting back her tears. Wrapping her arms around her grandmother, she told her she loved her. "What happened to your mother?"

"It's hard to say for definite," said Alexa sadly. "I wrote to the Red Cross for many years, in the hope of finding out what happened to my Mama, but the trail kept growing cold. There was information pointing to her having been sent to slave for the SS, but it must have been really bad for her, as she was listed as having been admitted to a German hospital in 1944 with serious wounds, after multiple beatings. That's the last solid piece of factual information I have. The hospital was liquidated near the end of the war, and if she had still been alive then, she'd have been a victim to one of two horrific endings. Many of the patients were shot and buried in a mass grave in the hospital grounds, and those still able to walk were taken on a death march or transported to concentration camps to be finished off. Many years ago, I went to the location of the old hospital and took some of the earth from the sacred ground where the killings took place. There is a monument to all the people killed there, you know. But I'll never know for sure if that was her final resting place."

The room was silent. Neither of them said a word. There was a long pause. Both women wiped the tears from their eyes, and Alexa looked down at the ring on her finger. "My poor Mama."

Alexa told her granddaughter her entire wartime history from start to finish, uninterrupted. She stressed how important Psalm 91 had been throughout her nightmare and how it had given her inner strength, courage, and faith to endure. She had never really been alone because God was always with her; he had always rescued her, guided her in some way and kept her safe, and he had granted her a long life.

"We're made in God's image out of love, and we must always choose love over hate, my darling," said Alexa. "Never allow breeding room for hate. Hate is a toxic poison; always remember that."

Once she reached the part in her story when she visited Germany for the first time with Stasha in 1978, she talked about Hans. Rochelle was gripped by the story, especially when Hans revealed that he was the SS officer in the first-class train carriage all those years before and the one who had paid the remainder of her train ticket.

"Wow, that's amazing," said Rochelle. "I'm speechless."

"I know," said Alexa. "I was shocked, stunned, and in a state of total disbelief when he introduced himself that day and told me why he had done what he had done for me."

"Babcia, you should write a book. Your story is incredible. As you've sat and told me all about it today, I can see it play out vividly in my mind as if I'm watching a movie."

"Darling, I see my whole life's movie replaying in my mind's eye every day of my life," said Alexa. "And yes, I'm sure it would have made a great book, but I'm far too old to write it now. Look how my hands shake. But you, my darling Rochelle, you could write it for me."

"I will one day, Babcia, I promise you I will."

Alexa told her how Hans had given her the gift of his black suitcase to keep and bring back home to Poland with her. He had told her it was the very suitcase he had carried with him on the train all those years ago. Alexa pointed to the top of her wardrobe. "That's it up there," she said.

"Really? Can I lift it down and look at it, Babcia?"

"Yes, if you want, but it will be covered in dust, my darling. I don't use it for anything, and it's sat up there for years now. I have always stored it up on top of the wardrobe as a souvenir, so I never forget Hans and what he did for me."

Rochelle grabbed a wooden chair, placed it in front of the wardrobe, and climbed up onto it, reaching up for the suitcase. She carefully took a hold of its handle and lifted it down, placing it on top of the table in front of her. It did have a thick coating of dust on it, which she cleaned off carefully.

It had a hard, black exterior with two brown wooden strips running all the way around the case, on the top and bottom. Its dimensions were roughly 24 x 16 x 8 inches, and it had two small locks on the front. Rochelle tried to open the case, but it was locked.

"Do you have the key to open it, Babcia?"

"Yes, I think it's in the top drawer over there, in the little red heart box." Alexa pointed to her dresser. "But there's nothing in it, darling. It's empty."

Rochelle opened the drawer and located the little red heart box. Inside she found two small keys threaded together with a piece of red ribbon. She took them over to the case and turned them in both of the locks. The clips sprung free and she opened up the case. Inside the walls of the case was an elegant burgundy velvet lining, which due to the age of the case gave off a fusty, aged odor.

Rochelle noticed something that seemed odd to her. The inside of the case seemed to be a little shallower than the depth of the walls on the outside of the suitcase. She began feeling around the bottom of the inner part; it felt different from the inside of the lid of the case. She wanted to explore it more closely but was afraid her grandmother wouldn't want her to investigate thoroughly. Since the case belonged to Alexa, and her granddaughter would never have done anything to upset her, Rochelle said to her, "Babcia, I think there could actually be something in the bottom of the case."

"What do you mean?"

"I'm not sure but I think there might be an empty space below the bottom panel, under the lining, as it seems much shallower than the outside of the suitcase. Can I please cut along the edge of the lining and take a look beneath it? I promise, I'll sew it back up again when I'm finished."

Alexa was a little hesitant at first but eventually agreed her granddaughter could investigate its interior. Rochelle got a pair of scissors and carefully began to cut along the stitching of the lining in the righthand corner. Once she had it undone, she looked through the opening and saw there was a piece of hardwood the same size as the bottom of the case, which seemed to be screwed in place at its four corners. Rochelle slipped her hand underneath the velvet lining and used her knuckles to knock on the wood. The sound echoed a hollowness.

"What are you thinking, darling?" asked her grandmother.

"I'm not sure, but I'm thinking there may be something hidden underneath, Babcia."

Rochelle proceeded to unpick the rest of the velvet lining from its stitching and then asked Alexa where she could find a screwdriver. Once she'd found the screwdriver, she began to undo the four screws; finally, the piece of hardwood became loose.

Rochelle slowly and carefully lifted out the flat piece of wood to reveal a folded piece of paper inside, sitting on the bottom of the case. Alexa asked her granddaughter to hand it to her. Rochelle placed the piece of wood face down on the table and handed her grandmother the piece of paper. Alexa carefully opened it up and read it to herself.

"What does it say, Babcia?"

"It says, 'THIS IS FOR YOU, ALEXA, FROM THE KLAUSS FAMILY. SORRY!'"

Alexa eyes were wide with surprise as she stared at the handwritten note in her hand. She'd had the suitcase in her possession for so long, for all these years, never knowing or even suspecting there might be anything hidden inside of it which was meant for her. She wondered aloud if the note had been there since her train ride when Hans had paid her train ticket? Or, had Hans and the Klausses put the note there when she visited in 1978? She wondered why they hadn't told her, or why they hadn't said the word "Sorry" to her directly.

She would never know for sure because Herr and Frau Klauss had passed away several years before, as had Hans. Alexa had outlived them all.

Rochelle still had a puzzled look on her face. "Babcia, I think there is something else still hidden here for you. It doesn't make sense to go to all that trouble to hide a simple note you might never have found."

Rochelle began examining the rest of the interior of the case. She looked in the walls of the case and the lid but eventually had to admit there was nothing else concealed within the suitcase for her grandmother. She reached for the piece of hardwood, lifting it up off the table so she could put it back into the case the same way it was before she had taken it out, as she had promised.

As she tilted it backwards towards her, Alexa said, "Look, what's that on the back of the wood?"

Rochelle flipped the hardwood over and saw there was something attached to it. It was a large piece of what looked like old artist canvas, without a frame. It was held down in place at its four corners, so Rochelle quickly went into the kitchen to fetch a clean, blunt butter knife with which to try and release it. Very gently, she began to loosen the first corner, which didn't take too much effort to become unstuck. Next, she loosened the second, third, and fourth corners, one at a time, until the canvas sat loosely on top of the hardwood, face down.

"What is it darling?" Alexa asked.

Rochelle slowly and carefully lifted two of the adjacent corners to reveal an unframed oil painting. She carefully turned it over and laid it back down on the piece of hardwood, facing upward this time. The painting was of a young male in a straw hat, walking by open fields on a sunny day, with two large trees casting shadows on the ground. He was dressed in casual blue clothing, carrying a bag on his back and what looked like an artist's canvas under his left arm, with paintbrushes and paints in his right hand. The oil colors were bright, mainly blues and yellows, with visibly raised brush strokes.

"I can't believe you have discovered this," Alexa exclaimed. "All this time and I never knew it was there," she said, shaking her head in disbelief. "It's beautiful."

"Oh, my goodness, could it really be?" gasped Rochelle.

"Could it really be what, darling?"

"Look at the style of the painting, Babcia. Does it remind you of any one painter's style in particular?"

Alexa stood up to get a better look and hovered over the painting, examining it closely. Rochelle reached for her laptop and powered it on. She opened her search engine and typed "*second world war stolen paintings*" into the search box. After a few seconds, the results showed a list of the ten most famous paintings that had still not been recovered since the days of Hitler's pillaging and stealing of priceless art masterpieces across Europe for his planned museum.

Rochelle scrolled down the list of paintings until she stopped and gasped. There it was in front of her, displayed on the screen of her computer, a detailed description and photo of the very painting they had just discovered in the suitcase: Vincent van Gogh's *Painter on His Way to Work*, dated 1888. And there it was, what appeared to be the original oil painting, sitting on her grandmother's table in front of them, in all its splendor. One of the great missing masterpieces, by one of the great masters.

"Babcia, this is a Van Gogh! Do you have any idea what it's worth?"

Alexa had to sit down. She couldn't believe her eyes, and she couldn't believe she'd had this masterpiece in her possession for all these years without even knowing it. She could clearly hear Hans's words to her, after he had given her the suitcase. "It's from my family to your family," he had said. Now his words made sense to her, as did the note of apology from the Klauss family.

"I cannot keep it," Alexa said to her granddaughter without any hesitation. "Because it's not mine. It rightly belongs to someone else and was stolen from them and their family. Just like the room full of treasure in the church all those years ago at the end of the war when I was offered whatever I wanted—the same principle applies: it's not mine to keep. We will have to see that it's returned to its rightful owner. No, no, I can't keep it," Alexa repeated, shaking her head.

Rochelle knew her grandmother was right. Firstly, her fine-tuned conscience would never allow her to even think about keeping it. If word got out that she had it sitting in her small apartment, it would become a target for every thief in the country; it was far too valuable. Further, it was far too famous to ever be sold to a collector or buyer without causing a tremendous media frenzy, world-wide. And finally, this was a priceless, beautiful work of art by the great Vincent van Gogh and it deserved to be appreciated by art lovers around the world. So, Rochelle agreed with her grandmother and told her she would begin researching on her computer as to with whom she could get in touch about returning the painting to its rightful owners, and how to go about it.

Alexa nodded, satisfied with her granddaughter's plan. "But darling, can you first go make us a fresh pot of tea and bring the special box of chocolates from up in the cabinet? For now, the painting is ours, and we are fortunate enough to get to be alone with this great masterpiece of Vincent van Gogh's. Let's sit and enjoy it and truly appreciate it for now, together, before we have to give it away. You know he's my favorite artist, don't you? Why do you think I painted so many sunflowers?"

Rochelle agreed it was a splendid idea. She quickly made her way into the kitchen and returned a little while later carrying a silver tray with her grandmother's best china teapot full of freshly-brewed Earl Grey tea, two clean glass cups and saucers, along with sliced lemon, a sugar bowl, and fresh milk jug, accompanied by a plate of fine Belgian chocolates. She placed the tray down on the glass coffee table and positioned the painting across from them on the larger wooden dining table, at eye level.

Alexa told her to lock the door so no one could come in and disturb them. Rochelle turned the key in the door, then poured them both a hot cup of freshly brewed tea. Alexa told her to open her display cabinet and bring out the small bottle of Spirytus Polish vodka, which she kept for medicinal purposes, and had her pour them both a small crystal shot glass each. Having done so, she rejoined her grandmother on the sofa.

"To Vincent," Rochelle said and they both raised their glasses, took a sip of their drink, and smiled the biggest smiles as they turned back towards the masterpiece. They still could hardly believe what they had uncovered as they feasted their eyes on the priceless oil painting before them.

Alexa raised her glass again. "Here's to you, me, and Vincent," she toasted. "Three artists in one room!"

The End

PHOTOGRAPHS

Alexa
Gdansk, Poland, 1965

Alexa and Antoni's
wedding photo
Paris, France, 1945

Antoni's grandparents with their family
Top left is Antoni's father, Fritz

Alexa and Asha
Kraków, Poland, 1992

Rochelle and Alexa
Kraków, Poland, 1989

Asha, Rochelle, and Alexa
Kraków, Poland, 1993

Alexa wearing Rochelle's gift of the BKNY tee-shirt
Kraków, Poland, 2000

Alexa
Słupsk, Poland, 2008

Alexa
Słupsk, Poland, 2008

Alexa's amethyst engagement ring,
which was stolen in Glasgow, Scotland, in January 2012

Alexa was finally laid to rest in Słupsk, Poland,
on April 18, 2019,
next to Antoni, who passed away on November 11, 1994

The author, Rochelle Alexandra, at Alexa's grave, 2019

ACKNOWLEDGEMENTS

First and foremost, my thanks go to my grandmother, Alexandra, for sharing her story so openly with me, and for her unconditional love and fine example of not holding onto malice or hate.

Secondly, a massive thanks goes to my amazing mother for always taking me to Poland on vacation as a child, so that I could grow up knowing and loving my grandmother, and for her 110% enthusiasm for this project and many others of mine. I couldn't imagine my world without you in it; thanks for all that you do for me.

Next, my thanks go to my great friend, Dorothy Robertshaw, for her continued support, encouragement, love, and wonderful friendship. Thanks also to her beautiful family and fabulous NY/CT tribe who have all received and encouraged this novel with much excitement from the very beginning.

Thanks to Ruth Griggs for her precious and priceless friendship and helpful contacts in Massachusetts, especially Janice and Sarah. Thanks also for snapping my author pic at Rob's place.

Thanks to Magda, Cece, and Anita for Polish translation assistance. Thanks to the very talented Heywood Gould for his writing advice at the start of my author journey. A massive thanks to Helen Izek for her full edit of this, the updated version, and to Iris Hart for her copy-editing and proofreading assistance. Big thanks to Kristin Bryant, my designer, for her creative talents in producing such a wonderful book cover. Thanks to my beta readers, all of whom gave great feedback, valuable input, and genuine excitement for my manuscript. Wilma Voois—your support and friendship have been fabulous. JJ, thanks for your assistance.

My deep gratitude goes to the fabulous #1 Best Selling International Author, Heather Morris, who has graciously promoted and recommended my novel to her own readers worldwide. I honestly could not have penned a more beautiful endorsement than the one Heather has written for the new back cover. We must tell these stories for future generations.

Thanks to the many people with whom I've verbally shared this story over the years, mainly at dinner parties, and who have all listened intently and encouraged the vision of it reaching a larger audience one day. Finally, that day is here.

Thanks to the whole fabulous team and tribe at Author Academy Elite (AAE): Niccie Kliegl and Brenda Haire for all their coaching assistance, and especially Kary Oberbrunner for his wisdom, advice, coaching, and encouragement on the publishing, marketing, and business side of producing this book and making it become a reality. I must once again thank Helen Izek, from the bottom of my heart, for handling this final edit. Her wonderful word skills, attention to POV (within the constraints of a second edition), and genuine desire to keep the integrity of my grandmother's story, were the perfect balsam needed to rectify the errors missed and made by my previous editors.

Last but not least, thank you to everyone who accommodated, tolerated, and assisted me during the process of writing this novel. There were so many. I began writing the first chapters in Scotland, then travelled with it on my iPad and continued writing in Paris, Poland, and Spain. It neared its completion in New York and Massachusetts, and was finished in Westport, Connecticut. It was written on trains, planes, buses, and in cars, hotels, restaurants, cafés, and at bars, in trendy apartments, and fancy houses, at office desks, and on comfy couches. So, to all of you friends and strangers who helped along the way:

THANK YOU KINDLY.
XOXO

ENDNOTES

[1] The reference to Psalm 91 at the end of Chapter 1 is a mix of all the verses in the chapter combined and written out into one long verse. It should be noted this version is not a direct quote from any one source. Rather, it is a combination of parts from several Biblical versions including The King James, The New World Translation, and The American Standard Version, for easier understanding and comprehension throughout the story.

The 91st Psalm Alexa recites and refers to throughout the novel is an old Polish Church song taken from the renowned 16th Century Polish poet, Jan Kochanowski, widely learned by young children in school. The English translation of this version is written below. It is the version that Alexa, up until the age of 92, continued to recite off by heart as her daily prayer.

Who will give himself up to His Lord,
And trust in Him sincerely from the bottom of his heart.
Can say boldly: I have protection in God,
No scary awe will ever come at me.

He sets you free from the traps
And saves you from infected air,
In the shadow of His wings He'll keep you forever,
Underneath His feathers you will lie safely.

His stable shield and a solid buckler,
Standing behind them, neither about a nightmare,
About a fright nor about any arrows don't you care,
Which we are lavished in on the way in broad light.

A thousand heads turn to You from here,
The imminent sword will not reach You,
And You, amazed by what Your eyes saw,
You will live to see the unavoidable revenge over the sinners.

If you say to the Lord, You are my hope,
If the Highest God is your escape,
No bad experience will ever come your way,
And no damage will happen to your home.

He made His angels watch over you,
Wherever you step, they will care about you,
Will carry you in their arms, so while you're walking,
No sharp stone can hurt your feet.

You will tread on impatient
Venomous snakes and slow worms safely.
You will mount the vicious lion without fear.
And you will ride a giant dragon.

Hear the Lord speak: "Anyone who loves Me
And honestly walks along with Me,
Then I will love him back in all his trouble.
And I won't forget and will indeed help him."

His voice won't be condemned in Me,
I will protect him in the fight,
Let him be sure of happiness and good heartedness,
And of long lifetime and of My thoughtfulness.

Get your free digital gift, which I am giving away
to readers of *In Alexa's Shoes*.
All you have to do is send me an email requesting it,
or click the offer on my website.

XOXO

It has been such a beautiful surprise to receive so many
lovely and inspiring messages from so many
fabulous readers. Feel free to get in touch by email,
or via my Facebook Author page if you'd like.

Email: RochelleAlexandra@outlook.com
Visit www.RochelleAlexandra.com
OR www.InAlexasShoes.com

Scan QR Codes

2019	1000 #1's	2020
Top 10 Finalist	and counting . . .	2nd Place Winner

If you dream of writing, publishing,
and marketing your own best-selling book, do it as I did:
https://vt226.isrefer.com/go/aaevtrng/RochelleAlexandra/

Made in the USA
Middletown, DE
06 July 2022